Perchance

2 DREAM

Copyright

MARSHGRASS PUBLISHING
ST. MARYS, GA

Dedication

I dedicate this book to my beautiful bride, my wife of over 43 years, Mary. She is my inspiration for Wendi's temperament, attitude, looks, and smart comebacks.

I also dedicate this book to the memory of my parents, Jacob and Dagny Zimmerli, who were married for 72 years and were impeccable role models for what a husband-and-wife team should look like. My dad passed away in February 2024, at age 98, hurrying to catch up with his bride, who went to Glory in December of 2018.

ALSO BY MICHAEL K. ZIMMERLI

Zamboni Is Not A Pasta – Blue Bridge Mystery #1
Wanted: Dead or Alive (Again) – Blue Bridge Mystery #2
To The Last Breath – Blue Bridge Mystery #3
Perchance 2 Dream – Blue Bridge Mystery #4
The Annunciation – A Biblical Historical Fiction about the Birth of Jesus (Fall 2024)

One Soldier's Story – Jacob Wesley Zimmerli's WWII Memoirs with Michael K. Zimmerli

Contents

Acknowledgments

ONCE AGAIN, IT TAKES a village—or, in my case, a small city—to produce a story.

Robert Nicholson – a friend since 2005, has been an invaluable resource for weapons and automobiles, plots and their holes, editing and proofreading, hints, helps, and more. He is also a big encourager.

And thanks to Robert's daughter, Sarah Nicholson, for getting your dad the first Blue Bridge Mystery book and sharing your nursing expertise with him and me so the hospital and medical scenes can be correct.

Roberto "Pepé" Perez – thank you again for letting me borrow your name and for your encouragement. Thank you for your insights about firearms, the police, the Navy, and security—some things that "normal" people don't need access to. And my thanks to your wife, Karen, for letting the book's Pepé have a wife. It's only right that the character's wife, Gwynn, be almost as sweet as you.

Steffens Restaurant appears again in this book—not as it looks today, but as it did in 1948 when it first opened: a two-story building with a gabled roof, a sign advertising Restaurant, Souvenirs, and Air Conditioning. This first version of the iconic eatery had gas pumps under a Café sign out by the road, complete with a pig wearing a chef's hat.

To my beta-readers: Trisa & Keith Chancey, Lana Beck, Paula Veno, Barry Allen, Jimmy & Sandra Street, and Karen Perez – thank you, thank you, thank you! You're the first readers to enjoy the story and the last eyes to see the manuscript before I publish it.

To all who have cheered me on and encouraged me to keep writing stories and to all who have asked me when the next book is coming out, this is for you.

And to my wife, Mary, who encourages me and pushes me forward to be better: I think each book gets a little better, just like each year we've been married.

A BLUE BRIDGE MYSTERY

Perchance
2 DREAM

MICHAEL K. ZIMMERLI

Marshgrass Publishing
St. Marys, GA

Prologue

WENDI PULLED INTO THE parking lot near the Staples store a few doors from Lyst Publishing. The first time Jimmy tried to find the little publishing company, Wendi told him to go to Staples and turn right. Even with such *precise* directions, he had to ask an employee from Staples where Lyst Publishing was. He discovered it was almost completely hidden between two buildings next to Staples. There was just a small entrance door, and then a narrow hallway led back to Hillary and Wendi's offices.

That was then. Now, Jimmy could find the office in his sleep.

They exited Wendi's car and walked toward the buildings. It was quiet, like evenings here usually were. Most people were at home, eating dinner. Very few cars were in the parking lot, and no one was on the sidewalk in front of the stores. Jimmy looked to his left and thought about steering Wendi toward the little Peterbrook Chocolatiers shop but decided to wait until another time. Turning back to his right, he noticed a black SUV suddenly stop in the driving lane. Jimmy assumed it was letting them cross, but he couldn't see the driver through the darkly tinted windows. Jimmy cheerfully waved nonetheless.

The SUV's doors flew open, and The Man's three-person goon squad piled out from inside. They rushed toward Jimmy and Wendi, and they didn't look friendly or cheerful. From within the SUV came The Man's electronically disguised voice.

"I'm going to let Hank off the hook, but you and I need to have one more dance, Mr. Favreaux. I'm getting very tired of your meddling."

Jimmy hurried Wendi across the lane toward the office door, hoping to get inside and avoid a confrontation, but the hoods arrived quicker. It was obvious they weren't looking for conversation, so Jimmy tossed his cell phone to Wendi and said, "Call 9-1-1."

She caught it one-handed, tossed it back, and said, "*You* call 9-1-1, and while you're at it, call Merry Maids to come and take out the garbage."

Jimmy was caught off-guard but caught his phone without bobbling it and slid it back into his pocket. Everything from that moment on seemed to occur in slow motion.

As Dimebag rushed Wendi, she took a couple of quick steps and met him halfway, threw her purse in his face, and followed it up with a kick to his knee that bent his leg backward, forcing his head down involuntarily. She brought her knee up to meet his chin as he doubled over. His teeth cracked loudly as his jaws crashed together, and his head snapped straight up and back as he went down.

Reacting to what was happening, Wheels rushed over and made the same mistake Jimmy had made three weeks before, grabbing Wendi's arm from behind. She whipped around, shot her arms straight up in the air to dislodge his grip, and stepped *closer* to the thug. Jimmy saw her fingers become as stiff and rigid as a solid wooden stake, then strike her opponent's Adam's apple perfectly, just as she had done to Jimmy.

Watching it happen was different than being on the receiving end. Jimmy noticed that as she lashed out with her deadly fingers, she simultaneously gave a little shout. He had read once that martial artists gave a little yell to concentrate the power into their kick or strike. It intimidates their opponent, removes air from their diaphragms, and gives their attacks more speed and power. All Jimmy knew was that it worked.

Wheels went down the same way Jimmy had, his hands grasping in vain at his throat to pry it open and get air flowing into his lungs again. Jimmy almost felt the blow in his own throat again as he watched. Wheels looked pale and like he was about to pass out, just like Jimmy had when Wendi struck him the same way.

Dimebag was struggling to get back up and had reached his hands and knees. Wendi turned toward him and, with a form that would make an NFL field-goal kicker jealous, used Dimebag's head as a football. After her perfect kick, he was sprawled out on the sidewalk, the second man to go down for the count.

Suddenly, Jimmy heard a roar and, from out of the corner of his eye, saw Kingpin charge toward him just before the gargantuan man scooped Jimmy up the way a normal-sized person would scoop up a toddler. Kingpin hoisted Jimmy over his head as easily as he would a throw pillow and, with both hands, hurled him against the side of the building. Jimmy's head hit first with a sickening sound, and he blacked out, sliding down the wall and pooling into a motionless heap.

Wendi screamed angrily and ran full speed at the giant gangster. She launched herself into the air, hoping to wrap her legs around his head and use the strength of her legs to get the giant off-balance and throw him to the ground or at least get him down on one knee. If that failed, Wendi hoped to let her momentum slingshot her behind his head and onto his shoulders. From there, she could smash the heels of her palms against his temples, clap his ears, and try to pop his eardrums, hopefully cutting him down to her size. The behemoth was just too big to take on one-on-one.

As Wendi flew through the air, Kingpin swung one massive arm out like he was playing handball and swatted her to the ground, knocking all the air from her lungs. He grabbed the front of her shirt and pants, hoisted her about four feet off the ground as effortlessly as lifting a toy doll, then body-slammed her back to the concrete sidewalk. Wendi landed hard on her back, unable to brace herself. The back of her head bounced once on the sidewalk, and she groaned and lay still.

Kingpin stomped over to Jimmy, grabbed him by the hair, hoisted him to a semi-standing position, shoved him against the building wall, and sat him down hard against the building, facing Wendi. He slapped Jimmy roughly across the face several times. Jimmy's head rolled down against his chest, and he slumped over. His head landed hard on the concrete sidewalk, scraping his cheek and leaving skin and blood behind.

"Wakey, wakey, Jimmy!"

The oversized beast reached into his coat pocket and pulled out a handgun. It looked like a toy in his massive fist.

"I'm going to eliminate you, Favreaux. But first, I'm going to get rid of your cute little girlfriend, so open your eyes."

Jimmy tried to do as he was told. His head felt like it was splitting in two. He forced one eye open partway. The other eye wouldn't respond. Through a haze, he saw Kingpin turn toward Wendi and point the handgun down at her still form.

"Are you watching, Favreaux? Because it's going to be good."

Jimmy was powerless to do anything, not to stop Kingpin, sit up, or even watch. One eye fluttered open and shut several times, but things were growing dim, and a smoky gray mist covered what little he could see. As his good eye lost its ability to stay open, Jimmy heard several loud gunshots, but he couldn't force his eye open to see what had happened. He was powerless to open his eyes, not even a slit. The sides of his head were throbbing, and his forehead felt like someone was holding a hot frying pan against it. The top of his skull felt like it was about to come off. Time had slowed to a crawl. There was only pain.

Just as everything was nearly black, Jimmy heard one more gunshot. It sounded distant and incredibly close simultaneously, and the sound echoed like someone had too much reverb turned up on their guitar amp.

His head! It was pounding continuously, and his eyes felt like they were about to pop out of their sockets. As he heard the last gunshot, time seemed to slow to almost a complete stop. Jimmy's world momentarily turned bright white, then changed to black with no fade out, as quickly and efficiently as if a light switch had been flipped.

Unlike people with near-death experiences who reported seeing a bright tunnel, Jimmy experienced no sounds, lights, or bodily sensations – except his head, which felt like it was about to burst.

Then, there was nothing.

Introduction

"WHATEVER IT TAKES, DOC, you do it. This is my best friend in the whole world. Put his bill on my insurance if you need to. I've got military insurance. Give him private nurses around the clock if necessary. You do whatever you need to make him better."

"I wish we could move people on and off other insurance policies that easily, but that's not how things work. I assure you, Mr. Perez, we're doing everything possible. Mr. Favreaux has suffered a traumatic brain injury. The neurosurgeon said Mr. Favreaux's brain was injured significantly when he was thrown against that building. His skull was cracked. If you've heard the term depressed skull fracture, well … now you've seen one. He is in ICU, where we have intubated him, placed him on a ventilator, and put him in an induced coma to reduce the swelling of his brain. Shutting down many of his brain functions can give it time to heal. We're helping his brain and body to do what they normally do independently. Mostly, he's going to need time."

"Okay, I got it. How's Mrs. Lyst – Wendi?"

"She's doing fine. We're going to hold her overnight for observation. She sustained a concussion, but it's very mild. The overnight hold is just to make sure nothing crops up. She may have mild amnesia about some recent events or not. We just can't say for sure. But you can see her tomorrow. We have her lightly sedated right now. She's resting comfortably, I assure you."

After the doctor left, Hillary walked into the waiting area and straight to Pepé.

"How did it go with the cops?" Pepé asked.

Hillary shrugged and looked down the hospital hall before answering.

"The police are going to need to see you. In-person, I'm afraid. They're only giving you some leniency because they know Jimmy, Wendi, and me. They already have our guns, but they explicitly said they needed to see you personally within the next twelve to twenty-four hours. I also informed them that you were a former Charleston police officer and Naval watch commander, and, like Jimmy, you are a private investigator. Telling them those things may not have helped, but they didn't hurt. I don't foresee any difficulties, Pepé, but remember, we just killed a man."

"It was a righteous shoot," Pepé said when Lyst finished. "We did what we had to. That giant ape was about to kill Jimmy and Wendi. We put four shots in his center mass— two from each of us—and he was still moving. He was still trying to take a shot at Wendi. I had no choice except to try a headshot. I cut Pinocchio's strings, and he finally went down."

"And you did it perfectly, right behind the earlobe like they teach you in marksman school. Wendi is alive because you took the shot, and so is Jimmy. Now tell me about Jimmy's condition."

"Jimmy is in an induced coma. Traumatic Brain Injury, the Doc said. A depressed skull fracture. The neurosurgeon says the coma is the best thing for him. Jimmy couldn't talk right now anyway – they have a tube down his throat. I guess he's on a ventilator, too. And Wendi has a slight concussion, so they're holding her overnight. After that, we'll just have to wait and see how they do."

"To sleep, perchance to dream. Ay, there's the rub."

Pepé looked at Hillary and raised his eyebrows. He didn't have to say the words. His new friend knew what he was asking.

"Hamlet, Act Three, Scene One," Lyst explained. "I wonder what adventures our sleeping colleague might be experiencing."

:: ::

I FELT LIKE I had been run over by a steamroller. In the back of my mind, I wondered if I looked as flat as Wile E. Coyote did after being run over by an Acme steamroller in the Roadrunner cartoons.

I tried to open my eyes, but there was something wrapped around my head. Reflexively, I reached one hand up to determine what it was.

Gauze.

It was wrapped around my head so many times I figured my head looked like a bowling ball under the Christmas tree.

Okay, so they don't want me to see anything. I can deal with that.

I lowered my hand down away from my head and rested it on the bed by my side. I could feel the crispness of the sheets, starched and smooth. My pillows – there was one behind my back and one behind my head – crinkled when I moved. I didn't know if it was from extra starch or if the pillows were encased in plastic inside the pillowcases.

I inhaled through my nose. Despite the gauze wrapping, my nose was assaulted by the antiseptic scent of a hospital, a mixture of Lysol, betadine, and bleach.

I listened carefully and heard soft voices. Were they actually speaking softly, or were they distant? It was hard to distinguish. I heard a tiny squeak every once in a while; it was a familiar noise, but I couldn't quite place it. It finally came to me: it was made by the soft rubber soles nurses wear and the shiny, well-waxed floors they walk back and forth on each shift. I was positive if I woke up during the night, I'd hear the hum and click of a floor buffer as a janitor shined the soft paste wax on the tile floors to a high gloss. Unfortunately, the wax would dull from foot traffic in only a few days and would need to be buffed again, but that was good news for the janitor.

As I listened to the sounds around me, I realized something was missing: there was no beep from a machine keeping track of my vitals. I took it as a good sign. I wiggled all my fingers and realized there was no pulse-ox monitor on my index finger. I squeezed my fingers and hands into fists, held them for a moment, and then let them relax. Another thing I noticed: there was no stinging, pin-prick sensation in the back of my hand or in my forearm, so I didn't have an IV. That's another good sign, but somewhat surprising.

I leaned back and relaxed against the crinkly pillows. The clean smell of the hospital was comforting. The quiet was peaceful. Even the lack of beeping and alarms was soothing. I tried to reach around for the bed controls but couldn't find the remote for them. No matter.

I had no idea how long I had been here. Hours? Days? Was it possible I've been in here longer than a few days? I could have been here months, and I wouldn't know it.

But at least my head didn't hurt anymore.

Wait. Why did my head hurt?

I tried to remember, but the effort created an achy feeling behind my eyes. The more I thought about it, the more the ache spread.

I tried to relax and turn off my brain. The more I thought about it, the more it made my head hurt, and the minor exertion exhausted me. The gauze wrapped around my head kept my world pitch black, but even so, I intentionally tried to close my eyes. I couldn't really tell if I was successful, but I didn't want to think about it. Thinking made my head hurt.

So tired.

In less than thirty seconds, I was asleep.

: : : :

THE NEXT TIME I woke up, the gauze seemed thinner, like someone had unwound some of it. Tiny little stars of light were shining through it in the thinnest areas.

I immediately thought about the Twilight Zone episode with the beautiful girl who was classified as ugly by the people of her planet, who all had misshapen faces. I recalled the scene when they took her gauze wrapping off to see if the plastic surgery was successful.

"No change. No change at all!"

I chuckled as I remembered the old TV show.

"Well, someone's feeling better, aren't they?"

A woman's voice. Soft and melodic.

I was about to respond when a smooth hand with cool skin took my wrist and felt my pulse.

"Good. Strong and even. Open your mouth and put this under your tongue."

Something about her voice was familiar, and I did as I was told.

After a couple of minutes, the woman – a nurse obviously – took the thermometer from my mouth and announced, "98-point-4. That's very good."

I felt a sense of satisfaction about my near-perfect temperature. I didn't know why. Maybe it was her tone. It was like she was singing when she spoke. It was …nice. With just her voice to go by, I thought she sounded like a brunette. I was looking forward to seeing her when they took my bandages off.

"I'm going to wash your arms now. Hold out your right arm, please."

Again, the smooth, cool hands took ahold of my arm, and a warm, sudsy washcloth was rubbed up and down from shoulder to fingertips, followed by a slightly rough towel to dry off. My left arm received identical treatment.

"Now you lie still and rest. The doctor will see you in just a few minutes."

And she was gone.

True to her word, a man came into my room and stood beside the bed.

"Are you ready to get those bandages off, young man?"

Young man? Has he seen me without this turban?

"Yes," I answered simply. My tongue felt thick, like I hadn't spoken in a while, and I swallowed.

"All right. I'm going to turn the lights off so your eyes don't get overwhelmed by too much brightness when the bandages are removed. Now, young man, keep your eyes closed."

Several minutes of careful unwinding followed.

There must have been more gauze around my head than I guessed.

No change, no change at all!

A giggle escaped my lips. I couldn't help it.

"Something funny, son?"

"No, not really. Just a show I was remembering."

"Oh. Okay." There was a brief pause, and the doctor spoke absently as he worked.

"There. Good. Fine. Now, hold still. Okay. Here goes the last of it. Keep your eyes closed."

I could see the light through my eyelids and wanted to open them wide, but I did as I was told.

"Okay, now slowly open your eyes. If it's too bright, go ahead and close them."

I slowly opened my eyes, allowing just a little light in at a time, allowing them to adjust. Then, after a moment, I realized they were open normally. The room was dark and subdued.

"I'm going to turn on the lights now," the doctor said.

The room blazed, and everything flared white for a second, and there was a tickle of an ache behind my eyes, but then things settled down, and the hurt dissipated.

The sudden flash of white …

Something about the sudden total whiteness sparked a memory, but it was gone as quickly as it came. It was like trying to hold water in my hand. It trickled out between my fingers before I could examine it.

I turned my head and looked at the doctor. He wore a white doctor's coat with a stethoscope hanging around his neck. He was wearing dark slacks that were pulled up too high, a white shirt, and a dark tie.

I thought, *Like someone else I know,* but that thought drifted away before I could inspect it, too.

The doctor wore heavy black glasses, and the coke-bottle lenses made him look bug-eyed. His dark hair was combed to one side with a very sharp part, and he had a thin, dark mustache.

He looks like Floyd, the barber from Mayberry.

The doctor leaned over the bed and said, "I'm going to look in your eyes with this little light."

He sounds like Floyd, too. And I swear I smell Barbasol on him.

"Your eyes look fine. How's your head?"

"Good, I guess."

"Excellent. One more question. Do you suppose you could tell me your name?"

My name? I thought. *I've been in here for Lord knows how long, and you guys haven't even figured out who I am?*

"It's Jimmy. Jimmy —"

Nothing came.

"It's Jimmy … Well, that's just stupid. I should know my own name. It's Jimmy—" I was starting to get agitated and angry, and my head was beginning to ache again.

"That's all right, son. Don't you worry about it. I'm sure it'll come to you soon."

"What do you mean don't worry about it? Where I come from, if you can't remember your name, that's definitely something to worry about."

"Where do you think you come from?"

"What? No. That's just an expression. Besides, I come from —," but I couldn't complete the sentence, which made me even more exasperated.

"Now, don't get yourself all riled up, young man. That'll just make things worse."

The doctor had turned around and was preparing something or getting something from a little table on wheels next to the bed. He turned back around and quickly injected my arm with a syringe.

Ow! You might want to sharpen that needle!

"We'll talk again later, Jimmy. At least you know your first name. That's a good start, you know. You nap now, Jimmy, and I'll be back to see you soon."

Great. I'm in Mayberry with Floyd, the barber, for my doctor. But what's my name? Jimmy what? Jimmy —.

Everything whirled and twirled, and I felt the too-familiar fog wrap around me as I drifted off to sleep.

: : : :

THE NEXT TIME THE doctor came back, I was ready for his questions.

"Can you tell me your name, son?"

"It's Jimmy. Jimmy Marlowe. I'm a private eye. I do a lot of work for insurance companies."

"Oh, that's very good. Pleased to make your acquaintance, Mr. Marlowe."

"Thank you, doctor. Can you tell me how I ended up in here?"

"Oh! Oh, my. No one told you? You've had a severe concussion. When they brought you in, it looked like someone used your head for a battering ram," Dr. Floyd said. "They dented your head and cracked your skull. Oh, yes. It was bad."

"But I'm fine now?"

"Oh, yes. You're much better. And since you remember your name, I don't see any reason to hold you here. But I need to ask you another question: do you know your home address?"

"Of course. 1313 Mockingbird Lane."

"Hmm. I'm not sure where that's at, but you answered so quickly and with such assurance that it must be right. You wait here a few minutes, and I'll discharge you."

"What about my clothes?"

"Yes, that's a good question. Let me just look in this closet … There you are. Neat and crisp, freshly laundered and ironed. We do have wonderful support services here, don't we?"

Dr. Floyd shook my hand and shuffled out, closing the door behind him.

He even walks like Floyd.

I scrambled out of the bed and went to the closet. I pulled a pair of khaki pants off the hanger and slipped them on. They fit, so they must be mine. The shirt came next. It was a loud Hawaiian shirt with palm trees, grass huts on little islands, and a sky-blue background. *Whatever!* As I was buttoning it up, I heard the door open.

A beautiful blonde head peeked around the door and said, "I guess this means no more sponge baths for you."

The beautiful brunette voice I had heard when my eyes were covered in gauze had attractive blonde hair, but it worked just fine because everything else I had imagined about her was spot on.

Ain't that a kick in the head …

At the thought of an actual kick in the head, my head responded with a twinge of pain. I ignored the sudden ache and concentrated on the scene unfolding before me. The blonde nurse opened the door all the way and stood sideways in the doorway, her arms folded across her chest, one leg pulled up partway, bent at the knee, her foot resting against the door jamb. I stopped buttoning my shirt and looked at her. There was something familiar about her, but I couldn't say what. There was also something very <u>un</u>-familiar about her, and I knew what.

Instead of the usual hospital scrubs I was expecting, she wore a crisp, white dress that fell just below her knees, white shoes, and white nylons on shapely legs. The top of her head was adorned with a little white cap. It was either Throwback Thursday or this was a very old-fashioned hospital, but I wasn't sticking around long enough to find out which. I resumed buttoning my shirt.

"You never know," I answered Florence Nightingale's remark about the end of sponge baths for me. "I could get hit by a car as soon as I walk out of here. Then I'd be right back in here, and you'd be back in the geisha business, baby."

Baby? Geisha business …?

"The doctor said you remembered your name. Is that true?"

I offered her my hand, saying, "I'm Jimmy. Jimmy Marlowe, private eye."

Her eyebrows raised, but she took my hand in hers. Her skin was smooth and cool.

"Well, Jimmy, I, for one, will be sad to see you go. Maybe we can get together outside the hospital for a drink or dinner. Or both."

"You never know what fate will throw your way, do you, sweetheart?"

Sweetheart? What the …? And the nurse didn't seem surprised by my choice of words.

I slipped my shoes on, tan wingtips with pink shoelaces, and gave her a wink and a smile before I strolled out of my room. I followed the signs in the hallway to the exit, my pace increasing the closer I got to freedom. *Walk, don't run!* I had to remind myself.

Pushing through the exit door, I noticed the sun was shining, the sky blue and clear, and birds were singing cheerfully in the trees.

I took a few steps down the street and stopped to sit down on a bench conveniently located outside the hospital's entrance. My head had begun throbbing again almost as soon as I got outside, and I felt dizzy and nauseous. It was probably the bright sunshine. I decided to try and 'walk it off,' like my Little League baseball coach always said.

The sunshine and blue skies were too bright for my eyes, so I held a hand up like a visor over my eyes. For a moment, everything went white again. I closed my eyes to the brightness for a few seconds and opened my eyes again.

I wasn't sure how I had gotten here, but I knew I wasn't where I thought I should be. Somewhere in my brain, I knew that the old hospital had been behind the funeral home off Atlantic Avenue. And I had been at that hospital. I had! But now I was walking downtown, nearly a mile from where I had been and supposedly should be.

My surroundings looked like an old movie set. All the cars appeared to be from the late forties or older. The old downtown looked similar to TV's Mayberry, except even older. The main street looked wider than I remembered, and it was brick or cobblestone. There were even tracks where trolleys had run at some time.

Most of the buildings lining the street were two-story brick constructions, and the one on the corner proclaimed Thompson Sundries. A large mural or billboard on one side of the Thompson building advertised a Luncheonette inside. A few doors down from Thompson Sundries, I saw a Western Union sign. *Telegraph? No, tele-gram.* Those messages that came in yellow envelopes carried by young kids or teens. They were cheaper than a long-distance call but not as immediate.

At the end of the street, the long concrete fishing pier on the Amelia River was missing; there was just a squat white building that said US Coast Guard on the roof. Live oaks and crepe myrtles inhabited each side of the street, and the stately live oaks were festooned with Spanish moss.

All the men walking among the business establishments were wearing suits, complete with hats like my grandpa used to wear. I was starting to feel out of place in my Hawaiian shirt and khaki slacks. Most of the men I saw were walking arm-in-arm with women, and most of the women were wearing dresses that hung below the knee; none of the women were wearing slacks. Nearly all the women had shoulder-length hair, but a few wore scarves tied over their hairdos while others had large, wide-brimmed hats. Some were carrying brown paper bags that I would have bet held groceries for supper or 'sundries' from Thompson's.

I had no idea what was going on. Some things felt familiar but not quite right, and I felt very out of place. Maybe someone was shooting a motion picture, and I had inadvertently wandered onto the set.

I decided I could worry about that later because my first order of business was to sit down before I *fell* down. I made it to a bench next to a grassy area and flopped down hard, panting. My head was throbbing, and I felt like I was going to throw up.

Chapter 1

"Are you all right, son?"

I didn't open my eyes. The sun was too bright, and I was busy napping on a bench. *Napping on a bench?*

Someone prodded my shoulder, and the voice spoke again. "I said, are you all right, son? It's okay if you want to set and rest a spell, but we can't have you lying down, sleeping in public. 'Round here, we have laws about vagrancy, y'know."

Whenever someone starts talking about laws, it's usually because they either make them or enforce them.

I opened my eyes, and a wave of nausea rolled over me. Maybe "rolled *up* me" would be a better description since it felt like it started in my toes and climbed my body toward my head, gathering force and speed as it passed my stomach. I felt a bit like a tube of toothpaste, and someone was trying to squeeze out the last pea-sized dab left inside.

I sat up, partially because the man had asked me to and partially because I was hoping that being vertical might alleviate the queasiness that had come over me. For about five seconds, I thought I had made the right choice. Unfortunately, it was like everything inside me had just rolled backward temporarily – like watching a wave in a bottle – and the wave was now advancing toward the exit rapidly. I knew this would not end well.

I spied a wire mesh trashcan next to the bench and scooted toward it, reaching around it to position my head over its opening.

"Uh-uh. No, sir." It was the voice of the law again.

I released the trashcan, sprang to my feet, and got about two feet away onto the green grass of a lawn when my stomach achieved liftoff velocity. What I lacked in substance, I made up for in power. I vomited across the grass, grateful I wasn't inside a building.

I was bent over, hoping I was done. From the corner of my eyes, I saw a pair of black shoes peeking out from under a pair of legs encased in tan pants. They were functional, practical shoes and utilitarian pants such as a law enforcement officer might wear, able to hold a crease and withstand brambles and briars during a manhunt or while chasing down a felon.

"I asked if you were all right, son. A simple yes or no would have sufficed. I didn't need a physical demonstration."

I pulled up the bottom of my shirt and wiped my mouth, then placed both hands on my knees and stared down at the grass where my watery, mostly liquid vomit was, thankfully, already soaking into the sandy soil and disappearing. I still wasn't ready to attempt standing in a fully vertical position and remained bent over while the officer watched.

"Are you ready to try this again, son? Let me ask you again: are you all right? Have you been drinking, by any chance?"

I shook my head no, a movement that made my head throb. What had the doctor said? Someone had used my head for a battering ram? But there was more. He – the doctor who looked like Floyd the barber, whoever *that* was – said I had a depressed skull fracture. I may be unable to remember my last name, but I knew fracturing your skull wasn't good.

I put a hand to my head where it throbbed, and I felt … a soft bump. *That's different!* I had bumped my head many times, but the resulting bumps had never felt soft like this – like someone had blown a bubble with my skull and scalp instead of bubble gum. I don't know how I knew that I'd been hit in the head many times since I couldn't remember any of them. I just did.

Feeling that oddly soft bump, I recalled seeing an archeological exhibit with long-dead Native Americans, including one skull with a gaping hole in it. The tour guide said the skull's original owner had been on the receiving end of some sort of club, and it had driven pieces of bone into the poor man's brain, killing him. That was a depressed skull fracture, but more extreme than mine. I had a cracked skull with an accompanying concussion. No bone fragments were jabbing into my brain. Not that I knew of, anyway.

For some reason, I remembered that someone with a concussion shouldn't be allowed to sleep, and throwing up was a sign of a particularly bad concussion. But I'd slept in the hospital, and the doctor even gave me a sedative to knock me out. I didn't remember throwing up in the hospital, something I was fairly confident I would remember since vomiting was something I hated with a passion. I took pride in the fact that I had not vomited for many years.

Another thing I know but don't know how *I know.*

"I'll ask you again: have you, by any chance, been drinking, son?"

It was that voice again. Neither high nor low-pitched, and firm but not demanding or threatening. From my semi-squatting position, with my hands on my knees, I managed to provide a weak reply. "No, sir. I have not been drinking."

"Okay. Are you sick?"

"Sort of. I have a concussion."

"Someone hit you over the head?"

"Something like that. The doctor said someone tried to use my head as a battering ram. He said they hit my head so hard they cracked my skull."

"And that's why you were lying down on the bench there?"

"I guess. The concussion gives me headaches, makes me dizzy, and makes my stomach do cartwheels. I may have temporarily passed out."

"Sounds to me like you should be back in the hospital, not out here puking on the grass by the train depot."

"Train depot?"

"Right over there. Built by David Yulee himself – both the depot and the railroad."

"As in Yulee … like the town?" I asked the tan pants with black shoes, afraid to stand up straight for fear of having a repeat performance on the lawn. Somehow, I knew there was a town called Yulee and that I was in Fernandina Beach, Florida.

"As in *Senator* Yulee, both before and during the War of Northern Aggression. He was farsighted enough to know we needed a railroad for this part of the state that didn't just go north and south, so he built one from Cedar Key on the Gulf of Mexico to Fernandina. During the war, a Union boat came up the river and shelled the port down here, blowing up the last train heading out, the tracks, and even some of the passengers. After the war, workers pulled up the tracks to use for a new line from Live Oak to Lawton, Georgia. The Florida governor had approached Senator Yulee about rebuilding Florida's railroads, and he did, starting with rebuilding his personal favorite, the Florida Railroad from Cedar Key to Fernandina. He also built some others, including the First Coast Railroad, which connects with CSX. They call Senator Yulee the Father of Florida Railroads."

I pulled my hands off my knees and slowly straightened up. The pain in my head had disappeared for the time being, and with it, most of the nausea.

"I'm really terribly sorry about getting sick on the lawn," I told the officer. Now that I was standing, I could see that the law enforcement officer wore a tan shirt that matched the color of his pants, a short black necktie with a sword-shaped tie clip, a thick, black, heavy belt with a service revolver on the left side, its handle facing forward, and six extra cartridges occupying built-in bullet loops on the right side. He had a badge on his cap, a matching one on his chest, and his patrol car was parked at the curb, proudly advertising its affiliation with the Fernandina Beach Police. *Is that car an antique?* I wondered.

"It's okay, son; most of it is already gone. Fire ants gotta eat, too." The officer crossed his arms over his chest. "By any chance, do you have a name?"

I turned to face him. Turning my head too quickly caused a touch of vertigo, but it dispersed nearly as fast as it came.

"Yes, sir. My name is Jimmy Marlowe. I'm a private investigator." I gave him the same name I had given the doctor, who told me he couldn't release me until I remembered who I was. Marlowe was the first name that seemed to fit, so I went with it.

"Marlowe, you say? Like that P-I on the radio? What's his name? *Philip* Marlowe?"

'Raymond Chandler would be proud that someone knew of his creation,' I thought. I was getting used to knowing things I didn't know that I knew.

"That's the one. It's just a happy coincidence, officer. I'm not as big or as tough as Philip, my cases aren't nearly as exciting as his, and I don't usually get the girl, either, if you know what I mean."

"That's 'cuz he's on the radio, and we're real life, Mr. Marlowe." The officer had already acknowledged my sideways membership in law enforcement, saying *'We're* real life.'

"I suppose you're right, Officer …? I'm sorry, I never caught your name."

The officer uncrossed his arms and extended a hand to shake mine. "Officer Crane. Officer William Crane of the

Fernandina Beach Police, but most people call me Bill. I also help out with the fire department. The police department, fire department, and city hall are all together in one building. It's just over a few blocks, on the corner of Third and Cedar. It's a beautiful red brick building. The original one was built in 1878. The deed was signed by former Senator David Yulee."

There was something about the police department that seemed familiar to me, like I had been in it before or had seen it. But the thread of memory was so distant and tenuous that I couldn't grasp it, and it faded as quickly as it made itself known. I shook his hand and released it.

"Fernandina Beach Police. Just like it says on the car," I said with a slight chuckle.

Looking over his shoulder at his squad car with the town's name emblazoned on it, Officer Crane replied, "Just like that."

He took a step or two toward his car before another thought seemed to strike him, one he decided needed clarification. He turned back to face me.

"Just one more thing, Mr. Marlowe. I assume you're on your way home, you know, to rest up and get better after having your head used to break down a door." Crane gave a long pause as he watched my face for signs that I was building a less-than-truthful story in response.

"Actually, I thought I had a ride lined up with someone," I answered, "and I was waiting for them to come and pick me up. The doctor said I shouldn't drive right away."

"No, I suppose you shouldn't. Where do you—"

"—Jimmy!" It was the blonde nurse from the hospital, and she was waving and walking toward Officer Crane and me. Except she wasn't wearing the nurse's uniform now. She had changed into a dark skirt, white blouse, and sensible shoes with a small heel. She wore a single strand of pearls around her slender neck.

The nurse leaned in close to me, bringing her face near mine as though expecting a kiss on her cheek, so I obliged, hoping the officer didn't notice my hesitation. She straightened back up and stepped in next to me, placing herself between Officer Crane and me. It felt nice, and it felt normal for her to stand alongside me. Part of me knew we had stood like this before.

"I'm sorry I'm late," she said to both Officer Crane and me, but didn't explain her tardiness. She just smiled at Crane as we stood under the Florida sun. She didn't offer any more explanation, and Crane lost the stare-down.

"Well, I guess I'll be on my way, Mr. Marlowe. I'm sure we'll see each other again, what with you being a private investigator and all and me a cop. We probably move in the same circles from time to time. Who knows, maybe we can even help each other out someday?"

It seemed to me that Officer Bill Crane ended a lot of sentences with an inflection that implied a question. He touched the brim of his hat and dipped his head slightly to the nurse as he did. "Ma'am?"

He walked over to his patrol car, which had prowler sirens that sounded like a kazoo on steroids when switched on. The nurse and I waved and smiled as he pulled away from the curb. When Officer Crane was out of sight, I turned to the nurse.

"Thank you for rescuing me, Miss, or should I say Nurse …?"

"Carter. Gwendolyn Carter. My mom was a big fan of the Peter Pan stories when she was young and wanted to call me Wendy. You know, after Peter Pan and Wendy? Except Wendy with an 'i' to be different. Guess what. Everyone calls me Wendi except my mom. She calls me Gwen!" Her smile was brighter than the sun but warmed me internally rather than on my skin.

"Okay … Wendi," I said tentatively, rolling the name around in my mind; it felt *natural* and right.

She wrapped her arm around mine and started walking toward the train depot. We walked a short distance, turning right at the depot and continuing across the street. The sign said Centre Street. The other half of the sign read Front Street. We were Front and Centre. Just like when the school principal called your name in the office. He wanted you front and center. *Yet another partial memory.*

When we reached the corner on the other side, I stopped and asked, "Where are we going, Nurse Carter?"

She scrutinized my face, shifting her gaze from my right eye to my left, then replied, "Oh, you really did get your brains scrambled, didn't you?" She started walking again, her arm still wrapped in mine as we strolled up the block.

"Well, that's what the Doc told me," I answered. "And judging by my continued headaches and dizzy spells, he's probably right."

I stopped dead in my tracks. "Why are you doing this, Nurse Carter?"

"Why was that policeman talking to you?" she replied.

"I asked you first," came my quick retort.

I felt my face grow warm, and I knew it had turned a shade pinker than usual. There were some aspects of our banter that seemed normal and natural, but I still felt like I was overstepping with someone I didn't know—or couldn't remember, anyway. I kept looking at her lips and thinking how much I wanted to kiss them.

Maybe when I get my memory back, I'll find out I'm some kind of a pervert. I shuddered at the thought.

I glanced over my shoulder to see if anyone was following us before explaining to Nurse Carter how I became acquainted with the police officer. I started walking again, our reflection tagging along in the store windows.

"It seems that 'round here, we have laws about vagrancy, y'know," I said, imitating the officer and his choice of words. "I was lying on the bench, waiting for my head to straighten out, when Officer Crane came over and told me that sitting on the bench was okay, but lying down was not kosher. Apparently, only vagrants lie down since he mentioned laws about vagrancy. If you've ever wondered what the difference is between a bum and a vagrant, now you know. Vagrants lie down, but bums don't."

"So, what did you do when he said you were a vagrant?"

"I sat up, which was *completely—absolutely!*—the wrong thing to do. Sitting up made my head worse, and it dragged my stomach along for the ride. I knew I was going to throw up, so I grabbed the trash can by the bench, but the officer made it clear that it was not acceptable to throw up in there. To make a long story short, I ended up spewing what little I had in my stomach on the train depot lawn. At least I didn't splash any on his shoes. So, tell me, what's the big deal with the trashcans? Are they just there for pretties? You're not supposed to actually *use* them?"

"The mayor's wife lobbied for them. Or, more correctly, she *told* her husband that he was going to get them. You see, Fernandina's esteemed first couple had been out for a post-dinner stroll early one evening, and she noticed a build-up of trash in the waterfront area, so she decided to clean up the downtown. It was her new mission. People getting off the train or who moored their boat at the dock might think a bunch of ne'er-do-wells live here. Or backward savages or uneducated louts. I think that was the phrase she used. Yes, that's it: 'Uneducated louts.' Anyway, thanks to the efforts of the mayor's wife, we have pretty, shiny new trashcans scattered about downtown. But we're not supposed to use them because that would get them dirty. And dirty trashcans imply a dirty town."

We stopped walking and stood idly in front of a store of some sort. I couldn't tell if it was a clothing store or a restaurant until I looked up and saw the sign on the awning that read: Palace Saloon.

"Do you want to go in, Jimmy?"

"Not particularly." I watched her face for clues, then asked, "Should I?"

She stepped closer and stared deep into my eyes again. I had the impression that she knew more about me than she was telling. I still wanted to pull her close and wrap my arms around her, but rather than act on my loutish urges, I turned and saw the saloon's name emblazoned in olde tyme script on a pair of wooden doors—stained, not painted, and possibly oak—under the awning: *Palace Saloon.*

"Let's go in," Wendi said. "I'm thirsty. Who knows, maybe a little drink will loosen your memory."

"I guess that's okay. Unless we discover some things about me we don't like."

"I'm willing to take that chance," she said, giving me another smile paired with a wink this time.

Hooking our arms together again, Wendi led me to the wooden doors under the awning and stopped. We stood together briefly before she gave a quick double-nod of her head toward the door. I finally realized what she meant and opened the door for her. She thanked me, dipped her head in a miniature curtsey, and we went inside.

The Palace Saloon's inside seemed bigger than the outside, another phrase that rang a tiny bell in my Swiss cheese memory. The walls seemed to stretch up and up, finally stopping when they met the embossed tin ceiling. The ceiling had been painted white once upon a time but was now a dirty, yellowish tan color from decades of cigar, pipe, and cigarette smoke rising from below. Ceiling fans hung down from the embossed ceiling on long down rods. It was surprisingly light inside, owing to the many windows near the front door, but the deeper one went into the establishment, the darker it became. The area by the back wall looked as dark as night, shrouding the tables in that part of the saloon with secrecy. I wondered what sort of deals were worked out within the dim, dusky lighting. Had bathtub gin and other liquor been ordered from here during Prohibition? Had whiskey been ferried here from Canada, where they looked at our Prohibition as an opportunity to provide what the people wanted regardless of the law? How many lives had been shortened by orders handed out from these darkened tables? How many beatings had been handed out here? How many under-the-table payments had exchanged hands?

Nurse Carter tugged on my arm. I realized I had stopped just inside the doorway, soaking in the ambiance and writing a history for the room stretching out before me. As I began moving forward again, I turned my head to view the saloon's pride and joy: the bar.

It was long and curved, made of very dark wood, and it looked impossibly heavy. I wondered if it had been built in place, right here. Something in my head said, 'Mahogany,' which I didn't dispute because it felt comfortable and right. I was starting to accept that there were things people inherently knew – things that I knew, too – that had no effect on one's ability to remember one's identity. Those items fell under the heading of General Knowledge.

Behind the massive bar was a substantial mirrored wall, and attached to the mirror were a pair of carved, "undraped" busts of women carved from the same wood as the bar. I thought they would have looked appropriate attached to the bow of a ship. For all I knew, maybe that was where they originally came from. This establishment was just a few short blocks from the docks, ships, boats, and the men who worked on them.

Running all along the base of the bar was a shiny brass rail. I was positive it had seen more feet than I ever would, but it was somehow still shiny. Someone had to spend time every day polishing it. I also noticed something curious: white towels hanging from the underside of the bar. The only way I could rationalize their presence was that men who drank here weren't supposed to utilize their sleeves to wipe away the foam deposited on their upper lips by their mugs of draft beer. The clientele was probably not limited to merely sailors and dockworkers but was probably a frequent watering hole for local downtown businessmen.

A man in a white shirt and suspenders stood behind the bar, a white bar towel in one hand and a shiny, clean shot glass in the other. Wendi nodded to him and said, "Hi, Uncle Charlie."

He nodded but said nothing.

My eyes looked down, and I noticed the floor was covered with tiny, white mosaic tiles. I turned to look back at the double doors we had come through when we entered. In addition to the large windows on the walls, there were large paintings of red-coated soldiers and eighteenth-century folk in between the windows.

Wendi tightened her grip on my arm, bringing me to a full stop.

"Anything?" she asked.

"Anything what?" I replied. "Do I want anything to drink? Is that what you're asking?"

She sighed and pouted a little. "No. I was hoping this place would jar your memory back to where it belongs."

"Do I come here a lot?"

"You might say that." Wendi stared at my face briefly, looking for something. "Come on, Jimmy. Let's take a little walk. Head toward that door in the back wall."

It was a little surprising to me how quickly I had accepted my surroundings – the whole town, not just the saloon or the park. I felt out of sync with many of the things I encountered, like they should be old and worn, not new and shiny. I couldn't understand why, though. The people I had met were just people. It was the bulk of my environment that felt off, even wrong. For instance, Centre Street seemed much wider than I expected it to be, but if you asked me why I thought that, I couldn't begin to form an answer. It was just a gut feeling I got as I looked at it.

Wendi steered me to the door at the back of the room. As we passed the bar, I noticed a young woman with high cheekbones, her raven-black hair braided and pinned up. She stopped drying a shot glass long enough to notice our passage but didn't make eye contact with either of us. She seemed familiar, but I couldn't place her. Her features looked Native American to me. Wendi continued toward the door in the back, so I didn't have a chance to introduce myself to the dark-haired barmaid. Any introduction would have been quite clumsy: '*Hi. I don't know who I am. Do you?*'

Wendi led me to the back of the saloon, and this time, I remembered to open the door for her. Opening the narrow door revealed an equally narrow staircase, its steps leading upward. Wendi motioned for me to lead the way through the door and climb the stairs.

Chapter 2

THE STAIRCASE WAS NARROW enough that we had to climb the steps in single file. I got the feeling that the stairs were an afterthought, as in after the place was built. The stairs only went up one floor, ending at another door at the top. That door opened out into a hallway, its wooden floor rough and bare, as though anyone living up here wasn't concerned about aesthetics. There was a hint of old varnish along the outside edges of the floor, so it had definitely seen better days, but not recently. The walls were painted, but what color had been used was anyone's guess. Like the embossed tin ceiling downstairs, the walls here were a nondescript dirty, tannish beige, regardless of what color they had been originally. Scuff marks scarred the walls from knee level down to the floor.

We walked down the hall, our shoes clomping on the bare wood and echoing in the open space. The corridor was populated with doors every so often, each door identified by a brass number tacked onto it. There were no windows in the doors, and the hallway had only a single bulb overhead. The only other source of light came from a filthy, grime-streaked window at the far end of the hall. The air in the hallway was unmoving and stagnant, laden with rancid cooking odors.

Wendi—Nurse Carter—had stopped partway down the hall. She was standing next to a door with a brass number six tacked about head height. I waited for her to make the next move. This was her domain; I was just a visitor. At least, that's how it felt. Besides, she seemed to know about the people and places in town, while I felt like I had just fallen off the train. *Literally.*

"This is it, Jimmy. This is where you live and work. Number six over the Palace Saloon." *My place? I live and work here?* She reached into a handbag I hadn't noticed her carrying and pulled out an old-fashioned skeleton key.

"I got the key from your pants while you were in the hospital. Not that you really need it. If you give a little lift on the door knob and a little shove, the door opens right up without a key. But we'll pretend to be civilized." She held out the dark, tarnished key toward me.

I took it from her and, rather than fitting it into the lock, dropped it in my pants pocket.

"What? You're not going in?" she asked, her eyebrows arching slightly as she watched my actions.

"I thought maybe we could go downstairs and get something to drink. And talk some more."

"Sure," she replied, but she looked a bit frustrated. "I can't stay very long, but I can sit with you for a while and maybe answer some more questions. I'm assuming you have some questions. Let's go back down the stairs we came up. There's another stairway there at the end of the hall, but it goes outside."

She brushed past me, and I caught a faint smell of her perfume. I started to put my arm up to block her way, but at the last second, I forced my arm down at my side.

When we returned to the stairway, our shoes were just as noisy as they had been when we came up. The echoing, hollow passageway stood in marked contrast to the whisper-quiet hallways of the hospital.

When we reached the stairway door, I asked, "Are all the apartments filled?"

"Mostly. It changes from month to month – sometimes from week to week. Most of the tenants are single guys, but there's a married couple in one apartment and a single gal in one." With that, Wendi opened the door and descended the steps. I followed behind after turning my head for a last glance down the hallway. All the doors looked the same to me. There were no clues to tell who was living in which room, and other than counting the doors, there was nothing to make them stand out from each other.

:::::

Wendi and I sat at one of the empty tables downstairs at the Palace Saloon. A few guys were sitting along the bar, their dirty shoes resting on the shiny brass rail a few inches above the floor. A few crumbles of dried mud littered the floor underneath, apparently scraped from work boots as people sat or stood along the bar.

The girl I saw working behind the bar when we came through earlier came over to our table. She still looked familiar to me and still looked Native American.

"Just a lemonade for me, Danny," Wendi told her. "I have to go back to the hospital to cover for someone tonight."

This was my first opportunity to really get a good look at the barmaid. She was thin, but not too thin. I noticed her high cheekbones again, and as she turned to look at me, I saw that her eyes were dark brown and slightly almond-shaped.

"Yeah?" She had caught me staring at her.

"Excuse me?"

"You gonna have something to drink?"

"Oh! Um … yeah. I'll have a lemonade, too."

She rolled her eyes, turned around, and walked back to the bar. 'Uncle Charlie' looked at us as the girl relayed our orders. He rolled his eyes, too.

"Isn't Danny a little unusual for a girl's name?" I asked.

"It's short for Danielle. Danielle Egly. She goes by Daani. She spells it D-a-a-n-i. She told me once that she has a little Indian blood from her mom's side."

"More than a little, if you ask me. Her hair, cheekbones and her eyes give it away, but especially the hair. Her hair is so long, but it's all braided and pinned up on her head. I wonder how long it is when she lets it down."

"I've never seen it down. And as far as that goes, I've never seen Daani anywhere but here at the Palace."

I watched as the girl brought our drinks over. She was wearing a simple, short-sleeved blue dress with a white apron over it. Her heavy black oxfords clomped on the floor, just like our shoes had done upstairs in the hallway. Her shoes were dusty and looked more gray than black as a result. It had obviously been a long time since they'd seen any polish. *What had my grandpa called shoe polish? Bootblack?*

The barmaid set the tall glasses of lemonade on the table, one in front of each of us. No ice and no straws.

"How much?" I asked.

"Ten cents," Daani replied.

"Each?" I asked. Another eye roll.

"For both," she answered.

I leaned back and was going to dig in my pants pocket, but Wendi had already dug a dime out of her purse and added a second one as a tip. Daani nodded and smiled at Wendi as she picked up the coins. She glanced at me, and the smile evaporated. Daani spun on her heel and was back behind the bar a few seconds later.

We sipped our lemonades and settled back in our chairs. After a long, uncomfortable stretch of silence made longer by my looking around the near-empty saloon, I said, "You know what would go well with this lemonade? Sweet tea. Mix them about half and half."

Wendi took another sip of her lemonade and then turned and caught Daani's eye. The young girl came back to our table and bent down near Wendi. There was a quickly whispered exchange that I couldn't hear, and Daani headed back to the bar. A minute or two later, she returned with a single glass of tannish-golden liquid and a spare empty glass and placed them on the table. Wendi pulled out another nickel and handed it to the barmaid.

Daani returned to her station but stayed on the customer side of the dark, heavy wooden bar so she could watch what transpired at our table.

Wendi took the glass of tea and poured half of it into the empty glass. Then she filled the glass the rest of the way with lemonade. Before I did the same with my lemonade and the remaining tea, I took a sip of the brewed liquid. It was definitely sweet tea – not so sweet as to make your teeth hurt, but there was no doubt about its sweetness. I filled the tea glass up with my lemonade and gave the glass a couple of swirls to mix the two liquids. I lifted my glass in a salute to Wendi and then turned and lifted it in a wordless toast to Daani before taking a large gulp. It was perfect.

Wendi took a sip of hers and smiled. She took another drink, longer this time.

"That *is* good, Jimmy! I can't understand why no one ever thought to do that before."

"Oh, I'm sure other people have done it, but maybe only at home. Or maybe no one made a fuss about it. But that's the way I like it."

"Do you call it anything? Or just tea and lemonade?"

There was another name on the tip of my tongue, Arnie or Arnold something, but I couldn't get it through my damaged brain and down to my tongue. I tried, but nothing came, so I just said, "Half and half."

She looked at me over the rim of her glass and raised her perfectly arched eyebrows. "Like the milk and cream you get from the dairy?"

"Sure. Why not?" I took another drink.

She took one, too, and stared at her glass like she was waiting for something from me. I cleared my throat and obliged her.

"How do you know so much about me?" I asked.

"What makes you think I know a lot about you?"

"You had the key to my apartment. You said you took it from my pants when I was in the hospital."

"Well, you needed it, didn't you?" she stonewalled.

"How did you know where I lived? The doctor didn't know. He asked me where I lived, and I gave him a made-up address because he said I couldn't leave until I knew my name and where I lived. I made up answers for both questions, but it worked, and I got out of the hospital."

"Yes, it *technically* worked, but you might have left the hospital a little early," Wendi said, staring into the now half-empty glass of tea and lemonade before her.

"Why do you say that?"

"Your head injury is a pretty bad injury. The fact that you're still getting light-headed and throwing up on the lawn tells me that the best place for you would be back in that hospital bed."

"So you could give me sponge baths?" I asked with a smile.

"I think you liked that more than I did."

"That sounds like you *did* like it, even if I liked it more."

She took another drink of her tea rather than answer me. It was dark in the saloon, but I could tell her face was a shade pinker than it had been a moment before.

I asked again, "How *do* you know so much about me?" Her answer surprised me.

"Because I work for you."

My mouth dropped open.

"Y—you what?"

"I said, 'I work for you.' Usually, a couple of days a week. I take care of your books and calendar, and I answer the telephone if anyone calls while I'm there."

"Like a secretary?"

"Like a secretary."

"Then you know my real name?"

"I know the name you told me, but I don't know if it's your real name. I've heard you give people so many names during investigations that I'm not a hundred percent sure *you* even know what your real name is."

"That's just it: I *don't* know what my real name is."

"I know. That's the brain injury's fault. But that'll straighten out eventually. Besides, I kind of like the sound of the name Jimmy Marlowe."

"What?! You're not going to tell me what my real name is?"

"It's better if you recover your memory on your own. Plus, Jimmy Marlowe is better than most of the others I've heard you use: Jimmy Dollar, Jimmy Spade, Jimmy Regan, Jimmy Friday, or Jimmy Valentine. Thank goodness you didn't pick Jimmy Holmes or Jimmy Poirot." Wendi took another drink of her tea and lemonade mixture.

"This is really quite good," she said.

I heard her, but I was lost in my own thoughts. I knew I wasn't Jimmy Marlowe, but who *was* I? And who was Wendi to me, really? *In for a penny … time to ask.*

"You say you're my secretary?"

"Sometimes. Other times, I help you solve cases. And other times …" She paused and didn't continue.

I waited. "Yes?"

"Other times, I—don't take this wrong, Jimmy. Other times, I help keep you alive."

"What? You? How?"

"Yes, me, and with these." She held up her hands. "Just these. I'm not the kind of girl who usually carries a gun. I mean, I know *how* to use one, but I don't often *need* one."

I couldn't imagine her punching anyone. I knew from my hospital stay and sponge bath how soft her hands were, but I also knew they were strong. I just wasn't sure they were protect-someone-strong, was all.

"What time is it?" Wendi asked. She looked over her shoulder toward the clock on the wall, which made me think of school. Something about the style of the numbers.

"4:30. Shoot. I'm going to have to go back to the hospital soon. I'm pulling a second shift today. I'm covering for Vicky Hanson. Jimmy, tell me how your head is feeling, and tell me the truth."

I looked at her suspiciously. On top of withholding information about me, she knew too much about me already, but somehow, I knew telling her the truth was for the best.

"My head feels okay right now. No headache, no dizziness. My stomach even feels okay. I'm not sure I'm ready for a seven-course dinner, but I wouldn't say no to a sandwich."

"Okay," she answered. "That's a good sign if you're hungry. Do you have any money on you?"

I reached into my pockets and turned them out, one by one. Empty. *The story of my life. Some things never change.*

"Of course, you don't," she said. "I should have remembered that from when I took your key for safekeeping at the hospital. You also don't have your wallet." She stopped talking and thought for a minute. "That's okay. You have another wallet in your office with a little cash in it—but not much—plus a driver's license and a library card, I think, but that's about it. But that'll work for now."

"What's happening now?" I asked.

"Now? Like I said, I'm going to go back to the hospital, and I hope there aren't a bunch of new patients tonight. You – on the other hand – are going to go to your apartment upstairs, take off those tourist clothes, and put on a different outfit – dark slacks, a white shirt, and a sports jacket. Then get your extra wallet from the bottom right desk drawer, and finally, you are going to walk down the street to the little diner and have a light meal. But keep it light. You don't want a repeat of your performance on the lawn this afternoon. Once you've eaten, I want you to go back home and go to bed. You need sleep to heal your brain. I know you think you got plenty of sleep and rest in the hospital, but you need more."

"Okay, fine, but why do I have to change outfits?" I looked down at my tan shoes with pink shoelaces and the flowery South Seas shirt. "Never mind. I think I get it. I'm trying to blend in, not stick out."

"Like a sore thumb," Wendi answered. She lifted her glass of tea and lemonade – a half and half – and drained it. "Don't worry about me. I'll eat something at the hospital. I may even come by after my shift and make sure you're sleeping okay. If you're lucky, I might even tuck you in." She gave me a wink.

Something about the way she said she might tuck me in made my heart speed up. I also felt guilty because I *wasn't* worrying about her. I hadn't given any thought to where she might eat, how tired she already undoubtedly was after her previous work shift, or how she would get back to the hospital.

"How are you going to get back to the hospital?" I hadn't seen her drive up in a car when I was by the train depot talking to Officer Crane. She had just sort of *appeared*, walking across the lawn to where the Fernandina policeman and I were talking. *Like she was walking into a scene in a Hollywood movie. Or a dream.*

"I've got your car. After all, you're not in any shape to drive. Doc told you that, right? No driving for a few days after a serious head injury. We don't want you passing out and killing people."

I tried to remember what kind of car I had, but my internal registry was blank. Another detail the head injury had stolen.

Wendi got up and came around the table. She leaned over, and for a second, I thought she was going to kiss me on the lips, but at the last second, she changed direction and kissed me on the forehead. A motherly type of peck.

"Remember—go upstairs and change clothes," she said in a commanding tone, mouthing the word 'wallet' silently so no one else in the saloon would hear. Then she continued,

"Eat something light at the diner, and head back to your apartment to sleep."

I resisted the urge to salute and say, 'Yes, ma'am.' Our eyes met briefly, and she knew I was agreeing.

She turned and headed to the front door of the Palace Saloon. The late afternoon sun silhouetted her in the windows. The sun prevented me from seeing anything except her dark silhouette, but I knew she turned briefly and looked back my way for a second. The door opened briefly, and she was gone.

I brought my glass of lemonade and tea to my lips and drank most of the remainder in one swig. Out of the corner of my eye, I caught Daani looking at me; her mouth was turned down in a frown. I gave her a thumbs-up as I finished my drink, but she turned away, not acknowledging my existence.

For some reason, I couldn't imagine Daani anywhere else but in an establishment like this. It was like her presence in a bar ticked some checkbox in my broken brain. This environment was where she belonged. But why? I didn't know the first thing about her, even though there was something naggingly familiar about her.

:::::

THE DINER HAD MEATLOAF with mashed potatoes and brown gravy. It may have been the best meatloaf I ever had, but I couldn't say for sure since I couldn't remember anything before waking up in the hospital sometime in the last couple of days. But even if I only had a few days' worth of memories, it was still the best meatloaf I had eaten as long as I could remember!

I asked for and received another half-and-half lemonade and sweet tea. I could have had coffee, but I didn't want it to keep me up all night. Not that I really *knew* if coffee kept me up at night, but better safe than sorry, I decided. Thinking about Wendi coming by to check on me, I almost changed my mind and got the coffee. *I might not want to be sleeping too deeply.*

Even though she told me to have a light meal, the meatloaf, and the chess pie for dessert, were too good to pass up. The pie's custardy filling was perfect, and the crust was flaky and handmade. *Of course, it's handmade. How else would you make a pie crust?* I thought. The idea of dedicating a factory to making pie crust stuck in my head and bothered me far longer than it should have. Something about it seemed right but seemed out of sync at the same time. Something told me that there would come a time when 'homemade' would go out of fashion in favor of profits and simplicity.

The cute little waitress brought my bill. She looked about fifteen to me, and I figured she was probably working after school for her parents. She laid the bill on the table in front of me; it was time to look in the wallet. Wendi said it had a little money but not much. I hoped there would be enough to cover the meal.

The bills compartment of my wallet held three ones and a five. *She was right about not having much!* Folded several extra times and stuffed down in one corner of the bill compartment was a ten-dollar bill. I didn't know if that was for emergencies, taxi fare, or buying information from a snitch. The me-with-memories had apparently hidden the bill in there for a reason, so I shoved it back down where I found it.

I looked through the rest of the wallet. There was a section with acetate sleeves made for pictures and ID cards. The picture section was empty, which was no surprise. There was a private investigator license in the ID section that said—I nearly fell off my counter stool when I saw it—*Jimmy Marlowe.*

All I could figure out was that it was my go-to alias when I wasn't using my real name. It was obvious that my mind wasn't going to help me out of this memory wasteland in my brain. I was on my own.

I looked at the bill from the waitress. It had very neat handwriting.

Meatloaf, mashed potatoes, & coleslaw special …50¢
Lemonade …15¢ *(the special includes tea or coffee)*
Pie …15¢
Total …80¢

I took a single dollar bill from the wallet and left it on the counter with the tab. That included a 20¢ tip. I was either going to be ridiculed or loved. I stood up, tugged down my sports jacket to straighten it, and walked out the door. I turned right to walk the half-block back to the Palace Saloon and my home that felt nothing like a home.

The waitress picked up the tab and the dollar and smiled broadly, then shuttled the plate, glass, and silverware to the kitchen.

Chapter 3

INSTEAD OF GOING THROUGH the Palace Saloon and up the steep back stairs in the back part of the bar, I decided to use the outside staircase that Wendi said was in the back. As I walked around back, I could see through the Palace's windows. It was full, but I didn't want to have any long conversations with people I should know but couldn't remember.

I knew I wasn't a drinker – not out of any strong moral objections to alcohol, but just because the thought of the taste made my tongue want to curl up and hide down my throat. Offer me sweet tea or a shot of whiskey – even "good" whiskey – and I'd take the tea. Given the choice between a beer and a lemonade, I knew I'd pick the lemonade every time. Beer is bitter to the point of 'why bother?' and most mixed drinks make me wonder if someone siphoned gas out of a car to make them. There is one other reason I prefer non-alcoholic drinks: to the best of my ragged knowledge, I've never gotten a hangover from drinking half-and-half's.

Even though Wendi had said to go straight home and go right to bed, I decided to walk a little more in the night air, and headed toward the waterfront. As I got closer to the docks, I could see a few ships tied up at the wide, sturdy piers. Some of the ships had big nets hanging down from long arms like sails. *Shrimp boats*, I thought. I knew that shrimpers moored at the waterfront, but early every morning, they'd untie and move back into the river channel, quietly sail around the curve and into the St. Marys River, sliding out between Fort Clinch and Cumberland Island before heading out into the Atlantic Ocean to places only the shrimpers knew to drop their nets for a haul.

I stood at the corner, about a block away from the waterfront, then decided to do what Wendi said and meandered back to the Palace and around back. It was quite dark, and I had to feel around to find the stairway, but I eventually found it, my eyes taking a long time to adjust to the darkness.

Suddenly, someone burst out of the door at the top and stomped down the stairs. The light spilling out onto the steps caught me by surprise, and I had to clamp my eyes closed against the glare. I opened them a slit and caught a quick glimpse of a man as he hurriedly pushed past me. He was taller than me, a bit overweight, wearing dark pants, a white shirt, a dark coat, heavy boots, and a bow tie. I didn't recognize him. I may have if I had gotten a better look at his face, but it didn't matter. He had already pushed past me and was gone.

Standing alone in the dark at the bottom of the stairway, I started up the steps. The ancient wooden treads creaked as

I climbed them, and the railing wiggled so loosely in my grasp that it was almost better not to use it. I was sure that more than one person had supported all their weight heavily against the railing after enjoying too many drinks inside the Palace.

I caught myself slanting to one side a tad and realized I was slightly nauseous after my meal. It was larger than it should have been. *I should have listened to Wendi and just had a sandwich and a drink.* But the meatloaf was so good, and its homey aroma hit me the second I opened the diner door, and I knew I had to have it. My mind may not have been able to affirm it with experiential confidence, but my body sure did: I was a meat-and-potatoes guy. There was no need for anything green on my plate; just give me meat and potatoes. The fresh chess pie was the perfect sweet follow-up. Perfect any time, that is, except after a severe head injury. The meal's components were conspiring to push me over the edge into debilitating queasiness.

Despite squeezing my eyes against the glare from the opened door, the familiar bright white light behind my closed eyelids began to assault my brain. I clutched the railing more tightly. I wished it was fastened to the wall as tightly as I was gripping it. I was about ten feet off the ground – not enough to kill me if I fell, but bad enough to mess me up pretty good, especially if I hit my head again. In that case, a fall from here might kill me.

After a few seconds and some deep breaths, my stomach and head settled down enough that I could continue the last few steps to the top. I opened the old weather-beaten door, surprised that the light that seemed so bright a moment before was emanating from a single small bulb in a wire cage in the middle of the hallway.

My shoes sounded heavy and hard in the hallway, just like earlier when Wendi and I came up from the Palace to introduce me to my digs. Although my head was slightly better, it still hurt, so I was glad I was almost home. I needed to go in and lie down.

I tried to walk down the hallway in a straight line, but I kept caroming off the walls, bouncing from side to side as I worked my way toward door number six. At least twice, I thought about sliding down the wall and sitting on the floor until Wendi came to check on me. She could help me get to bed.

The thought of Wendi brought a smile to my lips. She was beautiful, but she was familiar, too. *Probably just wishful thinking.* But no, she said she was my secretary. She "knew things" about me, but she wasn't willing to tell me those things. It would be better for my brain, she said. I should figure out who I am on my own, she said. *I don't think I like it when other people tell me what to do!*

I lurched ahead again, moving several feet down the hall toward my apartment. When Wendi and I came up the inside stairs, we approached my room from the opposite direction, coming from the other end of the hallway.

"I should be there by now, shouldn't I?"

And just like that, I was at number six. I plunged my hand into my trouser pocket for the key that Wendi gave me. I was about to insert it into the lock when I noticed a dim light peeking out from under the door. Even with my damaged brain, I knew I hadn't left any lights on inside.

I tried the doorknob. It rotated easily in my hand, and the door opened silently. I did my best to slip inside as noiselessly as the door had opened. I left the door slightly ajar to avoid causing any noise by letting it latch when it closed. I walked warily across the darkened room. The light was coming from the back room – my bedroom. Anyone trying to rob me would be sorely disappointed. Other than the hidden ten-dollar bill in my wallet, I had a total of seven dollars to my name.

Suddenly, I stumbled and tripped over something on the floor in front of me and fell forward. My brain wasn't helping my balance, and I crashed face-first onto something—no, someone! It was a person, and whoever it was, they were soft and warm and smelled of very feminine perfume. I reached out with my hands to get up and accidentally gripped her upper torso, her chest, to be more precise. I had accidentally gotten luckier with a body on the floor than I ever did with a girl in high school! And, whoever she was, she didn't react to my accidental groping.

The door to my bedroom opened, and light flooded out, illuminating the scene in front of me. It was a woman's body – a very attractive brunette – but a very *dead* attractive brunette. She had a small, neat hole in her left temple. It was a small caliber bullet hole; my brain said probably a .22 caliber as my mind automatically analyzed the information coming in without my permission or persuasion. I tried to push myself up and away from the body, my brain continuing to catalog more data as my eyes took in the scene thanks to the torrent of light pouring from the bedroom. I slipped and got another handful of her chest.

"Sorry," I whispered. I was nearly face-to-face with her.

I saw there were powder burns around the wound, so the gun had most likely been pressed against her head when it was fired. There was a dark circle around the wound to her temple, which I guessed was from a silencer, a tiny version of a car muffler screwed onto the gun barrel. There wouldn't have been a great deal of noise from the small caliber gunshot even without the silencer, but the silencer would have muffled it more. And, with a busy bar downstairs, no one was going to notice a stray, tiny thump from somewhere upstairs.

I saw that the woman's eyes were still open, as was her mouth; she looked surprised. From her makeup and evening dress, she looked like she was going out for the evening or to meet someone. She wore small, tasteful earrings and a matching necklace; they were sparkly, but I was pretty sure it was costume jewelry, not the real deal. *Don't ask me how I knew; I couldn't tell you.*

Her dark brown hair was arranged stylishly and was still in place despite being shot and ending up on the floor. Whoever killed her had probably been holding her by the arms and eased her down after firing the gun. There were probably two people involved in the murder.

In my mind's eye, I could visualize how each person held one of the dead woman's arms. The person on her left had raised the gun, placed it against her temple, and pulled the trigger. The killers let her sag to the floor; her descent slow, easy, and quiet. There had been no thump to hear in the saloon down below. One thing was for sure: it was *not* a crime of passion.

With that thought, four hands – two pairs – gripped my sports coat and hauled me upright. Even as they did, I was still looking at the body of the woman I had stumbled over, still taking mental snapshots of the tableau.

"Hey! You ain't supposed to be here!" an angry voice barked at me.

I stammered something nonsensical, "I—I didn't know. I—I had to see, b-but I'm in the wrong place…"

I looked at the two men in my apartment, which I now realized was not my apartment. *How did I end up here?* I wondered. *Where's my apartment?*

One of the men who grabbed me had a wild shock of curly red hair, and the other sported a slicked-back ducktail as black as midnight. Both men wore similar non-descript dark suits, dingy white shirts, and dark ties. The curly-haired man wore dark leather gloves, which was a little unusual since it wasn't cold outside, but I was pretty sure he had only worn them in the apartment.

Curly, the one with red curly hair, chastised me again angrily. "Hey, numb-nuts! I said you ain't supposed to be here! That's supposed to be your alibi, don't you remember? You need to be on the train, not stumbling around in here in our way!"

"Yeah, not getting in our way!" echoed Slick, his dark-haired companion. His hair looked like it was coated with about a cup of used motor oil. He periodically ran a hand through his dark, greasy coiffure, his fingers combing it straight back.

"I— I-uh, I had to get something I forgot. I didn't want to turn on the light, so I tripped … over …" My voice trailed off. This was obviously a planned murder, and they thought I was her husband or lover, who was apparently involved in the setup.

"Hurry up and get whatever you forgot, then get out! You need to be on that train before it leaves in ten minutes. That's what the boss told us."

This was definitely not my apartment, but it was laid out the same, so I turned and hustled into the back room, the bedroom. I saw a wedding picture standing on the nightstand. This was the bedroom of the married couple Wendi had mentioned to me as she counted up the tenants. A terrifying thought sprang into my head and pinballed around inside. I was neither of the people in the wedding picture on the nightstand. I knew the two thugs would come to the same realization. No one could be obtuse enough to not notice. Once they figured out I wasn't the husband—or whoever set up this murder for hire—there were going to be two bodies in that front room very soon, one of them mine!

I looked around the room hurriedly, spinning to see what I could grab as the thing I "forgot." I needed to get out of this apartment fast and get out of their way. As I whirled, I accidentally knocked a small container off the makeup table. It landed on the floor more loudly than I expected.

"Hey! What's going on in there?" Curly shouted.

"N-nothing. Just getting what I came back here for," I lied.

The container was full of makeup powder but had spilled all over the thin rug covering the bedroom floor. Then I saw it: a bundle of some sort, covered in powder, half-hidden under the overturned container. I picked it up and blew some of the powder off.

It was a wad of money. Depending on the denominations involved, it could be fifty bucks, several hundred, or more. I rubbed the bundle on a frilly nightgown hanging from the closet door to clean off some of the excess powder and then shoved the money into my coat pocket. I stepped back over near the nightstand just as Slick poked his head in the door.

"What's taking you so long?"

I grabbed the small wedding picture from the nightstand and shoved it into my other coat pocket, the one not holding the bankroll. "Nothing. I've got it now."

"Gimmee." Slick held out a hand. I hesitated. He pulled back his coat to reveal a dark, ugly handgun in a shoulder holster. I recognized it as a Luger, probably WWII surplus. I held up my hands, pulled out the wedding picture, and handed it to him.

"Why do you want this?" he asked after giving it a barely cursory glance in the darkened room. Most people don't examine a wedding picture too closely. They all have a bride and groom, and most couples don't look like they did when the picture was taken.

"Think about it," I said. "Who's going to suspect a guy who brings his wedding picture along on a trip?"

Slick looked at me for a moment, trying to follow my line of reasoning. He finally shrugged, let his coat fall closed over his gun again, handed me the picture, and stepped to one side of the bedroom. "Awright. Now get out!"

I shoved the picture back in my pocket and left the room as quickly as I could, squeezing past Slick and stepping out into the front room. Curly was looking around the room, pulling open drawers, emptying them out, and looking behind books on the bookshelf.

"Where is it?" he asked.

I was almost to the door. I stopped, swallowed hard, and turned back because I knew his question was for me, and I needed to answer.

"Where's what?" I asked, taking a step backward from the door and my freedom.

"I figure there's gotta be some cash in here. Angelo and I deserve a bonus since you've caused us so much trouble."

So much trouble? Yeah, right. But that's not what I said.

"I-uh, I don't have any. I spent it on the train ticket. Speaking of which, I *really* need to get on that train."

"C'mon. Don't give me that. Anyone willing to spend a couple of hundred bucks to have their wife whacked is gonna have some more hidden away." Slick had come out of the bedroom and was standing near Curly. Except now I knew his name was Angelo, not Slick.

I pulled out my wallet and made a big show of pulling out the five and two ones. "Seven bucks. That's all I've got, fellas."

Curly crossed the room in two steps, and his glove-covered hand flashed out. I thought he was going to hit me, but he grabbed the seven dollars instead.

"That'll buy us lunch this week, Sean," Angelo said.

Curly sneered at the remark. He jammed the bills into his pants pocket. I made a quick mental note that his name was Sean. Sean and Angelo. Curly and Slick.

"We still need a *tip* for doing you this favor, Mr. Brody," Curly said, deftly stepping between me and the door.

How would <u>Philip</u> Marlowe have answered them? *I'm sorry, boys. I don't know any Mr. Brody. I'll just be on my way. You can show yourself out after you straighten up in here.'*

But <u>Jimmy</u> Marlowe said, "I… um, I could write you a check … if that'll work."

"I dunno," Angelo said.

"Yeah. That'll work," Curly answered.

"It will?" I said, incredulous. "I mean, yes, it will. Good. Just let me get my checkbook."

I hoped the checkbook would be in the desk I had seen. I pulled open the middle drawer, and sure enough, there was a checkbook. I remained standing as I leaned over to write the check. I figured it would be too easy for them to prevent a quick getaway if I was sitting behind the desk.

"Make it out to Cash," Curly said.

"Gotcha," I answered.

"And make it out for five hundred."

"Five hundred?" I gulped. "I don't know that I can—"

Curly pulled his coat open, putting his hand on his gun. I could see that the silencer he had used on the gun when he shot the unfortunate woman lying across the room was still attached, the gun's barrel poking out through the bottom of the shoulder holster.

"Five hundred it is," I answered. I wrote out the check to Cash for five hundred dollars and no 100s, drawing a wiggly line over to the right. I was just going to sign the check when I suddenly froze. I had no idea what Brody's first name was. They would figure it out, and there would be two bodies on the floor. All my scenarios ended up with two bodies on the floor, one of them mine!

Time suddenly slowed to a crawl. I glanced around the desk's surface and saw an envelope addressed to K. Brody.

'Names that start with K,' I thought. *Kent. Kurt. Karl. Kevin. Just pick one! Kayden. Kaiser. No … King!* Something itched at the back of my brain at the thought of the name King. It belonged to a big guy, but I didn't have even two seconds of time to invest in trying to remember who it fit, and I shooed the thought away. Time began ticking again, tripping along at its regular breakneck speed.

I was out of time. I picked a name and signed the check as though I had done it a million times. "Kenneth Brody," I wrote, finishing with a big flourish on the y at the end of Brody. I handed the check to Curly and stepped away from the desk.

"I—uh, think I have a train to catch."

Curly made a show of folding the check in half and sliding it into his shirt pocket.

"Yeah, you do that, Mr. Brody. Enjoy your trip to Chicago. And say hi to Julie for us."

"Yeah," Angelo added, "and eat a hot dog for me and Sean."

Curly rolled his eyes under the mop of red hair. Even though I knew his real name was Sean, I thought Curly fit him better. Maybe if I saw him do a jig or sing *Danny Boy,* I'd change my mind. I hadn't noticed much of an Irish lilt in his voice, but we hadn't spent much time getting to know each other socially.

I hurried out the door, ran for the stairs, and flew down the steps. No grass was going to grow under my feet! I looked over my shoulder as I came around the front of the Palace building and saw Curly, aka Sean, looking out the window of the apartment. I still had no idea how I ended up in that apartment instead of mine, but it was clear that I needed to get on the train and get out of town. Curly was still watching my progress as I hustled across the street and down the forty or fifty yards to the train depot.

I ran over to the ticket window and finally got a small break. The ticket agent's window was on the side of the building, away from my apartment window, shielding me from Sean and Angelo's suspicious gazes. They could no longer see or track me.

"One ticket for the nearest stop," I said.

"That'd be Baldwin, just outside of Jacksonville," the ticket agent answered.

I said that was fine and paid my two dollars for the ticket, ran for the door where the conductor waited, and hurried up the little portable steps into the train car. I must have been the last one for the night because the conductor picked up the steps and climbed in after me.

I stumbled into a seat and sat down, sweating profusely and huffing and puffing. Mercifully, my head wasn't hurting, and my stomach was no longer queasy. After a minute, my breathing started slowing down. I pulled a handkerchief from the interior pocket of my coat jacket and mopped my brow.

I stared out the window as the train jerked and began moving. I watched the boats at the waterfront as we slowly pulled away. *I'm going to make it!*

Soon, the boats, ships, nets, and heavy ropes fell behind us, and the river disappeared, replaced first by the salt marsh and then by tall, straight pines. There were no houses back in among the pines, but something in my mind whispered, *Someday!* I didn't know if I was just acknowledging the inevitable progress that would someday fill this area with houses, restaurants, and other assorted businesses or if this was another of those future memories I had been having. There was no need to fixate on it, though, so I settled back in my seat and closed my eyes.

I was suddenly assaulted by a loud voice right next to my head.

"Hi, Marlowe!"

Who could that be? I opened my eyes and turned to look. It was the man with the bowtie who had run down the stairs in the back of the Palace as I was starting up the stairs. He was no longer masked by shadows, but I still couldn't ID him. Unfortunately, he obviously recognized me.

"I've seen you around the apartments a few times, but I've never had the opportunity to introduce myself. My wife and I live in apartment nine. I'm Kendall Brody."

I suddenly felt sick to my stomach, but not from my head injury. I had taken a huge gamble when signing the check in Brody's apartment, going all in as I signed *Kenneth Brody* on the signature line. I had bluffed, and I had lost.

'K' also stood for KENDALL!

Chapter 4

I WAS PART OF Brody's alibi. I hadn't understood it before, but it was clear now. A good alibi has people who can recall seeing you at a certain time and place. A great alibi has people who can recall seeing you backed up by a paper trail with dates and times, like the train ticket I held in my hand as I waited for the conductor. When the cops came to my door asking about Brody's wife, I would be an integral part of his alibi.

It was Kendall's wife lying dead in their apartment with a bullet hole in her left temple. She was the same woman with the wad of bills hidden in a container of face powder on her vanity table. The same wad of bills that were now in my coat pocket, minus the two dollars for the train fare to Baldwin.

Brody stood there, holding out a hand, waiting for me to shake it. I smiled weakly and, almost as feebly, shook his hand.

"Kendall, you say?"

"Kendall Brody. On my way to Chicago. Business trip, you know. Well, business *and* a little pleasure." As he mentioned pleasure, he grinned and winked at me, like I should understand what he was referring to.

Right. Pleasure. Because you just got rid of your wife.

"I'm Jimmy. Jimmy Marlowe, private investigator."

"You mean like a cop?" Kendall asked.

"Not really. Most of the work I do is for insurance companies. People trying to collect insurance money they don't deserve." *Shut up, Jimmy! The guy just had his wife killed!*

Kendall grimaced, and his eyebrows rose. My heart and attitude sank. He knew that I knew.

"Are you referring to anyone in particular, Mr. Marlowe?"

"No, not at all," I backpedaled. "Most of the time, it's not even anyone in Fernandina. I usually have to check on people over in Jacksonville. As a matter of fact, that's where I'm going now. Jacksonville."

Brody's smile had faded, and he stared darkly across the short gap between us. It was one of those cars where the seats faced each other rather than like an auditorium where all the seats faced the same way. I guessed it was supposed to be better for families or groups on long trips. It was intended to be easier for conversations.

"Did you know that Jacksonville was originally called Cow Ford?" I asked in a lame attempt to change the subject. "There was a low spot in the river where farmers could drive their cows across to take them to market. Then they didn't have to pay for a ferry or go further upstream or downstream to take their cattle across."

I hadn't been paying close attention before, but now I noticed that Brody was holding a folded overcoat in his lap. He saw where my eyes were looking, and his smile returned, but it wasn't the kind of smile that said, 'I'm so glad to see you.' It was a sad smile that said, 'I wish you hadn't said anything.'

With his left hand, he lifted the overcoat slightly, and I could see a handgun of some sort held by his right hand. It was another small caliber gun with a slender barrel. After Angelo's and Sean's, baby made three; it was the third one I'd seen that evening. It was not the kind of show-and-tell I liked. And since Brody knew I knew, it was time to lay our cards on the table. *In for a penny ...* I thought.

Our train car was almost empty. Apparently, there wasn't a big call for trains to Jacksonville at this time of night. Automobiles could get there just as fast or faster. Despite the semi-privateness of our car, I leaned forward into the gap between us and kept my voice down so only he could hear.

"That's the third one of *those* I've seen tonight," I said in a hushed voice. "Except yours doesn't have that little muffler on the barrel. You wouldn't want to use that thing in here; it would draw way more attention to you than you want."

"I'd really rather not use it at all," Brody replied. "But I can't have you messing things up for me."

"Trust me, I'd rather you not use it, too!" I answered.

We stopped talking for a bit, both of us listening to the click of the train's wheels on the track, feeling the car's addictive rhythm as it swayed and bounced lightly over the rails.

After an uncomfortable pause, I said, "I believe you, and I don't honestly think you're going to use that. You didn't use it earlier tonight – *at home*," I added pointedly. "I think if you could have, you would have. But I don't think that's who you are."

Then an unsettling thought hit me: *'Maybe he couldn't because he knew his wife for a long time and still had feelings for her. But me? He doesn't know me from the dog lying in the middle of the street in the afternoon sun. He's got no reason to keep me around.'* I forced the thought out of my brain, choosing not to let my notions continue down that trail.

"We've got some time," Brody said. "Let's just sit here and talk and get to know each other. Maybe we'll figure out something that works for both of us."

Spoken like a true businessman. Let's make a deal.

Kendall Brody looked over his shoulder at the rest of the car. There were barely a handful of passengers, and most appeared to be dozing. I didn't figure there was a sleeper car attached to this train. Most people who took this short hop would get off in Jacksonville and go home or to a hotel before boarding another train destined for a distant location. I just hoped I could pay another two bucks and return to Fernandina. If Kendall was truly going to Chicago like he said, he'd probably switch trains in Jacksonville and pick up a northbound one.

It would have been convenient to have some tracks going directly north from Fernandina, but the St. Marys River lay in the way, and it was affected by tides several times each day, an action that could take a heavy toll on a train trestle. To go straight north up the coast from Fernandina would be to cross the St. Marys at its widest. It was easier to stay on dry land and go to the big city of Jacksonville and catch a train leaving in whichever direction you desired to go. That was fine for most passengers, but I didn't want to go anywhere except back to my apartment and see Wendi when she came to tuck me in after her shift at the hospital. *What if Slick and Curly are in my apartment when Wendi comes?*

I struggled to push thoughts of Slick and Curly from my brain. They'd been in Brody's apartment, which meant they could wait in my place just as easily. I decided to step into the lion's den like Daniel. *Will I see morning like Daniel did?*

I screwed up my courage and uttered a one-word question across the gap between Brody and me: "Why?"

I let the question hang uncomfortably between us. I didn't care how he interpreted the question, as long as he quit thinking about the gun in his lap pointed in my direction. I didn't want him to think shooting me was even a remotely potential solution to this scenario we had discovered ourselves in. There were myriad ways out if we thought about it. *So, let's think about it.*

Kendall answered, slowly at first, but he answered exactly as I figured he would.

"She wanted different things than I did, a different life. When I go on business trips, she hangs around at her precious country club. She talked one of her girlfriends into nominating her for membership, and then the girlfriend pushed it through. She got voted in as a member and could hobnob with all the businessmen's wives. I make a decent living, right? But I'm not on the same level as the 'captains of industry' at the club. They're men who own and run paper mills, like the Gilman Paper Company across the river in St. Marys or the Rayonier pulp mill that started here just before the war. That pulp machine was a godsend to Fernandina. And because Rayonier opened a plant here, Kraft opened a container plant here about the same time. The population of sleepy little Fernandina jumped by almost twenty percent between 1930 and 1940.”

"What did it do for you, Kendall?" I asked, using his first name like we were old friends. He probably recognized the tactic from Salesmanship Class 101. Whether he caught the bit of familiarity or ignored it, I couldn't say. He kept talking, which meant he wasn't shooting.

"I make a good living, and the container factory, pulp mill, shrimping industry, and the pogy plant up on the island's north end ensure that. I'm a plumbing wholesaler. I started out as a plain old plumber, but I saw the handwriting on the wall and switched from *doing* the work to bringing in the raw materials for *others* to get their hands dirty. Plumbers and builders and factories and industries all buy from me. So, yes, I make a very comfortable living. But it wasn't enough for Catherine." His mouth turned down in a sad frown.

Catherine! That was the name of the body – the woman! – I had tripped over in their darkened apartment.

"She spent practically every minute at her darling club whenever I was on a business trip. When I was at home, she always told me how much more I needed to do to grow my business – how much more I could do if I applied myself. As if she had any idea what it was like working and traveling for meetings. What she really meant was how much more she could *spend* if I brought home more. The woman bought closetfuls of dresses, and she only wore most of them one time for a party at The Club. She bought cheap costume jewelry and passed it off as genuine. Thank goodness for small favors."

I remembered the sparkly earrings and the "diamond" neck choker Catherine was wearing when Curly and Angelo ended her life to fix Kendall's fiscal and marital problems. Even to my amateur eye, I had picked out the jewelry as fake.

"It was at one of those parties at the club that she met Doyle. She went on and on about Doyle. She told me he was young but ambitious – much more ambitious than I was. She said he was trying to make something of himself – as if I wasn't!" Kendall's face turned darker, his complexion redder. I could tell he was getting riled, talking about his wife and whoever this Doyle was.

I noticed that whenever Brody mentioned Doyle's name, my scalp began to itch, like the name was trying to trigger a memory, but my cracked skull kept short-circuiting, preventing me from adding two and two together. I knew it must mean something, though. I'd just have to wait and hope someone could make sense of it for me. Meanwhile, Kendall, the consummate salesman, was still talking.

"I finally met this Doyle – he was just a young kid, actually. But, in all honesty, he is truly ambitious. He told me he could help me with my 'problem' with Catherine. 'What problem?' I asked him. 'Her lack of respect for you,' he answered. And there it was. In less than thirty seconds, he had boiled it down to its simplest form."

Kendall turned his head and looked over his shoulder again. Most of the people in the train car had their heads down on their chests, lulled to sleep by the train's hypnotic rhythm as we chugged toward Jacksonville. No one was listening to our conversation.

I kept still and quiet in my seat, not making any move to wrestle the gun away from the former plumber. Any sudden movement I made would probably cause a reflex reaction, namely, Brody pulling the trigger on the handgun aimed in my general direction. He was so close that there was no conceivable way he could miss me, even if firing the weapon by accident. *Let's not have any accidents!* I kept quiet and let the plumbing supply salesman talk. It occurred to me that he was probably a good salesman; he liked to hear himself talk.

"Doyle told me he could make my problem go away for a couple of hundred bucks—quietly disappear was the actual phrase he used. I told him I wanted no part of anything like that. At first."

Brody got a faraway look in his eyes and continued, "But the seed had been planted in my brain. It was all I could think about, especially on my trips to Chicago."

He paused and looked out the car's windows as dark silhouettes of occasional trees or telephone poles flew past. I waited, watching him with what I hoped was an expression of interest. I had a gut feeling about where he was going next in his confession. I honestly hoped he would disappoint me and reveal something other than what I expected.

From our "encounter in the dark," I knew Catherine had a pretty face, even with her final expression of surprise. She was petite, with a tiny waist and nice curves where they belonged. I knew because I had accidentally checked them out trying to discover what or who I had stumbled over in the dark. I felt my face warming, and I looked out the window and concentrated on the dark shadows flitting past in the night so he wouldn't notice me blushing and ask me about it.

Brody continued his tale. "There's another woman—her name is Julie—up in Chicago. I met her in a tavern one night on a business trip. I didn't mean for anything to happen. It was all innocent at the time. It just happened. You know how it is. You're a man, Marlowe. A lonely man in a big city, far away. We've got …needs, right?"

"I've traveled to and from faraway places," I replied. *I think I have, anyway.* "And I haven't let my 'needs' – as you call them – make me do foolish things."

I stopped. I didn't want to make him angry now and decide to pull the trigger and take his chances with the small group of people in our car. His coat would act as a silencer, and with the pops and bangs of the train rolling on the tracks, no one would probably even notice.

Brody's face had turned a deep red. I didn't know if it was anger or embarrassment over his admittance that he couldn't control his base urges. I needed to get back on his good side, a colleague who could empathize.

"But I wasn't married to Catherine," I said quickly, trying to soothe him. "I have never even been married, for that matter." *Not that I know of, anyway!*

"So, you don't know what it's like!" Kendall said harshly, briefly pulling the gun out from under the overcoat and flashing it my way to punctuate his sentence. He suddenly realized what he was doing and shoved it back under the coat, looking around the car as he did. No one had stirred or looked in our direction. The train continued gently rocking its passengers in their slumber.

"Tell me about Julie," I said calmly, even though I felt a drip of sweat run down my back.

He glared at me for a second, and I thought he was going to ignore me and just keep me sitting across from him until he came up with some way to get rid of his other problem: *me*. He cleared his throat, swallowed, and spoke again, this time of Julie.

"She's everything that Catherine is not—or was not. Julie is authentic, sincere, and satisfied with her station in life. She doesn't need fancy gowns, jewelry, or dress-up parties to be happy. It's like she can read my mind. Julie thinks I'm rich enough; she says money isn't everything. She says money makes people do stupid things. Julie says love is what counts. She thinks love is all we need. She's a little naïve, I guess, but when I'm with her, I don't need anything or anyone else."

I was glad Kendall was talking again. I needed him to think happy thoughts, not contemplate how to get rid of me and make good his escape. He wasn't even actually escaping; I was the one trying to escape. Kendall Brody was just going on a regular business trip like he had done many times before. Except this time, his wife was dead on the floor of their apartment, a neat, round hole in her temple where the bullet had entered her skull.

"Recently, Julie said she couldn't continue with things the way they had been. She didn't want to be 'the other woman' and hide away from people, meeting in hotels and bars. She said I needed to make a decision: choose Catherine or her. She left me in my hotel room all week. Alone. She said she wanted me to think seriously about what I wanted.

"When I returned to Fernandina, Catherine had a surprise for me and not a good one. She said she had hired a private investigator to tail me in Chicago—" He suddenly paused, and his eyes narrowed to a pair of slashes on his face as he glared suspiciously at me. "Was it you, Marlowe? Did she hire you?"

I thought he might shoot me at that moment just because of my profession.

"No! I've never even met Catherine!" I didn't want to tell him I had 'met' her earlier that evening, but it had only been memorable for me; she was already dead. Brody still had no idea I had been to his apartment, and I wasn't going to tell him.

Kendall scowled at me for the span of a few breaths, then said tersely, "Catherine told me the detective had seen me with Julie and saw her go with me to my hotel room. She said she could forgive my little indiscretion, but her hired detective also investigated my financial information." This last revelation made him grimace. He looked like he was going to spit something bad from his mouth.

He rolled his neck and shoulders, the bones making cracking and popping noises, and continued. "We've been living in that miserable apartment for several years, waiting until I had enough saved up to build my dream home, sell the business, and quit working. All fine and true, except I had told her the apartment was all I could afford for now, but if she was patient, we'd get something nicer someday, which was kind of true. But thanks to that *detective*," he said the word like it was a curse, "she knew I had cash and investments worth half a million. Money was not really as tight as I led her to believe. I kept her in the dark because she would have spent it all in no time. She informed me she wanted three-quarters of the money I had in the bank, half of my investments, and a thousand dollars for a monthly allowance. And a divorce, of course. That's when I remembered what Doyle had told me. Two hundred lousy bucks could fix my problems."

"So, you took him up on his offer?"

Brody nodded, a grim smile crossing his face. "It wasn't as hard a decision as you might think. Two hundred bucks in cash versus nearly three-hundred-and-seventy-five thousand hard-earned dollars? I'm a businessman, Mr. Marlowe. For the price of a couple of business trips to Chicago, I could keep my business and all my money *and* have Julie to boot. Are you familiar with the expression a win-win situation?"

I nodded, but he continued without noticing my tacit answer.

"I met with Doyle and a couple of other guys he said worked for him. One had red, curly hair—"

"—and the other had jet black hair, oiled up and slicked back, right?"

"That's them. Sean and Angelo. I gave Doyle three hundred dollars—he said the price had risen slightly—and he said the boys would take care of everything. He told me to take a trip to Chicago to see Julie and give her the good news, and when I came back, I'd be a free man. This trip was supposed to be my alibi. I couldn't kill Catherine if I was over a thousand miles away, could I?"

I shook my head. I didn't want to tell him that ordering the killing of his wife was still murder, even if he didn't personally pull the trigger. But something else about what he had just told me was bothering me.

"When did you tell Doyle about Julie? By name, I mean?" I asked.

Brody thought about it. "Come to think of it, I never did. I wonder how he knew her name?"

"And how much did he originally say it would cost to get rid of Catherine?"

"Two hundred dollars. But he said there were 'complications,' so the price had gone up."

"Complications like a wife who had already paid him two hundred dollars to get rid of *you* until you saw her bet and raised it a hundred. That meant Doyle got *five* hundred dollars to kill your wife, not two or three. Two hundred dollars came from your wife to kill *you,* and three more were from you to kill *her*. Doyle kept her money and took yours to boot! Whoever had the bigger bankroll was going to be the big winner. Lucky you! You had more in the bank than she did! Ultimately, though, the big winner was Doyle."

Kendall Brody turned red, then suddenly went white, as he realized how close he had come to being the lump on the floor I had stumbled over, which he still didn't know I had tripped over.

Everything made sense to me. I had nothing to lose by telling him what I had figured out, so I did, telling him about my accidental visit to his apartment earlier.

"Even without much light to see by, I knew there were no signs of struggle in your apartment. The two hired killers were neat and efficient, and I saw the look of shock etched permanently on Catherine's face. She assumed the two hoods were waiting for you to give you what you deserved. No doubt her astonishment came when they delivered the big surprise to her instead. That's why there weren't any signs of struggle in your place: they were all pals. It was a business deal, nothing more."

I told him their mistake was in assuming all she had was two hundred. She had at least five more C-notes in that wad of cash I found in the makeup powder. She could have seen Kendall's offer and raised him another hundred. Doyle would have garnered seven hundred, and I wouldn't be sweating on this train with a gun pointed my way. Mister trying-to-make-something-of-himself settled for the low-hanging fruit. He got greedy and impatient. Unless he didn't care because he had other plans.

"Another thing," I said. "I have a gut feeling Julie was in on it, too." I watched him for signs of anger at that revelation. Nothing. So, I continued.

"I wonder how many traveling businessmen who regularly visit Chicago have received similar ultimatums from the same Julie. Maybe she was double-booked the week she left you in your hotel to 'think about your situation.' Or maybe there's a whole fleet of Julie's, all of them working with Doyle."

We rode in silence for a long time, both of us drawing connections in our brains we didn't want to make.

The conductor came through the car and announced that we'd be pulling into the Baldwin station soon. That's where I wanted to get off, hopefully under my own steam. It was time to find out if I had planted enough seeds of doubt in Brody's mind for him to let me go.

I stood up.

"Sit down, you!" Kendall snapped.

"No!"

I was taking a chance, standing up to him, refusing to do what he asked.

"Why you—"

"What? D'you still want to kill me? Why? All I did was accidentally go into your apartment instead of mine and stumble onto your little murder-for-hire scheme. By my reckoning, I did you a favor. If I were you, I'd forget about Julie. I have a feeling she's not expecting to see you back in Chicago anyway."

"You really think she was in on it, don't you, Marlowe?"

"Even if she wasn't, is she really the marrying kind, Kendall? Once a cheater, always a cheater. Could you ever trust her completely?"

Brody glared at me, and I saw his hands fidget under his overcoat. I was taking a big chance, playing on his emotions this way. Angry men do things they wouldn't do when they were calm. I had no guarantee how he would react.

The train lurched as the brakes grabbed hold as the train came into Baldwin, just outside Jacksonville. The jolt threw me into Brody, and I shoved him to my right, toward the windows, while I dodged left and ran to the other end of the car, betting that he wouldn't fire at me when I was amid the other now-awake passengers.

I opened the door and stepped across the gap between the two cars, opened the door to the next car, and dashed inside. I didn't care if a conductor yelled at me for running between cars. Words couldn't hurt me nearly as much as a bullet.

I performed the same feat in the second car, putting two cars between us. Then I slowed to a fast walk, repeatedly looking over my shoulder to check if Brody was following me. There was no sign of him. However, he could still be waiting outside for me when I got off, and all my running would be in vain.

Once the train was nearly completely stopped, I pushed ahead of the other passengers to get to the door. I didn't care if they thought I was rude. I didn't bother with the steps the conductor was positioning for passengers. Instead, I jumped out of the door and down to the platform. I nearly knocked the conductor down as I landed. He hollered something at my back as I dashed into the depot, but I didn't hear and didn't care. I hurried out the other side of the depot.

I kept walking until I reached Baldwin's little downtown a few blocks away, continually checking behind me for signs of Kendall. He had apparently taken my words to heart and given up on catching me. He was thinking of Julie and what might or might not be waiting for him in Chicago.

Then I thought of something that heaped a new pile of worry on me: he knew where I lived and could just take his time going back to Fernandina. If he didn't go to Chicago, he could wait for me at my apartment, downstairs in the

Palace Saloon, or outside in the alley – any number of places. And he still had his gun.

But that was a future worry. For now, I was alive.

I waited in a shop doorway until I heard the train leave the station, then waited a half hour more before going back to the depot and buying another two-dollar ticket back to Fernandina. Unfortunately, the train that had just departed was the last train for the night. I couldn't leave by train until 7 a.m.

After getting the station manager's reluctant approval, I settled back onto a hard, wooden bench lining the inside of the depot. I was going to keep my butt glued there until it was time to leave in the morning.

With so much time on my hands, I worried about Wendi. She said she was going to come and check on me after she finished her shift at the hospital. I wished there was some way to get a message to her so she wouldn't worry.

Instinctively, I reached into my inside coat pocket, surprised that it only contained my wallet. I wasn't sure what I was reaching for in my pocket. It seemed like a natural movement; I felt like I'd made the same move uncounted times before under similar situations. My muscle memory was reaching for something, but what?

I thought, *'It would be great if I had a portable telephone; then I could call her. Like Dick Tracy.'* Portable telephone? *You're thinking crazy thoughts, Jimmy!*

I got up and went to the depot window, where the station master sat. He was wearing a white shirt with elastic arm bands above his elbows and a visor on his forehead.

"Can I send a message to Fernandina?" I asked.

"Western Union?" he replied.

"Sure," I said, though I wasn't. I recalled seeing the Western Union sign near the saloon, though, so maybe I was on to something.

It was half past eight p.m. Wendi was still working for another hour and a half.

"Send a message to Wendi Carter at the hospital in Fernandina." *What's the name of the place you were just a guest at?* I tried to remember.

"Nassau County General?" he asked.

"Yeah, that's it. Send it to Wendi Carter – she's a nurse there. 'HAD TO LEAVE TOWN. BE BACK IN THE MORNING. JIMMY.' How's that?"

"It works fine for me. How does it work for you, young man?"

"Um—I think it's fine. Will she get it while she's still on shift tonight?"

"How late is she working?"

"Until ten."

"Western Union will get it there on time."

"Great! Thank you. How much do I owe you?"

"Let's see …ten words. One dollar even."

I turned around and pulled the wad of money I had found in Brody's bedroom out of my coat pocket. I peeled a single away from its companions and turned back to the window. I handed the station master the bill. I didn't mind paying for the message with Kendall's money or his wife's. It was their fault I was in Baldwin. They might as well share the cost.

The station master thanked me and went back to doing whatever a station master did. I went back to my hard wooden perch and sat down. There was a newspaper nearby, the widest newspaper I had ever seen. I understood why they called newspapers broadsheets. No one else was in the train depot, so I picked up the paper and started reading.

There was another Big Four Conference in London to discuss the future of Germany and Austria. Meanwhile, the last indictments in the Nuremberg Trials were filed. Thirteen generals and one admiral were charged with war crimes and crimes against humanity.

There was a big stink over Major League Baseball's Most Valuable Player award. Joe DiMaggio of the New York Yankees won his third American League MVP award despite Ted Williams of the Boston Red Sox earning the league's Triple Crown.

I stopped reading and closed my eyes. I couldn't believe how tired I was. A few seconds later, I was asleep.

A second later, it was morning.

Chapter 5

Pepé was sitting next to Wendi's bed, his chair between the bed and the windows. Hillary was on the other side, holding his former daughter-in-law's hand. Pepé had just come in to sit with Hillary and Wendi. She had a bruise on her chin and a black eye, but the real danger had been inside her head. Like Jimmy, she had suffered a concussion as she had battled The Man's goon squad.

After her self-defense classes, she had felt pretty indestructible, but she had never gone up against anyone as enormous as Kingpin. She discovered there was a limit to her ability to take down an opponent. Like her other bruises and contusions, that discovery stung, too.

"I found something," Pepé told the other older gentleman. "I went to the Nassau sheriff's office and found nothing on The Man, but then I went down to the Fernandina Police Department – the PD – and they let me go through their ancient records, the stuff that hasn't been converted to digital yet. It took me all night, but I finally found what I was looking for."

"Which was …?" Hillary asked.

"Any information or mention of Doyle Abaddon I could find. He does not exist in the digital age. It's like he's been wiped clean, erased. He probably owned people at the PD over the years, cops he did favors for, or maybe he bought their services—"

"Blackmailed is more likely," Hillary interjected.

"My thought, too. Anyway, I found a traffic stop from 1948 in Fernandina Beach. Doyle Abaddon – no middle initial – birthdate August 15, 1928, in Quebec, Canada. He became a naturalized U.S. citizen in 1946 when he was eighteen. Pretty handy – right after World War Two – all the soldiers who had fought in Europe and the Pacific were home by the end of '46. The draft was in a kind of a holding pattern. The Korean Conflict hadn't gone super-hot yet, so no one was looking at this young, able-bodied former Canuck."

"What did he do?" Wendi said from her bed, her eyes still closed.

"Do?"

"To get stopped by the cops," she asked, opening her eyes.

"Basic traffic stop. He rolled through a stop sign."

"That's it?"

Pepé slipped into his imitation of a Southern highway cop. "We take our traffic laws very seriously in this country, in this state, this county, and especially in this city, Mr. Abaddon. I don't know how they do things up in the Great

White North, but down he-ah, we love our mamas, salute the flag, bow our heads, and remove our hats when someone's prayin.' We also stop at stop signs and observe the speed limit. Until it's inconvenient, that is." Pepé smiled broadly at Hillary and Wendi, who both grinned back at the former cop. Pepé was glad to see the young woman's smile.

"So, what have we got?" she asked.

"Almost bupkis. Just a tad north of nothing at all. But we finally know Abaddon exists; we know how old he is, when he was born, and where. And we know he was living in Fernandina in 1948."

"You're saying the electronic voice we heard from the car at the cemetery is from a ninety-five-year-old man?" Wendi asked incredulously.

"I know it's hard to believe, but that's what the paper trail says. I guess ninety-five is the new sixty."

Hillary held up a finger, indicating his desire to add to the conversation.

"I just read about a study on SuperAgers – men and women over the age of eighty with the mental faculties of people decades younger. It's not just a trite cliche that ninety-five is the new sixty; it's quite possibly true. These SuperAgers' brains are aging at a much slower rate than the average person's. Part of it is genes, and part of it is the environment. What I found fascinating was the discovery that up until these people reach ninety, their aging, or lack thereof, is more dependent on exterior factors. Our behaviors — things like diet, exercise, and sun exposure — account for three-quarters of what gets us to ninety, and our genes make up the other one-quarter. Beyond ninety, though, the script flips like a Romanian gymnast, and our genes play a decisive role in taking us the rest of the way to one hundred."

Pepé looked at Hillary for a moment, making sure he understood everything his friend had said. "You mean, Doyle Abaddon – The Man – could be a …what did you call him? A SuperAger?"

"Absolutely, and it's simply the luck of the draw – at least, after ninety. Before that, it's quite dependent on how well we take care of ourselves. Smoking is a big no-no, excessive drinking, too, but so is living in towns and cities with air pollution, high crime, reduced access to nature … in a word, stress."

"So, because I was a cop and a Naval security guy, I'm going to shuffle off early?"

"Yes, and no. If you take care of yourself for the next twenty-five years or so until you become a nonagenarian …" Hillary paused and grinned at Pepé's confused look. "A nonagenarian is someone who's ninety, Pepé. Once you reach ninety, if you come from a line of centenarians – people who live to a hundred or longer – you stand a much better chance of coasting across that finish line with three numbers behind your name. How old was your dad when he died?"

"He didn't. He's 93. He's outlived three wives, too."

"Bingo! There you go, sir. If you have longevity in your family, you stand a better chance than if everyone died in their fifties or sixties."

"So, Doyle is ninety-five but looks and acts about twenty years younger?" Wendi asked.

"If he actually *is* a SuperAger. We don't know. He could be on the verge of keeling over any moment. But remember, we don't know that, either. Don't forget, I said stress is a big factor. Running his little crime syndicate could cause him a tremendous amount of stress. Having his plans foiled by you and Jimmy could cause a big pile-up in his stress department, generating tons of cortisol – a hormone your body produces in response to stress. Everyone has high cortisol from time to time, and your levels will vary throughout the day. It's part of your body's natural response to threats of harm or danger. However, a body that consistently makes too much cortisol usually indicates an underlying health problem. The fact that Abaddon is in his mid-90s and 'seems' to be going strong speaks to the idea that he has good genetics."

"Speaking of being healthy," Wendi interjected, "I think I am. Healthy, that is. I think it's time I get out of this fancy, *expensive* hospital bed, get dressed, and go to see Jimmy before I run home for a change of clothes. How is our boy this morning?"

Pepé and Hillary exchanged a wary glance before Hillary answered.

"I'm afraid there's been no change in his condition, Wendi. He's in the ICU in an induced coma and intubated. But he's stable. His doctor says he's physically quite healthy …" Hillary paused and searched for words.

"From the neck down," Pepé finished.

Wendi didn't say anything right away, letting the news sink in before finally answering. "Well, today's a new day. I'm going to think positive thoughts and believe something good is going to happen because … it just is. The sun is shining, and I'm getting out of the hospital."

Wendi shooed the two men out of her room so she could get dressed. More than clean clothes and coffee, she needed to see Jimmy with her own eyes.

:::::

THE STATION MASTER was hollering at me from the window. I had only just fallen asleep a second before.

"If you're going to be on the train to Fernandina, young fella, you'd better get up!"

I leaped to my feet. I was just as bone tired as I was last night, or was that only a few seconds ago? Had I even slept? When I stood up, the newspaper I had been reading fell off my lap onto the floor. I had apparently used it for a lap blanket.

I checked my shirt pocket. I still had my ticket for Fernandina. The sun was up but not very high yet. I would have killed for some coffee, but I suddenly realized I had an even more pressing physical need, and coffee wouldn't help. Liquid—coffee in particular—would only exacerbate that urgent need. I turned back toward the ticket window.

"Excuse me, sir. Is there a—"

"It's around the corner. Don't take too long, though. The train won't wait for you."

I dashed out the door and quickly found the men's room. There were three urinals and two toilet stalls. I stepped over to the first urinal. I did what I needed, washed my hands, splashed a little water on my face, and then discovered there were no towels. Being ever resourceful, I pulled my shirt out of my pants and used my shirttail to dry my face quickly, then tucked everything back in, trying to make myself look respectable.

Outside, I saw a water fountain and bent down to use it. As I did, I saw a sign above it that read, WHITES ONLY. I no longer felt thirsty. I stood again and walked briskly to the train and, with a short backward glance at the water fountain and its sign, climbed aboard.

I didn't see Kendall Brody anywhere in the car as I boarded. Hopefully, he had gone to Chicago as he had planned or maybe he decided to go somewhere else without a Julie or a Catherine. If he was going back to Fernandina this morning, I'd see him on the train. Hopefully, I'd see him before he saw me.

I was looking forward to a short, uneventful trip. There was no sign of Brody as time passed and the outdoor scenery changed gradually from tall pines to coastal wetlands. Brody had either found another way back to Fernandina or had decided to keep to his itinerary and travel north. I doubted he'd be gone very long, though. If he was lucky, the local Chicago PD would contact him about the discovery of his dead wife back in Fernandina Beach, Florida. If he was *very* lucky, they wouldn't ask him if he knew anything about it.

That chain of thought brought Catherine Brody back to my mind again. I hadn't even known her name until I was on the train with Kendall, and he mentioned her by name. From the brief look I got of her in the dim apartment, she was attractive, but I knew that looks only went so far. She could be an attractive shrew or an attractive tramp or slob. Looks can open doors, but it's your character that keeps those doors open.

I hadn't heard the complete story of Kendall and Catherine last night, at least not about their early days, so I couldn't make any informed judgments. Actually, I didn't need the whole story to pass judgment since they both tried to hire someone to bump each other off. Whatever they had when they first got married was already dead and buried, like Catherine Brody would be soon.

I wondered if the cops would grab me up for questioning upon our arrival. They were probably quizzing anyone who lived over the Palace Saloon, so I guessed I'd meet a couple more of Fernandina PD's finest when I stepped off the train into the depot David Yulee built and rebuilt.

Officer Bill Crane might be there to greet me. I wasn't sure if that was a good thing or bad. At least he knew I was a private investigator and that we were on the same side of the law, except when it came to vagrancy and heaving your guts out in the mayor's wife's trash cans.

The Amelia River came into view on the left side of the train, the west side. I had a 50/50 chance that left was west. I was usually directionally savvy, but some towns left me scratching my head and wandering in circles. If a town wasn't platted out on a north-south or east-west axis, it messed with my brain. I would have made a terrible homing pigeon.

A few minutes later, the train pulled into Fernandina's small depot near the corner of Front and Centre, and I waited until most of the other eight passengers had disembarked before I took my leave. I looked out the train car's windows before I exited, checking for signs of a certain plumbing wholesaler hanging around to finish what we started last night. Not catching sight of Kendall Brody, I stepped down from the car to the ground via the removable steps the conductor put out for passengers.

"Jimmy! Jimmy!"

I swiveled my head toward the sound of my name. Luckily, it wasn't Kendall, and, even luckier, it was a beautiful blonde nurse who said she worked for me from time to time.

"Jimmy! I was so worried about you. I barely slept a wink last night," Wendi said as she hurried over to where I was standing. "Where did you go?"

"Ever been to the big metropolis of Baldwin?"

"Baldwin? Right outside of Jacksonville? Why did you go there?"

"It turns out this train doesn't actually go *into* Jacksonville. It goes *near* Jacksonville. At least, that's what I was able to figure out when I needed to leave Dodge in a hurry last night. Speaking of leaving, are the cops done upstairs at the Palace?"

"Police? Why would they be there? Did something happen?"

She looked at me with genuine concern in her eyes. I liked seeing that look more than I expected. I was quickly arriving at the conclusion that we didn't have a normal boss and secretary relationship. I would have loved to take some time to discuss our work relationship with her, but her question and the fact that she was unaware of anything happening at the Palace Saloon apartments last night took precedence over my desire to spend unstructured time with my personal nurse.

"Hold on, Wendi. Are you telling me there was no dead body found in the apartments over the Palace last night or this morning? A woman – one named Catherine Brody?"

"Catherine Brody? No. She lives in apartment nine, just a few doors down from your place."

"Number nine? It must be missing a nail or something because when I came up the back stairs last night, the number on the door I entered was definitely a six, which should be my place, but wasn't. I went in – the door was unlocked and partially open – and I stumbled over her body."

The scene replayed in my mind of being practically nose-to-nose with Catherine on the floor of her apartment. I didn't feel a pressing need to enlighten Wendi about my backseat-style encounter with Catherine's corpse, so I jumped ahead to the part about my encounter with Sean and Angelo.

"There were two goons in the apartment, the ones who killed Mrs. Brody. One had red, curly hair, and the other had black hair, slicked back with enough pomade for several Dapper Dan's. Curly – the guy with the red hair is really named Sean, and the one with the black oil slick is named Angelo. At least, that's what Sean called him, and I have no reason to doubt him. Angelo kept running his hand through his greasy hair like he was stressed."

Wendi was thinking, probably trying to place the two thugs. Lots of people on the wrong side of the law needed occasional fixing up, and Nassau County General was the most likely place in town for that kind of fixing. It was possible that Wendi could have seen them before. After thinking briefly, though, she gave a little shake of her head to indicate she was drawing blanks, so I continued with my story. I hoped she'd believe it.

"They thought I was Catherine's husband and said I wasn't supposed to be there. They told me I was supposed to be on a train for Chicago. They said it was supposed to be my alibi. The theory was, if I was on the train going to Chicago, I couldn't also be in our apartment in Fernandina Beach, Florida, putting a bullet into my wife's brain, could I?"

"What did you say to them? What did you do?"

"I said I had forgotten something for the trip and went back into the bedroom. I figured it was laid out like my place, and it was, except there was a double bed instead of a single in the bedroom, and there was a makeup table with a little bench and a mirror, whereas mine has a shaving mirror and stand for a basin and towel. I guess Mrs. Brody used the makeup table a lot because it had a large jar of some kind of face powder, and I accidentally knocked it onto the floor. That's when I found 'it,' a wad of bills—money—rolled up tight and hidden in the powder, stuffed down inside the container. I guess Catherine Brody had been socking cash away for a rainy day, and I think she must have been hearing thunder from an approaching storm."

"I'm not following you, Jimmy. Mrs. Brody had money stashed away for what? In case she had to leave town suddenly?"

"That would be one way for a wife to deal with a philandering husband, but she chose a more violent and long-lasting route. She wanted to stay in Fernandina and send her husband away. Permanently. The ironic thing is, Kendall Brody chose the same route for her."

:::::

P EPÉ AND HILLARY WAITED outside Wendi's hospital room while she dressed. She looked better when she came out, but she still looked like she'd had a rough night – which she had.

Together, the trio walked to the Intensive Care Unit (ICU), just around the corner from where Wendi had been kept overnight for observation, just one room outside the ICU ward, but close enough for extra help if conditions warranted. She led the way to Jimmy's room, the two men trailing close behind.

Wendi may have looked better when she emerged from her room, but Jimmy didn't look any better and may have even looked worse. When they arrived, a nurse was in his room. She looked their way when the door opened, then held up a palm like a traffic cop to keep them out. The group reversed course and went back into the waiting area. Once the nurse finished checking his vitals and writing notes on a chart, she hit the automatic door closer button, stepped out of the room, and addressed Jimmy's friends.

In a soothing, smooth voice she had probably developed from years of working in the ICU, she told them that they could only go into Jimmy's room one at a time. If he had been able, Jimmy would have argued with her, pointing out that it wasn't like they were going to tire out the patient because the patient wasn't participating in any physically taxing activities. But Jimmy stayed silent, and the nurse insisted on one at a time. She also told them to limit their visit to fifteen minutes total, which meant about five minutes for each of them to sit next to Jimmy and try to think of cheerful things to say in case he could hear them.

There was no argument about who would go in first.

At first, Wendi stood next to the bed and just stared at him, trying to comprehend what she was viewing, watching Jimmy lying completely still in the bed. Both his eyes were blackened, and one ear looked like it had been viciously scrubbed along the wall of a brick building. The skin color of his face around his injured eyes was various shades of yellow, green, and purple, but mostly black. One arm was under the sheets, and the other was on top – the arm with the IV plugged in to give him fluids and a sedative; the latter kept him in an induced coma. The doctor had explained to Pepé and Hillary that the induced coma was a deep sedation designed to quiet Jimmy's brain and give it time to rest and heal.

There was a quiet knock on the door behind Wendi. She turned as a doctor entered the room, smiling at her. He wasn't wearing scrubs; he was wearing a white shirt and tie with dark slacks, and wore a long white medical coat over his clothes. He looked like he had stepped out of a TV medical show. He introduced himself and asked if Wendi had any questions about Jimmy's condition or care.

Before she could ask anything, he said, "By the way, you look a lot better than you did when they brought you in last night. I'm glad."

Wendi blushed a little but then glanced at Jimmy and became serious again.

"How long will he be in this … induced coma?" she asked.

"Just a couple of days. We don't like to keep patients in a coma any longer than we have to. One-to-two days is usually as long as we go."

"Does that mean he'll be fine in a couple of days?"

"We hope so, but we can't say at this point. But let me assure you, Miss Lyst—"

"Mrs. Mrs. Lyst."

His eyebrows lifted almost imperceptibly, but he didn't stumble or make any comment about her name. He had encountered all kinds of relationship situations as a doctor.

"Let me assure you, Mrs. Lyst, that his best chances for a complete recovery are after his brain has been on a couple of days of forced vacation. We aim for only a couple of days in an induced coma, as I said, but we have also seen rare patients who have recovered after six months in a medically induced coma."

"What about the tube down his throat?"

"We initially talked of going with the little cup-style oxygen mask, but because of where the fracture is on Jimmy's skull, we decided to err on the side of caution. The sedatives we're using also repress his breathing system, so we needed to intubate him. In a day or two, when we start to bring him out of the coma, we'll remove the tube and switch to an oxygen mask once we take him off his sedation."

The doctor looked at his smartwatch and said, "I'm sorry. I have to go. I just got a text from the nurses' station, and I'm needed in a patient's room. I'm sure I'll see you again and will answer more questions for you then." As quickly and quietly as he had come in, the doctor slipped out.

Alone now, Wendi stepped to one side and sat in the chair next to Jimmy's bed. She dug under his blanket and sheet and found his hand. She gripped it and squeezed, giving it several pulses. She waited, hoping, but Jimmy didn't squeeze back. There was just the quiet sound of the respirator breathing in ... and out.

Wendi put her head on the bed and quietly wept.

Chapter 6

"CATHERINE – MRS. BRODY – WAS saving her butter and egg money to buy her freedom, not a treat from the general store. She was tired of her husband Kendall's ultra-frugal, penny-pinching lifestyle, and she wanted out so she could live a little. Especially after she discovered his real financial situation. What do you do with a man who pretends he has nothing and gives the same amount to his wife? First, you take out life insurance on him without his knowledge. Second, you hire someone to help move him along in the direction of an untimely but lucrative demise. Third, you make sure the person you're paying to murder your husband doesn't get any counter-offers from the intended victim. Catherine Brody forgot about number three."

Wendi and I were walking slowly up Centre Street toward the Palace Saloon as I explained the drama that had taken place a mere three doors down the hall from my place. I had been in my apartment/office above the saloon exactly one time—at least, once that I could remember. It was late yesterday afternoon; I went there to change clothes before going to the luncheonette for supper. Any previous times had been left smeared on a brick wall. I had to rely on Wendi's memory because nobody had tried to find out which would break first: her head or a wall, like they had attempted to ascertain with my head a few days earlier.

After the wrecking crew finished trying to demolish the wall with my head, I woke up with a splitting headache – literally, since I received a depressed skull fracture. *Received! Like it's a gift!* I was reminded of Red Skelton as the Mean Little Kid, crying, "They bwoke my widdle head! They bwoke my widdle head!"

It was when I woke up in the hospital that I discovered the vision of beauty standing next to me: Nurse Wendi Carter, a blonde knockout who says she works for me part-time. I'm sure we have more than a normal working relationship, but unfortunately, I can't remember!

As we walked, I told Wendi, "What I can't get out of my mind is the look of surprise on Catherine Brody's face. I'd be willing to bet the last conscious thought she had was the realization she had been double-crossed and the cold, hard metal pipe suddenly pressing against her temple was a pistol."

Wendi walked silently, letting me ramble on. I babbled, more to myself than her, "I wonder if she knew the guy she paid to kill her husband had given Kendall an opportunity to make a counter-offer, and he had seen her bet and raised it so the boys would knock Catherine off instead? Maybe her last thought before the gun went off was that Kendall was just plain lucky. Or maybe it was pure anger. I know I'd be angry."

Wendi knew I needed to talk my way through the details. I had a feeling it was part of how we worked. I could examine that theory later. For now, I filled her in on my late-night train ride to Baldwin with my unplanned seatmate.

"Kendall Brody talked to me on the train last night – mainly because he was holding a gun on me, and he was the one feeling chatty. He told me how Catherine wanted to rub elbows with a more elite set of people, the kind who spent their days at the club and didn't live in a tiny, dirty apartment over a saloon. He also told me he had met a girl in Chicago named Julie, a girl who loved him just the way he was. Supposedly."

"And?" Wendi prompted.

"And when Brody got back from Chicago the last time, his wife told him she had hired a private detective to follow him, and she knew all about Julie and his other bank account. Catherine was going to ruin his little love triangle. But then Kendall remembered a guy Catherine had introduced him to named Doyle Abaddon."

"Where does he fit in?" Wendi asked.

"Brody's wife had been going on and on about this young guy with big dreams. What she didn't know was that this guy she introduced to Kendall had told him confidentially that he could make his problems with Catherine go away for a couple of hundred bucks."

Halfway up the block, we saw people going in and out of the luncheonette for breakfast. We were in no hurry; there was more story to tell. I continued talking as we walked.

"Doyle had already offered his services to Kendall even before Catherine ever found out about Julie, but Kendall didn't take him up on it at the time. Once the private dick Catherine hired told her about Julie in Chicago, Doyle told Kendall he could fix his love-life problems for three C-notes, not two. While we were riding the rails to Baldwin last night, I figured out that Catherine had paid Doyle two hundred to make Kendall her 'late' husband, but Doyle gave Kendall a chance to turn the tables on her for *three* hundred, a sweet deal for Doyle since he pocketed five bills. Even my broken brain knows you don't need an advanced degree in accounting to figure out that five is better than three is better than two."

"That's why Catherine looked so surprised just before she died: she thought she had a deal with Doyle," Wendi said, putting things together. I nodded and concluded my report.

"She didn't know that Doyle's services are always available to the highest bidder. It's a matter of supply and demand; whatever the market will bear," I finished. "It's almost never personal."

"Kendall Brody won the poker hand this time," Wendi interjected. "But it could have just as easily been Catherine if Kendall hadn't taken the bait from Doyle. Did you explain that part to Mr. Brody?"

"I did. He turned as white as the sheet they would have wrapped his body in when he realized he coulda been lying on the floor of his apartment instead of Catherine. I told Kendall that Doyle had played him when he told him to take the train to Chicago as his alibi and enjoy some time with

Julie. Kendall had never mentioned Julie. I figure she's working with Doyle for a slice of the pie. There's just no honor among thieves, Wendi."

We stood on the corner by the Palace as I finished my story. We strolled back to the alley to go upstairs to my place. One look told us there were no cops back there—none in the back, none out front, and probably none upstairs. I was willing to bet there was no dead body upstairs anymore, either.

Without talking, Wendi and I climbed the stairs with the rickety railing, the same place I first met Kendall Brody as he came charging down to beat it out of town on the train to Chicago. The stairs looked different by daylight—worse, to be honest. There were stains on the bare wood like multiple people had thrown up or bled on them while using the stairs.

I had no idea how old the saloon was. They could have been the original stairs and railing, for all I knew. Judging from the ambiance of the saloon, though, I'd peg it at about fifty years old – the late 1890s. It was mainly because of the bar: individual towels for wiping foam off your mustache and the brass rail and matching brass cuspidors were not modern conveniences.

At the top of the stairs, the hallway looked almost the same as it did at night, just slightly less dim. We walked toward my apartment, stopping first at number nine, Kendall and Catherine Brody's place. And, just as I guessed, the brass nine on the door was missing the top nail, and it had slipped upside down, tricking me into thinking it was apartment six – my place. In my defense, my head had been hurting, my stomach was trying to decide which way was up, and I had never walked toward my door from this direction. Or not that I could remember.

What a convenient excuse! I thought to myself. *I wonder how long I can use it?*

When we reached my door, I checked the knob to make sure it was locked, wiggled the brass six to make sure it was securely attached, then took out my key and opened my door. Wendi and I went inside, and she closed the door behind us, her back to me as she threw the deadbolt for the door. When she turned around to enter my apartment and "office," she crashed into my back because I had stopped in place rather than turning on a lamp. The impact caused us both to stumble forward in the dim light.

"Jimmy? Why are you just standing there?" She tried to step around me but stopped when I threw my arm out to the side.

"I'm sorry, I didn't mean to startle you, Mr. … Marlowe, was it?" The man speaking reached across my desk and pulled the chain on the lamp, illuminating my little living space.

He was young, trim, and good-looking with a square jaw. He had dark hair that was styled nicely, not like a bowl had been placed over his head before they cut his hair. He wore a dark three-piece pin-striped suit with a starched white shirt and dark tie that coordinated nicely with his suit. His shoes were shined, and he had a watch chain hanging from his vest that you just knew was attached to a real, working pocket watch inside his vest pocket. The young man looked ambitious and like he was 'trying to make something of himself.' That's how Catherine had described Doyle Abaddon to her husband. She wasn't wrong.

My heart rate and breathing skyrocketed at the shock of finding someone in my apartment. I lowered the arm holding Wendi behind me and took a few steps deeper into my apartment, making sure to keep myself positioned between Wendi and Abaddon.

He sat behind my desk, looking like he owned the place. *Maybe he does!* I couldn't see anything on the desktop, so either he hadn't been sitting behind my desk very long, or he hadn't been snooping. More likely, there wasn't anything to snoop through. Wendi probably kept anything snoop-worthy somewhere other than my desk.

I finally found my voice and answered him. "Yes, I'm Jimmy Marlowe. And you had better give me a real good explanation for what you're doing behind my desk in the next ten seconds, or you're going to find yourself going down the stairs on your nose." I didn't know if I could make good on my threat, but I had to make it sound believable for Wendi.

"I don't think anyone's going to go down the stairs on their nose, Mr. Marlowe," a second, more familiar voice said. "Unless *you'd* like to try it."

I gave my head a half-turn and saw the same curly red hair I had seen the night before. Sean. I wondered if Angelo, aka Slick, was in my bedroom snooping around.

Sean opened his suit coat to give me a quick look at the butt of a gun jutting out of a leather shoulder holster, still with a silencer screwed on. I recognized the gun from last night, and had seen its handiwork on Catherine Brody's temple.

Someone rapped lightly on the door behind me.

"Mr. Marlowe?" Abaddon asked smoothly and cordially. "Would you be so kind as to unlock the door behind you and let Angelo in? I like to cover all my bets."

I continued to stare at Abaddon while Wendi unlocked the deadbolt. Angelo opened the door when he heard the bolt unlock, but he didn't come in yet. He just stood there, filling the door frame and blocking any exit.

Wendi slowly pressed her back against mine so we could keep eyes on everyone, fore and aft. Not that our eyes were going to do that much good against a couple of Ruger semiautomatic .22 caliber pistols in the hands of a couple of wannabe gangsters. With the silencer, no one in the saloon below would even hear the shots. Anyone downstairs would more likely hear the muffled thud of us crumpling to the floor than the subdued noise of a silenced pistol.

"Jimmy, who is this guy?" Wendi asked.

"Remember the guy I was telling you about who was so eager to help the Brodys resolve their marital problems? This is him. Meet Doyle Abaddon. A real marriage counselor," I said sarcastically.

Abaddon did a little head nod in Wendi's direction. I hoped she wouldn't be taken in by his good looks and good manners.

"It's rude to break into someone else's apartment, Mr. Abaddon, to say nothing of illegal," Wendi said, acid dripping in her normally cheerful voice. So much for good looks and good manners always winning the day.

"No one broke in anywhere, Miss Carter."

I tried not to show my surprise that he knew Wendi's name. He ignored any reactions and continued.

"The owner of the Palace Saloon is a very good friend of mine and *volunteered* the use of his master key so we could wait comfortably inside Mr. Marlowe's office,"—he spread his hands to indicate the borders of my work area—"while awaiting his return," Abaddon replied, his own voice coated in syrupy sweetness. His tone matched his fancy suit, starched shirt, freshly styled haircut, and shiny shoes.

I decided to take a chance and pretend I had a little backbone, and I walked a couple of feet over to the extra chair in my office area and sat down, exhaling and thinking, *No one shot me. So far, so good.*

Since I couldn't remember, I guessed that I usually sat in this chair when Wendi was working here for me; the telephone was on the other side of the desk. I assumed it was her job to answer the phone. On the days and nights that she worked at the hospital, I probably sat in the other desk chair while working alone. But like most things, I was just guessing, with no amount of certainty for any of it.

"What are you up to, Abaddon?" I asked brusquely.

Curly-haired Sean quickly stepped over and tapped my head with the butt of his gun. It was a light tap, but after what had recently happened to my head, it was like he had dropped a cinder block on my head from five feet above me. The room flared white, and I had an immediate headache.

"Hey!" I yelled.

"Sean!" Abaddon's voice had a sharp edge to it. "I'm sure Mr. Marlowe meant no disrespect. Did you, Mr. Marlowe? Notice how I have referred to you as *Mister* Marlowe since your arrival? Not Jimmy or Marlowe, but *Mister* Marlowe. It's a term of respect. Sean was simply trying to let you know – in his rather raw and unsophisticated way – that he thinks you should afford me the same courtesy."

Wendi stepped close to me, holding my face between her hands and looking into my eyes. Her eyes moved from side to side as she looked at mine one at a time. I noticed that Angelo had left the doorway and come into the room and shut the door behind him when things suddenly became noisy.

"*Mister* Abaddon," Wendi said through clenched teeth, "please instruct your henchmen to keep their hands off Mr. Marlowe. He was just released yesterday morning from the hospital for a serious head injury."

"We know," Angelo said from behind her. "Who do you think gave it to him?" He grinned broadly at Sean, who chuckled momentarily but immediately sobered up when Abaddon scowled at the pair. Angelo looked like a petulant child who'd been slapped across the face and lowered his head, announcing, "Sorry, boss."

Doyle Abaddon glared at Angelo. "It's Mr. Abaddon, not 'boss,' you oily-haired buffoon!" He spit the words in Angelo's direction. I had a feeling he would have slapped his hired help across the face if we hadn't been there. Not that I was all there, but my head was starting to settle down again.

I waved a hand at Abaddon. "Don't worry about it, Mr. Abaddon. I'm all right. It takes a lot more than that to put me down. My mom always said I had the hardest head she'd ever seen. Now, why don't we quit dancing here and get to the main event? Why are you and your boys in my office, and what can Miss Carter and I do to hasten your departure?"

"My boys, as you so eloquently refer to them, were looking for something in the Brodys's apartment last night when you stumbled in."

"I got that feeling. Unfortunately, I was distracted by the presence of the recently deceased Mrs. Brody on the floor between us. Besides, your boys made the mistake of assuming I was Mr. Brody. They didn't ask who I was; they just assumed I was her husband."

"Yes, they admitted their faux pas, but they also told me that *you* didn't correct them. I'm willing to overlook your little charade if you would be so good as to hand over the object you took from Mrs. Brody's bedroom."

At the mention of the bedroom, I turned my head to look at the door to my bedroom. Sean was still standing there, his gun once again holstered, but a visible lump under his coat, as visible as the scowl on his face. I imagine Abaddon had verbally skinned both men for failing to bring back the wad of cash I had in my possession when I departed.

"Jimmy? What's he talking about?" Wendi asked. "What object did you take out of the Brody's apartment?"

She was still looking at my face but not checking my eyes or the condition of my head this time. In hindsight, she probably should have since I could only attribute some of my recent bonehead moves to my serious brain injury.

On the other hand, who knew that the stash of cash hidden in Catherine Brody's face powder wasn't fair game for all scavengers? Finders-keepers had always been the highest rule of the playground.

I reached into my coat pocket, pulled out the wad of bills, and bounced it up in the air on my palm a couple of times like I was weighing it. A few small clouds of face powder escaped from it before I tossed it across the desk to Abaddon. He snatched it out of the air in one smooth move and dropped it into his suit pocket without even looking at it. His eyes barely left mine the whole time.

"Jimmy! That's a roll of money!" Wendi gasped.

"And it's all there," I said to Abaddon, "except for four dollars for my trip to Jacksonville and back. And one more for a telegram."

"I'm sure the loss of five dollars won't be a hardship, Mr. Marlowe. Besides, Sean and Angelo told you that you were supposed to be on the train. You were just following orders, right?"

As smoothly as a cat, Abaddon rose to his feet and motioned to Sean and Angelo, and the trio began funneling toward the door.

"Hold on a second," I said, my voice a little louder than I intended, but I had just lost a bunch of money I hadn't even had the opportunity to adequately count. My guess was it was Catherine's two hundred dollars plus several hundred more. Curly and Slick must have finished their job before being paid, which was why they were looking for the cash so diligently. With her two hundred, Doyle would have his five hundred, but with the extra in the roll of bills, he'd probably have closer to eight hundred. An easy payday.

Abaddon paused and looked my way. "Something else, Mr. Marlowe?"

Rather than belabor the money issue, I asked, "What happened to Catherine—Mrs. Brody's—body? And why aren't there any police here?"

"Oh, that. You missed all the fun, Mr. Marlowe. It was quite comical to watch our local Keystone Kops manhandle Mrs. Brody down the back steps in the middle of the night. They took good care of her – at least once they reached the bottom of the stairs. She should be glad she couldn't feel the manhandling they gave her or the bumps and bruises from being dropped more than once. I'm sure when Mr. Brody returns from Chicago, they'll let him know where her remains are should he desire to hold a funeral service in her memory."

Doyle tapped Sean lightly on the shoulder, and they continued out the door. Angelo was last in line and winked at Wendi as he reached out to close the door behind them.

And then they were gone, their steps echoing briefly in the hall before a door slammed to punctuate their exit from the building.

:::::

I WAS STILL SITTING in the chair I had occupied during our impromptu interrogation. Wendi came and sat behind the desk where Abaddon had sat. I looked at the clock on the wall. It wasn't even nine in the morning yet, and I'd already been insulted, threatened, knocked on the head, and lost what I was sure was a sizable sum of money.

Wendi swiveled in the desk chair and stared out the window for a bit, looking down on the foot traffic and cars traveling up and down Centre Street.

It was actually kind of nice, just sitting there quietly, enjoying each other's company. There was no pressure to impress anyone. It was Wendi who broke the silence. She had apparently been thinking different thoughts.

"You know, Jimmy, that thug could have really hurt you by knocking you on the head with his gun. You know that, don't you? You're not indestructible like Superman. And what was the deal with the roll of money?"

I sighed and told her. "I told you before: it fell out of Mrs. Brody's jar of face powder last night, and I instinctively grabbed it. I shoved it in my pocket without counting it or anything. It came in handy when I had to leave town, though, because those two thugs cleaned me out last night. They thought I was Brody, and they said they wanted more money. I pulled out the seven dollars I had left, thinking it was too little to mess with, but they grabbed it. They didn't know I had just found the cash Catherine kept hidden in her face powder. They knew there was money someplace in the apartment because they insisted on it last night, and today they came back for it. Or maybe it's because ..." and I trailed off.

"Because what?" Wendi asked, still looking out the window but holding a letter opener in her hand, its point poking into the desktop.

"I, um, kind of wrote them a check."

She stopped fiddling with the letter opener and turned away from the window.

"For how much? And on whose account?"

"Well, since I was in the Brodys's apartment, whose check do you think it was?"

"You wrote Tweedledumb and Tweedledumber a check from Kendall Brody? For how much?"

"Five hundred dollars."

She looked completely flabbergasted. She said nothing.

"Except," I said, "I didn't know Kendall's first name."

"So, you just signed it, K. Brody?"

"Nope. I went all in. I signed it, *Kenneth* Brody."

"You're kidding!"

"No, I'm not, and I figured that was why they showed up here, if you must know. I'll bet they went to the bank first thing this morning, hoping to get the money Catherine owed them and three hundred extra for their trouble. But then, the bank turned them down because the signature was wrong. They had to tell Abaddon, and he would have looked at the check and realized the name was wrong. But if they haven't been to the bank yet, we could still see them again, wanting me to make good on the check."

"Oh, I don't think so. They know you're not Brody now, and they know you don't have that kind of money. Plus, they got the cash they were looking for."

I heard a skritch out in the hallway, like a leather-soled shoe on a sand-covered wood floor doing a soft shoe. A moment later, there was a light tap on the door. I jumped out of the chair and was across the room in two giant steps.

I hurled the door open to find Angelo half-crouched over, looking embarrassed.

He held out some crumpled bills toward me, and when I didn't immediately take them, he shook them slightly.

"Sean said we need to give this back since you gave us the real money we were looking for last night."

Numbly, I took the bills. Angelo turned and walked quietly down the hall. I reversed back into my apartment and bumped into Wendi, who had come to see what was going on in the hall.

I turned around, and we were face to face, scarcely an inch apart, my eyes gazing into hers. Her head was tilted slightly, and it felt like the most natural thing in the world as I leaned forward, took her hand in mine, and, in one swift motion, erased the space between us, my lips finding hers.

: : : :

WENDI SNIFFLED SLIGHTLY AS she quit crying, blowing her nose with a tissue from the table next to Jimmy's bed in the ICU. Her visiting time with him was nearly up; either Pepé or Hillary would come in and sit with Jimmy next.

She took Jimmy's hand in hers and then, with the thumb of her other hand, rubbed the back of his hand gently. She heard a noise behind her and looked up. Hillary was in the doorway, looking at her questioningly, trying to see if she was coming out. She nodded and stood up. She squeezed Jimmy's hand several times. Just as she was about to let go and retreat into the hallway, Jimmy squeezed her hand ever so lightly.

She quickly squeezed his hand again but got no response. She tried several more times but without a response.

Hillary could see the excitement on her face. "What is it?" he asked softly.

"I squeezed his hand, and he squeezed back! Hil, he's still in there!"

Chapter 7

WENDI AND HILLARY WENT back out into the waiting area, and Pepé replaced them on watch in Jimmy's room. Wendi could hear Pepé telling Jimmy a story about something, but she couldn't quite make out any of the details as the door swung closed quietly and efficiently behind her. Hillary came over to her and wrapped his ex-daughter-in-law in his arms.

"What did the doctor tell you when he went in with you?" Hillary asked after a moment.

"He said this course of treatment is the best thing for Jimmy right now. His brain needs a rest, and that's what a medically-induced coma does – it gives the brain a rest. I'm starting to think I need something like that, too. Hil, I'm so worn out and tired. I feel like I could sleep for a week, but whenever I close my eyes to catch some sleep, I see the fight. I see that horrible big man tossing Jimmy and me around like we were toys."

Hillary hadn't heard Wendi call him by his special nickname for a long time, maybe not since his son, Charles

– Wendi's nearly ex-husband – had died. When she and Charles were together, she said she wasn't comfortable calling him Dad, so they had settled on Hil. No one else called him Hil; only Wendi. In that way, it was as personal and intimate as if she *did* call him Dad. He hadn't heard it for a while, and he realized he missed it.

Even though they saw each other nearly every day at their small publishing house, it was like a computer program they ran repeatedly. They had to attend to the daily business, which they did, putting their personal lives, loves, and hurts into boxes for the hours they spent working a few yards apart in their offices.

Hillary had been looking forward to Thanksgiving together with Wendi and Jimmy. And after the recent drama with The Man and his thugs, Pepé and Gwynn would be joining them for Thanksgiving. Hillary had considered asking Wendi if they should invite Hank and Aleesha, but he didn't want to overburden her.

Thanksgiving was about families, and even though their group – soon to be called Blue Bridge Investigations – had been through a great deal together recently, it still wasn't quite a family. Jimmy, Wendi, and Hillary fit together like pieces of a puzzle. They felt like a family to Hillary. No, not *a* family; they felt like *his* family. When Pepé stepped into the picture to join their investigative group, Hillary realized he was someone who understood and could empathize with parts of Hillary's past rarely shared.

Thanksgiving was only a few days away, and Hillary was still looking forward to it, but he wasn't sure how it would work with Jimmy in the hospital. Now, it was as if Wendi could read his thoughts.

"Hil? I still want to do Thanksgiving."

"Are you sure? What if Jimmy's still in the hospital? Or worse, still in the ICU?" What he didn't ask was, 'What if Jimmy's still in a coma?'

"Then we'll bring him a turkey leg to gnaw on when he wakes up. This is a medically induced coma, and the doctor told me earlier that they have more control over bringing him out of it than if he was in a non-induced coma. Either way, I want to be with the people I love on Thanksgiving, and I want to laugh and eat and be thankful for what we have. I'm believing and trusting that Jimmy will be there, one way or the other."

"Wendi, you *do* know he may have a long road to recovery—" Hillary started but then paused, his words hanging uncomfortably between them.

"Hil, he *squeezed* my hand. It was not a spasm. Just as you came into his room, he squeezed my hand when I squeezed his. He only did it once, but he did it. Jimmy's still there, and he still knows me. The doctors have said he could have short-term amnesia when he wakes up, long-term amnesia, or possibly none at all. Every case is different. But if he knows me and who *we* are – who he and I are together – we can make it, Hil. That's what I want to celebrate with him, and you, and Pepé and Gwynn. That's our family."

Hillary couldn't argue with her and didn't want to. He knew her attitude might not seem completely rational to people on the outside looking in, but it could be exactly what they all needed right now. She wasn't giving up hope; on the contrary, she was bringing a serious dose of positivity to the ICU.

: : : :

I OPENED MY EYES for a second and quickly closed them again. Wendi's eyes were closed, too, and she was kissing me back. *It isn't a one-sided thing! Kissing back is good!* I thought to myself.

Suddenly, Wendi broke our passionate embrace, stepped back from the doorway, and spread her arms out like a fence between us. "I'm sorry! I don't know what came over me."

"Don't apologize, Wendi. I kissed you first. If anyone should apologize, it should be me."

She turned around, crossed her arms, and faced the window across the room. I went over and stood behind her, putting my hands on her shoulders. I was afraid she might brush them off, but she didn't.

I told her, "Look, ever since I left the hospital, I've been thinking about you almost every minute. I can't get you out of my head. I can't remember my own last name or anything about … anything, but *you're* stuck inside my brain. Do you have an answer for that?"

She took a step away, walking out from under my hands on her shoulders. She kept her back to me as she answered.

"We've been … seeing each other, I guess you'd say. It's a fairly recent thing, but I guess you have a right to know. Especially now that you kissed me."

I told her, "When I turned around, and you were so close, I just couldn't help it. I've been fighting the urge to kiss you and hold you ever since I woke up and saw you in the hospital."

She continued to face the window. "There are people who might say I'm taking advantage of *you*," she said distantly.

"Well, thank goodness! I'd much rather have people say that than accuse me of taking advantage of you or that I caught you at a weak moment! That kind of thing. I have to ask you, do I have money? Like a *lot* of it squirreled away somewhere? Because that's about the only reason I can think of why people could say you were taking advantage of my amnesia: to get at me and money. But I don't have any money, do I? And you're not a gold digger." I watched her carefully, a small part of me hoping she would say I was an independently wealthy multimillionaire.

She turned around, her big, beautiful smile extending from ear to ear. "No, Jimmy, you don't have any money. You can barely make the rent on this awful place." She spread her hands to encompass the grungy apartment.

"Dang! Now I really wish I hadn't given those guys that roll of bills I found. I know there was at least two hundred dollars rolled up in it. Oh, well," I sighed, "at least they gave me my seven bucks back, plus I still have the ten hidden in my wallet for emergencies."

The thought of the ten-dollar bill reminded me I had been meaning to ask her about it, so I blurted out, "I need to know: is that ten bucks for emergencies or for buying information?"

She laughed, and I loved the sound of it. It was the best sound I had heard in … well, to my addled brain and Swiss-cheesed memory, it seemed like forever.

"Yes, Jimmy. That ten-dollar bill is for emergencies. But emergencies can be many things. You might need it to eat, or you might need it for a taxi or train ride, or you might need it to buy information from someone. Any of those things could be an emergency."

"Or I might need it to send a telegram to you, so you don't worry?" I asked, thinking back to last night. "When I was at the Baldwin depot, I knew I needed to get you a message, and then I remembered the Western Union office near here. That's really very handy, by the way. Of course, if we could take our telephones with us, that would be even more handy."

"Who do you think you are? Dick Tracy with his wrist videophone? Honestly, Jimmy. Telephones are tied to the wall with wires. What would we do, carry a spool of wire around that was connected to our homes? How would we get it wound up again? No, I think telephones are going to stay on the wall right where they belong."

"Maybe in the future," I answered, trying to imagine what a phone with no wires would look like but failing. It was like there was a wall between the damaged part of my brain and my memories, and it was a wall I couldn't climb or leap over.

"Well, in this girl's future, you're taking me out for breakfast. Or lunch. What time is it? Good heavens, it's nearly ten o'clock, Jimmy. If we don't hurry, we'll have to have pie and coffee and bars for lunch until they're ready to serve lunch. C'mon. Let's run over to the luncheonette."

Warm thoughts about last night's meatloaf swirled in my head, and my tastebuds recalled the delightful piece of chess pie I'd had for dessert. I could definitely go for another piece of *that* this morning.

I started out the door, but Wendi was picking up the telephone.

"Checking to see if you can bring the telephone along?" I asked.

My question earned me an eye roll. "No, goofus. I'm calling our service – *your* service. The operator who takes your calls and messages when you aren't available. You remember—wait, hang on. Hi, Barbara! It's Wendi. I'm sorry I can't chat, but we're in a hurry. Have there been any messages for Jimmy? There is? Okay. Give it to me." She wrote something on a piece of paper on the desk.

"Okay, Barbara. Thanks. I'll take care of it." She hung up the phone. I guess if we had an answering service, we didn't need to take telephones with us.

"What's the message?" I asked.

"She said a Dale Higgins called and wants to meet you tonight at eight o'clock on the dock near the Ship's Galley at the waterfront. The *Orange Coast* is tied up nearby. That's where your meeting will take place: on the docks."

"The *Orange Coast*. Well, that sounds like a Florida ship. I wonder what the meeting will be about."

"I couldn't tell you, but we're going to have to wait until noon to get anything to eat if we don't hurry. Let's go, and be sure to lock the door behind you, Jimmy."

"What good does it do to lock the door when the owner gives out the master key to every Tom, Dick, and Doyle who wants it?" I asked.

"That's a good point," Wendi replied. "Maybe we can get a locksmith to come in and change the lock and give you a key the owner *doesn't* have."

I locked the door behind me anyway, thinking, *'A new lock would only keep out the honest people, and not even all of them!'*

As we walked around the corner to Thompson's luncheonette, I was still thinking about the idea of a telephone you could take with you. I couldn't figure out why the idea intrigued me so much.

I forgot all about telephones when we reached Thompson's Luncheonette. My nose picked up the aroma of freshly baked pies and other goodies mixed with the heady bouquet of freshly brewed coffee.

"Over there, Jimmy," Wendi said, tugging on my arm.

"There's already someone sitting at that table," I replied.

"I know. That's *why* I want to sit there."

The man sitting at the table stood up and extended his hand. As I took it, Wendi introduced us.

"Jimmy, this is Hillary. Hillary Lyst. Hillary, this is my friend Jimmy, the one I was telling you about."

Hillary wore round glasses with gold wire rims. His sandy hair was thinning, and he had a sandy-blonde goatee that was nearly white. He wore black slacks and a white shirt but no tie. A black suit jacket was draped over the chair behind him. The elbows of his shirt looked thin and worn. The sight of his threadbare shirt elbows told me he worked at a desk, either as an accountant or something else, where he laid his arms on a desk all day long.

"Jimmy," Wendi said, "Hillary loves writing and books. His dream is to own either a newspaper or run a library. But he'd settle for anything to do with books."

Hillary and I shook hands, and we sat down at the table.

"How about a bookstore?" I asked. It just seemed like a natural alternative.

Hillary looked at me over the tops of his glasses. His eyes crinkled, but his goatee partially hid the smirk that had invaded his face.

"I think that falls under the heading of *anything* to do with books," he answered.

"I take it you're a big fan of words."

"The biggest, most substantial, and immense type of enthusiast," Hillary replied. "Without words, *War and Peace* is just a big coloring book."

"Did you know that John Steinbeck's *Of Mice and Men* has less than thirty thousand words?" I asked.

"I did. Were you aware that Victor Hugo's novel, *Les Misérables,* contains a single sentence that is 823 words long?"

"Does that sentence come with time off for good behavior?" I asked, doing my best to keep a straight face.

"I'm going to buy you both some food and coffee—" Wendi began, turning back toward the counter.

Hillary stopped Wendi by holding up one finger.

"Correction," she said. "Food and coffee for Jimmy and food and _tea_ for Hillary."

Hillary's smile lit up their little corner of the luncheonette. "Thank you, my dear. You know I'll pay you back someday. As soon as I'm gainfully employed with some semblance of regularity."

"Yes, you will. Probably in ways neither of us can imagine."

She leaned down and kissed the top of my head. *Not my first choice for her to kiss.*

"Be good, Jimmy. Don't get hit on the head anymore today. I have to go to work for a few hours, but I'll be back this afternoon unless something comes up at the hospital. Regardless, I'll be back before supper for sure."

She stood and looked at the two of us at the table for a moment, like she was setting a picture of the moment in her memory, then turned on her heel and left. As she did, she cast a lighthearted, "You word-boys have fun!" over her shoulder.

I watched her as she walked across the room toward the door. She stopped at the cash register and talked to the waitress. She pointed briefly at Hillary and me, then pulled out her pocketbook and gave the waitress a couple of dollars for whatever she had ordered us for lunch. A second or two later, and she was out the door.

"How long have you known Wendi?" I asked Hillary.

"It seems like forever and as though we've only just met for the first time, simultaneously," he answered.

I looked across our small table for two at him. "I know what you mean. I feel the same way. There's something about her that makes me feel as though I have always known her … or been looking for her … but at the same time, I feel like there are infinite depths still to explore."

The waitress brought my coffee along with Hillary's hot water and a tea bag. We put our conversation on hold while she set the cups on the table in front of us. Once the waitress departed, Hillary picked up the conversational thread again.

"It sounds like you have a different relationship with her than I do," he said.

I was putting cream and sugar in my coffee as I answered him. "I don't honestly know what kind of relationship I have with her yet. She seems to know everything there is to know about me, but she won't tell me much. And I can only remember the last couple of days with her – in the hospital and then down here along the waterfront."

Hillary repeatedly raised and lowered his teabag in the cup of hot water the waitress had brought. I had already finished doctoring my coffee and took a tentative sip; it was still hot enough to blister my lips and tongue. I let it sit to cool.

"Wendi says you love books," I said to the bespectacled man. "What can you do with that? Can you parlay a love for books and reading into something that'll put food on the table? And not just for one but two? And maybe more as time marches on?"

"I've been toying with the idea of trying to hire on with the local newspaper. I did some writing during the war …" His voice trailed off.

His eyes took on a far-away look. I'd heard soldiers call it the ten-thousand-yard stare, but I really didn't understand. *Wait! Which soldiers had I talked to? Which war?* But like all my transient memories, this one ran out of the room and slammed the door shut behind it just when I wanted to have a conversation with it.

"Which newspaper were you thinking of working for?" I asked my brunch companion as I sipped my coffee. I was interested to hear what Hillary's plans were, but I was equally curious to see what Wendi had ordered for us since it was now significantly closer to noon than 7 a.m. I was hungry.

"Well, Jimmy—can I call you Jimmy? Or would you prefer Mr. Marlowe?"

"Jimmy's fine. And if anyone asks, I'm Philip Marlowe's second cousin."

Hillary's eyes twinkled at the mention of the radio and literary character, and he continued.

"Fernandina used to be north of where we are now, but the whole town moved in 1853 after David Yulee was building his railroad. He said the railroad couldn't cross the salt marshes around Fernandina, what became known as 'Old Town,' so the town moved. Such was the charisma and influence of David Yulee. There have been dozens of newspapers here on the island known as Amelia, but they have merged and remerged so many times, that no one is exactly sure when they became the Fernandina Beach News-Leader, a blending of the Nassau County Leader and the Fernandina Beach News."

Hillary gave his tea bag a few more dunks and, after squeezing it out slightly into his cup by wrapping the string around the bag and his spoon, lifted the cup, pausing in mid-air. I thought he was smelling his tea, but then realized he was waiting for me to join him in a toast. I lifted my coffee cup, and we clinked our cups together lightly. Then, we both blew on our beverages to cool them slightly before sipping from them.

Hillary set his cup down after a very brief sip. He sat back in his chair and looked over his glasses at me. "Did you know," he began, "that Fernandina's first newspaper was in Spanish? It was called el Telegrafo de las Floridas."

"I didn't know that, but it really doesn't surprise me in the least. Fernandina has been under seven or eight different flags since people started living here. Some more than once."

"Indeed. Florida was under colonial rule by Spain from the 16th to the 19th century and was briefly under Great Britain's Union Jack during the 18th century. Since Florida became a U.S. territory in 1821, over twenty-one newspapers have been published here in Fernandina, the longest running being the News, started by Senator David Yulee in August of 1854."

"The train guy," I added.

"Indeed. Trains, newspapers, politics, and more."

Hillary tried his tea again, slightly cooler from a minute earlier, but it was enough. He could sip his tea less tentatively now, and without wincing afterward.

Meanwhile, I had nearly drained my coffee, so I caught the waitress's eye and raised the white cup to about eye level, placing it directly in the line of sight from my eyes to hers, breaking the contact and sending a message. She nodded. Communication received.

Less than a minute later, she was at our table, refilling my cup. She glanced at Hillary's cup to check the liquid level while she resupplied me.

"I'll have your food in a few minutes, maybe sooner," she said. She gave me a genuine smile, the lines around her eyes revealing an age the rest of her face didn't. She was the same waitress who served me last night when I enjoyed the meatloaf and chess pie. I had figured she was about fifteen when I first saw her, but now, in the light of day, I could see that she carried an internal burden and a few more years I hadn't picked up on before. I had no inkling what that burden might be, but she carried the load stoically.

She was trim and tiny, with dark brown hair and brown eyes. The strings of her apron wrapped around her waist more than once, revealing how very slender she was. She wore a navy blue skirt that went down to her mid-calf and a mostly white blouse with a collar and a tiny, delicate blue floral pattern. The blouse was long-sleeved, but she had rolled them up like a farmer who rolls up his flannel sleeves to let the air reach his skin when he's hard at work.

The waitress was hard at work, too. I wondered how many miles she walked every day in the luncheonette, moving back and forth from table to table, to the kitchen, back to the tables, and to the cash register. She rarely stopped moving. She was a waitress, hostess, bus person, and dining room manager, all in a tiny package. I had no doubt she also performed many tasks in the kitchen, too.

"That's Alice," Hillary said.

I forced my eyes to change their focus from the waitress to Hillary's face. He was looking directly through the lenses of his glasses at me rather than over the top for a change.

"Who is Alice?" I asked.

"The waitress. This is her restaurant."

Something about that statement struck me as incredibly funny, and I barked out a sudden laugh but tried to cover it as a cough. My batting average hadn't been very good lately when people told me things.

"*This* is Alice's Restaurant?" I asked. I waited, but he didn't seem amused by the name, and I couldn't tell him – or myself – why I found it so humorous.

"As previously noted, her name is Alice. Alice Mortel. Emphasis on the last syllable. Mor-tel'. It's either French or English. A name intimately associated with death. It could possibly be Italian, but I think it's much more likely French or English, and I would put my money on French; if I had any money, that is."

I looked at Hillary, who seemed to spout encyclopedic information in little bursts when you weren't expecting it. I looked back at the waitress, who was hopefully on her way to our table. She was carrying two plates and a coffee pot, the coffee in her right hand and the plates in the other – or rather, one plate in her left hand and the other plate on her left forearm, tucked in close to her body in case she got jostled and needed to balance it.

She smiled as she placed the plates on our table, one in front of each of us.

"Wendi told me how much you liked this last night, and I told her we had a few pieces left in the icebox – enough to make a couple of sandwiches."

The aroma of meatloaf reached my brain. I looked down and saw that it was the meatloaf I had enjoyed so much the night before but placed between two pieces of Texas toast. I saw a dribble of ketchup sneaking out along the cut edge of the bread and meat. The meat had a slightly smoky smell to it, like a good steak that's been cooked on a hot, flat piece of steel. The twin triangles of meat and bread flanked a pile of french-fried potatoes in the middle of the plate. There was no gravy, but the waitress reached into a front pocket hidden in her apron, brought out a bottle of Heinz Catsup, and sat it on the table to accompany the meatloaf and the fries.

"I had Cook throw the meatloaf on the griddle and heat it up. It gets a good sear, a little char, and a tasty little crust from browning the meat a little and caramelizing the tomato sauce. I hope you like it. I wish I had some more chess pie for you, but the last piece went out a half-hour ago. We *do* have fresh banana puddin' if you're so inclined, and Wendi left enough money so you could have some dessert, too."

Something incredibly familiar about the girl made me think I had met her before, and I don't mean the night before when I came in to eat. There was something—

"Splendid, my dear! A repast fit for royalty!" Hillary practically shouted, reaching out and placing his hand on hers briefly. "You've refreshed my faith in humanity."

Alice blushed and tucked her chin down like she wanted to hide. Her face was turning red when someone in another part of the luncheonette called out, "Oh, Miss..." and she spun around and hurried off to restore someone else's faith in humanity. Or refill their coffee.

"You made her day, Hillary."

"Indeed? I meant every word. It was not idle chatter."

I wasn't about to argue with him. The food smelled too good.

"Let's eat, Hillary."

"An excellent idea, Jimmy. As the British say, let's tuck in."

For the next ten minutes, there was no talk about words, newspapers, books, backgrounds, or plans. There was only eating and the sheer enjoyment of it. I made sure to keep a scrap of Texas toast to clean my plate at the end. Some people may find that uncouth, but I wasn't about to leave anything but memories and wishes behind on that plate. As in, "I wish I had a little more."

Alice returned to our table. "Puddin'?" she asked.

"Yes, please," Hillary and I answered in unison.

Her face lit up like we'd given her a five-dollar tip. She returned shortly with bowls of creamy, yellow banana puddin' smothered in meringue topping and baked under the broiler to give it a toasted marshmallow flavor.

Hillary took a bite and moaned. "My dear, you've outdone yourself! I didn't think it possible after that culinary masterpiece you created from something as pedestrian as meatloaf, but this dessert is remarkable. Truly stellar quality."

She turned from Hillary toward me. I stopped with a spoonful of pudding mid-point to my mouth. "It's really, really good!" was all I could get out. I felt like an eighth-grade boy when he encounters a cute girl in the hall and tries to speak, but nothing comes out but a tiny squeak – if *that* much.

She laughed a laugh filled with genuine mirth, wrapped her hands in her apron, and walked back to the kitchen, signaling OK with her fingers – letting Cook know they'd 'done good.'

Chapter 8

WE FINISHED OUR MEAL in relative silence and then had Alice freshen our drinks. I'm always surprised by how much better coffee tastes when it's hot and how bad it can taste when it's cold.

Alice brought Hillary another cup of hot water, and he made another cup of tea. While it steeped, he leaned back in his chair. "I understand you have not had an easy time of it since arriving here in Fernandina," he said across the now-cleared table.

"I appreciate you acknowledging that, but I can't say for sure that it's been all bad. I don't remember anything before a couple of days ago when I woke up in the hospital with my head wrapped in gauze, thanks to a skull fracture courtesy of—" I tried to remember the name. For a brief second, I got a glimpse of a large man with hands twice as big as mine. He had a scowl on his face, and his eyes looked like two pools of pure evil, if evil could be a liquid.

I almost had a name to go with the face, but then the face dissolved, taking along with it any chance of applying a name. It left a sudden twinge of pain in its wake.

"Dang! I almost had it."

"Almost had what, Jimmy?"

"I almost had the name of the guy who smashed my head against the wall. But then I lost it."

"Perhaps if you try *not* to think about it, it'll return on its own. Like cats in particular, and a few dogs, some memories can't resist being ignored. It's as though they want to be noticed. Maybe your memory is the same."

I smiled weakly at his theory, rubbing my temples. At least the ache was easing, and there had been no bright lights this time. And thank goodness there had been no nausea! Alice's food was far too good to waste feeding the ants across the street in the grassy expanse near the train depot.

"If I may ask, what else has been happening to you since you woke up in the hospital, Jimmy?"

"Well, some lowlife guys killed a woman and mistook me for her husband. I took the train to get out of town, but I met her husband on the train. He tried to kill me, but I got away. Later, the thugs were in *my* apartment with their boss, and I had to give them a wad of money I found in the dead woman's apartment. So, you know, just the usual, run-of-the-mill, everyday stuff."

Hillary stared at Jimmy for a few seconds, then shook his head for a long minute, a high-pitched laugh coming from his mouth. He took off his glasses and began cleaning them with a handkerchief he pulled from his pocket.

"I can't tell if you're telling me an enormously tall tale or the truth."

"Trust me, it's the truth. But I didn't even tell you it all. The cops are in on the whole thing. They helped take the dead woman's body out of the apartment. No muss, no fuss, and nobody's the wiser because there's no corpse! Kendall – the husband – may have gone to Chicago, but he could be back anytime. My problem is that I don't know if he thinks he needs to get rid of me because I saw the guys in his apartment who bumped off his missus. He also may want me out of the picture because I know that he knew about the murder and was just going to Chicago for an alibi. Well, his alibi, yes, but also to see Julie, who might also be in on it."

Hillary was laughing even more, a strange high-pitched sound, and took his glasses off again and set them on the table in front of him.

"Do you know what you need, Jimmy? You need a biographer to tag along with you and write down all these outlandish things that occur to you and around you. They could be serialized in the newspapers."

"Speaking of newspapers, Hillary, what do you want to do at the News? You said you wrote some stories or something during the war?"

"Indeed. I was a war correspondent in the Pacific Theater. You know, I've always disliked the term theater when describing a war area. It always sounds like I went to watch a play or some Kabuki shows while I was overseas. But I didn't. I was attached to an infantry unit, similar to the war correspondent Ernie Pyle, except I came home alive."

I knew who Ernie Pyle was. He had been killed on Okinawa in 1945. He wasn't even a soldier. He was a Pulitzer Prize-winning journalist. They called him the voice of the American Soldier. All the dogfaces—soldiers—loved him because he wrote about the ordinary guys who were over there fighting and dying to protect everybody back here in the States. *Why can I know about Ernie Pyle but not my name?*

"I'll bet you have some incredible stories you could tell," I said to Hillary, at the same time wondering what stories I could tell if I could just recover my memory.

"Incredible, indeed, but I hope I never have to tell anyone those stories. No one would believe me if I wrote down the things I saw or the things I heard. That's why our troops were there – so the people we love back here need never be exposed to atrocities like the ones we experienced abroad."

His eyes took on that blank, faraway look again, and I knew he was staring back in time, no longer sitting in the little luncheonette watching couples finish their meals while he and I enjoyed our coffee and tea.

After a brief moment, he snapped back to the present, and he said, "But these days, I want to write about good things, normal things, the activities and routines we take for granted here. I want to write about babies being born, people getting engaged and getting married, celebrating anniversaries, store openings, band concerts, winning ribbons at county fairs, and if I have to write about death, I sincerely hope it's a quiet death at the end of a very long, fulfilling life, surrounded by loved ones and friends." He paused and then whispered, to himself more than to me, "I'm done watching young men die. I've had a bellyful of that."

"Hillary," I said, "the News-Leader would be lucky to get you. Any newspaper would be lucky to have you on their news staff. How are your prospects looking?"

"Well," he said, "I have an interview with the publisher and general manager on Friday – two days from now. In the meantime, I'm taking advantage of my furlough to wander this fine town and take in its many sights and wonders. I'm spending time at the local library, reading about the town's history and the people who made that history, from the indigenous peoples to pirates to captains of industry and visionaries."

"Like David Yulee?"

Hillary smiled. "Yulee was definitely a big influence on this region of Florida. He was a man who made something of himself and this region he admired."

I began thinking about a young man in a pin-striped suit with shiny shoes who was trying to "make something of himself." I wondered if Abaddon would succumb to the daily grind—the need to pay bills and put food on the table. Some men were not destined to be fathers and family men. Some found honorable ways to meet their needs, and some did not.

"Do you know what Jean Ribault said about this area?" Hillary asked me.

"I don't even know who Jean Ribault is or was. Is she a singer, dancer, or actress?"

The eyes crinkled, and the high-pitched laughter snuck out fleetingly again. "It's Jean – the French John. He, Jean, was a French explorer who came to this area a scant seventy years after Columbus discovered America. Ribault came across Amelia Island, and is reported to have said, 'It's a place wonderfully fertile and of strong situation.' I believe he was right on both counts."

"It sure beats snow and cold," I said.

Hillary took a final sip of his tea and asked, "So, you have experience with snow and cold?"

"Beats me, Professor. It just popped out. Like I was saying it without thinking, just a gut reaction."

"Indeed! Perhaps you haven't always lived here. Perhaps you've spent some time dwelling in a colder climate. Who knows – you might even hail from a completely different country."

"Well, if I do, there's no residual accent."

"No, that's not quite true, Jimmy. Your inflection is as flat as a Midwesterner's but not as broad as someone from Wisconsin or Michigan. That in itself is a kind of accent. You could be from a large, north-central region that includes North and South Dakota, Minnesota, Wisconsin, and Michigan, even parts of Canada."

We sat for a few more minutes, watching the post-lunch-rush cleanup and marveling at how promptly the frantic restaurant had returned to being a drowsy little café in a sleepy little town.

After watching Alice and Cook for a bit, I stood up. "I'm glad we got to meet, Hillary. I hope we'll see each other again. I'd like to know how you make out with that job at the newspaper. I'm going to stroll around the block to my apartment, and if I'm extremely lucky, I'll be able to catch a nap after that fine lunch."

"I plan on walking over and spending some time at my favorite place in the entire world, the local library," Hillary responded. "If I'm lucky, I imagine I'll be there the rest of the afternoon. Please pass along my appreciation for the repast to Wendi if you should see her before I do, Jimmy."

"Indeed!" I said and smiled broadly. We shook hands, and I headed out the front door of Alice's Restaurant. Something about the name still tickled my brain and my funny bone. I hummed a little tune I had no words for and no idea where it originated.

: : : :

I STROLLED DOWN THE sidewalk in the sunshine and decided against going directly to my apartment, opting to meander down to the waterfront first. I'd be meeting Dale Higgins there after dark tonight, so a little daylight reconnaissance seemed prudent.

I didn't have any trouble finding the *Orange Coast*. It was a big ship, and, obviously built for carrying passengers, not fruit like the name implied. The multiple deck levels had rows of foldable canvas deck chairs lining them, and I was pretty sure if I wandered around a bit, I'd find a shuffleboard court somewhere on the ship. For now, though, I was just a tourist having a look from afar.

While I walked leisurely along the boardwalk, eyeing the ship and trying to look like your average sightseer, a man dressed in a blazingly white suit came out from somewhere on the big passenger ship and walked over to the railing. He looked down at the people walking around the waterfront. He was probably thinking how odd life must be for those anchored to the land, unable to roam from port to port or from one warm tropical town to another. The people looking up at the big ship with the man dressed in white were probably thinking how odd life must be for someone with no house to call home, forced to live on a boat as large as a factory, a floating city that never stayed anywhere for more than a few days.

A boy of about twelve years old came running up to me, a Western Union cap perched on his blonde head. There was a pencil in a loop on the cap, and he wore a white button-down shirt with a black four-in-hand tie. His pants were dark, ending just below his knees. *Knickers?* But instead of socks and shoes, he was barefoot.

"Are you Mr. Marlowe?"

"I am. What can I do for you?"

"Telegram, sir. From Dale Higgins."

I took the yellow envelope from his hand and tore it open. The message was short. "CHANGE IN PLANS. MEET ME AT THE BAR IN THE SHIP'S GALLEY. SAME TIME. DALE."

I thought for a second. Was Dale Higgins asking me to meet him in the galley of the *Orange Coast,* or was he asking me to meet him at the dockside seafood restaurant and bar called the Ship's Galley?

I suddenly realized the message boy with the Western Union cap was still standing in front of me. He had pulled a book of telegram blanks from his back pocket and had his pencil at the ready.

"Any reply, sir?" he asked.

"No. That's fine. No reply."

The boy put the blanks back in his pocket and pencil back in his cap, but he didn't leave.

"Is there something else I can do for you, young man?"

He looked at me uncomfortably and held his hand out briefly, only extending his arm out about halfway. It was the universal sign for *I'm waiting for a tip, you jerk!*

"Ahh. I'm sorry. I'm a little off today. Got knocked pretty hard in the head the other day, and I'm still recovering. Hang on." I dug in my trouser pockets and pulled out a quarter. I hoped it would do. I handed it to him. His eyes lit up as he saw what I was giving him.

"Two bits? Really? Gee, thanks, Mr. Marlowe. If you need anything else, just ask for me by name. I'm Ralph."

"If you can be of any help to me, I'll keep you in mind, Ralph. And you can call me Jimmy."

Ralph took off running up Centre Street, rushing back to the Western Union office located a few doors down from the Palace Saloon. I tried to figure out if he was being sarcastic about the tip I gave him, but finally decided he was genuinely happy to get twenty-five cents for delivering an envelope to a stranger on the waterfront. I couldn't remember my own last name, but I knew when I was a kid, I would have been ecstatic to get paid a quarter for running around.

I saw the Ship's Galley up ahead. It wasn't too far down the boardwalk from the *Orange Coast*. I wondered what connection the big passenger ship had to this person named Dale Higgins. Had he come to Fernandina on the ship, or was he just using it as a landmark? I decided I'd find out in a few hours and moved it to the back of my mind.

I walked back to the Palace, continuing past the front doors to around back with the rickety stairs and the "private" entrance – at least it was more private than walking through the saloon while people watched you walk to the back and enter a door with a narrow stairway. I always hated people knowing where I was going, especially when it was a tight space where someone could make trouble for me from above or below.

I wondered which entrance my "second cousin," Philip Marlowe, would use. He'd probably walk through the Saloon, stop at the bar to get a shot of whiskey, and set up a date with the most beautiful woman in the whole place.

That made me think of Daani, who could easily be the *only* woman in the place at this hour. She was kind of cute, but she usually had such a sour look on her face that I couldn't imagine spending much time talking with her. I was curious about her long black braids, though. I wondered where her ancestors had come from. She had more than a drop or two of American Indian blood in her veins; I was sure of that.

When I arrived at my apartment, I checked the six on the door to make sure it was actually a six and not an upside-down nine. Then, I looked down the hall toward Kendall Brody's apartment.

I wondered if he was back from Chicago yet. I wondered if he was coming back at all, but I already knew the answer: he was. He had too much invested in his business here to walk away from it. And, since Doyle, the young man in the pin-stripe suit, had already taken care of the police, there was no reason for Kendall to stay away. Except for Julie. But maybe Brody would bring her down here from the Windy City to get a taste of the warmth and sun that didn't disappear when you flipped the calendar from August to September.

Out of the blue, I wondered what Julie looked like. Catherine Brody had been a fine-looking woman, even dead and with a neat but fatal hole in her temple. I felt bad for her. But not too bad. She *was* trying to have Kendall killed, after all. He had simply had a little more disposable income than she did, and he had disposed of her.

In my office, I walked over to the desk and patted all my pockets. I had a strong urge to take something out of my pocket and lay it on the desk, but I realized I didn't have anything in my pockets I needed to set aside. It just felt like something I did regularly, but I couldn't figure out what I might habitually leave on my desk. I only had the door key, the one for this apartment, and my wallet, which was pretty thin. Seven dollars. No need to toss either of them on the desk.

I decided I'd try to catch a few z's before supper and my evening meeting. I went back to my bedroom and threw myself on the bed, but before I could nap, my brain started asking questions. *Wait! Am I supposed to have dinner with Dale at the Ship's Galley or just drinks? What about money?*

I checked my wallet again. The ten dollars for emergencies was still there. *Phew!*

I was so tired I felt like I hadn't slept in days, but I knew I had. There were big gaps of darkness in my memory that I was sure were the times when I had slept. After all, the doc at the hospital had given me a hypo and put me out. That should count for sleep, shouldn't it?

And at the Baldwin train depot, I had slept, hadn't I? Although come to think of it, I only remembered closing my eyes and discovering it was suddenly morning. It was as if time had compressed, and I had skipped the middle part, the deep sleep part, the part containing rest and rejuvenation. It was like I had skipped directly from beginning to end. It was the same way in the hospital: every time I closed my eyes, I'd immediately wake up again, but it'd be hours later.

Well, I had hours to sleep right now before I needed to find Wendi for supper. She would probably come up here so I wouldn't have to try and find her.

I closed my eyes.

A second later, I opened my eyes again, and the sun was no longer high in the sky, no longer streaming through the window shade with the holes and tears in it. If you told me I had napped, I couldn't testify to it. I didn't feel like I had slept at all. I felt more like I *thought* about sleeping more than I actually slept.

I didn't get up immediately, choosing to lay there thinking and listening, trying to figure out if I was still sleeping and not dreaming or not sleeping and dreaming everything. *What's the line from Shakespeare? "To sleep, perchance to dream. Ay, there's the rub." So, which am I missing, the dream or the sleep?*

I rubbed a hand over my face. I had a little beard stubble but not enough to worry about shaving before supper and the meeting with Dale Higgins at the Ship's Galley. I didn't know if I should have a light supper with Wendi and save room for dinner with Dale or if our meeting at the Ship's Galley was just that: a meeting, and I should have a full dinner with Wendi.

I swung my legs over the side of the bed and sat up. My head gave me a momentary touch of vertigo, but it passed quickly, so I stood to my feet. I walked out into the other room in my apartment, the front room I liked to call an office, and I strode over to the desk. I pulled back the age-yellowed lace curtains and looked outside. A few people were walking on the sidewalk, but it was that lull that came before the dinner hour. People were either at home for a homemade meal, deciding where to go for dinner, or – having decided – walking to the restaurant because it was such a nice day.

I heard the tiniest of noises, as soft as the swish of an owl's wing overhead at midnight as he glides from tree to tree, looking for signs of a rabbit or a mouse moving furtively on the ground. It also sounded like the rustling fabric made when a dress brushed against a chair or a desk. Like it would sound in a small room like this one.

I turned to find Daani in my apartment, standing a few feet away, staring at me. She wasn't scowling, sneering, or rolling her eyes. She looked younger than she had in the saloon. And the long braids of hair were no longer in a bun but trailing down, one on each side of her head, falling past her shoulders and down to her chest.

"You have seen him, haven't you?" she said to me.

"Seen who?"

"The Wendigo."

"Wendigo?" I was about to ask her if a Wendigo was some kind of bird when I realized some part of me already knew what a Wendigo was. An evil spirit. The Ojibway and the First Nations in Canada described it as a flesh-eater of the forest. *How do I know that?*

"Yes, a Wendigo," she answered, not realizing I already had a working definition. "You might call it a bogeyman. But he's much more than that, and he's much worse."

Chapter 9

In the dim light of my apartment, with her braids released from the bun they had been bound up in before, I analyzed her high cheekbones and brown eyes, and I confirmed what I had seen earlier. Danielle Egly was an Indian. Maybe not full-blooded, but at least half.

"Who's a Wendigo?" I asked. "And while we're exchanging pleasantries, why don't you tell me how you got into my apartment."

Daani rolled her eyes at my second question, and her mouth turned down in a frown.

"I work downstairs, and there's a master key for all the apartments up here." She pulled a key out of a pocket on the front of her work dress. Dresses for going out to dinner or a show either had no pockets or had hidden pockets on the sides. Work dresses had square pockets in the front about waist-high. The word that came to my mind was utilitarian.

"And do you frequently let yourself into other people's apartments?" I asked, taking a slow, easy step closer to her.

Her frown turned down even more, becoming an angry scowl.

"I only came up here to warn you to keep your head on a swivel because a Wendigo is nothing to take lightly. But I see now that I'm wasting my time. You don't need anyone's help, or so you think. But if that's what you think, you're in way over your head."

I shifted slightly and moved slightly closer. She matched my movements in reverse, like we were dancing, and moved closer to the door and hallway. I held up my hand to show I wasn't going to try anything. Her features relaxed ever-so-slightly, and I saw her shoulders lower a tad.

"Where's blondie?" she asked.

"Wendi? She had to work a shift at the hospital this afternoon. She should be back soon. Why don't I sit over there at my desk, and you come in and sit in this chair here? You can tell me about the boogeyman. I'm sorry; you can explain about the *Wendigo*."

Her eyebrows pinched together as she narrowed her eyes at me, trying to discern if I was really interested in a creature from Native American folklore.

How do I know that? Some part of my brain was still working, or pieces of my memory were starting to shift into place again.

I decided to take the first step, literally, so I turned slowly and deliberately, went to my desk chair, and sat down. I gestured toward the other chair, and she looked at it briefly before giving a little shake of her head – a tacit way to say, *'I'm fine where I am.'*

"What makes you think I know what a Wendigo is?" I asked her, trying to match my question with a smile to keep her from bolting from my room.

"You *know*. You actually know about more things than you know. You used to live where these things are taken seriously, where creatures of his type are feared, and where children are taught at an early age to keep their eyes open and be on the lookout for him. Wendigos are always on the lookout for a human to possess, to compel them to commit murder by filling them with intense greed and hatred. You *used* to know this when you lived where the Wendigos walked in the forests and hunted in the cities, seeking the tender flesh of children foolish enough to stay out after dark. *After seven o'clock when the streetlights came on.*"

Her words made my scalp itch. On some visceral, gut level, I knew what she was talking about, but I couldn't put any facts, dates, or places together with those feelings. *Where did I come from? What's my last name?* Those were fundamental questions I needed answers to, but none would come. If there was someone like a Wendigo wandering around unrecognized, it could be harmful to my health if I didn't have all my faculties.

"How do you know these things about me?" I asked.

"I just do. You shouldn't even be here, but your mind needed a rest, so you came here. But it cannot be an extended rest. The Wendigo is still stalking the vulnerable, weak, and especially the foolish. It's become even easier than ever for the creature to harvest prey because people have decided it's irrational to believe in such things. It's become a simple thing for the Wendigo to take them before they even smell its foul stench."

She was holding the master room key in between her fingers and turning it over and over. The scowling and frowning that had made her features seem hard were gone. She was a handsome woman with strong features, but if she would just let her hair down, I was sure she would be an attractive young woman. She caught me looking at her and frowned again. I smiled. After a second, she gave a half-smile back. I was right. Hidden in there was a pretty girl. Then I frowned.

"Who is the Wendigo?" I asked.

She shook her head. "It's not my place to tell you. You know him. He masks his true nature with nice clothes and a handsome countenance. But his anger and hate are never far from the surface. He is young now, but he is strong and patient. All I can tell you is to be careful and keep watching. You'll know him when you see him if you concentrate on perceiving with your heart instead of your eyes. Remember, a Wendigo has a heart of ice, filled with hate and anger, and an insatiable desire for human flesh. It has always been that way, even when you were young."

Just then, I heard a door open down the hall. It was the door from the rickety outside stairs. It must be Wendi.

Daani dropped the key she was holding. I bent over to pick it up, and when I rose with the key in my hand, she was gone. The apartment door was closed, but I hadn't heard it open or close.

There was a light tap at the door, and it opened. Wendi poked her head in and smiled at me. She opened the door fully and entered the room. I caught a faint scent of her perfume mixed with disinfectant and soap when she came near me.

"Anything going on? Did you have a nice lunch with Hillary?" Wendi asked as she sat down in the chair that Daani had refused to sit in a few minutes before. I decided not to tell her about the barmaid's visit; not yet, anyway.

"Hillary and I had a great lunch. Thank you for springing for that. The meatloaf sandwiches were great, and the banana pudding was the perfect ending."

"I wondered what Alice would feed you. We talked briefly before I left, and she said she knew what you liked and would take care of you. It sounds like she did."

"What's her story?" I asked.

"Alice's story? It's really not that long. A girl graduates from high school and falls in love with a guy who is only using her. The girl gets pregnant, the guy leaves, and the girl has a baby and lives a hard life from then on, tasked with being the sole provider and both parents to the child. Sound familiar?"

"Yeah. I think I've heard it more than a few times. In some versions, the guy marries the girl out of a sense of duty but then resents her for crushing his dreams. It doesn't matter that her dreams were shattered, too. He usually takes up strong drink and chasing loose women as hobbies. Eventually, they either get an ugly divorce, or he wraps his car around a tree in a drunken stupor, leaving her with a huge bill for a funeral, or worse, he survives the crash but needs constant care from her. I'm glad I've avoided that path."

Wendi looked at me and raised her eyebrows at my last remark.

"What?" I asked. "I have avoided that path, haven't I?"

She paused a beat too long before answering, "Yes, you have. So far, anyway."

"What aren't you telling me?"

"What did you and Hillary talk about?" Wendi asked, deftly trying to change the subject.

"Words. Books. Newspapers. What aren't you telling me?" I repeated my question.

She took a big breath and exhaled before answering. "Who's to say whether any of us are truly awake or if we're dreaming? How would we know?"

I didn't like her answer. Having woken up to find myself in a hospital with gauze wrapped around my head and then the unsettling feeling that I'm not where I'm supposed to be, her answer hit too close to home. At times, I felt like it wasn't so much not being *where* I was supposed to be as it was not being *when* I was supposed to be.

"What do you want to do for supper, Jimmy?" She changed the subject again and was looking at me as I sat staring off into space, ruminating over her questions.

"I've already eaten at Alice's twice in the last twenty-four hours," I answered. "Is there any law against eating there again? I don't know if I just don't remember that I've eaten there before or if I truly never have until this week."

"There is no law against eating every meal in the same place as far as I know. Is that what you want to do?" She stood up and took the several steps required to cross over to my desk and put her hand on mine, her skin soft and warm. Suddenly, I wasn't thinking about supper anymore.

I stood quickly, took her in my arms, and said, "This is what I want to do." I kissed her for a long time, and I was grateful and relieved again that she kissed me back.

When we broke from our kiss, she buried her face in my shoulder, and I could tell she was crying. *That's a real ego booster. Not!*

"Hey! Hey, hey, hey. Here now. Was it that bad?" I asked her quietly.

She gave a little half-laugh and shook her head.

"Then what is it? When I kissed you, it felt like the most natural thing in the world. Isn't that how you feel?"

She nodded and looked up at me. "Yes, Jimmy, it is. But until you get your memory back, I don't want to push you into a relationship you might not want. This amnesia you have might be a blessing in disguise … for you. If you don't remember *us*, you can have a do-over."

I stepped back and held her at arm's length. She was beautiful, even when she had been crying, and her nose was slightly red and sniffly, and her mascara had run slightly and smeared, darkening her eyes.

"Did I get you pregnant, and we had to get married? And then I became a drunk and got in a car wreck? And now I'm in a hospital ward somewhere with no memory of our little boy or girl, and you have to take care of me and our child and …" She put a finger on my lips to stop my rambling.

"I didn't get pregnant, we didn't get married, and you don't like alcohol," she said.

I wanted to see her face, but Wendi turned away and said, "I just don't want to take advantage of you, Jimmy. I have all the memories, while you have none. For you, it's like starting from scratch. Maybe this time you'll want to do things differently." She sniffled.

"Nope. I still want to go to Alice's Restaurant," I said, and it was like a puzzle piece slid into place in my brain. I knew I wanted to be with Wendi. "C'mon, Wendi. Let's go. I still have seven dollars in my wallet. I'll buy."

I slipped my sports jacket on, and another thought hit me. "Wait right here," I said.

I went back into the bedroom to the closet I had looked in earlier before my alleged nap. When I stepped back into the front room, Wendi broke out laughing.

"What?" I said with mock indignation. "You don't like it?"

I had found a big Panama hat in the closet, complete with a purple hatband, and I was modeling it for her. "I see other guys wearing hats."

"If we're going to be seen in public, the hat stays here," she said emphatically.

"Fine," I said, tossing the hat onto the desk. "But I'm still buying supper."

"Fine," Wendi answered.

I turned out the overhead light as we left.

:::::

THE LUNCHEONETTE WAS BUSY. Alice was there. I realized this was probably her life. For the lucky few, work is what you do, not who you are. But the vast majority of people are defined by their jobs. In other words, work is not only what we *do*, but work is *who* we are.

I wondered if that was why I was struggling to remember who I was. I knew I was a private investigator, but beyond that, I was at a loss. Was that all I was? Did I play the piano, paint pictures, cook like a chef, write poetry, make furniture by hand, or all of the above? Maybe all of the above, but badly? *That could be!*

And where did Wendi fit into that picture? And what about other people in my life? *Were* there other people in my life? What about family? I must have had one. *Had or have?*

Suddenly, I felt weak. I had a thought that would have stopped me in my tracks if I wasn't already sitting at a small table for two in the little eatery. What if Wendi was the "other woman," and I had a wife somewhere? What if I had a wife and a kid—or kids?—and I had simply forgotten them? Would Wendi tell me the truth about that? Is that why she said she didn't want to take advantage of me? Why did she say my amnesia was like getting a do-over?

No, not *like* getting a do-over. She said I could *have* a do-over.

What if Wendi was my *wife,* and I had left her for someone else? Could that be what she meant by a do-over? We could get back together, and I could just walk away from some other woman. How do you walk away from someone you can't remember?

"Jimmy? Are you okay? You look a little green."

I didn't know if Wendi was my wife, the "other woman" who had busted up my marriage, a girlfriend, or just a *very* friendly secretary.

I leaned across the small table toward her. She looked at me for a second, then realized I was serious and leaned closer to me. I was grateful because I didn't want to broadcast our conversation for the whole supper crowd to hear.

In a hushed voice, I asked, "I need you to tell me something straight up – no dancing around the issue. Deal?" I felt a little sweaty, and I wasn't sure I wanted to hear the answer, but I had to know for the sake of little Jimmy Junior.

Wendi sat up straighter but kept her voice low. "I can't just agree to answer whatever you ask. It depends on the question. You know that."

"No. No, I don't know that. You keep dancing around the issue of my identity, but I need to know something, so I need you to be honest with me. Okay? Please?"

She took my hands in hers and looked into my eyes, searching for something in them that might tell her whether she should answer or not. She must have seen the seriousness in my eyes because she said, "Okay, Jimmy. I will answer your question."

She continued to hold my hands across the little table. I was having trouble getting the words out. I didn't want to ask the question. What if I was a total jerk? What if I was a lowlife sleazeball? What if I was a womanizer, chasing anything on two legs in a skirt? I didn't *feel* like I was. I didn't have carnal urges every time a woman walked past. Except for Wendi.

I sat there with her hands in mine.

"Well, are you going to ask me?" she said.

"Yes. But you have to be honest."

"Jimmy! I already said I would."

"Okay. Here's what I want to know—"

"Do you guys need menus? Or do you just want to get the special?" It was Alice. She had impeccable timing.

"Can you bring us a couple of waters, Alice?" Wendi asked. Alice nodded, and Wendi added, "And if you could give us a few minutes before asking for our order? I'll give you a sign when we're ready."

"That's fine. I have a lot of other people to take care of."

"Go. Take care of them. We're not in a hurry."

Wendi had kept ahold of my hands the whole time she was talking to Alice Mortel.

"Well? Are you going to ask me or not, Jimmy?"

I took a deep breath, wishing Alice had already brought us some water.

"Am I a sleazeball, Wendi?" I blurted out.

"W-what? What are you asking, Jimmy? That's not your real question, is it?"

"Yeah. I guess it kinda is. You said my amnesia could give me a do-over. A chance to change things. What things, Wendi? Tell me the truth: do I have a wife and a family I can't remember? Are you 'the other woman?' Or are you and I married, and I left *you* for someone else? Which I can't believe I would ever do, but maybe I was really stupid, and now the cracked skull fixed me. Is there a Jimmy Junior? Is that what your talk about a do-over is all about?"

Wendi looked at me for a long minute, still holding my hands across the table, and I noticed her lip starting to tremble. *'She's going to cry,'* I thought. I had nailed it. I was a sleazeball, a jerk, and a womanizer. But which one?

Suddenly, Wendi burst into loud laughter. I yanked my hands back across the table. She was laughing so hard she couldn't talk, and tears were leaking from the edges of her eyes. I pulled my arms in and crossed them over my chest, and I waited for her to get it out of her system.

She finally composed herself again, dabbing at the corners of her eyes with a paper napkin from the little dispenser on the table.

"Oh, my. I needed that. Thank you, Jimmy. I haven't laughed like that in ages." She paused and wiped her eyes some more, then added, "Not since you walked out on little Jimmy Junior and I!" which threw her into another fit of laughter.

That was about all I could take. I stood up, and she grabbed my hand. "Sit down. Please, Jimmy? If you sit down and let me, I'll explain some things while we have a nice meal. Okay? I know I shouldn't have laughed, but you looked so serious, and I couldn't help it. Especially the part about Jimmy Junior." She covered her mouth with her hand to hold back the laughter.

I sat back down, glancing around as I did. People were looking at us, some with smiles, some looking very confused.

"Just a little impromptu dinner theater, folks. Come back tomorrow night for another show. We'll be here all week," I said in my smarmiest lounge lizard voice.

Wendi had raised a hand and caught Alice's attention. The petite brunette was alongside our table in no time. She set our water glasses on the tiny table along with two sets of silverware.

"Do you know what you want?" she asked.

"Just give us the special, Alice," Wendi replied. "Jimmy's paying, so money's no object."

"Two specials coming up," the waitress and proprietor responded, spinning as gracefully as a dancer and hurrying back toward the kitchen window.

"Any idea what the special is?" I asked when we were alone again.

"None whatsoever. But have you had anything bad since you've been coming in here?"

I had to admit I hadn't. Plus, I had seven whole dollars burning a hole in my wallet, and I knew that we could eat well and for a long time on that amount of cash.

I was still smarting a little from her outrageous laughter at my serious questions. She had no idea how frustrating and disconcerting it was to try to tell someone your name and grasp at nothing but air, to know nothing about your past.

"Let's get back to our previous conversation," I grumbled.

"Where do you want me to start? With Jimmy Junior? Relax. There is no Jimmy Junior." She let that hang in the air between us for about ten seconds. "You have a little girl instead," she said with a giggle.

I started to stand, but she grabbed my hand and pulled hard on it, holding me in place.

"I'm sorry, Jimmy. I'll stop. Honest."

I pulled the chair back under my lower half, hoping it would look like I had just adjusted the chair slightly.

"The truth is … there's no jilted wife, abandoned family, no other woman, and … when you kissed me today, well … that was the first time you ever kissed me. I mean, *really* kissed me."

The first …?

Chapter 10

"WHAT? YOU SAID THAT we were seeing each other. Am I a priest or a monk or something? Do I have a physical problem that makes me unable …"

Wendi turned a bright shade of pink. "No! Nothing like that. We've just been going slow. They used to call it courting, Jimmy. I know younger people always seem to be in such a rush to get married, but if you look at us, you might notice that we're not teenagers. Besides, there's the other … thing."

The other thing? What the—? Is there something else wrong with me besides having no memory? I tried to remain calm and cool on the outside, but like a duck – who looks so calm and serene on top of the water – underneath the surface, his feet are going a mile a minute.

I took a drink of my water. I set it back on the table and, without taking my eyes off the glass, asked, "Um … what other thing?"

She leaned across the table, but since I was staring at my water glass, I didn't notice immediately.

"Pssst," she hissed at me to get my attention. I looked up and saw she had leaned almost halfway across the table. It was my turn to be late to the party. I leaned over so our heads were almost touching. I leaned to her right so her mouth was near my right ear.

"You're really going to make me say it?" she whispered.

"I really *do* have amnesia," I whispered back.

We held our positions for a short five count, and then she whispered, "I used to be married, Jimmy."

"You what?" I replied in a voice considerably louder than hers and many decibels louder than I intended, but her declaration was a big surprise to me.

She shushed me and crooked her finger to get me to lean in again. "I got married to Charles Jeffers just two days before he left for the Philippine Islands in 1944. He died on the Japanese island of Okinawa on the second of April in 1945. Easter was on April first that year."

I leaned back and sat up straight. She did the same. I looked at her for a long while. Finally, I said, "I'm so sorry."

Her eyes dropped to the table, breaking eye contact with me. I didn't know what else to say, so I kept my mouth shut.

Her voice was soft as she continued, but at least we weren't leaning over the table anymore.

"That's why I became a nurse. They told me ..."

"*Who* told you ...?"

"The War Department. They told me that Charley was gravely wounded on the first day when they began the assault on the island. I talked with a couple of guys from Charley's company after they came home. They said the sky was filled with rockets and mortar shells streaking overhead, and assault crafts were riding the waves over a reef that surrounded the area where they were landing. They said there was no response from the Japanese. They only encountered two machine guns as they moved inland, and they took care of them quickly with grenades."

I took another drink of my water and waited for more of the story. I was not disappointed.

"Charley's buddies said that they were moving inland, and it was getting dark when word came down from the scouts in the lead that they would have to move through a minefield before they could dig in for the night. Everyone had to be careful to stay on the path that had already been cleared, but Charley hooked his foot on a root or something and fell off the path. He landed on a mine. They sent for a medic and stretcher, and he was transported out to the hospital ship offshore, but his injuries were too severe. He died a little after midnight on April 2, 1945. He never regained consciousness."

I was still mute. I didn't know what to say for one thing, and for the other, I had no idea that she had gone through such a tragedy.

"Can't you see, Jimmy? To some of the people, I should still be in mourning, even though it's been over two years. I wasn't just married; I was married to a local war hero. For me to have feelings for another man doesn't sit well with some folks in town."

I took another drink of water. Wendi must have thought I was incredibly thirsty when, in fact, I just didn't know what to say.

"That's kind of a big load to lay on you all at once, isn't it?" she asked.

I cleared my throat before speaking. "I don't mean to be insensitive, but it still doesn't help me know who I really am, though. Can you understand?"

"You're someone I care deeply about, Jimmy. That's why I'm giving you the opportunity to step out of the picture if you need to. You may never fully recover all your memories, you know. What if the new you without your old memories can't take being compared to the local town hero? The man I married who went to war and died defending not just our country but our town and everyone in it."

She leaned back over the table and lowered her voice to nearly a whisper. "It's not easy being the widow of a hero. Sometimes it feels more like he was a martyr than an unfortunate casualty."

I leaned across the table, and this time, I took her hands in mine. I lowered my voice and said, "I have known since the first time I saw you that you were something special to me. The more I am around you, the more certain I am of that. The feelings I have for you don't just involve my brain; they are buried in my heart, insulated from skull fractures and concussions, protected from people who narrow-mindedly think I shouldn't be kissing a woman whose husband died years ago. How many of them would be willing to take up a life of total celibacy and close themselves off from any intimacy because their husband or wife died?"

A thought struck me, and I firmly held her hands as I asked it. "When did you and I become 'you and I?' Before or after you received word of Charley's untimely death?"

She lowered her eyes to the table and, after a quiet moment, tried to pull her hands back. After a second, I let them go.

I turned in my seat and faced the front window of the café. I wished I smoked. Or drank. I needed something to do with my hands and something to numb the burn that had just ignited in my core. *Is she saying she and I started seeing each other before Charley died?*

As I sat in silence, staring out the window, Alice came out of the kitchen with our food. Tonight's special was tube steaks: hot dogs served with French-fried potatoes and coleslaw. Alice placed our plates on the table and pulled a bottle of catsup and a bottle of mustard from the pockets in the front of her apron.

"Can I get you anything else right now?" she asked.

"No, Alice. This is great. I haven't had a good hot dog in years," I said.

Alice looked at me, a little confused, and said, "Of course not. Not with rationing and all. We just started getting the good ones again recently. You know, the ones with the casings on. We could only get skinless franks during the war."

"Right, right. Yeah. That's what I meant," I said, reaching for the mustard. I ran a line of bright yellow mustard along my hotdogs and then waited. Wendi hadn't made a move or a sound since I asked about our past. And now Alice was standing next to the table, watching me.

"Is there something I can do for you, Alice?" I asked.

"No. I was just waiting for your reaction to the hot dogs. There's nothing like a hotdog in a natural casing. They snap so good when you bite into one ..."

She let her comment trail off, and I thought maybe she wanted to sit down and eat with us. Instead, I picked up one of my hotdogs and took a bite. Sure enough, the snap was delightful, the salty, juicy rush of flavor taking me slightly by surprise. I smiled involuntarily. Alice smiled, too.

"See? Nothing like a hotdog with a natural casing. The skinless wieners were fine during the war because of rationing, but these are the real deal. Am I right?"

I set my hotdog down on the plate as I chewed. After chewing and swallowing, I said, "Yes, ma'am. These are the real deal."

She was about to leave, but she leaned down and said, "Try some coleslaw on the next one. I call it a slaw dog. You get the sweet and salty flavors along with the soft bun and crunchy cabbage. It all goes together really well."

"Thanks," I said. "I'll try it."

Alice smiled broadly and moved back to the front to take care of someone at the cash register. I saw her give a thumbs-up to the cook. I felt like a food critic that they were trying to impress. Of course, I *had* come in for three meals in a row.

I looked at Wendi. She was staring down but looking at nothing. I reached across the table and squeezed her hand. She looked up, and our eyes met. I tried to make my eyes convey all the acceptance and grace I could channel to her.

"You should try your hotdogs, Wendi. They're really quite delicious. Besides, don't forget that I'm buying. You don't want them to get cold."

She gave me a half-hearted smile, not the genuine kind that warmed me from the inside out. After pouring a thin line of catsup and an equally thin line of mustard the length of her hotdog, she took a bite. I could hear the snap of the skin as she bit into it. Orange-colored juice ran down her chin, and she clamped a napkin to it before it could drip on her clothes.

"Oomph!" she declared. "Thass good!"

I chuckled and said, "That's all the matters right this minute. Anything else, we can deal with later. For now, let's just enjoy our meal."

She was still chewing, so she just nodded. I saw that her eyes were shiny, but no tears escaped.

: : : :

AFTER WE FINISHED OUR hotdogs, French-fried potatoes, and coleslaw *(Wendi liked the slaw dog. Me? Not so much.),* Alice talked us into some coconut cream pie for dessert and fresh coffee. Altogether, I burned through two bucks with the tip. 50¢ for the dinner special, 15¢ for the pie, and a dime for the coffee, all multiplied by two, along with a very generous 50¢ tip. It was no wonder Alice enjoyed seeing me come in the door: I had no clue how much to tip, so I always erred on the generous side.

We were still sitting, enjoying our coffee. The clock over the door had a blue neon tube inside it that gave it an ethereal glow, a sweep second hand, and large, easily readable numbers. In the middle, it read, "We Serve Maxwell House Coffee. Good to the last drop!" It was clearly visible from anywhere in the café. I still had an hour before I needed to meet Dale Higgins at the Ship's Galley down on the waterfront.

"How would you like to go for a little stroll with me, Wendi? It'll help settle our stomachs."

She nodded her agreement, but just as we reached the door, we heard a crack of thunder, and it began raining.

"I guess we can sit and drink some more coffee," I said.

By that point, there was only one other couple in the restaurant. We walked back to our little table, and Alice came and asked if we wanted coffee refills. We said yes, and a minute later, our cups were filled with steaming brown liquid.

When we were alone again, I said, "Tell me about how you and I became 'you and I.'"

"You're really going to make me do this?" Her eyebrows were raised as she waited to see if I was serious.

"I can't do it for you, Wendi. I have no memory. Someone big and ugly knocked it out of my head. And by the way, I can sometimes see the big, ugly guy's face, but I have no name to go with it."

Wendi picked up her coffee and took a sip before she began telling me a story I should have known.

"You know that I married Charley Jeffers just two days before he shipped out with his division for the Philippines and Japan—"

"—When did you get married? The month?" I interjected, making sure I got all the details.

"It was July 16. Charley had gotten ten days' leave and travel time, so it was actually about sixteen days off for him. Two days after we were married, he got on the train to return to Camp San Luis Obispo on the opposite side of the country in California. From there, his unit was supposed to sail to Hawaii to do some jungle training and mock beach landings before going on to the island of Yap. While they were in Hawaii, their orders were changed from Yap to Leyte in the Philippines. That information is all after the fact, of course. At the time, we didn't know where he was going. No one did. I didn't find out he was over there until his letters arrived."

I held up a hand to interrupt and ask a question. "Here's something that's been bothering me: why didn't I go? Why wasn't I drafted, or why didn't I enlist?"

Wendi looked down into her coffee cup for several long moments. Finally, she looked up and focused on me.

"You were too old, Jimmy. That's all. If things had gone differently over in the Pacific Theater, they might have come back and taken you, but probably not, since the war was over in Europe, and they had all those trained soldiers ready to take on Japan. They could have just reassigned them."

"I suppose you're right. And while I don't like hearing that I'm too old, I guess it is what it is. There's nothing I can do about that. We don't choose when we're born."

"I thought you knew."

"I don't know my birthday or where I was born or anything. I don't know how old I am, for Pete's sake. My life – *this* life – started the day I woke up in the Nassau General Hospital in Fernandina Beach, Florida. Tell me again when Charley died."

"April 2, 1945. The American troops landed on Okinawa on April 1 – Easter Sunday morning. He died just after midnight, in the early minutes of April 2. He never regained consciousness after falling on that landmine, so there were no last-minute deathbed messages or requests. He just ... died. They said he was already dead when he got to the hospital ship; his brain just didn't know it yet."

I could appreciate that last statement. I knew it was hard for her to recall and relive this painful period of her life, but I didn't have any of it in my head.

I glanced at the neon Maxwell House clock: 7:20. I looked outside and saw that it was no longer raining, just drizzling. That was good. It would probably stop raining completely soon, well before my meeting down on the docks. Besides, I was only five minutes away. I could wait until the last minute if I needed to.

I needed more information about us. "When did you come to work for me?"

"Right after Charley left for California, Hawaii, and the South Pacific. I needed to do something. I couldn't just sit around and worry about my ... husband."

She stumbled over calling Charley her husband.

"You ran an ad in the newspaper, Jimmy. When I came in for an interview, you picked up the telephone and called the newspaper and told them to cancel the ad because you had found your secretary. You did it before we even talked. You did it right in front of me. I didn't know what to think."

"But I was right, wasn't I?"

She smiled a sad smile. "Yes, you were right. We just clicked, I guess. Sometimes, you'd say we were a match made in heaven. It was like you didn't remember that I was married. And sometimes … I forgot, too."

I suddenly felt like a heel. *I was a homewrecker!* That sounded more like Philip Marlowe than Jimmy … *Crap! I still can't remember my name!*

I tried to stay calm and not let Wendi know how frustrated I was inside. I took a sip of coffee that was only lukewarm now. I pushed it away on the table; I'd had enough anyway.

"When did you and I move on from boss and secretary to … something more?" I asked. Wendi was avoiding my eyes, staring into her coffee cup.

"April 6. A Friday. Four days after Charley died, but I didn't know that yet. We were celebrating a big case, and I stayed with you all weekend."

"Did we …?"

She shook her head. "No. You said you couldn't do that. And I couldn't either. But even though we didn't … you know … my heart no longer belonged to my husband."

I felt like a rat. *And I should!* But I had to know more, even if it hurt her – and us. "How soon after Charley … *it* happened did you get the news?"

"It took a long time for them to get telegrams out to inform spouses and families. It was Monday, May 9, 1945, at 9:45 in the morning. It was a week after he died."

"So, Charley was already dead when we spent the weekend together …" I said lamely.

"It didn't matter," Wendi continued. "I didn't know he was gone, so I shouldn't have stayed with you. In my mind, I was still a married woman. Not in my heart, but I was in my mind. And until that Monday morning when I heard the news, I was still Mrs. Charles Jeffers."

I looked at the clock again. Twenty minutes left before I had to meet Higgins.

"And now, you're offering me a do-over," I answered, "a mulligan in the terminology of a silly game with a little white ball played by rich business executives with too much time on their hands. You're giving me a pardon because I can't remember the details of that weekend. Or what happened between us in the two-plus years since. Let me tell you this: from the moment I saw you – even having no memory of previous engagements or attachments – my heart recognized you and drew me to you. My mind and memories aren't required for that fragment of truth. My feelings go beyond thinking and reasoning."

Teardrops began to slowly dot the table between us. Wendi grabbed a napkin and wiped at her eyes and her nose.

I kept going. I had to. I posed a question to the woman who was willing to let me leave, even though I never asked for a reprieve.

"The question is not whether I want a do-over or a second chance; the question, ironically, is, do you? I'm sure my reputation has not been damaged by our relationship, but I can't say the same for you. Being with you has probably *boosted* my reputation."

She took my hand in hers and held it, squeezing it repeatedly, like she was trying to send me a message. Finally, either out of desperation or a lack of understanding, I squeezed back, and her smile lit up the room.

Alice came over to our table, and I could have sworn she said, "Visiting hours are nearly over."

I must have misheard. But it was approaching 8 p.m., and I had an appointment, so I stood. Wendi rose, threw her arms around me, and held me tight.

Trying to sound like a tough, hardboiled detective, I said, "Don't worry about me, baby. I'll be back. I promise I'll always come back to you."

Chapter 11

The earlier rain shower enticed the fog to roll in, and it arrived thick and clingy, shrouding the docks and making everything blend into indistinct gray shapes. The nearer I came to the waterfront, the worse the fog got. Hoping to be seen by my client, I stood under a streetlight that would ordinarily be blindingly bright, but the fog diffused it to a murky glow.

Boats and ships creaked and bumped against the docks, creating a percussive background soundtrack to the sound of people talking and laughing, their voices escaping from the Ship's Galley, a dockside restaurant. Every so often, someone swung the door open to go in or out, causing the sound to swell and recede with the action of the door, like waves gently lapping on a beach.

I decided to take a look at the nautical-themed bar and restaurant for myself. The door opened on the bar side of the establishment, revealing people inside standing hip to hip, shoulder to shoulder, talking loudly but laughing even louder. The place was filled with a blue haze from the smoke of untold cigarettes, and there was a sour smell of whiskey and bitter beers that eventually ended up on the floor, some spilled and some after having been consumed.

Whoever's idea it was to put a bar and restaurant down on the docks was a genius. How could it possibly fail? You had the crews from the workboats and the passengers off the private yachts and commercial cruise ships, plus you had the locals who liked to hop from tavern to tavern and back again. By bar hopping, they never wore out their welcome in any one place. Or, nearly never.

The Ship's Galley had a big guy positioned right inside the door. He was not exactly a doorman and not entirely security, either. Sometimes, he helped over-served people find their way out of the bar. For the most part, he just made sure people didn't get out of control or start any fights. Crews from shrimpers and other working-class boats were frequent customers at the Galley, and it was normal for alcohol to cause tempers to flare. When that occurred, the big guy would step in and bounce the offending person out the door. No one got too fuzzed up over it because there were plenty of other bars or saloons willing to take their money.

The doorman didn't overtly acknowledge my presence, but I saw his eyes shift slightly in my direction. He probably saw that I was alone, not very big, and not dressed like I worked on a shrimp boat. He probably labeled me as easy to manage if whiskey or beer made me think I was bigger and stronger than I actually am. *And he'd be right!*

The bar's gatekeeper had probably also compared my face with his mental list of previous troublemakers. He made no effort to detain me, so I decided I could check off "not prone to causing disturbances in the local pubs and taverns" from my list of amnesia questions. *Good information to know, but not very surprising.*

I took a couple of steps inside, looked around, and gave the big guy a slight nod as I exited through the same door I had just entered. Outside in the fog again, I looked up and down the docks stretched out before me. The fog made it impossible to see twenty feet down the wooden planks, let alone to the end of the docks, and the dinghies, boats, and ships moored there were mostly hidden, silent dark hulks taking advantage of the shroud of mist and the moonless night to remain concealed.

"Marlowe." A man's voice called out my name. *Or the name I was answering to, at least.*

I turned my head in the direction I thought it came from. I was rewarded by the sight of a man in a dark overcoat walking in my direction from the Ship's Galley. It looked like he simply appeared out of nowhere, a gray figure walking out of a wall of gray fog and night.

"Is there something I can do for you, sir?" I asked.

"I'm Higgins," he replied as though that was enough of an introduction. In this particular case, it was.

"Mr. Higgins," I answered and reached out my hand to shake his. "I'm a few minutes early, but so are you."

"Yes. I was raised by a man who said if you weren't fifteen minutes early, you were late. I've been strolling along the dock as I waited, looking at some of the yachts tied up here. I don't know how much they cost, but I know I can't afford to rent one for a day or even an afternoon, to say nothing of entertaining thoughts of purchasing one. But like a beautiful woman, they are nice to look at, even if you can never possess one. Am I right? Hand-carved woodwork on many of them, even the service railings on the decks. The below-deck staterooms and kitchens are all outfitted with the amenities of a fine New York hotel."

"I don't believe I've ever been to a fine New York hotel," I replied, "on the water or off."

"Oh, you'd know if you'd been to a good one, Mr. Marlowe. And you'd never forget a bad one."

"I take it you don't have a boat, Mr. Higgins?"

"Nothing on the order of these vessels, I'm afraid. No, mine is just barely bigger than a fishing boat. It's tied up on the bay out in the fog here. I can't afford a slip here on the dock, so I just take a dinghy out to the boat when I'm going to use it and bring the boat over to the dock for my passengers to board. It's convenient, and the price is right." I thought I saw him wink at the last statement.

It was my turn in our game of twenty questions. "Let me ask you something, Higgins. Why do people pack into a place like the Ship's Galley? I've never seen the attraction."

"Don't ask me. I'm not a psychologist. Let's take a walk on the docks, Mr. Marlowe. We can talk as we walk."

"That's fine," I answered. "But please call me Jimmy."

"Okay, Jimmy," he responded as we began the odd, stiff-legged saunter that people often do when walking slowly on docks. In my mind's eye, I imagined we looked penguin-like, tilting from side to side as we went.

"Your message sounded urgent," I said as we passed the yachts trimmed with teakwood and probably dozens of coats of enamel paint and varnish and endless coats of wax.

"Yes, well … I'm afraid that was a bit premature. I, uh, I don't think I'm going to be needing your services after all. When I contacted you by telephone and talked with your answering service, my wife and I thought we might need help in locating her daughter – her stepdaughter, actually. The girl arrived on the *Orange Coast,* a regional passenger cruise ship that sails out of Tampa Bay, and then she disappeared for a few days without saying a word to my wife."

"How old is your — stepdaughter, did you say?"

"Yes, my wife Amelia's stepdaughter. The girl is Amelia's late husband's daughter by his first wife, but Amelia is the only mother she's ever known. Amelia was his housekeeper, but married him soon after his wife died – for the baby's sake, you know. Then I married Amelia several years after her husband died. I had been his groundskeeper and chauffeur. We tried to give the girl a stable home life – when she was home, that is. The girl's been away at boarding school for the last seven years—six now since her father died. She's nearly twenty-one now, and Amelia and I wanted to see her since it had been a couple of years since she was last home. I'm afraid she's a little confused right now, but I believe she'll settle in soon. If not, we'll take her to a psychiatrist for some help."

"Your wife's name is Amelia, just like the island we're on." *Very observant, Captain Obvious,* I said to myself.

"Yes," Higgins replied dryly. Thankfully, he left my unnecessary observation lying on the dock to die. We walked silently for a minute or two, rocking like penguins past more yachts and sailing vessels that neither of us could afford. I was thinking of another question to ask when Higgins broke the silence.

"I intend to pay you for your time, of course," he said.

"Did my service tell you my rates?" I asked, hoping they had because I didn't know what they were.

"Yes. She said $25 a day plus expenses and mileage. Obviously, there wouldn't be any expenses or mileage since we just met here at the docks and walked around, discussing the case, although there really isn't a case for you after all."

"Yes," I agreed. Higgins seemed to be more on top of things than I was, but he probably hadn't suffered a severe concussion in the past few days like I had.

"Is cash acceptable?" he asked.

"It always has been," I replied.

"I believe I have the exact amount here. Yes. Ten and ten and five makes twenty-five. I apologize again for bringing you out here when there is not an actual case for you to investigate, Mr. Mar—Jimmy." He handed me the three bills, and I slipped them into my pocket. *Easy money!*

"Don't worry about it, Higgins. Yours has been the simplest case I've worked all week." *And that's no lie!*

Our meanderings had brought us around full circle to the Ship's Galley again. The door continued to periodically open and close, the light, loud voices, and music swelling and subsiding whenever it did. Higgins and I shook hands again before I walked off the docks and headed for Centre Street.

Higgins turned in the other direction and walked down one of the long docks that ran perpendicular to the one we had been on.

I turned up the collar on my stereotypical private investigator trench coat I wore to ward off the chilly fog. The train depot was just across Front Street from where I was, its light beckoning like a friendly, familiar smile after a long day. There was a man wearing a dark pea coat standing under the depot's small porch overhang, holding a sailor's sea bag. I could see his bell-bottomed dungarees beneath his dark pea coat and the white Dixie Cup hat on his head – the kind some people call a dog dish or a bucket hat.

His hat and uniform made me think of a Frank Sinatra and Gene Kelly movie in which Gene Kelly danced with the cartoon mouse from Tom and Jerry. The name *Anchors Aweigh* flitted through my brain, but I couldn't come up with any details, so I let it float away.

As I walked across the street, I decided to greet the sailor. Something about him looked familiar. '*That's a hoot!*' I thought. '*A guy with no memory saying people look familiar!*'

I crossed the street and raised my hand in a little wave to the sailor. Just then, someone called my name.

"Mr. Marlowe! Wait, Mr. Marl—"

It was a girl's voice, and something cut her off in mid-sentence, like someone had clamped a hand over her mouth.

I turned around to look but could see nothing in the fog and darkness. I ran in the direction I thought the voice had come from but stumbled in the murky fog and nearly fell on my face. The streetlights were just barely visible, dirty yellowish orbs hanging above me like distant, nearly-exhausted suns.

I took a few more careful steps and tried to listen for the sounds of someone else moving around in the night. Nothing. I couldn't even hear the waves from the marina a hundred feet away. The Ship's Galley had disappeared from my sight, all except a single dull brownish-yellow light above the front door that normally shined a bright white on a typical, fogless night.

I couldn't hear or see anything out of order, so I turned around and walked back toward the train depot. I wanted to talk to that sailor I had seen. I took a longer look as I came closer; he still looked familiar. This might be promising.

"Did you catch them?" he asked me as I approached.

I strode toward the depot with its tall windows doing their best to illuminate the area on this foggy night.

"Excuse me?" I asked, unsure of the sailor's involvement.

"Did you catch whoever you were chasing?" the sailor asked again.

"You heard someone call my name, too?"

"Yeah. It was a girl, but I couldn't see her. But I heard her, and then you took off. And now you're here, so I guess you didn't catch her."

I was under the depot's portico with the sailor. He was just slightly taller than me, but his hat gave him the appearance of a couple of extra inches. I could see dark, tight curls sticking out from the bottom of his hat. He wore dark blue pants with wide legs, a matching wool jumper with a square, striped collar flap, his dark wool pea coat, black

Oxford shoes, and the white Dixie Cup cap that stood out like a shining lighthouse beacon.

I stretched out my hand to shake his. He looked at my hand for a heartbeat before taking it, almost like he was checking it for a weapon before taking it. His grip was firm and strong, but he didn't try to overpower me or show me who was stronger.

"Welcome home, sailor," I said as we shook hands.

"Thanks," he replied. "I hope I'm going to like it here."

We dropped our hands, and I looked at him. He still looked familiar, but my memory was too riddled with holes to place him or even know for sure that I knew him from somewhere.

"What do you mean?" I asked. "You don't live here? Are you just passing through on your way to another port?"

"No, I came through here on my way back from leave once. I got on the wrong train and ended up here. I had a couple of hours to knock around, so I did. I wandered all over, and I guess I kind of fell in love with the place. So, when my hitch was up, I decided to come back here."

"Where are you originally from?" I inquired, trying to get the whole story.

"I was born and raised in Brooklyn—that's in New York."

"Yes, I'm aware."

"I enlisted near the end of the war, just before Japan surrendered. What luck, huh? Anyway, I was assigned to a Liberty ship to bring our guys home from the Pacific. We were part of Operation Magic Carpet. That went from September of '45 to September of '46. After all our boys were brought home, I still had another year to go on my hitch, but when that was done, I didn't re-up. I decided to come back here. I kind of got used to winters without snow in the Pacific, so I thought I'd give Florida a try. You know, have a palm tree Christmas."

"Well, let me say it again: welcome home, sailor."

"Thanks, Mr. …?"

"Marlowe. Jimmy Marlowe, private investigator."

"Hey! That's just like that other guy. The one on the radio. Philip Marlowe. What's that thing he says at the beginning of each episode? 'Get this and get it straight. Crime is a sucker's road, and those who travel it wind up in the gutter, the prison, or the grave. There's no other end, but they never learn.'"

"Yeah, that's it," I said. "But I'm Jimmy Marlowe, not Philip. He's my second cousin."

"Aww, you're making fun of me now. He's just a character on the radio."

"I'm not making fun of you, honest. I used to imagine being a private detective and calling the girls 'baby,' 'doll face,' or 'sweetheart.' But honestly, most of the time, I don't have time for girls. I mean, *dames*." I chuckled at my tiny joke. Those terms just didn't flow off my tongue. "But it's nice to get swept away in the make-believe sometimes because it's a lot nicer than reality."

"Yeah," the sailor agreed. "Even though I wasn't in any of the fighting, I saw lots of guys who were, and some of them were shot up pretty bad." The sailor looked down at the ground for a minute, and I let him light a mental candle for the ones who didn't make it back.

"You didn't tell me *your* name, sailor."

"Gosh. I'm sorry," he said, his head rising and a big smile stretching from ear to ear. He stuck out his hand again, and we shook again, only he held onto my hand a little longer this time. There was something intimate and urgent in his grip.

"It's me, Jimmy. It's Pepé. I came to make sure you're not goldbrickin'."

I stared at him and gave my head a little shake. "What did you just say?"

"I'm Robert. Roberto Perez, actually, only everybody on the ship called me Pepé. Like the cartoon skunk, you know? Except I don't stink. My company commander called me Pepé because I was always chasing after girls whenever I got a pass. Just like Pepé Le Pew in the cartoons."

I couldn't help but smile. This young sailor was proud to be nicknamed after a skunk.

"So, tell me … Pepé, do you know anyone here? Do you even know where *here* is?"

"Sure. I mean, I know this is Fernandina Beach, Florida. There's the intercoastal river on the north end – the St. Marys River that connects with the Amelia River, which is what we have right out here with the docks. And Fort Clinch, which was used during the Civil War, is up on the north end of the island, too."

His enthusiasm was infectious.

"That's great if you're going to be a tour guide. But I mean, do you *know* anyone here?" I asked again. Pepé looked down at his shoes for a second.

"No, I don't. I mean, I met some people when I was here that one time, but I just spent a couple of hours wandering around, sightseeing, you know?"

"Do you have a place to stay? Any plans to get a place to stay?"

"Do they have a YMCA?" he asked. "I stayed in one in New York City once."

"No YMCA here that I've seen," I answered.

"I could just sack out on that park bench over there," he said, pointing at the bench where I had been nursing my broken head when I met police officer Bill Crane.

"Uh, no, you can't. They have laws against vagrancy here, and that includes sleeping on a concrete bench in downtown Fernandina Beach. Of course, if you get desperate, you could *try* sleeping there because, eventually, a nice police officer will come by and take you to jail, and then you'll have a place to sleep, with free meals, too. Just like in the Navy."

"You mean the brig? Oh, no, Jimmy. I don't wanna do that."

I thought about it for a minute. I had been in a similar situation when I woke up with my head covered in gauze. I still wasn't sure what was going on, but going with the flow was better than trying to fight upstream.

"Listen," I said. "If you don't find anything in a while tonight, you can bunk with me for a night or two. I have an apartment above the Palace Saloon, just up the street from here, right on Centre Street. It's apartment six. You can either go up the stairs inside the saloon, or you can come around back and take the outside stairs there. Apartment six.

Like an upside-down nine," I said, thinking back to my initial run-in with Sean and Angelo.

"Hey! That would be swell. Are you sure you don't mind? I wouldn't be any trouble. I don't even need to sleep in the bed. I can bunk in a chair or on the floor. And it would probably be just one night," Pepé replied enthusiastically.

"Sure, that's fine," I said, but I was backing away, my attention diverted by a noise.

I had heard someone moving around up the street a short distance away, and I started moving in that direction to intercept them. I wouldn't ordinarily do that, but I don't usually hear my name being called out by a fog bank under normal circumstances, either.

"Mr. Marlowe!" The voice hissed my name in a stage whisper, and I tried to zero in on where it was coming from. Then I saw a dark figure dart around a corner. And when I say a figure, I mean a figure, as in a dame … I mean *a girl*. Some girl was calling my name and trying to get me into an alley. I wanted to know why. It usually works the other way around – a guy trying to get a girl into an alley.

I rounded the corner and saw her. She wasn't moving away anymore. She was standing in a doorway, and the door behind her was closed.

"They're going to kill me," she said. Her voice was urgent, but the volume was barely above a whisper. I wondered if that was how she always spoke. Maybe she was used to whispering and still being heard if necessary.

"Who is trying to kill you?" I asked, slowly edging closer to the doorway where she stood. Just like with Daani, this girl wasn't having any of that. She took a step to the side, moving halfway out of the doorway. *I need to work on my edging skills!*

"Stop!" she hissed, "That's close enough. I don't know if I can trust you, so I can't risk you getting too close. How do I know you're not working with … them?" Her head swiveled quickly from right to left as she spoke like she was checking for possible escape routes if she needed one.

"Working with who?" I answered, stepping slightly to one side to cut off her egress in that direction. I figured I could let the wall stop her on one side, and I could grab her if she tried to get around me on the other side.

"Right now, I'm not working *with* anyone or *for* anyone. So, listen, Miss…" I wanted her to make a connection with me and stop thinking about running. If she was answering questions, she'd be less likely to pull the frightened rabbit hundred-yard dash.

"Higgins. Miss Dale Higgins. But you know that," she said in her breathy but forceful tone.

"You're Higgins? I thought the man I talked to a little while ago was Higgins. I'm sure he told me his name was Higgins. My answering service said the message was from Dale Higgins, and this guy I met by the Ship's Galley said he was Higgins."

"He's not Higgins! I'm Higgins. *Miss* Dale Higgins. I was named after my father. The man you were talking to on the docks is Val, Val Sackett. He's married to my stepmother, Amelia. And they're trying to murder me! The two of them! That's why I needed to see you tonight."

I tried getting a little closer again.

"Stop! I told you not to get any closer. You'll try to grab me, and then you'll turn me over to them, and they'll kill me. So, stay back, Mr. Marlowe!" Miss Higgins snapped at me from her doorway refuge in the dark, foggy alley, her voice a little louder and more forceful now.

I raised my hands in the classic 'don't shoot; I'm backing up' pose. Despite my pose, I didn't back up. I held my ground. Mainly because I didn't see any gun in her hand.

"Why would your mom—"

"—*Step*mom!"

"Okay. Why would your stepmom and this Val Sackett want to kill you?"

"I've been gone for seven years, and I came home because I am about to turn twenty-one. What happens when a person turns twenty-one, Mr. Marlowe?"

"Well, Miss Higgins, since we're not talking about blackjack, you must be referring to the tradition of being considered a fully mature adult at age twenty-one."

"Exactly, Mr. Marlowe! And do you have any idea what will happen to me on *my* twenty-first birthday?"

"Let me guess. Cake and balloons and pony rides?"

"Very funny, Mr. Marlowe. No, on my twenty-first birthday, I'm going to—watch out!"

Why is it that when someone yells 'watch out,' our first inclination is to look where they're looking, not duck to avoid whatever prompted the warning? I was turning my head to look at whatever Dale had seen when something hard slammed into my jaw, and the girl and the fog and the questions all disappeared like someone blew out the candles on a birthday cake.

Chapter 12

The intensive care room was quiet, just as intended. If things suddenly turn noisy in the ICU, it's not usually a celebration. Frantic activity and people hollering for help are not the hallmarks of a good night in the ICU. Pepé slipped out of the room containing his friend and walked to the small waiting area where Wendi and Hillary sat.

"Anything new to report?" Wendi asked as Pepé dropped into one of the Naugahyde-covered chairs.

He shook his head. He stretched his arms up over his head until his shoulders popped audibly, then brought his arms back down and tilted his head from right to left several times to loosen the muscles. He'd been sitting in Jimmy's room for only about ten minutes, but the stress made it seem like an hour.

"One thing," Pepé said to his companions. "I held his hand while I talked to him, and I'm pretty sure he gripped my hand after I told him it was me sitting with him. I said,

'It's me, Jimmy. It's Pepé. I came to make sure you weren't goldbrickin,' and I swear he gripped my hand for a second."

Wendi reached out and took his hand in hers. She was so grateful to have these two men in her life for support and to console her as they waited for Jimmy to wake up. She squeezed Pepé's hand, then reached out with her other and took Hillary's. He wrapped her hand in his, then placed his other hand on top of their embrace, symbolically adding another layer of shelter. She knew he was silently affirming his promise to support and protect his family, even though it was now just the two of them after the loss of his wife and grown son, Wendi's ex-husband.

"Did the nurse come by and tell you that visiting hours were almost over?" she asked Pepé.

He shook his head.

"She did when I was in there. I didn't know that visiting hours applied to family in the ICU, so I just didn't pay any attention. Luckily, nobody came back and tried to kick me out."

Hillary patted her hand with his. Pepé gripped her hand a little more firmly on the other side. Each man had silently noted her use of the word 'family' in describing their little ad hoc unit. Both men approved.

: : : :

JUST LIKE THE OTHER times, I didn't register any passage of time as I slept or was unconscious. I opened my eyes and realized I was looking up at Pepé, the sailor I had met just moments before. *Or was it hours?*

"You gonna make it, Mr. Marlowe?"

"What happened, Pepé?"

"Some guy came running out of the alley and clocked you on the fly. He didn't even stop to do it, either. He was running, and he just kept on going. It was some guy with a bowtie, and it sounded like he said something about Julie."

'Brody!' I thought to myself. *'He must be back from Chicago!'*

I rubbed my jaw and felt around my teeth with my tongue to see if any were missing or loose. Everything seemed complete and solid, but my chin would have a bruise tomorrow; of that, I was sure.

"Where did the dame go?" I asked. "I mean, the girl."

Pepé looked at me, confusion clouding his features. Or maybe that was the fog, still masking the night. He shrugged and stretched out a hand to help me get to my feet.

"I didn't see anyone but the big guy with the bowtie that punched you, and he didn't hang around for tea and crumpets, if you get my meaning."

I was on my feet, and I felt my jaw again just to confirm that I was okay. I was glad Brody hadn't hit me in the same part of my head where I had received the fracture.

I tried to remember what part of my head that was and reached my hand up and touched the right side of my head, toward the back. I was rewarded with a stab of pain and the odd, mushy feeling of a soft bump – not a firm one – a *soft* bump. Feeling it made my stomach do flip-flops. I fought to keep my supper down and was thankfully successful.

"No, I don't suppose he would stay, Pepé. I doubt that guy was very inclined to hang around and chew the fat. I've been kind of wondering when and where he would pop back up. I guess I got my answer." I felt my jaw again, glad my injuries weren't worse.

"Was he one of your cases?"

"On the contrary, he was merely a spin on the wheel of misfortune. In other words, it was just plain bad luck that threw us together. I walked into his apartment by accident and walked in on a dead body who happened to be his wife. Unfortunately for me, the two guys who had done the job were still there. The only reason I'm still walking around on the right side of the grass is because they thought I was *him*."

I let that sink in for a bit to see if Pepé would do the arithmetic. He did.

"He was in on it? He croaked his own wife?"

"And she was good-looking, too. A doll. It turned out that she and her husband were the bidders in a silent auction for the two hit men's services, only neither spouse knew about the other. It could have just as easily been him I stumbled over on the floor as her – that is, if she had had a little more butter and egg money. But he was the breadwinner, and he was allowed to make a counteroffer, which he did. And she quickly became a dead loser."

"So why is he sore with you? Did you call the cops or something?"

"No, not the cops. I figured everything out pretty fast and hightailed it out of there, which was, ironically, the advice of the two guys who had offed Brody's wife."

"Brody, huh? Is that his name?"

"Yeah, but it's not something you need to know, so there's no need to try and hang on to it."

I was trying to protect the young sailor, and something in my mind or gut told me this was somehow a reversal of our usual roles. But I couldn't figure that out, so I shoved it down in my sack of things to figure out later and continued my story.

"I ran across the street and down the block and jumped on the train – the same one you just got off tonight – and was headed to Baldwin, Florida, just outside Jacksonville, when who do you think I met on the train?"

"Brody? Or the two killers?"

"Brody. He said he recognized me from the apartments over the Palace Saloon where we lived, but I couldn't recall ever seeing him. By seeing him on the train, I became a part of his alibi. He couldn't have killed his wife because he was on a train to Chicago, and he talked with me on that train. I would have to tell that to the cops when they came around to ask me if I heard anything that night from my apartment down the hall. But then I let the cat out of the bag about his wife and the two killers. Brody decided he had no choice but to try and kill me."

"Whoa! But you're not dead, and neither is he. How does that work?"

"He told me about a girl he saw semi-regularly in Chicago, a girl named Julie. I came at it from the angle that Julie could be part of the whole thing. Like she wasn't really interested in him for himself; just for his money. I suggested she was probably in cahoots with the boss of the two killers. I put enough layers of reasonable doubt in his mind that he couldn't shoot me or throw me from the train. I jumped off at Baldwin—literally—and I guess he went on to Chicago. But if tonight was payback for messing up what he thought he had going with Julie, then I got off easy. The way I figure it, Julie didn't want to be his one-and-only if that meant really being his only one. Seeing him once or twice a month was probably enough for her. Maybe she has her own one-and-only in Chicago that she sees all the rest of the time when Brody's not in town. Or maybe she has a whole fleet of Brodys, and he was there when it was supposed to be some other guy's turn. It wouldn't be the first time that's happened. Anyway, I'll keep my eyes open for a few days in case he wants to mix it up with me some more. If he had really wanted to, he could have given me a third eye while I was out cold on the ground after he cold-cocked me."

I lifted a hand and made a gun with my finger and thumb and placed it against Pepé's forehead in case he wasn't sure what a third eye was. He went cross-eyed, trying to see my finger.

I liked Pepé. There was something familiar and comfortable about the sailor. But like everything else since I took early departure from the hospital, it was murky and fuzzy, just feelings and instincts with nothing concrete to back them up.

The fog outside had gotten thicker. It felt like being swaddled in a cold, wet blanket. Visibility was only about six feet, partly due to the darkness but mostly due to the fog.

"Mr. Perez?" I asked. "I'm going to walk up the street to my apartment. Do you remember where it is?"

"Aye, aye, sir."

Ingrained habit, I told myself.

My sailor friend continued, "Apartment six above the Palace Saloon. Take the stairs in the back. Make sure it's a six and not an upside-down nine." I was afraid he might salute.

"Right. I don't think you're going to find a cab in this weather tonight, and I don't know of a rooming house or anywhere else that could put you up at this late hour. I don't know about your finances, either, but we can worry about that tomorrow."

"Aye, aye … I mean, yes, Mr. Marlowe." He caught it himself that time.

As I started to walk up the street, I turned around to say one more thing before I faded away into the fog. "Oh, and Pepé? One more thing: If you see a white nurse's cap hanging from the doorknob at my apartment, don't knock. Just make yourself at home on the welcome mat in the hallway."

"Sir …?"

I gave a little wave of my hand and kept walking, chuckling to myself and knowing I was already out of sight in the fog.

It was nearly ten p.m. when I rounded the corner to the back alley stairs behind the Palace. And for the second time in one night, someone cold-cocked me. A few seconds later, I woke to a different set of scenery.

When I opened my eyes, instead of Pepé, I was looking into the eyes of a woman, but it wasn't Wendi. This woman had very plain features, her brown and gray hair pulled tightly into a bun on the back of her head. She was wearing a white blouse with a black sweater over it. The only term that fit to describe her was matriarchal.

"Oh, good, Mr. Marlowe. I'm glad to see you're awake," she said.

Just like my previous attempts at sleep or other people's efforts to knock me out, I was aware of a disconcerting lack of a sense of elapsed time. I had no idea how long I had been out or if I was just speeding from one scenario to another with scant seconds in between, like in a dream world.

"Yes, I am," I answered with a groan. "You have me at a disadvantage, madame. A – you know my name, and B – you probably know *where* we are."

"I'm sorry. I'm Amelia Higgins, and you're in our suite at the Keystone Hotel."

I suddenly realized I wasn't lying on the ground. That was a nice change.

"Higgins?" I spurted out. "Is everyone in Fernandina named Higgins this week?"

She smiled, and it actually softened her features a great deal. She still looked matriarchal but more grandmotherly than like a stern mother-superior figure.

"I'm sorry. It's technically Amelia Graves Higgins *Sackett*. I was married to Dale Higgins for fifteen years, and it's an ingrained habit. I'm Dale's stepmother. The poor girl's mother died giving birth to her, and I married her father when she was barely six months old. I was his housekeeper and took care of young Miss Dale, so my life didn't change drastically when I got married. Actually, my life barely changed at all. Mr. Higgins – who was also named Dale –

died when Dale was fifteen. Oh, dear. That sounds a tad confusing, I'm sure."

I struggled to raise myself up on one elbow, but lifting my head made me feel worse, so I left my head on the pillow where it was.

"What happened?" I asked. "To me, I mean. I was almost to the stairs leading to my apartment when … bam! Next thing I knew, I was here."

"Oh, dear. I'm so sorry. I'm sure she didn't mean to hurt you."

"She? She who?"

"Dale, I'm afraid, Mr. Marlowe."

"Dale did this? She hit me and knocked me out? With what?! A pier?!?"

"Oh, dear. She doesn't mean to do things, and when she gets upset, she doesn't know her own strength …"

"Apparently, I don't know my strength, either, or should I say I don't know what *happened* to my strength. It's hard to believe I let a little girl cold-cock me."

"Well, she is going to be twenty-one, and she works hard with the nuns—"

"—Wait. Nuns? I thought she was in boarding school."

"It's a private school run by nuns at a convent in Key West. It's called the Basilica School of Saint Mary Star of the Sea. Dale began attending when she was fourteen and stayed on after graduating. She helps with the younger students and works in the kitchen and gardens with the nuns."

"She must lift weights, too."

"I'm sorry, Mr. Marlowe. She's high-strung and often violent. But I'm sure when Dale realizes what she's done, she'll be sorry, too. She has a tendency to imagine all sorts of things, and when they come to a head, she just blows up."

I made a little explosion sound with my mouth to add sound effects to Amelia Sackett's story. She ignored it and continued.

"Now, don't you spend any time worrying about Dale; that girl's my problem, Mr. Marlowe. I don't want to worry you with any of our troubles. You just get a nice rest." Mrs. Sackett patted my shoulder perfunctorily before letting herself out of my room. Her actions were without any warmth or emotion, like an actor playing a role. I heard the key turn in the lock as she left.

Great. I'm locked in, I thought. *Oh, well, I might as well take a nap while I'm here.*

I closed my eyes and opened them a second later. Just like the other times, it seemed like a second later. However, the lighting in the room had changed again, so I knew that time had elapsed, but to me, it seemed like I had just closed my eyes for a second, like a slow blink.

I turned my head toward the window and discovered the cast of players had changed, too. Instead of Amelia Sackett's matronly countenance, I locked eyes with a much younger woman. She looked to be in her late teens or early twenties, with a slim frame, light brown hair, and greenish eyes. She had a healthy complexion with a spray of freckles across the bridge of her nose, and her face was devoid of any makeup. *But do twenty-one-year-old girls actually need makeup?* I didn't think so. She spoke before I could clear away enough cobwebs in my broken head to know what to say.

"Mr. Marlowe!" It was that same theatrical whisper that guaranteed she could be heard across a crowded room. However, there was no one in the room but the two of us.

"I need you to know that I did not put you here. I had nothing to do with you being bludgeoned. That was Val. I was hiding in the shadows under the stairs to your apartment to talk with you and saw him step out from behind a car. He swung something at you, and you went down. It looked like a man's stocking, and he hit you with it. You went down like a puppet with his strings cut."

"A sock, you say? Drop a roll of quarters in a sock, and you have a makeshift sap."

"Sap? Like from a tree?" she asked.

"No, a different kind of sap, like a blackjack. A leather club filled with lead shot or a metal rod. When used by someone who knows how to use it, it can knock a guy out with one swing. If used by someone who doesn't know what they're doing, you could easily have a dead body on your hands. Cops actually used to use them to even the odds when they were faced with a much larger perpetrator. The sap could be easily hidden in an officer's back pocket. Some people say it's called a blackjack because the 'dealer' always wins."

"Is that a playing cards reference? I don't know anything about cards. But I saw Val swing that thing at you, and you fell down. He slipped it back in his pocket – just like you said – and then put you in the car he'd been hiding behind. He got in and drove you here. I heard Amelia tell you that I did this to you. I want to assure you, I did not."

"Your stepmother. Yes, she said you get wound up and turn violent. But she said you'd feel sorry about doing it."

Dale Higgins crossed her arms over her chest and exhaled forcefully through her nostrils.

"I'm sorry you're here, Mr. Marlowe, but I'm not sorry I did it because I didn't do it. Val did. Mr. Marlowe, I'm afraid Val's going to kill me, and my stepmother might be in on it."

"Whoa," I replied. "Why would Val want to kill you? What did you do to him?"

"It has nothing to do with anything I did. It's about my inheritance from my father … the one I get when I turn twenty-one in a few weeks. I don't know what—"

She stopped abruptly. Her hand flew to her mouth, a single, slim finger going to her lips to warn me to be quiet. I listened and heard the sound of footsteps in the hallway and then the sound of a key turning slowly in the lock. The door opened, revealing Val Sackett in the dark wooden doorframe.

"Hello, Mr. Marlowe. Hello, Dale. I think it would be good to let our guest recuperate, don't you?"

"I'm not bothering him, am I, Mr. Marlowe?"

"Not at all," I said. "We were just beginning to get acquainted."

"Still, we don't want to tire him out, *Dale*," Sackett responded, emphasizing her name. "By the way, how did you get into this room?"

Dale fidgeted in place but answered his question. I think all that time with the nuns had hamstrung her ability to embellish the truth.

"I came in from the other door that goes into the rest of the suite. Amelia left the key on the table, so I used it. I needed to speak with Mr. Marlowe."

"I think we should let him rest some more. Why don't you come out this way, through *this* door this time?" Sackett intoned quietly. Although there was nothing sinister in his words, I had the feeling that there was a threat hidden within.

"She can stay, Sackett," I told him, putting myself into their battle of wills.

"I think it's for the best if she doesn't, Mr. Marlowe."

I started to throw back the sheet and blanket to confront Sackett and maybe pay him back for the sneak attack, but Dale stood up from the chair where she sat and stepped between us, stretching out one hand toward me to prevent me from getting out of bed.

"It's okay. I'll go with him, Mr. Marlowe. I'll talk to you later. I promise." She directed the last two words at Sackett, looking him square in the face like a challenge.

She slid quickly and quietly past Val, and I heard her steps fade down the hallway. Sackett didn't say anything more and was gone a moment later.

I lay back in bed, thinking about what Dale said about the threat to her life because of the inheritance she was about to get on her twenty-first birthday. I had no idea how much that inheritance was, but I had a sneaky feeling it was far more than Sackett was going to get.

I closed my eyes, and time shifted in my world again. It was still daylight, but the sun was no longer shining directly in the windows. Once again, I wasn't alone in the room, but it was Mrs. Sackett looking at me again, not Dale.

"I trust you're beginning to feel better, Mr. Marlowe?" It was both a question and a statement.

"Where's Dale?" I replied, ignoring her question. "She wanted to talk to me."

"I'm afraid she's … unavailable. She was very upset when she and Val left your bedside earlier, and he gave her a sedative. It's nothing unusual; we've done it for years to help manage her … condition."

I've always hated it when people pause and look for a word that is more acceptable than the unvarnished version. They always pull out something watered-down and bland.

"Is there something I can do for *you*, Mrs. Sackett?" I asked, wondering why she was here, hovering over me again.

"No, I just wanted to check up on you."

"My head is still not quite right, so if you don't mind, I'd like to rest my eyes for a few minutes," I replied.

"Fine. Very well …" She stood and backed out of the door. I heard it lock behind her again.

I wasn't kidding about my head not feeling right, but I also wanted to test a theory. I closed my eyes and let myself drift off to sleep. It seemed as though nothing was happening, though, so I opened my eyes.

The room was much darker than it had been just a second before. I didn't know how much time had elapsed because I couldn't see a clock, but it was no longer afternoon; we had moved into evening or even full-on night.

I swiveled around, swung my legs over the side of the bed, and let my feet find the floor. My eyes roamed around the room, and I discovered my clothes in a free-standing armoire, its doors ajar. I crossed the floor to it and was pulling my pants on just as I heard the doorknob turning. I continued dressing, aware of Amelia Sackett's eyes watching me as I did. *Get a good look, honey. I'm leaving.* She stood in the doorway, arms crossed, her plain face betraying her concern but saying nothing.

"Where's Dale?" I asked as I slipped on my shoes.

"She's still … asleep."

"You mean drugged. How much sedative did Val give her?"

"No more than necessary, I'm sure."

"Well, I'm not as positive as you are. I'd like to see her to check on her condition for myself."

"I'm afraid you can't. She's not in her room, and I don't know where she is."

"Let's ask Val."

"We can't." Her shoulders shifted as she spoke the words, and she twisted her fingers together. Her movements were like an odd juxtaposition of a little girl and an old woman. She obviously didn't want to complete the sentence.

"Why can't we ask him, Mrs. Sackett?" I was done dressing and was standing in front of her. I wasn't tall or menacing, but I was firm, and I was not going to be denied.

"Because he's not here, either!" she blurted out.

Chapter 13

"WHERE WOULD VAL TAKE her?" I quizzed Dale Higgins' stepmother.

"I don't know what you mean!"

"Let me explain it to you, then. Dale's not here, and Val's not here. Since Val drugged Dale, it only stands to reason that he took her somewhere since she couldn't wander off by herself. And since *you* are married to Val, it stands to reason that you might know where he has taken her and maybe even *why* he took her!" My volume was starting to rise. I was starting to get pretty angry and impatient. I was tired of being lied to, stonewalled, and misled.

"I don't know where they've gone. I'm sure they'll be back eventually." She said 'they' would be back, but by her distressed look, I wasn't entirely sure both people would return. I couldn't figure out why Val would try to get rid of Dale, except for the little information she had dropped about her inheritance being released on her twenty-first birthday.

"Mrs. Higgins," I said, "or Mrs. Sackett – whichever you choose to go by – I'm leaving. I appreciate everything you've done for me since my unfortunate, so-called 'accident,' but I have to leave here if I'm going to do anything about Dale's disappearance. I hope you haven't kept me in here too long already. Good day, madam."

As I strolled out of the Keystone Hotel onto Centre Street, I spied a guy hanging out across the street, leaning on a light pole. Something in my mind told me I knew him, but like most other people I'd encountered, I couldn't recall his name. *I can't recall my own name; why should I expect to remember anyone else's?*

The guy watched me expectantly. I nodded in his direction and turned toward downtown, pausing as I did and looking into the distance. I dropped my left hand to my side and quickly motioned for the guy to cross the street and meet me. I began walking down the street. He did the same on the opposite side of the street. At the corner, he hustled over to my side and quickly caught up with me.

Just as he was about to reach me, a frightening thought ran through my head: *What if I knew him because he was part of whoever gave me my concussion and amnesia? Or maybe he helped Sackett after he whacked me with a homemade blackjack. What if that's how I knew him?* I was about to find out, though, because he fell into step next to me.

"Long time no see, Jimmy."

"Longer than you know, Bud," I replied, forcing my eyes to look straight ahead.

The new guy was short, rail thin, and wiry. He probably only weighed a buck ten soaking wet, and his nose accounted for a sizable portion of that. He was wearing nubby brown slacks, a white shirt with an unbuttoned tan vest over it, and a tan pork pie hat on his head. A toothpick sprouted from his mouth, changing from side to side with great regularity. His shoes were utilitarian, good for working and walking. They were dust-covered, brown, high-top brogans badly in need of a shine. They could have been soldier shoes, but the man didn't have a military bearing or posture. Plus, he was probably slightly less than five feet tall and couldn't meet the height requirement.

WWII soldiers needed to be between five feet and six-and-a-half feet tall. Men less than sixty inches tall were classified as "nonacceptable." The military tried to say it was due to maintaining uniforms for the most common sizes. *Right.*

"Listen," I said after we had walked a few more paces. "I was in some kind of wild fracas, and I ended up in the hospital with a concussion – and a fractured skull. To top it all off, I've got a touch of amnesia. Okay, *more* than a touch. I'm having a hard time pulling up your name, if you know what I mean. It's nothing personal."

I stood and looked at him, and he stared back at me, the toothpick between his lips suddenly still. He was trying to read me to see if I was conning him or pulling some kind of gag.

I shrugged and held out my hands, palms up, in a "Whattaya gonna do?" motion.

The little guy was still for a few seconds more, then he stuck out his hand and said, "Pleased to meet cha, don't cha know. I'm Muff Benjamin. We go back a ways, you and me.

I help you out from time to time when you need information. I'm a finder."

I took his hand, and he smiled from under his giant nose as we shook hands. "Muff," I said, "I'm really glad to meet you, too. More than you know! I haven't met many friends since my accident."

We dropped into an easy stride down the sidewalk, headed for my place or somewhere in that neighborhood. I thought a quick stop-in at Thompson's Luncheonette might be a good choice. A little pie and coffee was always good, whether it was ten in the morning, three in the afternoon, or seven at night. Judging by the lack of direct sunlight, it was probably closest to the latter.

I surreptitiously felt my back pants pocket to make sure my wallet was still there. It was, so I relaxed some. After getting tagged in the alley and being undressed by someone else and tucked into bed at the Keystone Hotel, I knew there was no guarantee of finding it in its usual place. Perhaps things were starting to turn around for me.

When we got to the luncheonette, I asked Muff to hang on for a second, and I turned my back to him. I pulled out my wallet to have a look inside. Just because the wallet was where it belonged didn't mean my money was still there. But again, I was pleasantly surprised. I still had five bucks in my wallet and a hidden ten for emergencies. I felt something loose in my pocket: two tens and a five. *The money Sackett paid me the other night when I thought he was Higgins!* But that was business money, so I should probably leave it where it was until I could give it to Wendi. Meanwhile, I could spring for pie and coffee for Muff and me and still have four dollars to play with.

I opened the door to the luncheonette and held it for Muff. We went in and found a couple of empty spots at the counter. The stools had shiny chrome posts with red vinyl seats on top of the posts. The vinyl had a golden pattern mixed in, like a vein of gold ore in a chunk of quartz. The seats swiveled without squeaking. We sat down at the counter.

As usual, Alice was working. Her eyes darkened at the sight of Muff, but just for a second. She probably couldn't be too choosy about her clientele. She came over and stood in front of us on the other side of the counter.

"What are you in the mood for today, Jimmy?" she asked, keeping her eyes on me rather than my dining companion.

"Two coffees, Alice. One for me and one for my friend. I'd also love to hear what kinds of pie you have available to go along with those coffees."

She turned and looked at the case where the pies were stored. I knew she was reviewing what she had put in the case earlier and mentally tabulating what was still left.

"We have apple and peach fruit pies, coconut and banana cream pies, a slice of pecan left—" she pronounced it pee-can, the common pronunciation rather than the hoity-toity pih-kahn.

"—oh, and one slice of chocolate cream, too."

"What strikes your fancy, Muff?" I asked.

"As much as I love pecan pie, coconut, and banana cream pies, I'm going to snag that chocolate cream pie before it sprouts legs and hightails it outta here," the diminutive man with the oversized proboscis answered.

"And I'll have a slice of the coconut, Alice," I responded.

"Two coffees and two pies, coming right up," Alice said as she spun on her heel and went to get our orders.

While she was away, I leaned closer to Muff and said, "I need you to see what you can dig up on a Val Sackett and a man named Dale Higgins. Mr. Higgins has been dead for six years. He was married to his former housekeeper, Amelia Graves, who is now married to Sackett."

"So, the housekeeper married her old boss, and when he kicked off, she married this Sackett guy?"

"And Sackett was the groundskeeper for Mr. Higgins. Nothing like keeping it all in the family, or at least under one roof," I replied, finishing my description just as Alice came with our coffee and pie.

"Anything else I can get you two *gentlemen*?" she asked, putting a decidedly cold spin on the word *gentlemen*. I had a feeling she didn't care much for Muff, but I needed his services, so I ignored her attitude.

"No, darling," I replied. "This coconut cream pie will have to do until you're willing to run away with me and cook all day, every day, for me."

Alice snorted. I'm sure she had flippant offers like that on a regular basis, and she knew not to ascribe any weight to any of them. She gave another cool glance in Muff's direction and left us to eat our pie.

After a few more bites of pie mingled with sips of hot coffee, I leaned closer to Muff again and said, "In addition to uncovering what you can on Sackett, I also need you to dig up whatever you can on *Miss* Dale Higgins, age twenty-one, most recently from Key West."

"*Miss* Dale Higgins? You're saying the old man named his daughter after himself? And she's twenty-one and from Key West. Please tell me she doesn't *look* like her old man."

"She definitely does not. I forgot to add one thing about Miss Dale Higgins: for the last seven years, she's been living and working at the Basilica School of Saint Mary Star of the Sea – a school run by nuns."

Muff choked momentarily on his chocolate cream pie. I gave his back a few whacks to straighten him out.

"N-nuns?" he asked. "I don't know about that, Marlowe. I went to a parochial school, and the nuns were always on my case. They still make me nervous."

I licked and nibbled on a bit of coconut cream pie on my fork, grinning the whole time, enjoying Muff's discomfort.

"Better be careful, Muff. Investigating nuns could become a *habit*!" I said, laughing at my own stupid joke.

As I cleaned up the remaining pie on my plate, using my fork to squish together all the crumbs and bits of whipped cream, I knew playtime was over, and I had to get serious.

"Don't worry about the nuns, Muff. You're not going to Key West to the convent. Miss Higgins is here in Fernandina. Sackett gave her a sedative last night, and that's the last time I've been able to get a fix on her location. I need to know if he has a place here in Fernandina where he might hide her away, and I'd like to know if he's ever done something like this before."

"Does he have a boat? Rich people around here like to sail, and if this girl's been living away from her stepmother and her—what is he? A step-stepfather?—then I assume they're more well off than me."

"Yeah. You're on to something, Muff. He does have a boat, but he said it's barely bigger than a fishing boat. Maybe by fishing boat, he meant a shrimp boat or something on that order. That would be considerably larger than a rowboat or dinghy. But what would he be doing with her on the boat? I don't think there'd be any hanky-panky going on. She doesn't like him. At all. I picked up on that straight away when she said Sackett and her stepmother were going to kill her."

"She might not like him, but he might be using drugs to force himself on her, you know? But why would Mom and Pop want to kill her?"

"There's the big question, Muff. Right after she said they were out to kill her, she said something to me about her inheritance, but she never said how much she was expecting to get. It might be enough to murder for, though. I have figured out that she gets the dough in a few weeks when she officially turns twenty-one."

"It sounds to me like you've got everything figured out, Jimmy. We don't need to dig up a bunch of dirt on Sackett. I'll just go figure out which boat is his and see if he's on it and check to see if he's alone or with the sister, and by that, I mean a nun, not a sibling."

"Okay, Muff. You take care of that legwork, and I'll go hang out with Mrs. Higgins – I mean, Mrs. Sackett – in case Val contacts her. You can call me at the Keystone Hotel, in care of the Sacketts."

"Is this little excursion to be gratis, or do you have a little something for my time?" Muff questioned.

I reached into my pocket and felt the crumpled bills I had received from Sackett. I had hoped to give them to Wendi, but duty called. I pulled one bill partway out of my pocket and looked under the counter to see what my fingers had snagged.

"How's five bucks sound, Muff?"

"It sounds like you've got a bloodhound, Jimmy."

: : : :

AFTER I PAID THE bill at the luncheonette, Muff and I went in separate directions. I was on my way back to the Keystone Hotel to see Amelia Sackett, and Muff was going to nose around down at the marina to find out which boat belonged to Val. I grinned at the thought of Muff "nosing" around to ascertain if Sackett's boat was out to sea, at the dock, or being used for some other nefarious purpose.

However, after walking half a block toward the Keystone, I turned around. I decided to swing by my apartment/office, check the mail, and see if I had any messages. I wasn't sure if Wendi would leave me messages or if I needed to call the message service, and I had no clue what the number was, which made calling the service a little more problematic.

As I walked down the hall above the Palace Saloon to my apartment, I saw that the door to the infamous apartment number nine was slightly ajar. I figured I might as well take the bull by the horns and confront Kendall Brody and get things straightened out rather than have him blindside me again.

The door was only open about an inch, so I knocked and waited, but no one answered. I pushed the door open slowly and was greeted by the sight of Kendall Brody hanging from a rope tied around his neck. The rope was looped around the large light fixture in the middle of the room, and tied off to the radiator. A small dining table was shoved off to one side to make room below the light fixture. My first thought was to check for a pulse, but I could tell by the dark color of his face and the nearly-black tongue sticking partway out of his mouth that he was beyond any help or heroics from me or anybody else.

I decided it was best not to touch the body. I needed to call the police, but there was no hurry, so I decided to snoop around a little to confirm that the scene was as it appeared to be, or at least as it was supposed to appear: a suicide.

Brody had been involved with Sean and Angelo and that young thug, Doyle Abaddon, the person that the late Catherine Brody said was going to make something of himself. Kendall Brody had escaped Catherine's fate by paying them more to kill her than she paid them to kill him. To top it off, I had paid them an extra $500 of Kendall's money – first as a mis-signed check and then in cash that I had found in their apartment the night Catherine was killed. In total, if they got the check cashed, they made in the ballpark of fifteen hundred dollars to remove Catherine

Brody from the country club registry and from Kendall's marriage bed.

I didn't truly believe Kendall killed himself, and certainly not over the loss of his wife since he had paid handsomely to acquire that convenience. If he did it, maybe he did it over the loss of Julie, the girl he was seeing on the side in Chicago on his business trips. It sounded to me like she dropped him when he wanted to be exclusive, but I seriously doubted he would react with a hemp necktie. It was much more likely he would get rip-roaring drunk and spend a weekend in his apartment in his underwear, shacked up with a new girl to take his mind off Catherine and Julie.

I looked over the rope apparatus to see if it looked like something he could have done. One end was tied to Kendall, obviously, and then the rope went around the light fixture down rod and was tied off on a cast iron radiator. I wondered if my apartment had a radiator. It seemed like a funny thing to have in Northeast Florida, where there were no basements to house a boiler, to say nothing of the few hours a year when you needed heat. There was, however, a small addition on the backside of the Palace Saloon. That could house a boiler for the rare times the apartments needed heat. *Well, then, we won't worry about that.*

The rope came down from the light fixture and wrapped around Brody's neck. It wasn't a noose in the traditional sense, but it also wasn't simply wrapped around his neck. Just wrapping it around his neck would have made it too easy to spin out of it, either intentionally or unintentionally. That wasn't how you did it if you were serious.

I looked around for something to stand on. I wanted to examine the rope around Brody's neck. There was a tipped-over chair, but it was across the room. The chair made me stop and analyze the scene laid out before me.

It was possible Kendall had kicked the chair across the room when he suddenly realized he was actually about to die. Reaching out with his legs and feet to try and snare the chair and bring it close enough to stand on could have caused it to go skittering across the room, ending up on its side. It was too far away for him to have stepped off of it and ended up over here, straight down from the light. He'd have had to do a standing broad jump. The only thing I could come up with was that he had kicked it.

I hauled the chair over next to the body. Kendall Brody's feet were dangling about two feet off the floor. There was no way he could have stood on his tiptoes and clung to life. The chair's seat was about a foot and a half from the floor – eighteen inches, give or take an inch. Kendall hadn't used the chair to stand on. Someone had hoisted him up and tied the rope around his neck. Or he used the table. But why? Stepping off the chair would have left him with eighteen inches of air beneath his feet. Someone didn't measure twice and cut once.

Standing on the chair, I looked at the rope around the dead man's neck. I noticed a slight discoloration around the slipknot he had used. It had an odor, too, not totally unpleasant but totally unexpected on a piece of rope. It smelled like a hair product. There were numerous types on the market and sold in all the general stores: Dapper Dan, Wildroot Cream Oil, Vitalis, and Brylcreem. *But how did it get on the rope? When he slipped it over his head?* I reached out and touched Brody's hair. *Dry. He doesn't slick his hair up.*

Slick! Angelo! I had nicknamed him Slick when I first saw him and the quart of used motor oil he called hair. Maybe Angelo and Sean had been here 'helping' Brody with his last chore. I could envision them taunting Brody with a chair that was just out of reach of his feet. He would have been kicking like crazy to try and reach it. That could explain how it got across the room.

I looked more closely at Brody's neck, where the rope was against his skin. Something about it made my brain tickle. Something was missing. There was no rope burn. There was no sign of Brody struggling against the rope, trying to lift himself up or get his finger in between the rope and his neck. If you're fighting for your life and trying to get air into your lungs, you're not going to worry about whether you scrape your neck with your fingernails. You're going to try to get your fingers in and make some airspace. But I couldn't see any signs that Kendall had fought with the rope in his last battle with the Grim Reaper. There were no signs of a struggle at all. Except for the tipped-over chair across the room.

I climbed down and placed the chair back the way I had found it. There was an easy chair across the room next to a Philco floor-model radio. I went and sat on the front edge of the easy chair and looked at Kendall Brody's completely still corpse hanging from the light fixture. He was too high from the floor. There was the greasy stain on the rope and the smell of pomade or hair oil. There were no signs that he had tried to change his mind at the last minute when he could no longer breathe. That is, other than the tipped-over chair. And as I stared at the dead body, another thing hit me: Brody hadn't even wet himself.

It would take a good county examiner to prove me right, but I believed that Brody was killed by someone—either here or somewhere else—and then strung up to make it look like a suicide. If there were two attackers, one could have held his arms while the other choked Brody with a rope, possibly the same one they hung him with.

"Well, well. It looks like your stomach is better. Leastways, you're not pukin' at the sight of a dead man."

It was Officer William Crane of the Fernandina Beach Police Department, standing in the doorway looking at me sitting in Kendall Brody's apartment while the apartment owner's body hung from a light fixture in the middle of the room.

I casually crossed my legs, smiled, and gave him a tiny finger wave.

Chapter 14

"I'll bet this looks bad," I said to Officer Crane, not moving from my seat.

"That's a safe bet, young man. It doesn't exactly put you in the best light. Let me ask, did he do it hisself? Or did you do it?"

"Me? No, sir, I did not do it. But just between you, me, and Mr. Brody here, I don't think Mr. Brody did it, either."

Bill Crane came a few steps farther into the room and closed the door behind him. "No point in letting everyone who comes down the hall take a peek at him. We'll keep this just between the three of us for now."

He came over and stood next to the easy chair I was sitting on, and we both faced the body. Bill folded his arms over his chest, then just stood there quietly for a minute or two, his thoughts private.

"What do you suppose makes a man do this to himself?" Crane asked no one in particular. He wasn't looking at me, but I figured he wasn't talking to Brody, either.

"Well, sir, as I pointed out, I don't think he did it."

He waved one hand in the air to dispel my slight protest. "I heard what you said before, son. Even if he didn't tie the rope around his neck, though, ultimately, he *did* do this to himself. This is not the kind of thing a robber or a thief does, nor are these the actions of a second-story man. This is the kind of thing done by someone who's angry and wants to send a message to all the other people who might think they can ignore the men behind this evil act."

I had a strong feeling Bill Crane had a better-than-good idea who had been in this room a short time before I accidentally wandered in, but I opted to keep my opinions to myself. We sat and stood in respectful silence out of regard for the loss of another human being.

"Each man's death diminishes me," Crane said, quoting from John Donne's poem, *For Whom the Bell Tolls.*

I responded with the next line from Donne's immortal poem about death. "For I am involved in mankind."

Crane removed his tan service cap, still staring at Brody's unmoving form, still quoting Donne. "Send not to know for whom the bell tolls—"

I joined him in quoting the last line, "—It tolls for thee."

After another quiet pause, Officer Crane put his service cap back on his head and turned toward me. "You know I'm giving you some latitude because you and I are on the same side of the law, even though we go about it in different ways. But I'm going to ask you now to tell me what you know about this macabre scene we find ourselves a part of before I call it in."

I wondered if Crane sometimes put on a good ol' Southern boy act. Words like 'latitude' and 'macabre' and quoting John Donne didn't fit with it. I decided to cooperate.

I explained how I was on my way to my apartment to check my messages when I saw Brody's door partially open, knocked, and came in. The scene I discovered was virtually the same as he had walked in on. I pointed out the damning pieces of evidence I had noticed: the hair product stain on the rope, the victim's height above the floor, and the lack of signs of a struggle – specifically, no marks to indicate Kendall had struggled against the rope. His hands weren't tied, so there was nothing to stop him from reaching up and pulling himself up the rope, something anyone would do in that situation. The body's will to live is a difficult one to overcome. I told him I was of the opinion that Brody had been killed—either here or elsewhere—and strung up to make it look like a suicide.

He nodded several times as I gave him my theory, and he even stepped close to the body to look at the stain on the rope and at the condition of the dead man's neck.

"You don't think his neck snapped, killing him almost instantly?" Officer Crane asked.

"Honestly, sir, I don't have that much experience with dead bodies, but his neck looks fairly normal to me. I think you'll know for sure after the county examiner takes a look at him. The examiner or coroner should check the hyoid bone in Brody's throat. Most strangulations break the bone, but most hangings do not."

Crane gave me a sour look, then raised his eyebrows like he was thinking about what I just said. He was probably thinking about the reaction he would get from a county medical examiner if he told him to check a victim's hyoid bone. Trying to tell him how to do his job was one thing; using the term "hyoid bone" was another.

After a second, he said, "Shoot. We haven't buried Catherine yet, and now Kendall's dead. To the best of my knowledge, there's no family to contact, which means there's no point in an autopsy. We'll just clean them both up, dress 'em up nice, place them in a couple of pine boxes, and bury them. Their marriage may have been coming apart in real life, but we'll put them back together in death. Mr. and Mrs. Kendall Brody. Side by side for eternity."

"And that's it?" I asked.

"What more do you want? They're dead, and no one's going to mourn their loss. Shoot, you and I standing here quoting John Donne a few minutes ago is probably the most genuine mourning that's going to be done for them."

He moved around in front of me, his back to the body.

"Now, I'm going to need you to come over to the police station and fill out a statement. You're not a suspect or even a person of interest. You just happened to be the unlucky person who lives nearby and found him. You write out a statement to that effect, and then you can go on with the rest of your day and evening. Maybe see that pretty little nurse who's sweet on you."

Bill Crane went over and sat the chair back upright, the one I had found tipped over and used to stand on before replacing it exactly as I found it. I turned away, a little angry that nothing was going to happen but also relieved that nothing was going to happen *to me*. There was a bureau against the opposite wall with a small mirror on the top. I could see Crane looking at the body.

Suddenly, I heard a male voice say, "How is he today? Any movements or speech?"

I whirled around and said, "What did you say, Bill?"

"I said this has been quite the day. You should get a move on to the PD."

I figured I heard someone in another room or voices from downstairs or outside. I let it go.

Officer Bill Crane walked over to the telephone and called the station to let them know what he was dealing with and to send the hearse over from the funeral home to remove Brody's body.

I walked quietly out the door and headed for the stairs to go over to the police station.

: : : :

"How is he today? Any movements or speech?"

"Not anything intelligible, doctor," Wendi answered. She had slept on the chaise-style chair in the ICU room where Jimmy remained in an induced coma.

"That's not anything new," Pepé added, standing in the doorway.

"Excuse me?" the doctor replied, puzzled.

"Nothing intelligible. That's normal for Jimmy, 'par for the course' in medical terminology," Pepé said lightheartedly.

The doctor chuckled as he caught up to the conversation and the playful ribbing.

"He squeezed my hand last night," Pepé said.

"Mine, too," Wendi replied. "I was squeezing his and telling him to squeeze back, and all of a sudden, he did."

"I was just holding his hand and talking to him," Pepé clarified.

"Not to tear down anyone's hopes, but those could be just involuntary muscle contractions," the doctor answered. "But they could also be Jimmy reacting to your voice, your touch, or something happening in a dream, so don't stop talking to him. There's a lot we don't know about the unconscious mind. We're going to start weaning him off the sedative tonight to let him wake up slowly on his own. Then we'll assess him after he wakes up."

"What do you think the chances are that he'll be okay when he wakes up?" Wendi asked.

"I try not to get into talking about the odds. I'm not a bookie taking bets on a horserace."

Wendi's shoulders slumped a little at the doctor's words.

The doctor continued, "But there's no reason not to think he'll make a full recovery. It was a severe injury, but he was brought straight to the hospital, and we did everything right, including inducing his coma. Rest is still the best thing for his brain right now."

"What about amnesia or having full use of his faculties?" Wendi posed.

"It's too soon to tell. Again, I need to wait until he's awake, run him through some assessments, do another CT scan, and take new X-rays. Physically, his data all looks good – heart, blood pressure, and respiration are all looking fine."

"But you're monitoring his brain activity, too, doctor. Does that look normal?"

"What's normal for me or you may be completely abnormal for Jimmy or Mr. Perez. Everyone's EEG is unique. Groundbreaking research in 2020 revealed that neuroscientists can identify each of us by our unique brain signature. It's like a neural thumbprint. They discovered that you and I display our own distinct brain signature when we're processing information, similar to how our fingerprints distinguish us from everyone else on the planet."

Pepé looked at Wendi to see if she understood what the doctor had just said, and she gave a slight nod. Pepé shrugged. She could explain it to him if need be.

"I primarily wanted to let you know that we'll start weaning Mr. Favreaux off the sedation tonight. Then in the next twenty-four to forty-eight hours, we should have a much better picture of the future. But I am optimistic that things will be fine." The doctor turned to go but swiveled back to Jimmy's friends. "Did either of you have any questions while I'm here?"

They looked at each other briefly, then Wendi answered. "No, not right now. I appreciate you coming by and letting us know in person what the plan is and the timeframe so we know what's going on."

"In the meantime," the doctor said, "Mr. Favreaux is going to continue as he is, so don't be afraid to go home and shower and rest. We'll take good care of Jimmy." And with that, the doctor exited the room.

Pepé and Wendi stood in Jimmy's room, looking at him lying motionless in the bed, a tube down his throat to make sure his breathing was consistent, and an IV delivering drugs to keep him in a coma, while others kept his blood pressure normal, his heart beating smoothly, and prevented any seizures.

Wendi felt a little overwhelmed looking down at Jimmy.

Pepé said, "Coffee?"

"Who's going to sit with Jimmy?"

"Gwynn."

"Me," came the echo from the ICU sitting area outside Jimmy's room.

"Gwynn's here?" Wendi asked, turning and walking toward the seating area.

"I am," Gwynn replied, meeting Wendi partway, and the two women embraced briefly. They'd only met once before, after Carolyn Dawson's funeral, but death and injury had thrown them together, removing the need for small talk. They were automatically friends.

"I thought you might need a break," she said, "so I came with Pepé this morning. I've been where you are, so I know how important it is to be able to get a break every now and then. Trust me, I'll keep a close watch on him."

Pepé and Gwynn went into Jimmy's room, and Wendi went to sit down in one of the waiting area chairs. She was sitting there, staring into space and thinking, when Hillary came in.

"Who's in with our young friend?"

"Gwynn. And Pepé, too, right now. But I think Pepé and I will go find some coffee in the cafeteria. I haven't been awake very long, and sleeping on that fake sofa in Jimmy's room cannot legitimately be called sleeping."

"That's one of the few things that comes from being in the military during wartime: you learn to sleep anywhere at any time because you never know when the opportunity will arise again. If you and Pepé will have me, I'll accompany you to the cafeteria for a cup of tea."

Wendi reached out a hand to her former father-in-law, and he took her hand in his and gave it a slight squeeze.

Pepé emerged from Jimmy's room about the same time, and the trio walked to the elevators to find the cafeteria. On the way, they met a young man carrying flowers in a plastic vase for someone. The bouquet left an invisible trail of rose and lily scent in the air. Wendi took a deep breath, enjoying the sweet smells. Pepé punched the button for the elevator door, and they walked in and turned around. They could see the delivery person turn at the end of the hall, but none of them gave it any thought.

They spent about a half hour in the cafeteria savoring their coffee and tea along with large, fluffy cinnamon rolls. Wendi also ate an egg and cheese breakfast sandwich and a small cup of yogurt. She consumed nearly half of Hillary's cinnamon roll and was making motions toward Pepé's before he got her one of her own.

Revitalized by the ingestion of caffeine, sugar, protein and carbs, the weight of the world was no longer quite as heavy on Wendi's shoulders. The doctor believed Jimmy was going to be fine, and she knew in her heart of hearts that he would be. It was just a question of time.

On the elevator ride back up to the ICU floor, they could still smell the floral scent left by the flower arrangement. Jimmy had mentioned once that he enjoyed the smell of roses and the spicy tang of Asiatic lilies. He said his mother had kept both in her garden up in Winnipeg when he was young.

After a quick stop at the girls' room, Wendi walked into Jimmy's room to relieve Gwynn from duty. There on the corner table was the flower arrangement that the young man had been carrying. Wendi felt a slight tremor of alarm run through her.

"Where did the flowers come from?" she asked.

"A flower delivery person. He didn't say much. Just that he had some flowers for Mr. Favreaux and asked where to put them. I hope it's all right that I had them placed there," Gwynn replied.

"Yes, of course, it's all right. Was…was there a card with the flowers?" Wendi stumbled over the question nervously.

"You know, I didn't even get up and look. I just always expect to see flowers in a hospital room. You should look."

Wendi went over to the table, and sure enough, there was a small envelope tucked in among the greenery. She extracted it from the bouquet, her hand trembling ever-so-slightly.

The card was simple, with no girly frou-frou. Inside, in plain machine-printed type, it said, "Get better. There's more to come." It was signed, "Le Bonhomme Sept-Heures."

The 7 O'clock Man! The Man!

: : : :

I DIDN'T REMEMBER WALKING to the police station or how I got there; I just remember suddenly being there. Since the day I woke up in the hospital with my head bandaged, I've been having trouble remembering things. Especially going places. If I think about going somewhere, I quickly find myself there with no recollection of the trip, just being there. Unaware of the several blocks I must have walked, I was now walking up the sidewalk to the Fernandina Beach Police Department.

As I walked up to the police station, I saw a woman sitting outside. I wondered if she was waiting for a bus or a taxi. *Does Fernandina even have buses and taxis? They used to have a streetcar that ran up and down Centre Street, but that's been gone for a long time.*

Something about the woman seemed familiar, and I felt compelled to sit on the bench next to her.

"Hi, Jimmy. It's Gwynn."

I looked at the woman, but she wasn't looking at me. She was just staring straight ahead. It was weird, but I didn't reply. I wanted to see what was going to happen next.

She continued, "I just came to see how you're doing."

This time, she reached over and took my hand. I should have felt uneasy, but instead, the gesture seemed comforting and nice. Like I knew her from somewhere, and it was okay. Safe.

"Robert and I have been praying for you since this happened, and we know everything is going to be okay. Robert, Wendi, and Hillary went to get some coffee, and I told them I'd sit with you."

I began to get nervous, and my head ached behind my eyes. I started to pull my hand back, but she reached over with her other hand and began to gently knead the back of my hand.

"I'm going to tell you something, but you can't repeat it. It's been good for Robert to work with you and mentor you these last few years. He needed a 'project,' a reason to get up each morning. After his girls grew up and moved away and he retired from the Navy, he began to get listless. Working by himself helped, but working with you has really brought him back to life. So, I just wanted to tell you that I'm indebted to you for rescuing Robert. That's just between you and me, though. Okay?"

I smiled even though I wasn't sure exactly what she was talking about and replied, "Okay." I gave her hand a squeeze.

I don't know why, but she pulled her hand back like she'd been burned, and I became aware of the scent of roses and lilies. They reminded me of Mom.

: : : :

"JUST ABOUT THE TIME the flowers came, I was talking to Jimmy, and I was holding his hand, and all of a sudden, I thought he said, 'Okay,' and he squeezed my hand." Gwynn was telling Wendi about her short visit with Jimmy while she and the two men went to the cafeteria.

"Jimmy spoke? He's intubated. He can't speak."

"Well, not speech – a grunt or a moan maybe, but it was two syllables. Maybe I just wanted to hear him say 'okay,' so that was what I made myself hear. But he definitely squeezed my hand. I was so startled that I pulled my hand away."

"I'm sure he did, Gwynn. He squeezed mine, too, and Pepé said he squeezed his, too. I wonder what he's dreaming about in there."

While Wendi and Gwynn spoke in Jimmy's room, Pepé and Hillary were in the waiting area, looking at the card from the flower arrangement.

"At least he was nice enough to send flowers," Pepé said.

"Indeed. It seems only fair since it was one of his henchmen who put Jimmy in the ICU. But I don't like the implication of 'more to come.'"

"You and me both, brother, you and me both."

: : : :

I INHALED THE SWEET scent of roses and the spicy aroma of Asiatic lilies, wondering where the smell was coming from.

"You always did like my flowers, didn't you, Jimmy?"

The woman I had been sitting next to on the bench had transformed in the brief second I had looked away. I suddenly found myself sitting next to a completely different woman, and the sight of her made it feel like my chest was squeezing my heart, and my throat hurt like I had swallowed something too large.

"Mom?" I croaked, forcing the word past the lump in my throat.

"Yes, Jimmy." She placed her hand on top of mine, and unlike the other woman, she looked directly and deeply into my eyes, like she could see all the way into my soul. She saw me and knew me, even though I didn't know myself – *she knew me.*

"Mom, you're not supposed to be here. You're de—"

"—Shhh. Don't ask how, just enjoy it, Jimmy. Isn't it enough that we can be together for a little while? It's been such a long time since I've seen you. Let's just sit here together for a few minutes."

"But I don't understand, Mom …"

"Shh. You've always been my inquisitive boy, haven't you, Jimmy? You always wanted to know how everything worked. The world was always so full of wonder for you. Sometimes, though, we don't get the answers we want at the same time we want them. Sometimes we have to go on faith that things are the way they are for a reason, and we'll know that reason by and by."

I turned my head and saw Wendi in her nurse's uniform, walking up the street toward the police station, her blonde hair shining against her crisp white uniform. Mom nodded her head in Wendi's direction and said, "She's a good one, Jimmy. Don't let her get away."

I jumped to my feet and took a few steps in Wendi's direction. She smiled as she walked up the sidewalk.

"Wendi! I'm so glad to see you! I don't know how you knew that I'd be over here at the police station, but I'm glad you came. There's someone I want you to meet. I want you to meet my m—"

I wanted so badly to introduce Wendi to my mom, but when I turned around to look at Mom, she was gone. The bench where she had been sitting next to me was empty. And when I turned back to Wendi, she was gone, too.

Chapter 15

I SAT BACK DOWN on the bench in front of the police station and let the tears roll quietly down my cheeks and drop on the sidewalk below, looking like raindrops from a very small cloud passing overhead. I didn't sob or weep; I cried silently, mourning the loss of someone I probably couldn't tell you ten things about if you asked me. But I knew that she was gone and had been for some time. Just like I couldn't tell you my last name, I couldn't tell you her first or last name except for the one she had always been to me: Mom.

I had no memories to attach to her name, just deeply rooted feelings that I knew would flesh themselves out when my head healed and my memories came back. I knew that I would someday remember my real name and stop play-acting as Jimmy Marlowe. What I wasn't sure of was which things in my life were real and which things were a product of my amnesia and brain trauma. The doctor – the one who looked and sounded like Floyd the barber – had said it was more than just a bump on the head; it was a traumatic brain injury. He said it was a depressed skull fracture. Part of my skull had been broken and might be pressing into my brain.

As heart-rending as it had been to turn around and realize my mom was gone, it had been nearly as distressing to turn back and discover that Wendi had disappeared, too. Had I dreamt that she was coming to meet my mom? Was it because I wanted so badly for these two women in my life to meet, and part of me knew that it was never going to happen? Was I mourning the loss of my mother or grieving over something I wanted that could never be?

I wiped my face with my hands and then ran a sleeve over my eyes to further dry my face before going into the police station. I still had to give a statement about the dead man I had found – Kendall Brody. Bill Crane had called his report in already, so they should be expecting me. He said I could just give a statement. He said I wouldn't be interrogated as a suspect in Brody's death.

I trudged to the front door and pulled it open, walked through, and up to the dispatcher's window. I told him who I was. The man behind the window told me Crane had called it in, and I could just write my statement and be on my way.

He told me to go in a side door, and he met me inside. He led me to a small room with a table and a couple of chairs. It was an interview room, not an office, but there was just me—no one asking questions like they would in an interview. There was a pad of paper and a pen on the table. I wrote out my statement as clearly and succinctly as I could, keeping things in good chronological order, stating facts, and not bringing feelings into it.

I wrote that Officer Crane and I stood and looked at the body hanging from the light fixture for a few minutes but didn't add that we had quoted lines from a three-hundred-year-old poem by John Donne. I mentioned that I had met Officer Crane a couple of days before and introduced myself as a private investigator, and he had mentioned that we might see each other sometime when we were both working on a case since we were both on the same side of the law. I stared at those last words and then crossed them out repeatedly until I was sure no one could read them. I didn't want there to be any chance for someone to accuse us of collusion.

I read through the statement again and added a couple of lines at the end about walking over to the police station to give my statement, so it looked like I had messed up the ending and not about Bill Crane and me working together. I signed it, Jimmy Marlowe. *I wonder how long I'll be doing that?*

I took the pad of paper back to the dispatcher. He motioned for me to leave it on the desk near him while he talked to a patrol officer on the radio. I retraced my steps out of the police station and headed back to Centre Street. I followed it east until I came to the Keystone Hotel.

I went up to the Higgins/Sackett suite, and Mrs. Sackett opened the door so fast after I knocked that she must have been standing right next to it.

"There you are, Mr. Marlowe. Some man named Mutt or Duff or something has been calling for you," Amelia Sackett said as she let me in the room.

"Muff Benjamin," I said as I entered the room and looked around to see if anyone else was there. "Muff helps me track down information sometimes."

"And was he 'tracking down' information about us? And if so, what information did he come up with?"

"Yes, he was, but I don't know what he came up with. I asked him to gather information about Val and Dale, and I don't know what information he may have dug up because I haven't talked to him yet. If you don't mind, I'd like to borrow your phone. Did Muff leave a number where he could be reached?"

She pointed to a note next to the telephone with a number written in neat, perfect penmanship, the kind of writing only the teacher usually possessed when I went to school. At least, that's what I remembered. There were no faces or details to accompany the pseudo-memory, just a vague feeling that I suspected was a memory trying to work its way to the surface of my mind.

I dialed the number, and Muff answered on one ring.

"Yeah, Marlowe?"

"What? No hello?"

"Fine. Hello, Marlowe. I've been trying to get in touch with you for the last couple of hours. I checked with the harbor patrol, and they said Sackett's boat is the *Tortuga*, and it's moored temporarily at slip number fifteen. I'm down here at the Ship's Galley, keeping an eye on it. He's out there, Marlowe. I don't know if he's alone or with somebody, but he's definitely out there. I've seen him on deck a couple of times."

"Good job, Muff. I'll take it from here. You earned your money."

"I always do, Marlowe. Look me up when you need somebody else found."

"I'll do that, Muff. Maybe sooner than you think. Have you ever heard of a guy named Doyle Abaddon?"

"Sure, I've heard of him. Young up-and-comer. Came to town a couple of years ago. Trying to make a name for himself, but most of his capers are nickel and dime jobs with goons who got kicked off the B-squad, if you know what I mean."

"Big on brawn but short on brains? That kind of B-squad?"

"Exactamundo, my friend."

"Keep yourself available, Muff. Right now, I have to find out where a young woman is."

"Always keeping the best jobs for yourself, aren't you, Marlowe?"

I smiled before I said, "Later, Muff. Thanks again for finding Sackett." I placed the telephone back on its cradle on the desk and turned to Amelia Sackett. My smile disappeared.

"Where's Dale?" I asked in a stern voice.

She crossed her arms over her chest and tried to look stern, but I saw through it. She was deeply worried. The question was, who was she more worried about, Val or Dale? After trying to stonewall me for a few seconds, she crumbled.

"I don't know, Mr. Marlowe. I honestly don't know. I went to her room earlier to check on her, and she was still sleeping. I tried to wake her, but I couldn't. While I was checking on her, Val came in and told me he had given her some more of the sedative because he wanted to make sure she didn't cause any trouble. When I went back to check on her an hour later, she was gone, and I couldn't find Val anywhere, either. I checked the parking lot, and his car is gone. I don't have any idea where they've gone."

"What would you say if I told you I knew where he was?"

"I'd say, 'Tell me.' I'm begging you to believe me; I don't know where he's gone or if he's taken Dale with him."

"Does the name *Tortuga* mean anything to you?"

"His boat? What about it?"

"That's where he's at. Muff Benjamin located it down at the marina, and he's been checking on it from a seat at the Ship's Galley. He told me that Val's on board. Is he getting ready to leave port? Are you going to be joining him? Does he have Dale with him, or did he leave her some other place? How does this all tie in with Dale's inheritance? Do you even know if your stepdaughter is still alive?"

I fired the questions at her rapidly, trying to keep her off-balance, not wanting to give her time to think so that whatever answer she gave would be the truth because she didn't have time to think up a lie. That is unless they'd already planned for this. Val may have kept her in the dark so she couldn't tell me or the police anything.

"I don't know, I don't know, I don't know!" She swung her arms down by her sides, her hands balled into fists and hammering her hips with each "I don't know." I believed her. It wouldn't be the first time someone left a co-conspirator behind because it was easier to travel light, even when the partner was a spouse.

"How much is her inheritance?" I asked. When she didn't answer right away, I took a step toward her. I didn't intend to threaten her, but she stepped back, cringing like I was going to hit her. Maybe Val was in the habit of smacking her around. I took a step backward, so she knew I wasn't going to hurt her. But I needed to know about Dale.

"How much is it, Amelia? Enough to kill for?"

She was chewing on the inside of her lip, and then suddenly, I saw the dam break. A tear formed in the corner of one of her eyes, and I knew she was going to tell me everything I needed to know and maybe even help me catch Val and save Dale.

"Three-quarters of a million dollars. It should have been a million, but Val has been dipping into the trust fund as her 'guardian,' pretending to be a man of means. He bought that boat and a couple of cars, plus there's the summer home in Asheville and the winter home in Miami. Or was. He had to sell the winter home, but we've been living here in the Keystone for several months now, and that's whittling down his bank account fast. He pretends that he's got a bottomless well of money, but he doesn't. And even if he figures out some way to get Dale's money, it won't be enough for him."

"Do you have any idea how he intends to get Dale's inheritance?"

"I'm scared, Mr. Marlowe. I think he's going to kill her somehow and try to make it look like an accident. Then the money will go to me, and as his wife, he'll have complete access to it." She was rubbing her temples like the stress and worry were getting to her.

In case she hadn't figured out Sackett's next step, I decided to tell her.

"No, he won't have complete access to it. Not if you're still alive. So that means he'll have to get rid of you, too, so it all flows to him, nice and neat. With 750-thousand dollars, he can always pick up another wife."

She turned visibly pale as the truth of what I had said hit home.

: : : :

A NURSE CAME INTO Jimmy's ICU room, an occurrence that had become all too familiar in the past thirty-six hours. None of his friends even took notice anymore or stopped their conversations. Like the angels they are, the nurses work in the background, seeing things other people don't. A patient's facial expression or movements can take on much larger implications for these modern Florence Nightingales.

The nurse looked at the readout from one of the machines and moved closer to the bed where she could get a better look at Jimmy.

"What is it?" Wendi asked. Even though she tried not to actively notice the nurses, she couldn't help but mentally catalog their activity, and she knew when something was different. The nurses' demeanor changed, and they became tighter, less personable, and more like pieces of the healing machinery.

The professional wall of personality went back up, marked with a small smile. "I don't think it's anything to be concerned about. Especially since we're going to start waking him up later tonight. I just noticed that his brain isn't resting as much as we'd like. There's more activity than we usually see. I'm sure he's just having a particularly vivid dream."

She marked something on a chart as she answered Wendi's question and left the room.

"I would dearly love to have a window into his mind," Hillary said. "Think of the wild, imaginative stories he could be experiencing right now with his mind freed from all the usual worries and duties."

"I don't know, Hil. We have no way of knowing if they're pleasant dreams or nightmares. You, of all people, should know how terrible the dream world can be, how easily you can slide from a wonderful, sweet dream into something right out of a horror film."

"Indeed. The trauma of losing my wife and son in that car wreck brought about increased night terrors when my PTSD flared up. My therapist is a saint. I may contact him soon to have a little chat after all the excitement we've had recently."

"That's probably a good idea," Wendi agreed. "It wouldn't hurt to actually go see him, too. You could take a couple of days and drive down to West Palm Beach. If nothing else, it's good to get away sometimes and take a deep breath."

"You could stand to do the same, my dear – when this is done, of course."

"I was thinking the same thing. It would be nice to go up to northern Minnesota with Jimmy and spend a little time in his old habitat. But when I look at the weather reports for up there, I think, 'No way!' I'm a Florida girl, and I don't want to go somewhere they talk about hypothermia happening in three minutes or less!"

: : : :

W E TOOK ONE OF the Sacketts' cars down to the marina. I let Amelia drive because I still didn't trust my broken head. I almost changed my mind halfway there, what with her difficulties handling the clutch and close calls with stationary objects, but she never hit anything – she just came close. She also struggled to find the right gear at times, but at least the car's lurching didn't set off another headache for me. We parked as close to the Ship's Galley as we could, and Muff hurried over.

"He's out on the boat. I saw him on deck again a few minutes ago. He comes out, looks around, and goes back inside," Muff said to bring us up to speed. "It's like he's watching for somebody."

"Have you seen anybody else out there?" I asked.

Muff shook his head. "Just Sackett," he answered. "So, who's the lady you brought along?"

"I'm sorry, Muff. This is Amelia Sackett, Mrs. Val Sackett. Stepmother to Miss Dale Higgins," I replied.

"Oh, so you're the dame–I mean, the lady who answered the telephone when I called for Jimmy," Muff said to Amelia.

"Yes, I'm the 'dame,' as you put it. And I'm just another person in a line of people Val has tricked for years into providing him with money. But that stops tonight. He's gone too far."

"Hey, Muff," I asked, "how do we get the Coast Guard or Harbor Patrol or the cops to make a little visit to Val's boat, the *Tortuga?*"

"I'm glad you asked, Jimmy. Ordinarily, you'd know the answer, but since you've been on the receiving end of a hard knock on the noggin, I will enlighten you. All you do is drop a nickel in the slot of the nearest payphone and ask for which branch you want, and they'll be down here in short order, on account of this is a port city, and they're all nearby."

"Here's what I want you to do, Muff. Give me five minutes to stroll over to the slip where the *Tortuga* is moored and then drop that nickel and call the Coast Guard. That'll give me time to have a little chat with Val and make sure Dale is okay."

"You're taking me with you," Mrs. Sackett insisted.

"Of course I am! It wouldn't be a family reunion without you, Amelia!"

I shook hands with Muff, who had more than earned his five bucks. Then Amelia Sackett and I started walking down the long dock toward the *Tortuga,* which means "turtle" in Spanish.

As we walked in the near darkness, I tried to keep my ears open for sounds that indicated the presence of someone else, and I soon heard them. They were faint, but they were there. While Mrs. Sackett and I walked at a regular pace, after every twenty feet or so, I'd hear quick little footsteps, like someone watching us and then running to keep up. We were being followed, but they weren't very stealthy. But then, maybe they didn't have to be.

I stopped beside a 1930 fantail yacht with beautiful woodwork accents and wood railings on both decks and gently took Amelia by the elbow. She looked at me, her eyebrows raised. I lifted a finger to my lips to signal her to keep quiet. To her credit, she did as I indicated.

"Keep going," I whispered. "I'm going to find out who's following us."

She nodded and kept walking toward her husband's boat, still a good distance away. Thanks to a little three-step removable staircase someone left behind, I stepped up onto the 1930 yacht's fantail. Then, I stood in the shadows and waited. It didn't take long.

A dark figure came tiptoeing by on the dock, and I quietly stepped off the wood-embellished pleasure craft. The figure had hurried up to the next slip, so I had to move fast to catch up.

The man in the dark clothes stopped and waited in the shadow of another yacht, and I made my move. I stepped forward and grabbed him by the shoulder, spinning him around. I cocked my arm back, ready to deliver a haymaker to whomever this less-than-silent tail was. But instead of throwing an uppercut or lashing out with a rabbit punch, I found myself looking down the barrel of a Smith & Wesson .38 Victory Special.

Chapter 16

FOR A SPLIT SECOND, I thought the roar of the pistol I was staring at would be the last thing I would ever hear, but luckily, it didn't happen. The gun turned to one side, and the hand holding it lowered it, and a hushed voice said, "Holy cow, Mr. Marlowe! Gee whiz! Don't do that! I coulda plugged you!"

It was the young sailor, Robert Perez, the one known as Pepé. He'd been shadowing us on the dock for reasons only he knew because I hadn't invited him to the party. He tucked the pistol into the waistband of his many-buttoned sailor pants.

"Robert!" I hissed. "What are you doing here?"

"Following you!" he hissed back.

"Why?" I responded with a little less sizzle in my voice. I noticed Amelia had stopped and was looking back at us. I held up a hand to her, and she began walking toward us.

"I've got your six, brother. I've got your six."

He was using the phrase of World War I fighter pilots who referred to a pilot's rear as the six o'clock position. Pilots in a squadron would inform the lead pilot before taking off that they were covering his backside, saying, "I've got your six." Straight ahead was twelve o'clock, three o'clock to the right, and so on. It soon became a universal military term and was later adopted by law enforcement. Pepé had my six; he had my back.

If anyone had checked, they probably would have discovered adrenaline dripping from our ears after our sudden near-disastrous confrontation. I took a step back, and so did Pepé. He bent over and let his head hang down a bit. While we both learned to breathe again, Amelia rejoined us.

"Is everyone all right?" she asked.

"All our dories are hunky," I replied.

I got a single raised eyebrow from her, but she said nothing.

"Let's keep going," I said. "Amelia, this is Pepé. Pepé, Mrs. Sackett. Stay with us, Pepé. Don't worry about our six right now. No one can sneak up on us out here anyway."

We moved quickly and quietly the rest of the way to the boat. No one spoke. There were lights on poles like streetlights, but they only had regular lightbulbs and didn't do much to illuminate the dock. We hurried through each little circle of light, trying to stay in the darkness.

We finally reached the *Tortuga*. There was a dim light in the lower cabin and a small light in the captain's bridge above us. Yeah, it was "barely bigger than a fishing boat," if the fishing boat is a forty-foot shrimp trawler carrying a four-man crew and sixty-thousand pounds of shrimp.

Val also told me he didn't pay for a slip, a spot on the dock, but I was beginning to believe that the man didn't know how to tell the truth because I was looking at his boat moored at the dock. Maybe no one checked the slips this far out very often, or maybe he just pulled up because he was waiting for someone – like Amelia. Or perhaps he pulled up to the dock because it was too hard to haul Dale from the dinghy onto the boat. I was ready for some answers.

"Keep that cap pistol of yours handy," I told Pepé in a soft whisper. "I have no idea if Sackett is going to be packing. I also have no idea what condition Miss Dale is in. There's also a slight chance that whoever Val was waiting for came while we were on the long march out here. They could have come from the other side of the boat and gone aboard, and we wouldn't have seen them in the dark."

Robert started to say 'Aye, aye' again but caught himself. Next, he started to throw an automatic salute before stopping his arm and giving me a frustrated look. All the automatic responses the Navy had drilled into him were no longer necessary.

I opted not to board the boat immediately. I wanted to peek through the porthole windows along the side and check out the guest list. Even more, I wanted to see whether the boat was hauling people sporting hardware, and I don't mean hammers and screwdrivers.

"You two stay here. I'm going to try and get a peek inside to get the lay of the land before we make like pirates and board her."

Pepé gave me a disgruntled look, so I leaned in and, in a hushed whisper, tried to placate him. "I need you to stay here with Mrs. Sackett. I don't know which team she's playing for yet." I gave him a wink, which I doubted he could see in the dark. Even so, he seemed more content to stay behind while I reconnoitered the situation facing us.

Pepé and Mrs. Sackett hid in the shadow of the 'barely-bigger-than-a-fishing-boat' *Tortuga* while I started moving furtively along the length of the craft, keeping one hand on the rope railing lining the dock. I walked on the outsides of my feet, rolling them to avoid making loud clomping noises someone on the boat might hear.

Through the first round window, I saw a small kitchen – the ship's galley – with a small dining table flanked by a bench on each side, like a restaurant booth. It all looked fairly utilitarian, not ostentatious like the larger fantail yacht we had stopped at on the way out here.

I moved to the next window, which gave me a view of the salon, the nautical equivalent of a living room. Jackpot! There was Val, his back to the window. Dale was sitting in a chair in front of him, a rope wrapped around her to keep her in the chair and, from the looks of things, to hold her upright. There was a handkerchief protruding from her mouth, and her eyes were closed. She wasn't moving or fighting against the gag in her mouth, and I feared she was still doped up by whatever sedative Sackett had administered.

I couldn't tell what Sackett was doing; his hands were in front of him, and he was facing away from me. Despite not being able to see what he was doing, I decided the odds were favorable for us to surprise and overpower him, subsequently rescuing Dale.

I slipped as quickly as I could back to where Pepé and Amelia stood.

"They're both in there – Val and Dale. She's tied up in a chair with a gag in her mouth. He's in the same room with her, but with his back toward me, so I couldn't see what he was doing."

I hadn't figured out a game plan yet when Amelia planted one foot on the top of the steps by the little gateway onto the aft deck and – like she had done it many times before – half-walked and half-jumped onto the deck before I had any chance to stop her.

"Val!" she called.

"Who's there?" came a rough reply from within.

Amelia walked carefully down the deck and into the lower cabin and galley. A sudden thunderous boom filled the air, and she dropped to the floor in a heap. Through the open doorway, I could see Val standing in the doorway to the salon where I had seen him with Dale. One hand held the Colt M1911 .45 caliber pistol he had just used to shoot Amelia. There was rage on his face, not despair or the anguish you'd expect from a husband who had just accidentally shot his wife.

Pepé looked at me, his eyes wide, and I put my hand on his arm to keep him from jumping aboard the boat and likely taking the next bullet from Sackett's weapon. As we stood on the dock, hidden by the sides of the boat, I could hear Sackett raging in the galley.

"You ... stupid ... stupid ... cow!" I heard him shouting. "Look what you did! It doesn't matter. I'll still get the money.

This was eventually going to happen to you anyway. You just didn't know it."

He turned around and walked back into the room with Dale. I motioned to Pepé to go in through the galley while I was going to get Sackett's attention through the salon's porthole window. He nodded and, with an agility that could only come from three years on board ships at sea in all kinds of weather, leaped over the steps and glided silently into the galley.

I hurried along the dock, past the first window, and then came to the second one. I took a big breath and held it. I had no desire to suffer the same fate as Amelia nor to see my faithful new friend, Pepé, join her on the galley floor.

In for a penny, in for a pound, I thought.

I stood up and shouted, "Hey, Sackett! She wasn't out here alone!"

From within the cabin, I heard Val Sackett roar, "Marlowe!" Almost simultaneously, his head and shoulders appeared in the window. I saw him spin around toward the window to find where I was. He fired at the window, which shattered, but the thick glass deflected the bullet, and it failed to find me. I dropped to the dock, keeping low and out of sight. I began crab walking as swiftly as possible back to where Pepé had leaped aboard.

Once I was adjacent to the galley window, I stood up again. I heard Pepé shout at Sackett to freeze, but Val must have decided to shoot it out because Pepé suddenly fired his sidearm, a SW .38 Victory Special. He fired not once but three or four times in quick succession. I was so startled I couldn't count the shots.

And then everything went quiet again, and there was just the gentle sound of waves lapping against the side of the *Tortuga*.

I ran to the gate at the aft portion of the boat and thought about jumping over the steps like Pepé and Amelia had, but knew I'd probably fall flat in my face, so I ran up the tiny steps. I felt like my legs were going a hundred miles an hour as I stepped on each of the miniature steps.

I hurried into the galley. I found Pepé in the middle of the room, facing the doorway to the salon. Beyond him, I could see Dale, still tied to the chair. Amelia Sackett was behind Pepé in an unmoving heap, looking as though she suddenly had squatted in place. Pepé still had his revolver aimed in the direction where Sackett had been standing mere seconds before. I took a step to one side and could see Val lying on his back in the salon, the front of his shirt slowly becoming soaked in dark blood.

I put a hand on Pepé's arm, and I felt him flinch at my touch, but he lowered his weapon. The small kitchen was filled with the acrid smell of cordite from Pepé's rapid-fire shooting and mixed with the rancid stench of fried fish from a not-so-recent meal. The combination of odors was hard to ignore, so I breathed through my mouth.

In a quiet voice, Pepé said absently, "They teach you to eliminate the threat, not just fire once and hope for the best."

"You eliminated the threat, Pepé. You and I are both unscathed, and I'm pretty sure Dale is, too. I'm going to check on her."

I could see Dale beginning to slowly squirm in the chair she had been tied to. Her jaw muscles were functioning, and she was trying to work the gag from her mouth.

I stepped past Pepé and into the salon. Even though I was sure Sackett was dead, I moved his gun out of reach to one side and then checked for a pulse. Nothing.

I went to Dale and pulled the handkerchief from her mouth. I untied the knot holding the rope in place, and she sagged to the side. I grabbed her and sat her upright again.

"Dale!" I said loudly, shaking her shoulders. "I need you to wake up." Her eyes were glassy, and her head started to slump again. I scooped her up and laid her on the divan.

I ducked back into the galley and hurried past Pepé, who was now sitting on one of the benches next to the dining table. He looked somewhat green, and I noticed he was holding his dog tags in one hand and mumbling. I slowed down as I strode by him and heard him intoning, "Holy Mary, Mother of God, pray for us sinners, now and at the hour of our death …" He was using his dog tags chain as a rosary.

I told myself to ask him about that later. In the meantime, I decided I needed to check on Amelia Sackett. With all the shooting and excitement, I hadn't checked to see if she was dead or alive.

As I moved toward Mrs. Sackett, Pepé paused from his chanting and said flatly, "She's dead." After a second, he began reciting the rosary in a hushed voice once again.

I stood next to Amelia and tried to assess what I saw. She appeared to be seated or kneeling on the floor, with her dress splayed out in a perfect circle around her. Her head hung forward, and her hair had all been swept forward, masking her face. Her arms hung at her sides, her wrists bent, and her palms on the floor as if holding herself in place. She looked very peaceful, almost as though kneeling in prayer.

I took one wrist and felt for a pulse. After a short duration during which I felt nothing, I stood and was about to lift her head when Pepé spoke again.

"She's dead, Mr. Marlowe. There's nothing you can do." He turned away from the scene in front of him, the one showcasing the deceased Amelia Graves Higgins Sackett.

I had spoken with ambulance drivers many times who told me that people often made a wrong pronunciation of death at a scene. The carotid artery in the neck is a much better indicator of heart activity than the wrist. Without saying so to Pepé, I was going to check Amelia's neck for a pulse.

I placed my hand on her forehead and gently lifted her head to give me access to her neck. Instead of checking for a pulse as I planned, I gently lowered her head again, scrambled over a few feet, and sat across from Pepé on the other bench.

"I told you. There's nothing you could do for her," Pepé said in his flat, emotionless voice. "Sackett aimed a little high when he shot her. Instead of hitting her in the center body mass, the bullet went through her jaw and neck. That big caliber bullet tore the bottom of her face off."

The sight that had greeted me when I lifted her head would likely haunt my dreams for some time. I understood why Pepé had looked queasy. While I was checking on Dale, he must have checked on Amelia, unbeknownst to me. Since he had enlisted in the Navy after the hostilities of war were over, this was probably his first time seeing violent death up close.

I noticed that Dale was sitting up on the divan, leaning forward, and holding her head in her hands. I rose and went to her, sitting beside her on the divan.

"My head feels as big as a basketball, but my throat feels as dry as a desert. What happened?" she asked.

"Val drugged you and brought you out here to his boat. You were right about the inheritance. Val was going to kill you and then take you out away from shore, weigh down your body, and toss you overboard. And that's *if* he was going to be nice to you. If he wasn't, he would have just tied you to some weights before you were dead and thrown you over the side to drown."

"But why? For the money?"

"That's the number one reason people kill people, Dale. Since you've been gone for so many years to the convent in the Keys, it wouldn't be a big thing to have you declared dead by the court, especially when you didn't show up for your inheritance hearing. Then Amelia would get the money. He wouldn't have let her enjoy it very long, though. Sackett would have seen to it that she suffered a tragic accident at sea, and as her husband, he would get all the money."

Dale was holding her head in her hands as she replied, "At the school that the nuns run in the Keys, they taught us that the love of money is the root of all evil. I guess that's true."

"More than you know, darling. The love of money is the perfect rooting medium for all kinds of evilness. I guarantee you're going to have a lot of people contacting you about sharing that inheritance with them. Do you know how much it is?"

She gave a small shake of the head.

"Amelia told me when we started looking for you. She said it's three-quarters of a million dollars. Nearly 750 thousand dollars," I told her. To my surprise, she didn't react to the huge number; she just sat on the divan, not moving or speaking.

After a long moment, she asked, "What am I supposed to do with it?"

"Well, kid, if you're smart – and I think you are – you'll do good things with it, starting with going back to the nuns and laying low while you think about how to use it for good. For the good of others. Maybe discuss it with the Mother Superior; see what she thinks you should do with it. Are there things the school could use?"

"Oh, yes! So many things!"

"Now you're thinking in the right direction."

So far, she hadn't looked around the two rooms at her surroundings. She was still kind of dopey from the sedative Val had stuck her with. I wasn't sure if she really knew about Sackett or Amelia. I was also wondering where the Coast Guard was. Muff should have called them a long time ago.

Suddenly, Dale let out a shriek. She had turned her head and saw the obviously dead body of Val Sackett on the floor of the salon.

"Mr. Marlowe! That's Val! He's been shot! Is he … dead?"

"I'm afraid so, kiddo. But don't spend a lot of tears on him. Like I said, he was going to kill you so he could get your inheritance. He was not a nice man."

"What about Amelia?" she asked, looking around the salon and then craning her neck to see into the galley.

"Don't. You don't want to see her, Dale. When we got here to the boat, she stepped up on the boat to confront Sackett. I had told her about his plan to kill you and then kill her. She decided to stand up to him, but he shot her. He didn't give her a chance to say anything. He just shot her. And she's dead, kid. I'm sorry. I know she wasn't your real mom, but she took care of you when you were little, so I'm truly sorry."

Dale leaned against my side and sobbed quietly. I had hit the nail on the head. Amelia had been the only mother figure Dale had known, even though she started out as the housekeeper. And even though Amelia had married Sackett after Dale's real father had passed, there would always be the memories of happier times. Or the feelings, at least, if not actual memories she could pull up. I knew what that was like.

Suddenly, I heard hushed voices outside. I hoped it was the Coast Guard finally coming to secure the scene. Even though it meant spending an hour or more writing a statement and fielding a barrage of questions, I, for one, would be relieved to have someone else in control of the situation.

I heard the shuffle of feet on the deck outside the salon. They sounded very unsteady, like every time a wave tipped the boat slightly, the people walking on the deck had to rearrange their feet to stay standing. I knew the waves against the boat were minimal, which meant whoever was out there wasn't used to walking on a boat. Whoever it was, they weren't the Coast Guard or the Harbor Patrol.

I caught a glimpse of red curls walking past a window, followed by a head of black hair slicked back with more oil than should be legal. It was Sean and Angelo!

Chapter 17

Wendi and Hillary were huddled together in a corner between a pair of windows, their heads close together and whispering when Pepé came out into the ICU waiting area. They were obviously discussing something important as Pepé came over but he was irritated about the flower delivery from The Man. As he approached his friends, they stopped talking abruptly and turned toward him, each giving a small but genuine smile. With no prelude, Pepé launched into a tirade about the flowers.

"I don't like it. And by 'it' I mean I don't like that The Man sent flowers to Jimmy. He only did it to needle us and get under our skin, as if showing us how easy he could get to us" Pepé said animatedly, his hands punctuating his sentences.

Hillary placed a hand on Pepé's shoulder. "Don't let him irritate you, Mr. Perez. If you let it 'get under your skin,' as you say, then he wins. Is that what you want?"

"No, of course not. But I've been sitting in that room with Jimmy for hours, and it's starting to make me a little stir-crazy. As much as Jimmy usually talks all the time, I'd give anything to hear him make a stupid dad joke right now. Even a knock-knock joke would be better than watching him sleep! When are they going to start weaning him off this sleeping juice, anyway?"

Wendi was just as tired as Pepé if not even more, but she gave him a little smile at his use of their group's term for the sedative the hospital used to keep Jimmy in a coma: sleeping juice.

"All they told me was 'sometime tonight,'" Wendi replied. "I don't know if that means six o'clock or ten o'clock or midnight. From what I've been able to pick up from the nurses and the doctor, it could still take several days before Jimmy fully regains consciousness. The first signs of consciousness by the patient tend to be simple, like basic responses in which they respond to simple changes in light or sound. Then he might be able to follow simple commands, such as blinking his eyes when asked to or moving a limb or a finger. Those first responses tend to be slow and inconsistent, but they should become more regular with time and healing. I'll know he's back for good when he tries to tell a joke."

"I don't think I'd use that for a benchmark," Pepé replied. "He's fallen asleep riding in my truck, and he tries to tell jokes in his sleep!"

The trio drifted back near the seating area, but no one was inclined to sit; they'd all been planted in chairs for too many hours straight. There was a vending machine in the corner, but no one wanted more coffee, either. Right now, they each wanted to walk around and limber up, to stretch their legs a bit. What they really wanted most was to feel normal again. *'This is worse than a stakeout!'* Pepé thought.

"Let's go outside and walk around the block," Wendi said, trying to sound cheerful even if she felt anything but chipper. "I really need to get out of this place for a little bit and get some fresh air. Are you guys with me?" The two older men agreed. Pepé stuck his head in Jimmy's room and told Gwynn where they were going.

Gwynn was watching an old Password episode on TV, one of the originals with Allen Ludden as the host, and his wife, Betty White, as a celebrity contestant. Gwynn beckoned Pepé over to where she sat; he bent down, and she gave him a kiss, her eyes leaving the TV just long enough to make sure she found his lips.

"Be good," she said as he turned to leave. "We'll be right here if anyone is looking for us." She patted the bed lightly to indicate that the 'we' included Jimmy.

Outside, it was a typical autumn day in northeast Florida, with sunshine and temps in the low 70s. Wendi was used to walking more energetically than Hillary and Pepé, so she maintained about a twenty-foot lead on the two men, frequently looking back over her shoulder to check the distance. Occasionally, she would stop and wait for them to catch up before she raced ahead again.

It was hard for any of them to believe it had only been a couple of days since they had been together at the Dawson house on Piney Island after Carolyn's funeral. The past couple of days had been intense.

Her thoughts returned to the run-in with The Man's thugs outside of Lyst Publishing, as they had often since the confrontation. What else *was* there to think about, especially with Jimmy lying motionless in that hospital bed? Her mind's eye called up the image of the impossibly strong man nicknamed Kingpin, who had swatted her to the ground like a mosquito. He had hoisted Jimmy over his head and thrown him against the side of the building like Jimmy was a ragdoll. Her memory of the sequence of events was fuzzy and incomplete after that. She couldn't remember anything definite between the incident and when she woke up in the hospital. Her doctor said that was normal. She might get partial recall of the events, total recall, or she might never recover that short time span.

As tired as she was of thinking about the events of the last few days, she needed to sift through them to make sense of them. Jimmy was in the ICU in a medically induced coma, and she had spent a night in the hospital for observation after sustaining a concussion from Kingpin's body slam. And then there was Thanksgiving …

Somehow, Thanksgiving was still two days away. It had become the holiday that would never come this year. Her lips trembled and her eyes filled as she wondered if they would have anything to be thankful for this year. She blinked away a tear and wiped her suddenly sniffly nose with a Kleenex she had decided to keep in her pocket. Tears had been coming too easily since this ordeal began.

She stopped walking and waited for the two men to catch up again. As she waited, she picked up snatches of their conversation as they approached.

Pepé was still going on with the same tirade. "I don't like it, Hillary. I don't like that The Man could get to Jimmy so easily in the ICU."

As usual, Hillary was the voice of reason. "But it wasn't one of his henchmen; it was just a flower delivery person."

"How do you know that? Huh? How do we know? We were down in the cafeteria getting coffee. The hospital needs to beef up its security; that's all I'm saying."

The two men came up short at the sight of Wendi standing in front of them, holding out a palm like a traffic cop stopping traffic.

"Do the two of you know what I want? I want to walk on the beach without worrying about finding spare body parts. I want to go out to eat, to a movie, put gas in my car, and go to the grocery store, all without having to constantly look over my shoulder. I want a quiet, peaceful life again," she explained to the two men who had joined forces to save her life and Jimmy's. "Most of all, I want Jimmy to just be … Jimmy. Is that too much to ask?"

No one answered the question. Instead, the trio walked in silence for a distance. Eventually, Hillary asked gently, "Do you suppose life can ever go back to being quiet and peaceful?"

: : : :

I HEARD SEAN AND Angelo's footsteps coming around the curve of the deck. It had been my distinct displeasure to meet the two thugs before, and they would be in the galley soon. I had to get Dale hidden, but where?

My eyes swept the salon before I stepped over to the galley and stuck my head around the doorway. Dale was right behind me, Amelia was lying in a crumpled heap in the doorway, and Val was spreadeagled on the salon floor about six feet away, but where was Pepé? The young sailor who had saved my life from the gun-wielding Val was nowhere in sight, and I didn't dare call out for him. Had he ditched us? Gone AWOL? Maybe the shock of killing Val was too much for the young man.

I whispered to Dale, "How well do you know the layout of Val's boat? Pretty well? Is there a closet or something you can hide in?"

"There's a small storage area in the salon," she answered, pointing past my head. "It's tight but I can fit. It's right behind the wet bar. There's an access panel in the wall."

"Hurry!" I told her, not bothering to look where she was pointing since it could only hide her. I was keeping my eyes on the galley door in case Sean and Angelo walked in before she was hidden. The young woman moved quickly and confidently, and I left her to hide herself.

Meanwhile, I stepped around Amelia and moved across the small galley as quietly as I could, dropping into a crouch next to the stove. If Sean and Angelo just poked their heads in and didn't come all the way into the galley to check for us, they might not find me. The stove jutting out from the wall should help conceal me if our pursuers didn't come all the way into the galley. I was counting on the dead bodies of Amelia and Val to occupy their attention. The arrangement of their bodies looked like they'd been in a duel with no winner.

A single corpse in a room demands a person's attention, but finding *two* dead bodies so close together can make a spectator miss all kinds of details. At least, that's what I was counting on. There was always the possibility that Sean and Angelo had caused more than their fair share of dead bodies and were so desensitized to the sights and smells of death that they would barely take notice of the Sacketts. That could be bad for me if they were on a first-name basis with the angel of death because I was hiding almost in plain sight in a corner of the galley.

Where is Pepé? My thoughts briefly turned to the young sailor. He couldn't have known about the salon's hidey hole, so he and Dale couldn't both be trying to fit into the same cramped spot. From her quick description, it wouldn't have held both of them anyway.

From the sound of the footsteps on deck, it sounded like the two hoodlums were nearing the galley door. There was nothing I could do except press myself into the corner between the stove and the wall, try to make myself as small as possible, and pray they didn't see me *(turning temporarily invisible would be best!)*.

I was jammed so tightly into the corner that I couldn't see much of the doorway without leaning out and revealing myself, but I saw the toes of someone's shoes cross the threshold and stop, hanging just inside the galley. I figured it was Angelo since Sean usually made the decisions. It was a rule of thumb that Angelo poked his head into places for a quick reconnoiter before Sean risked his head and ginger curls to take a peek. I heard Angelo's quick intake of air at the sight of the two bodies laid out before him, the toes of his shoes still in the doorway.

"Looks like two, Sean. Mrs. Sackett is right in the middle of the kitchen, and her mister is in the living room. I can't see where she got it, but I'm pretty sure she's toast, and Sackett took three to the chest. Nice grouping, too, all in the center upper quadrant. Personally, I would have given him a third eye for good measure, but that's just me, you know? I'm kind of an artist at what I do."

Sean snorted in derision. "Yeah, you're a real artiste," he replied, pronouncing it ar-teest, like the high society pronunciation.

The boat we were on was tied securely at the dock, but the waves striking it could still throw a man off balance, especially as the boat struggled against the ropes holding it in place. At times, the ropes held the boat in such dramatic fashion that everyone on board had to brace their feet and adjust their stance to maintain their balance. I got the feeling that the two outlaws were out of their element on the boat. My supposition was made even more evident by their physical reactions as several waves shifted the deck under their feet. Unless you were in California, you could almost always count on the ground under your feet to be stable, unmoving. The deck on a boat? Not so much.

Besides trying to keep an eye on Slick and Curly's whereabouts, I was also listening intently for the presence of anyone else coming on board, and I hadn't heard any other voices or feet. I had only heard two pairs of feet moving about on the deck. I knew approximately where Dale was, but I still had no clue to Pepé's hiding spot. Wherever he was, he was keeping absolutely still and quiet. There had been no shooting or struggling, which meant Pepé and Dale were still healthy. Now if we could just keep it that way.

"Go check those two stiffs out, Angelo. Make sure they're completely dead. The Boss is gonna want to know."

"C'mon, Sean. You can see that Sackett is lying dead in the living room. He took three in the chest. He's not going to get up and walk it off."

"It's a salon."

"What's a salon?"

"The room where Sackett is laid out. It's a salon, not a living room."

"Like where women get their hair and nails done?"

"Yeah, just like that."

"Why do they call it a salon if it's a living room?"

"I have no idea, Angelo. They just do!"

Sean was getting frustrated with Angelo's reluctance to check the bodies. I heard a muffled slap and, in my mind's eye, saw a meaty hand slap Angelo's upper arm. I envisioned Sean pointing across the room and Angelo reluctantly stepping into the galley.

Except I didn't have to imagine the last part as Angelo tentatively crept into the room, suddenly coming into my view around the stove. Just as I hoped, he seemed to only have eyes for the dead bodies. I kept perfectly still, doing my best to keep my breathing low and slow as I folded myself even smaller and pressed backward into the limited space in the corner next to the stove.

Angelo took a couple of giant steps, ending next to Amelia Graves Higgins Sackett's body. He leaned down, lifted her head slightly, then lowered it back down. He did not seem shocked. As he lowered her head, he said, "One to the lower jaw. Nothing very nice to see here. Probably dropped her straight down when it severed the spinal cord. The good thing is, she was dead before she hit the floor."

He straightened up, ran one hand through his heavily oiled hair, and reached Val Sackett's body after a couple more giant steps. A child's voice in my head chanted, *'The floor is lava ...'* as Angelo crossed the expanse with extra-large strides. I wasn't sure why he was taking such big steps unless it was his way of being stealthy when he wasn't completely sure he was alone.

He didn't bother bending over to check the dead man for a pulse. His "professional experience" finally came into play. From the position of the bullet holes and the amount of blood, he knew Sackett was dead. He had "retired" enough clients to recognize death. He reached down and picked up Val's pistol from where I'd kicked it and shoved it in his coat pocket. A pick-up was considerably cheaper than buying a throw-down.

Angelo paused to look around the cramped salon. I got lucky because he couldn't see me from his vantage point. Apparently, Dale was lucky, too, because Angelo said nothing as he did a quick half-circle to clear the small salon, turning clockwise. His rotation brought him back around, facing Sean and the doorway with Amelia Sackett's body to his right. I was on his right, too, but he wasn't looking around the galley. He had turned his head and was looking out the windows on his left. He'd either seen someone through the portholes as he cleared the room, or he didn't feel like looking at Amelia's body again. I didn't blame him. It would be some time before I would get that image of her decimated face out of my memory.

The black-haired goon somehow made it back to Sean in fewer steps than it took him to cross the room to check on the bodies. Surprisingly, I remained out of his line of sight during his trek.

"So, what are we going to do now?" he asked Sean.

"We're going back to the boss, and we'll tell him Mr. and Mrs. Sackett saved us the trouble of killing them."

"But what about the girl? Ain't we gotta find the girl, Sean? She gets the inheritance, doesn't she? I thought that's why Sackett brought her out here in the first place. He was going to kill her and dump her body out at sea, then come back and file the missing person paperwork with the local cops. Mrs. Sackett was supposed to get the money after they declared the girl dead, and then Mister Val was going to do an encore job on the missus so he would inherit all the money. And once he harvested the inheritance, we would exterminate him and relieve him of the cash."

"All true, Angelo, but we jumped ahead a couple of spaces on the board by not having to wait for the Sacketts to drop out of the picture. Like I said outside, they done us a favor by killing each other."

Angelo looked at Sean, his mind turning something over, examining it.

"What is it now, Angelo?" Sean snapped impatiently.

"Well, if Val was waiting for Mrs. Sackett to get the money, and we were waiting for Val to get the money, what happens to the girl? Didn't she have to go first to make the rest of the dominos fall down?"

Sean looked like he was going to tell Angelo that too much thinking was bad for his health, but he suddenly realized his partner was right. Without Dale's death to start the snowball rolling down the hill, there would be no avalanche of money and no payoff for them or Abaddon. Sean's features clouded over.

"We gotta find the girl, Angelo. If she shows up alive, the boss's plan don't work. The blocks won't stack up right."

"I don' know 'bout that, Sean. I've never killed a woman before, especially a girl."

"You didn't mind when I pulled the trigger on Mrs. Brody, though. How is that different?"

"Because I didn't pull the trigger, Sean, you did. I couldn't of done that one, neither."

"When did you grow a conscience, Angelo?"

"When the people we're whacking started being women. Young ones, pretty ones. I still got a mom, you know. She wouldn't like it if I started getting rid of girls or women."

"Your mom's had five husbands, Angelo, and the guy she's living with now ain't her real husband. Plus, I know for a fact that she offed at least two of her five husbands. Furthermore, I did another one for her, and the other two were lucky enough to die of natural causes, or so she says they did."

"But she always told me to be nice to women."

"How is that any different from her whacking husbands?"

"They weren't so nice to her, and they were men, that's how."

I had never expected to be eavesdropping on such a deep subject. Who would have ever guessed that hitmen had ethics or standards? But then I started wondering about Dale again and if she was okay. What if she couldn't hear them from her hiding place? If she thought these two goons were gone, she might pop out of her hiding place too soon, and they might actually finish what Val started. I couldn't let that happen, but I had no sure way of stopping it. Angelo had picked up Val's Colt .45, leaving me with nothing to protect myself with. Pepé was still armed, but I didn't know where he was. I had no idea if he was hiding or simply biding his time, waiting to see what the next scenario contained.

I didn't mean to, but I couldn't help but let the thought run through my mind: What if Pepé actually had snuck off the boat to find help, leaving just me and Dale against these two? Granted, they weren't the sharpest pencils in the box, but they were armed, and they were proficient with those arms, while we were neither. Angelo may have had objections to killing women, but neither thug had any reservations about killing men, which was the section of the population that included me.

A muffled thump came from somewhere on the boat, and both hitmen scrambled out the door to find it. From what I could tell, they didn't know I was on the boat with them. I counted that as a blessing.

My question was, who made the noise? Was it just the boat tugging against its mooring ropes and bumping against the fenders and the dock? Or was it Dale, Pepé, or the Coast Guard? Speaking of the local Coasties, where *were* they? If they had been punctual, there would have been at least one less death on Sackett's boat, but I'd seen no sign of them so far.

I wondered if I had misjudged Muff's abilities, but even more so, I hoped I hadn't misjudged his allegiances. However, there was another possibility: Sean and Angelo could have rendered Muff incapable of calling. That was something I didn't want to think about because I felt responsible for the diminutive man, but the thought took root anyway. Then it blossomed and grew in my brain, and I worried that Muff had received a better offer from the two thugs now wandering around on Sackett's boat.

It had been easy—and so cheap!—to get Muff to assist me with snooping around and digging into the background of the Higgins clan. Thanks to my lack of memory, I didn't know but what Muff could be on a retainer with Sean and Angelo—or even Abaddon. It was entirely possible that when they whistled, he responded to their every beck and call. I thought of the old RCA Victor logo with the dog sitting in front of the gramophone, listening to his master's voice. Was that Muff? Was he the dog? It wasn't such a wild idea, and it would explain why we were floating out here on the river with no backup.

I stood up from my hiding place to get a better look around and see if I could get a bead on where the two hitmen had gone. I could hear Angelo's voice, but I couldn't pinpoint his presence. I tried looking out the porthole window near my head for a visual, but I couldn't see either gangster. I couldn't see them, and Pepé and Dale were still unaccounted for, which meant they were hopefully hidden away, blessedly out of sight. Which left me, hiding in a corner of the galley. I slid back down into a crouch, much like Amelia Sackett's final resting position.

I didn't like hiding out alone in the galley, especially with two dead bodies only a few feet from where I was concealed. Dead bodies had a bad habit of attracting attention.

Hiding, I thought. *Yeah, right. I'm hiding—practically right out in the open.* The galley and salon were lit, but the world outside had become pitch black; whether cloudy, foggy, or clear, I couldn't say. All that mattered to me was that I was too visible in this lighted cabin. I needed to be outside under the dark cover of night.

I stood up partway to sneak another peek out of the porthole again and saw nothing, so I crept quietly across the galley to check out the other porthole before stealing over to the salon window to look. I tried to avoid looking at either of the Sacketts, but Val was spreadeagled in the middle of the salon, his body screaming, 'Look at me!' to anyone looking in the doorway.

Mrs. Sackett looked like she was simply kneeling on the floor with her head down, almost as if in perpetual prayer. I shuddered as I recalled the sight of her missing features. I was glad her head had sagged forward, covering up the nightmarish visage. The blood was hidden by the jacket she wore against the damp night air. She had been a plain woman—calling her handsome was being generous—but her face in death was horrific.

There was nothing to see out the windows, but I heard occasional, indistinct snatches of conversation from Sean and Angelo, so I dared not try slipping off the boat. I returned to my spot next to the stove. It didn't afford me much cover, but it had hidden me from the two mercenaries so far. Hopefully, they'd leave soon to report back to Abaddon.

I paused for just a moment before sliding down the wall into my baseball catcher's position again. I questioned my options. *Shouldn't I be trying to get outside? Not trying; doing! Just get outside before they come back and find you in here! You're hunkered down in the only two rooms on the ship that are lighted! Not the best choice for playing hide-n-seek!*

There were footsteps outside the galley. There were no options anymore. I had no time to try and escape to the darkness-shrouded deck outside. All I could do was squeeze further into my corner, mentally willing myself to become mouse-sized. I wrapped my arms around my legs and tucked my chin down into my chest. I tried to keep as still as humanly possible. I got a mental image from the stereotypical Western movie of a Mexican peasant dressed all in white except his bare feet, clad in sandals, wearing a big sombrero, and seated against a wall, taking a siesta. I had to force myself not to chuckle.

The footsteps stopped in the galley doorway. I hoped whoever was standing there only had eyes for the corpses. Since everything in the two rooms appeared exactly as they had left them a few minutes ago, maybe they would only give a cursory sweep of the rooms with their eyes.

'*Nothing to see here.*' I thought, trying to project that thought into their heads as I tried to blend in and become one with the stove. I didn't hear them leave the doorway, though.

I actually *felt* the presence of someone standing next to me before I heard them. People animate the space around them even when they're not moving or speaking. I knew the void in front of me had been empty when I squatted down, just as well as I knew it *wasn't* empty now. It wasn't that I felt their body heat or heard them step over next to me. There's just some kind of … what? Their aura? A presence? There's *something* palpable that identifies us as alive, something discernable by other people. Our living presence extends into and fills the space around us. While not truly tangible, it is not completely *intangible*, either.

I had been squeezing my eyes shut tightly the whole time, praying for the power of invisibility. Little children playing hide-n-seek often believe if they can't see you, you can't see them. After a moment, I cracked my eyes open into narrow slits. Peering through my eyelashes felt like looking through filmy lace drapes.

A pair of black brogans were almost toe-to-toe with my feet. I refused to move or acknowledge the person's presence for as long as I could. *I'm a sleeping Mexican peasant!* My holdout lasted only a few seconds before Angelo rapped his knuckles on the top of my skull. *Ow! Why do they always go for the head?*

"Knock, knock. Anybody home? Wakey, wakey, or you'll be sore and achy!"

I twisted and rotated my head enough to see the man with his trademark slicked-back hair standing in front of me, one hand resting on an ugly Luger pistol that resided in a shoulder holster under his coat. At least he hadn't knocked on my head with the gun barrel. *Thank goodness for small favors.*

"Hey, Sean!" Angelo called in mock good nature. "I found a turtle over here. Hey! Isn't that what the name of the boat means? Tortuga? That's a turtle, right? The way this guy's backed into this corner, I think he's trying to lay some eggs."

Angelo laughed at his own joke. I probably did look like a tortoise that had dug a nest in one of Fernandina's oceanside beaches. I thought about wrapping my arms around his legs and knocking him down, but before I could do anything so foolhardy, he grabbed me by my coat and hauled me to my feet. *Siesta time is over!*

I stood nose-to-nose and toe-to-toe with Angelo, my nose assaulted by the greasy kid's stuff he called pomade. There was no doubt in my mind about his involvement in Kendall Brody's 'suicide.' The greasy hair oil on the rope fit perfectly with Angelo's habit of running his hand through his hair, and the smell was the same as that on the rope.

Angelo pulled his German Luger P.08 from its holster. There were lots of Lugers available after WWII, and they weren't hard to come by. A sinister-looking gun, it had a detachable magazine for quick reloading. It also looked much larger up close than it did from across the room. I could smell cleaning oil from the unholstered weapon – it had a faint scent, almost like licorice – mixed with the acrid smell of ignited gunpowder. Any good craftsman kept his tools clean and serviceable, whether saws, knives, or a .9 mm pistol. For a brief second, I wondered if he used the gun oil in his hair or his hair oil on the gun.

Then the gun was moving, and I found myself staring down the barrel, unable to look anywhere else, my head following the business end of the gun like a doctor saying, 'Follow my finger with your eyes.' From my vantage point, my brain knew it was a small caliber weapon, but it looked huge, and the small dark hole in the barrel extended before me like a cannon barrel. Fatalistic thoughts went through my mind. *Would I hear it? Would I feel it or would it happen too fast? Would I see the bullet leaving the metal tube? Or just the flame? Would I see anything at all?*

A voice suddenly rang out. "I don't think so, buddy! Let him go!"

Chapter 18

The voice barking orders at Angelo to let me go belonged to Pepé, who now stood outside the salon, his service revolver aimed through the broken window Val had shot out earlier by firing at me a second before Pepé took him down. Unfortunately, Angelo and I had become a package deal from Pepé's vantage point. Although the young man did, indeed, have Angelo in his sights, by default, he also had *me*.

Faster than I believed possible for him, Angelo slipped behind me, wrapping his right arm around my head and shoulders, his right hand reaching across my chest and gripping my left shoulder to maintain control of me. I made a pretty solid shield; it was not a job I would willingly apply for.

With his right arm wrapping me up, he leveled the gun in his left hand at my head in a move that seemed fairly easy and natural for the man. Despite his lack of refined language skills, Angelo knew his way around a firearm and apparently had paid attention in class the day felons were taught how to use a human shield.

To his credit, Pepé didn't waver. His .38 caliber service revolver was absolutely rock steady. His dark-brown eyes, however, were as wide as the saucers at the luncheonette. I could see his pupils flick periodically toward the door on his left, where Sean stood as stiff as a Buckingham Palace guard. The ginger-haired crook had started reaching behind his back for his Luger—a twin to Angelo's—when he paused in mid-reach, realizing that Pepé could flick the gun toward him in less than a heartbeat. He looked like a football referee frozen in the process of throwing a flag on a play.

"Let him go," Pepé growled at Angelo, who didn't seem at all shaken by the doll-dizzy sailor's command.

"Nuh-unh. He's been causing too much trouble. I think we'd all be better off with him out of the picture. Whatta you think, Sean?"

"I'm not the one sailor-boy is aiming at," Sean replied. Angelo's eyes flicked toward his partner for a millisecond. His mouth turned down in an irritated frown, but Pepé spoke again before the walking oil-slick holding me could argue with his partner.

"There's no need for you to end up like the guy in the salon," Pepé said.

"Is that your handiwork?" Angelo asked.

"Yeah," Pepé answered.

"Nice grouping."

"Thanks. I didn't have a choice."

"Maybe I don't have a choice, either."

"You always have a choice," Pepé said. "The question is, will you make the right one? Every situation has a right choice and a wrong choice. Do you want to walk out of here alive? Because I promise you I can make you as dead as you're ever going to be. Take another look at Sackett."

I was holding onto Angelo's arm that was wrapped across my upper body. I felt his solid muscles bunched inside his coat sleeve. I was extremely aware of the hard metal authority of the pistol barrel pressing against my left temple. I had seen firsthand the result of what it could do at close range when I stumbled over Mrs. Brody in her apartment. It didn't make a big hole, but the size didn't make someone any less dead.

"We just want the girl," Sean said, opening a new channel of discussion and drawing Pepé's eyes away from Angelo. I was glad to have the spotlight off me, but I would have felt better with the gun gone, too.

"You want the girl for what?" I asked. The arm around my neck tightened.

"She's worth a lot of money," Sean answered.

"She's *almost* worth a lot of money," I replied.

Sean gave me a puzzled look. I smiled back at him, which confused him even more. Potential victims aren't supposed to smile. What did I know that he didn't?

I willed myself to remain calm, trying to shut out the voice in my head screaming that there was a pistol pressed against my head.

"Okay, I see now. You don't know, do you?" I said.

"Know what, smart guy?" Sean answered with a sneer.

"She doesn't have the money yet."

"Then why was Sackett going to bump her off and dump her over the side of the boat out where only the fish could find her?" Angelo growled in my ear.

"Because Val was way too greedy and not nearly as smart as he thought he was. Because he was an eager beaver, he couldn't wait anymore. His debts were piling up, and he needed the money, even if it meant not getting all of it. He'd already frittered away a quarter of a million dollars pretending to be a bigshot. Val thought he could force the situation to change and start the pendulum swinging his way."

I stole a glance at Pepé. He was rock-steady. *Atta boy, sailor. Pay attention and keep up with me.*

"The girl doesn't get the money until she's twenty-one, whether anyone is dead or not," I explained evenly, recalling an old saying that the truth shall set you free. There was no point in lying now. The truth would probably work better. I continued.

"You've got most of it right. Her birthday's not for several weeks yet. Sackett was going to kill her and then claim she had been missing for seven years and get her declared dead. Then the money would go to her stepmother, Amelia Sackett, and Val would kill Amelia and make it look like an accident so he could inherit everything. But he had been spending like he already had the money, and he was in over his head. Sound familiar?"

Sean didn't say anything, which I took as a yes. I could feel Angelo's grip relax ever-so-slightly. It's hard to maintain a tight lock on someone who's not resisting, and I wasn't fighting back against him at all. I wanted Angelo to get comfortable holding me, as creepy as that sounds.

I continued with Slick and Curly's lecture.

"Who's next in line to get the money? Since the Sacketts are out of the picture, that must mean your boss, the up-and-coming Doyle Abaddon, has somehow filed a claim on the money in case something happened to Val and Amelia. But things went all akimbo, didn't they? Everything turned topsy-turvy. Things aren't happening in the right order, and you don't know if *you* should kill the girl or leave her alone for now until you can haul her in to see Abaddon. That's assuming you can find her, which you haven't done so far. You don't know if you should wait on the boss for explicit instructions like you usually do or if you should try and make a play and hope it's the right one. My advice to you two clowns? Leave her alone. She's off limits until she turns twenty-one, anyway. You see, until her birthday, she's just another poor girl. Well, not quite poor, but not nearly as rich as she will be in a few weeks. If your boss is the wise owl he thinks he is, he'll wait until the candles are blown out on her cake before making any moves."

I dropped my left hand slowly, letting it come away from Angelo's right forearm and wrist and relax by my side. I was about to take the biggest risk of my life. As I talked to Sean, Angelo relaxed marginally, and I leaned ever-so-slightly to my right, mostly just shifting my weight onto my right leg. At the same time, I pressed slightly backward into Angelo so he would think he still had a tight hold on me.

I was still worried about the .9 mm Luger shoved against my head, but I was even more concerned with the .38 caliber aimed my way. I was about to tell someone I had known less than 72 hours to fire that gun at me.

"Pepé!" I nearly shouted his name, forcing him to focus on me. His eyes grew bigger than they already were. I gritted my teeth and made myself say something that might be the stupidest thing I had ever said, and that's saying a lot!

"It's time. Do it."

Pepé kept his aim fixed on Angelo and me, but his eyebrows had scrunched together in an unspoken question. Maybe I was expecting too much. Maybe my plan wasn't clear enough to him. Angelo refreshed his grip on me and turned slightly, making me the bigger target. I would have to deal with it. I tried again.

"His *watch* says it's time! Do it, Pepé!" Simultaneously, I leaned marginally more to my right into Angelo's embrace and turned my body even more into his, like I was getting ready to hug him.

Pepé fired his sidearm and at the same second I heard the gun's explosion, I felt the round shatter Angelo's right wrist next to his wristwatch. Angelo was a lefty and wore his watch on his right wrist. I had leaned far enough away to the right that Pepé's bullet missed me entirely. I rolled back to the left, pushing away the gun that was no longer directly pointed at my head. Angelo wasn't thinking about shooting me anymore; he was howling about his shattered wrist.

Pepé roared, "Stand down! Stand! Down! Don't make me shoot again! I will drop you right where you stand if you don't lose your weapon!"

Angelo dropped the gun and tucked his ruined wrist under his left arm. I saw Sean take a step back toward the door and finish pulling the black, sinister-looking Luger from behind his back. He was out of Pepé's line of sight but not mine. And I was directly in his line of sight.

"I really wish you hadn't done that, Marlowe," Sean said, bringing up his weapon and aiming it in my direction.

There was another huge explosion, and I saw the flare of a handgun from under a side table in the salon. Sean turned his head in that direction and began to swing his pistol around to return fire, but another blast came from beneath the table, and Sean jerked backward like he'd been hooked in his right shoulder with a fishing gaff.

He dropped the pistol involuntarily, his arm hanging limply by his side. He bent over to pick up the pistol with his left hand, but a foot stepped on the gun before he could reach it. Pepé had leaped from his firing perch in the broken window of the salon and dashed to the galley doorway, a distance of less than ten feet. Quickly stooping down and smoothly scooping up the pistol, Pepé waved Sean toward Angelo with his SW .38 Special. He tucked the .9 mil Luger P.08 semiautomatic into the waistband of his dungarees.

I looked back into the salon just as Dale Higgins crawled out from under the side table. I ran over and held out my hand to help her stand.

"You were just in time, Dale. Were you hiding under there the whole time?"

"No. I told you it goes through to a storage box. The storage box opens up on the other side. Once these two came in here to look around, I slipped out through the storage box. Pepé found me outside the salon. We kept them under our watch until they grabbed you. Then he got in position, and

I crawled back through the box and under the table. It was dark under the table, and with Val's body lying there, they couldn't see me open the panel partway."

"Where did you get the gun?"

"Val had several handguns hidden around the boat. I think he needed to have them close at hand in case the people he owes money to came out and caught him on the boat."

"Where did you learn how to shoot?"

"The nuns taught me."

"The nuns …?"

"There were always snakes in the garden, and some of them were pretty nasty. Mother Superior says there have been snakes in the garden ever since Eden. We don't have a flaming sword to keep them out, so we use the next best thing: a .38 Special."

"Whoa. Nuns packing a .38 Special? That's a lot of firepower to take care of a simple serpent or two."

"One of the nuns inherited her father's gun when he passed away. It was his service revolver when he was a cop with the Miami Police Force. I was already somewhat familiar with guns – I used to go skeet shooting with my father – so it became my job to evict any snakes we saw in the garden. I actually became a fairly good shot."

"Jimmy!"

The voice yelling my name from outside the salon belonged to Muff Benjamin. He came around the corner into the galley. His eyes opened wide when he saw Pepé holding a gun on Sean and Angelo, each thug wounded and bleeding. Pepé had given Sean a dishtowel from the galley to press against his shoulder wound, and Angelo's wrist and hand were wrapped in another.

"Boy, am I glad to see you, Jimmy!" Muff exclaimed. "And without any holes in you from the look of things! I heard gunshots as I was trying to get out here in time!"

"Where have you been, Muff? And where are the Coast Guard or the Harbor Patrol or whoever has jurisdiction down here on the river?"

He pulled his tan pork pie cap off his head, and I saw something red mixed in with his hair, matting his hair against his head. Someone had given him a lead-weighted sleeping pill like the one Val had given me.

"I was just about to call the Coasties when someone smashed me on top of my head with something. I went down hard, and I was out cold for a long while. If I were a betting man – which everyone knows I am not – I'd put money on the person responsible being the same guy with enough hair tonic on his head to grease up everyone in this room."

His eyes swept around the room, taking in the sight of Mr. and Mrs. Sackett in their separate final quarters for the first time. He gulped and amended his sentence.

"Make that enough hair tonic on his head for everyone in this room, dead or alive!"

"You're lucky we didn't feel like wasting a bullet on you, you runt!" Angelo groused in reply.

"Shut up, Angelo!" Sean growled, then moaned and pressed the dishtowel against his wound again.

I stepped over next to Muff, turning my back on Sean and Angelo, and asked quietly, "Okay, Muff, tell me this: is *anyone* coming? I don't have the authority to do anything with these two mugs that jumped us; plus, they both need medical attention."

As if on cue, we heard the sound of multiple feet treading heavily on the boat's deck, and three men appeared in the galley doorway, all wearing matching khaki shirts and pants, two with side caps and a third guy with a khaki-colored brimmed cap. I don't know ranks very well, but the third guy was probably a petty officer or warrant officer. He did the talking while the other two took charge of Sean and Angelo and their wounds.

"We got a call that there was some bad stuff going on out here. Some gunshots and other trouble. It appears whoever made the call was correct." He leaned in toward me slightly and lowered his voice. Tilting his head toward Pepé, he asked, "Is that man an enlisted U.S. Navy sailor?"

I shook my head. "Was, not is. He's already served his country and been honorably discharged. He just arrived here a couple of days ago. He decided to make Fernandina his new home, at least for now. I'm awfully glad he was here. I'd probably be dead twice over if it wasn't for him." I was suddenly interrupted by a voice that was becoming too familiar to me.

"Evening, Cyrus. Anything you need my help with?"

Officer Bill Crane from the Fernandina Beach Police had poked his head into the galley, which was starting to get crowded.

"No, thanks, Bill. At least not with those still living. But we have two dead bodies you're welcome to take charge of and see to it that they get to the county examiner's office."

"Can do, Cyrus. Those two make three tonight. That's three too many. I don't like to see this kind of thing happening in our town."

"I know what you mean, Bill," said the man Officer Crane had called Cyrus.

I didn't want to say anything to the Coast Guard officer, but I knew the thought was bouncing around in Bill Crane's head, too. I had been personally present at each of the three deaths that day, either during or soon after: Kendall Brody, Val, and Amelia, and I wasn't about to tell Crane that I had also been on the scene mere minutes after Brody's wife, Catherine, was murdered. He may have already suspected my connection to that one, though. From what Doyle Abaddon had insinuated to me, the local police were aware of the Fernandina underworld and chose to ignore it in exchange for cash, influence, and future favors. I wondered how high the corruption rose. I wanted to believe Crane was not an active part, but couldn't be completely sure yet.

Muff came over and stood next to me. "Sorry again, Jimmy. I hope you know I wouldn't leave you hanging out to dry like that. From the bump on my noggin and the Coasties that are here, you know I did what you asked as quick as I could. I'm just sorry it wasn't sooner."

"No harm done, Muff. It all worked out. Not so good for Curly and Slick, and even worse for the Sacketts, but none of it was your fault. I'm sorry you got bashed on the head. I know what that's like." I felt the bump on my head, smaller now but still weirdly soft.

"Yeah," he said. "I guess you're right. I'm glad to see you're in better shape than Sean and Angelo and *much* better than the Sacketts. I still feel bad, though, 'cause you were counting on me."

"And you came through, Muff. Will an extra five-spot make you feel better?"

"Gee, Jimmy. Yeah, that would be great."

"Fine. But you're going to have to wait a little while. I don't have it on me right now. I'm a little tight. But if you could loan me ten bucks, I can give you the five right away."

"Sure—hey, wait a minute ..."

We both laughed.

Things definitely can turn bad in a hurry when bullets start flying. It felt good to laugh. It meant I was still alive. Pain meant you were alive, too, but laughing was a much more pleasurable indicator.

I was grateful to have Muff, Pepé, and Dale Higgins, the nun with a gun, on my side.

Chapter 19

THE AFTERNOON SUN WAS drifting closer to the horizon, and Wendi and Gwynn were sitting in Jimmy's room in the ICU. Much of their time in Jimmy's room was spent in quiet reflection or small talk since Jimmy was not holding up his end of the conversation. They'd need to go find something to eat soon unless Hillary and Pepé brought something back for them. Suddenly, Jimmy moaned several times.

"What's he doing, Gwynn? Is he in pain?" Gwynn didn't know and shook her head.

Concerned, Wendi stood up and worked her way in between the IV tubes and the ventilator tube down his throat. She took Jimmy's hand in hers and stared at his face, searching for clues. She noticed that the corners of his mouth were turned up slightly in a small smile.

After a moment, Wendi turned and faced Gwynn, who had gotten up to stand next to her. Wendi knew that Gwynn could read the concern painted across her face and see the frustration from the impotence that filled her eyes. Gwynn smiled sympathetically and placed her hand over Wendi's hand as she held onto Jimmy's.

"If I had to guess, Wendi, I'd say he was laughing. Judging by that slight smile he's wearing, he's not in pain. We're out here worried sick about him, and he's somewhere inside there having a good time, laughing and carrying on. That's just so rude!"

Wendi's mouth opened to respond, and then she stopped, relaxed, and let the tension wash away. So far, it had been two days of non-stop worry and concern, topped off with a giant serving of helplessness. That was the worst part of this whole ordeal. Gwynn's light verbal swipe at Jimmy broke the tension and reminded Wendi that Jimmy was still with them and he was going to make a comeback. She was confident of that. For the moment, at least.

Gwynn eased back into her chair next to the bed. They had convinced the nurses to let them have two chairs next to the bed and to stand vigil over Jimmy in pairs rather than a single visitor at a time like the hospital originally mandated.

"Tonight, they're going to start weaning him off the sedative," Wendi said randomly, still standing alongside Jimmy's bed, her hand still holding his. Part of her felt she needed to maintain a physical connection to keep him with them; it was as if letting go of him physically would allow him leave in other ways. The doctors were upbeat about his prognosis and felt positive about his recovery once they took him off the sedative. Wendi wasn't as sure about the prognosis as they were.

"Mm-hmm," Gwynn responded wordlessly to Wendi's statement. There was nothing to add.

Wendi didn't look at Gwynn, keeping her eyes on Jimmy as she asked, "Do you think he'll be okay?"

"I do," Gwynn said without hesitation. "The doctors have said his vitals have been strong throughout the sedation period, and even though the induced coma is supposed to help his brain rest, his brain activity has remained at a fairly active level. That boy is on some kind of adventure in his dreams. Like Jimmy in Wonderland! But I believe that's a good sign, Wendi. As long as Robert and I have known him, he's always been a thinker. His brain is always working on the puzzles that his cases turn out to be. Who knows, maybe he'll solve something while he's stuck inside."

Wendi had noticed that Gwynn always called her husband Robert while everyone else called him Pepé. For his part, Pepé seemed to settle down whenever he was with Gwynn, becoming less of the "wild and crazy guy" and turning more introspective. It was like he took in the things happening around him and filed them away for closer examination later.

The two women were silent for a short time before Wendi broke the quiet again. She extricated her hand from Jimmy's after figuring out that he wasn't in pain and sat down.

"How do you do it?" Wendi asked Gwynn.

"Do what, dear?"

"Stay so positive. So upbeat. You're just so, so … unflappable." Wendi paused. "You know, I don't think I've ever used that word before, but that's the only one that fits. You, Gwynn, are unflappable."

Gwynn gave a little chuckle. "Thank you, but I'm far from unflappable. There are times when I'm very flappable. I run around like a chicken with my head cut off, or at least like a chicken with my neck on the chopping block! And I can't count the number of times Robert has caused me to dissolve into a puddle of tears and fears. Between his work with the police in Charleston and his time in the Navy, I never knew what the next day held for me, him, or us. You literally never knew if you'd have a husband the next day."

"I can't imagine that kind of life. That has to be so hard. How did you get from there to … here?" Wendi asked, spreading her hands apart like a model on the Price is Right revealing some fantastic item up for bidding.

Gwynn gave another little laugh. "You have a completely wrong impression of me, Wendi. I'm not in charge of anything, certainly not in charge or control of what's been going on in this hospital room the last couple of days. You're getting the wrong idea."

Wendi looked confused, and Gwynn could tell she was waiting for more explanation.

"I'm not in charge, Wendi, and I realize it. So, I let the One who *is* in charge do what He's going to do. And He always does what's best."

"You're talking about God, aren't you?"

"Mm-hmm. The Bible says His sheep know His voice and follow Him. Robert is one of His sheep, and he follows Him. Robert trusts Him to protect him in all situations."

Wendi had turned her head at these last words, and her gaze was fixed out the window somewhere. She started to speak softly. "I remember hearing those things when I was little, but I'm not a little girl anymore. Life's not that simple anymore."

The two women lapsed into silence again for a few heartbeats. The only sound in the room was the soft, rhythmic whooshing noise as Jimmy's ventilator made sure he received adequate oxygen while under sedation. The drugs they used to induce the coma also made his brain forget that he needed to breathe, which was why he needed the ventilator.

Wendi tucked her legs up under her as she sat next to the hospital bed where Jimmy lay completely motionless. After a bit, she spoke.

"I haven't talked with anyone about this stuff in a long time. I haven't been to church in years. The last time I went was for the funerals of my husband and mother-in-law. Before that … well, I can't remember when it was."

"Your wedding, maybe, or after?" Gwynn prompted.

Wendi thought for a minute, then raised one finger. "That's it. It was my wedding. But before that, I honestly couldn't say. It was probably when I was thirteen or fourteen. That was about the time I quit blindly accepting things and started questioning why some things were the way they were. It's not much different from now. Sitting here next to Jimmy, wondering and worrying about what's going to happen when they turn off the sedative and let him wake up."

"I believe he'll be fine," Gwynn said. "And worry won't change anything, you know. The Bible says, 'Don't worry about tomorrow; it can worry about itself. Each day has enough trouble of its own.'"

"I remember that," Wendi nodded. "But it's awfully hard not to worry about tomorrow."

: : : :

IT WAS WELL AFTER midnight before Muff, Dale, Pepé, and I got off Sackett's boat, *The Tortuga,* but at least none of us had to go to the police station for questioning, and none of us would spend the night in jail. And most importantly, we all walked off under our own steam.

We were just meandering along the dock, not in any hurry to get anywhere. None of us had any place we needed to be. Dale Higgins had a bed waiting for her back at the Keystone Hotel, although tonight, the room would be nearly empty – no Amelia or Val to share the suite.

"I'm exhausted," Dale said. "I hope you all don't mind, but I have got to go to bed. I simply can't take anymore tonight. This has been more stress than I've ever experienced in all my years with the nuns. And that includes when my father died."

Pepé offered to walk her up the street to her hotel. I had my apartment to go to, and I had offered to let Pepé stay at my place on the couch as long as he needed. He said he'd be back in just a few minutes to 'hit the rack.'

"The torture rack, you mean," I said after him. "I've slept on that couch before, too!" My remark made him laugh. The two young people quickly disappeared into the night, leaving Muff and me standing at the edge of the marina. I realized I didn't have any idea where Muff Benjamin lived.

"What's your plan for the rest of the night, Muff?" I asked.

"After all the excitement, I'll probably just go home and sack out. You?"

"Probably the same." I paused briefly before asking, "You know my memory is still a great big blank, don't you, Muff?"

"Yeah, sure."

"So … sorry I have to ask, but where do you live?" I asked, apologizing for needing to ask the question. After all, the guy had gotten clobbered on my account.

"Hey, don't worry about it. I have a room in a boarding house over on Sixth Street. The Strickland place. It's not as glamorous as your place, but it works for me." I didn't know if he was ribbing me or not, but I let it go.

"Since most of the other roomers are early risers and I'm not," he continued, "I don't even have to fight for the bathroom. Usually. And Mrs. Strickland cooks up some pretty good suppers, plus she makes a real nice Sunday dinner."

We had reached the end of the dock and were back at the junction of Front and Centre Streets. I could still hear the sound of people hooting and laughing over at the Ship's Galley, their laughter and noise drifting across to where we stood. They had no idea what had gone down just a few hundred yards away on one of the marina's boats that evening.

"What time do they close?" I asked, nodding my head toward the lights and sound from the nautical-themed bar and grill.

"I'm not sure they really do," Muff answered. "Officially, they probably close at two or three a.m., but if people are still partying or eating or a good band's playing—"

"They have live music there?" I asked, surprised that there might be room inside for a stage.

"Sometimes," Muff replied. "Sometimes they get some of the Black artists from down at American Beach. Some of them do a half-a-night over there and a half-a-night here. It's a little more sedate over here, but …"

"This is sedate?" The hooting and hollering from within the little shack on the dock was rising and falling like the waves on the shore.

"Compared to the jumping and jiving that goes on at the club over on American Beach? Oh, yeah. When they get somebody like Cab Calloway or Duke Ellington over there, the place is packed all night."

"I had no idea," I said, and I really didn't. I probably did once upon a time, but that was another part of me that had fallen out of my head recently. I let Muff fill in the gaps.

"It's been going strong for a dozen years now. They're calling it 'The Negro Ocean Playground' and a place for 'Recreation and Relaxation without Humiliation.' Folks from Jacksonville, Savannah, and Atlanta all make their way here, especially in the summer. In the fall, like it is now, it's a little quieter, but there's still a good contingent that comes up from Jacksonville. There's talk about a new place opening up next year – Evan's Ocean Rendezvous. It's going to be right down on the beach. Go for a little walk outside, and you're right there on the sand."

"And this club that's open now is someplace you've been? I asked.

Muff looked embarrassed. "Me? Naw. I sometimes catch the acts when they play here in the Ship's Galley." He looked around and then down at his feet. "They'd never let me in down there. Not that I'd try, you understand."

I thought back to the morning I had to catch the train from Baldwin to Fernandina and encountered the "WHITES ONLY" sign above the water fountain at the train station. The very thought of denying someone a drink of water because of their skin color made me angry. It came as no surprise, however, that the opposite would be true, too – the juke joints in American Beach weren't for white folks. To circumvent that, places like the Ship's Galley hired the Black artists who played at American Beach to come up to Fernandina to entertain, ironically in the same places where they couldn't get a sandwich, a beer, or use the restroom.

That'll change someday, I thought. *I hope.*

"You want to grab an early breakfast or a late supper at the Ship's Galley?"

Muff thought about it briefly before shaking his head. "Thanks, but no thanks, Jimmy. I'm bushed. I'll be lucky to make the few blocks up to my place without curling up on somebody's lawn for a nap."

"Well, if you do, someone will probably wake you up asking for a pot of gold, thinking they've caught a leprechaun!"

"Won't they be surprised?" Muff responded with a laugh. Then he got a serious look on his face that the streetlights illuminated. "I'm serious, Jimmy. I can't remember the last time I was this tired. I know getting conked on the noggin didn't help, but I don't know how you private investigators do it, living on the edge, your life always hanging in the balance, people shooting at you or trying to stab you to death."

I didn't want to tell him you get used to it because you don't. The truth was, I was exhausted, too. After the high from the rush of adrenaline, your system crashes big time when your body flushes the stimulant out of its bloodstream.

Instead of admitting I wasn't Superman, I said, "Some of us deal with it better than others. I'll see you around, Muff."

Muff turned to walk home but turned back to say, "Goodnight, Jimmy. Take it easy and be careful walking home."

When I turned back to tell him to do the same, he was already gone. I shrugged my shoulders.

I guess he was in a hurry.

I turned back toward the Ship's Galley and decided to go in for a bite to eat and to catch some jumping jive music.

What the heck. How badly could they ruin eggs, bacon, and toast?

Chapter 20

WENDI AND GWYNN WERE still sitting next to Jimmy's bed when the nurse came into the room. Stepping around the two women, she announced, "I'm going to start slowing the rate of the sedative drip into his IV." She fiddled with the little valve at the bottom of the plastic bag hanging on the pole next to Jimmy's bed. Picking up a clipboard hanging on the end of the bed near his feet, she wrote some notes on it before hanging it back on the bed.

As she moved toward the door to leave, Wendi asked her, "How long do you think it'll take before he wakes up?"

The nurse paused in the doorway. "It usually only takes about a day for someone to wake up from an induced coma. But I've also seen it take several days. Everybody's different. And 'waking up' is different for each person. You should ask the doctor the next time he stops in. He'll be able to give you a better answer." She hit the door opener and was gone.

Wendi got up and walked over to look at the bags of fluid hanging from the IV pole. "I have no idea what any of these meds are," she said to Gwynn.

"The one she fiddled with is obviously the sedative keeping him asleep," Gwynn answered. "What's it say on the bag?"

Wendi cautiously examined the bag without touching it. "Prop, PentoB, and ThioP. Do you have any idea what those are?"

"I had a friend once who was an ICU nurse. Her husband worked with Robert on the police force. I think those drugs are propofol, pentobarbital, and thiopental. The other things hanging on the pole are probably saline and nutrients to keep him hydrated and fed." She waited to see if Wendi had more questions.

Rather than questions, though, Wendi started pacing around the room. "I'm so tired of sitting and doing nothing. I have to go find Pepé and Hillary before I lose my mind. Is it all right with you if I step out for a bit and leave you with Jimmy?"

"I'll be fine for a little while. It's not like Jimmy's going to suddenly jump and run off to play pickleball. When you find Robert, ask him to come in and sit with me, okay?"

"I'll do that," Wendi answered. She paused as she opened the door to leave, like she was going to say or ask something else but then changed her mind and continued out to the waiting area without further conversation.

The two men were sitting in the waiting area, leaning forward, heads together, talking in hushed voices.

"Hey," she said as she approached them.

They looked up and smiled. "Hey, yourself," Pepé replied.

Both men stood to greet her as she neared. They were both from a generation that stood when a woman came into the room.

Hillary gave his former daughter-in-law a quick hug. "Do you want to sit with us?"

She shook her head, saying, "I'm tired of sitting." Hillary returned to his seat, but Pepé remained standing with her. Wendi said, "I was wondering if you'd come up with anything else on Abaddon."

"I'm looking," the former cop answered, "and I've got a couple of friends from the Fernandina Police and the Nassau Sheriff's office running some internal searches for me. The only thing I've got for sure is that traffic stop from 1948 in Fernandina that I found. It's not much, but that stop is like a fingerprint; it puts him in the system. It would be a whole lot better if I had all ten of his fingerprints, though, you know?"

"I think so. Has Abaddon been living here the whole time? You said he was from Canada and became a naturalized citizen in 1946, right?"

"That's what I said, but that may not be completely true or the entire story."

Wendi's eyebrows shot up. "Tell me more."

"He may have told people he became a naturalized citizen, but I can't find any record that he did. The people helping me haven't found any evidence yet, either. Even if he was, though, if he was committing crimes in the late 40s, he could have been deported for moral turpitude."

"Moral turpitude?" Hillary interjected. "That's an old term."

"Yeah," Pepé answered. "It could be used for a serious crime like murder or aggravated assault, but it could also be for – and I quote – 'a quality of dishonesty or other immorality that is determined by a court to be present in the commission of a criminal offense.' End quote. So, what does that mean, Professor?"

"That means if a court determined he was not of upstanding moral fiber, and that lack of good breeding and character was what caused him to commit criminal activity, then rather than incarcerate him in our jurisdiction, they could repatriate him to Canada."

Pepé looked questioningly from Hillary to Wendi. "You try," he said to Wendi.

"If The Man was arrested and the court said he was bad to the bone, they could just send him back to the Great White North rather than spending our dollars to keep him locked up down here."

"I believe that's exactly what I said," Hillary responded.

Wendi just smiled at that and asked Pepé, "Is someone looking into him from that angle?"

"Yeah, I've got someone looking into it. But now's when I really wish Jimmy could do more than just lie there in the bed. He loves poking through archives."

Wendi took a step away and turned her back on the two men. She wanted Jimmy to do more than just lie in bed, too. Much more. She pulled a tissue from her pocket and quickly dabbed at her eyes before turning around.

"Okay!" she said, trying to sound cheerful but it came out a little forced. "I was supposed to tell you, Pepé, that Gwynn would like you to come in and sit with her in Jimmy's room."

"Great," he said with zero enthusiasm. "Can you write me a note that says you didn't find me right away? So, she knows I wasn't ignoring her? I'm as tired of sitting around as anyone."

"I'll tell you what," Wendi answered. "You get a note from Gwynn that says you can come with us, and we'll wait for you."

"Deal."

: : : :

NOT ONLY DID THE Ship's Galley *not* mess up my breakfast, but they actually did a pretty good job of making it. The cook – the guy who was also a bartender and bouncer – whipped up the scrambled eggs with ham and toast in a jiffy, just the way they should be done. *I'm no slouch in the kitchen, but I'm no … that guy, you know … who always says … Aargh! This is getting really frustrating!*

I was sitting close enough that I was able to see the cook's secret: a couple of dashes of hot sauce just before plating the eggs and ham. Not enough to make my head sweat, but just enough to give the eggs a little style and pizazz. He also only used eggs – no milk or cream, water, or liquid of any sort. Just whip the eggs up, pour them on the hot flat-top griddle, toss in a handful of diced ham, and after a couple of chops and flips, you're done. You actually need to put your bread down in the toaster *before* you put the eggs on the griddle. Drop the toast, make the eggs, butter the toast while the eggs enjoy one last little sizzle, and plate the eggs and toast together in one smooth motion. Slide it all out to the customer, and wait for the smiles all around.

At least until somebody comes into the joint you don't want to see.

"Marlowe. You're quickly becoming a thorn in my side."

"I'm glad you think so, Mr. Abaddon. I'd hate to think all my efforts were going to waste."

"Always with the jokes. You need to learn that not everything is funny, Marlowe. Sticking your nose in my business is not funny. I thought you would have learned that by now, but apparently, you're a slow learner."

"And who's going to pick up the slack in my tutoring, *Mister* Abaddon?" I emphasized the Mister, a reminder that he had tried – and failed – to teach me manners on a previous encounter. "My tutors, Angelo and Sean, are currently indisposed after trying to kill me and my associates."

"Your *tutors*, as you refer to them, are getting patched up at the hospital and will soon be back at work following my orders, possibly as early as tomorrow. As I'm sure you know by now, they were merely out for a stroll on the docks when they heard gunfire and stopped to investigate on the off-chance that a citizen in distress might need their assistance. They had nothing to do with the two killings on Mr. Sackett's boat; they weren't even there when they happened. You know I'm right, don't you, Mr. Marlowe?"

I said nothing. My eggs and toast were cold now, but it no longer mattered because I had lost my appetite.

Abaddon continued talking. "You and your companions were there when it happened, though, weren't you? In fact, assuming the police told me correctly, that young sailor was directly responsible for Val Sackett's death. And I have no reason to doubt the veracity of the police department's statements, do I, Mr. Marlowe? My 'associates,' if I can borrow your term, were merely checking on the safety of the people on board the boat where they heard shooting and put themselves at perilous risk to apprehend the shooter – or shooters – until local law enforcement personnel arrived. If anyone should be worried about consequences, it should be you and yours, Mr. Marlowe. My men, acting as Good Samaritans, were merely defending themselves after being fired upon. Who fired on who is evidenced by who is at the hospital and who … is … not." He drew out the end of his statement for emphasis.

He made it look like we were the offenders and his men were innocent bystanders who jumped in to protect persons unknown who might be in duress on Sackett's boat. I couldn't believe he was trying to make that bird fly.

"Self-defense? That's what you're going with? Your guys are the wronged parties? I guarantee that if it weren't for the sailor you mentioned and the girl – the one your men were trying to kidnap and bring back to you – if it hadn't been for my friends, I wouldn't be here, and we wouldn't be having this conversation. I would be laid out at the funeral parlor with the Sacketts. Let me assure you, Mr. Abaddon, your guys are lucky they're just getting sewn up and not being prepped for a long dirt nap."

"We obviously have a difference of opinion, Mr. Marlowe," Abaddon said with a smirk. I wanted to take my plate of eggs and toast and smash it into his face. Because of him and his assassins, two more people had died, bringing the total to four: first Catherine and Kendall Brody and now Amelia and Val Sackett. Unfortunately, the link tying his goons to the Sacketts was tenuous at best, and, as an eyewitness, I knew that the Sacketts' deaths could not be directly attributed to Sean and Angelo.

Abaddon's back was to Wendi as she walked into the Ship's Galley during the sudden lull in our discussion. Seeing me, she said, "What the heck, Jimmy? Four bodies have come through the hospital morgue, and now the Bobbsey Twins are up at the hospital getting put back in working order, one with a bullet hole in his shoulder and the other with a shattered wrist—" She saw Abaddon and stopped speaking.

"Hi, Wendi. Mr. Abaddon was just telling me that his guys were trying to *apprehend* whoever was shooting on the boat. They were innocently walking by and ended up getting shot while selflessly protecting others. He's claiming they drew their weapons in self-defense. They should be lauded as heroes, not castigated as criminals."

She looked from me to Abaddon and back to me. "He's kidding, right? No one in their right mind would believe that load of horse manure. I talked to one of the cops, and he told me you were there, Jimmy, right in the middle of things again. Is that true?"

"I was there, and what Abad—*Mr.* Abaddon says is technically true. Surprisingly, Angelo and Sean were *not* responsible for the deaths of Val and Amelia Sackett, and it is also true that they weren't even on board the boat when those two deaths occurred. Val killed Amelia in cold blood and then tried to add me to the tally for good measure, but Pepé intervened on my behalf. Whether Curly and Slick felt they were being good citizens by becoming involved in what was going on isn't for me to say. I *can* tell you that Angelo tried to use me for a human shield and was about to shoot me in the head, but Pepé shot him in the wrist first. Sean was taking aim at me and about to finish what Angelo started when Dale Higgins popped up and plugged him in the shoulder. It's amazing how much more docile people are when they're bleeding from bullet wounds."

"Well, I just plugged those bullet holes, and the police are going to turn those two mooks loose after they finish asking them a few questions," Wendi replied, sparks practically shooting from her eyes.

"In that case," Abaddon said, "I should probably go and collect my employees. I'll need to tuck them in and make sure they get some rest after such a difficult day protecting the citizenry of Fernandina." He tipped his fedora to Wendi, and I watched him disappear into the throng of revelers still partying at the Ship's Galley. He worked his way through the crowd to the door and slipped out.

I stared at the gathering for a minute, marveling at the tête-à-tête that had just taken place. I called the cook/bartender/bouncer over and asked him if he could make me another order of eggs since the first one had gone cold while Abaddon and I talked. "Don't worry," I told him. "I'll pay for it. And bring an order for Miss Carter here, too."

"No problem," was all he said, and he got to it. Wendi climbed onto the barstool at the counter next to me and leaned against me. "I'm sorry I couldn't be there with you."

"Don't worry about it. I had Pepé and Dale. It turned out they were all I needed. Did you know the nuns taught Dale how to shoot the heads off of snakes?"

"They did?"

"Yup. The girl is a regular Annie Oakley."

After a surprisingly good breakfast, Wendi dropped me off at my place. Then she went home for a few hours of sleep before she had to check in at the hospital and see if they needed her that day. Such is the life of a nurse on call.

I went up to my apartment and discovered it was empty; there was no Pepé on the couch. He had told me he was walking Dale up to the Keystone Hotel, where she had been staying with Val and Amelia. It was also where I had stayed to recover after Val hit me with the blackjack, or rather where Val and Amelia kept me locked up after he tried to break my head for a second time in a week.

I wondered if the bill for the suite was open or paid in advance and how long Dale would stay since she no longer needed a whole suite of rooms for just herself. I figured Pepé had stayed there rather than on my ratty couch, and who could blame him? I figured they either stayed up talking, or she invited him to stay in one of the unused bedrooms since he didn't have an official place to stay. I wasn't worried about hanky-panky since she was completely exhausted, and Pepé probably was, too.

Alone in my room, I took off my shirt and lay down on my bed. It was already the wee hours of the morning but still night and still pitch dark. Not even boys with paper routes or roosters were up yet.

I listened to the quiet outside and let my eyes get heavy. My eyes closed slowly for a second … and reopened.

The morning sun was pouring in the window. I couldn't remember sleeping, but it was obvious that hours had slid by; once again, my brain hadn't recorded them. I had no recollection of dreams, no memory of waking and going back to sleep several times; it was just a quick scenery change – from one moment to another. The previous scene had finished, and now we were on to a new one after barely fading to black.

That had been happening to me ever since I woke up in the hospital with my head wrapped in gauze. It was starting to worry me. A single night without dreaming or really sleeping was one thing, but multiple nights in a row with no memory of sleeping was another.

My thoughts were interrupted by a knock on the door.

"Just a minute."

Before I reached the door, it opened.

Chapter 21

I WAS HALFWAY ACROSS the floor when Wendi strolled into my apartment, looking like she'd had the best night's sleep of her life. She was wearing a light blue dress that ended a couple of inches below her knees, along with a white button-up sweater as a hedge against cool breezes. She carried a newspaper in one hand and her pocketbook in the other.

"Why are you not up and dressed yet?" she asked, a question that should have been rhetorical since I was dressed and standing right in front of her, but I answered anyway.

"I'm up, or vertical, at least. And I have my pants on." I didn't want to admit that I had slept in my trousers last night. *Or was it this morning?* Either way, she didn't need to know about my sleeping apparel. Every relationship needs a little mystery.

"Did you sleep?" she asked.

"That's the sixty-four dollar question. I closed my eyes at some point, and the next thing I knew, it was morning."

"Did you dream?"

"Dream?"

"Yeah. You know, that thing people do when they sleep? It's part of the restoration process our bodies go through. Dreams let you figure things out or even go a little crazy sometimes, so you don't go crazy when you're awake. They reveal things you're worried about. You know – dreams."

"To sleep. Perchance to dream. Or perchance not."

"That's not the way the quote goes."

"I know, but I honestly can't remember sleeping and dreaming since I woke up in the hospital. I close my eyes, and suddenly, it's a new day."

"Are you tired?"

"No more than usual."

"It's not good for you to not dream. Dreaming is critical to your health, both mental and physical."

"So you've said."

"I'm not joking, Jimmy. Your brain needs time to heal itself, especially after a traumatic head injury with a concussion. Someday in the future, we may have a better handle on how to effectively treat injuries like yours, but for now, rest is the best treatment we can suggest. Rest, and avoid getting hit in the head again. You might have heard that they've figured out that a boxer who gets three concussions should be restricted from any more fights. I don't know how many concussions you've had in your lifetime, but you've had at least one big one now. You're going to have to be more careful from here on out."

"So, that's our plan for today? To sit around and talk about my broken head? Or is there something else you'd prefer to do?" I asked, drifting back toward my bedroom to throw on a fresh shirt.

"Well, I brought the car because I thought we might take a little drive up Highway 17 to Kingsland. There's a new restaurant I thought we could try. It's brand new. They just recently opened their doors. I read an article in the newspaper about it."

From the next room, I hollered, "I usually like to let them get the kinks all worked out before I go, but if you want to go, we'll go. What's the name of the place?"

"It's called Steffens."

It felt like I'd been struck by lightning. My knees became weak, there was a sudden ringing in my ears, and I couldn't catch my breath. I sat on the edge of my bed, causing the springs to squeak loudly.

"Jimmy? Are you okay? You're not going back to bed, are you?"

I tried to say I was okay, but nothing came out. My mouth was as dry as sand; I couldn't even work up enough spit to swallow. Suddenly, Wendi's head peeked around the door. She caught one look at me, and her eyes popped wide open. She rushed over to where I sat.

"What's the matter, Jimmy? Tell me what's happening. What are you feeling?"

I shook my head and motioned for a glass of water. She hurried out and came back in less than thirty seconds with a glass of water. "Can you hold onto it and drink it?" she asked.

I nodded and held out my hands. She gave me the glass, and I drank it with all the finesse of a toddler trying to feed himself for the very first time. I tipped the glass back too far, and water ran down my chin and all over my clean shirt. But it was cool, clear water, and my throat felt instantly better. Miraculously, everything began to relax. I slowed my drinking down and got the glass under control. I held the tumbler in one hand, resting it on my knee. With my other hand, I wiped my mouth on the sleeve of my shirt. As I did, I felt the roughness of my beard stubble and absently noted that I should shave before we went anywhere.

"Can you tell me what just happened?" Wendi asked.

I cleared my throat, and I said, "I dunno. It was like I stuck a fork in a light socket. It was a big jolt from the top of my head down to my toes."

"What were we talking about when it happened?" she asked.

"You had just told me about going to a new restaurant in Kingsland. Steffens, you said?"

"That's right. It's right on the edge of town, about five miles from the swing bridge over the St. Marys River. The Blue Bridge."

At the mention of the Blue Bridge, my head started to swim again, and black dots swam in front of my eyes like a swarm of black flies by the river at low tide. "Help me lie down," I whispered.

She gripped my hands and let me lie back at a slow pace. Then she sat down next to me before curling up alongside me, her mouth near my ear.

"What's going on, Jimmy?" she said quietly, her mouth so close I could feel her warm breath on my ear. At any other time, I would have found it very sexy, but there was nothing erotic about my situation.

I kept my eyes tightly closed as I said, "I dunno." My tongue and speech felt and sounded a little thick. "When you mentioned the restaurant and the bridge, something in my head reacted. There's something about those places …"

"Okay. You just lie there. I'll get you another glass of water, all right?"

My eyes were closed, and I swear Wendi was only gone for a heartbeat. I became aware of her return when I felt her lie down next to me again.

"Let me know when you want another drink, and I'll help you sit up," she said. I gave the smallest of nods but didn't try to sit up, talk, or drink. After a few minutes, I opened my eyes. I looked up at the poorly-painted, embossed tin ceiling above my bed. The once-white paint was too thin in some spots, too thick in others, and non-existent in others. I hoped I hadn't painted it; if so, it was not a good example of my finesse with a paintbrush.

I lifted my hands up so they were hovering in the air over my prone torso, and Wendi slid off the bed and took my hands in hers. She pulled slowly and steadily, and I gradually came up to a sitting position. After a minute with my head above my heart, I held out one hand and said, "Water, please," keeping hold of her hand with my free hand.

She obliged, and I drank about half the glass. After handing it back, I asked, "Do I know these two places? The Blue Bridge and Steffens?"

"Steffens just opened up, and I mean *just*. But I'm sure you've been across the Blue Bridge hundreds of times. You've told me more than once that you'd like to build a house next to it someday."

I felt a little zing in my head but not so bad this time. Either it wasn't as intense, or I was getting used to whatever was making my head twirl around the room. I put both hands on my knees and forced myself into an upright position. As I did, Wendi stayed close, keeping one hand on my elbow and her other hand poised to grab me wherever was handy if I fell. She slowly backed up as I came to a standing position. Hopefully, she could stop me from landing on the floor headfirst.

"If I fall, just push me backward, and I'll fall back on the bed," I said in a husky voice. I wondered if I sounded sexy. *Probably not.*

"You've always been a pushover, and you know it," she replied, but her expression gave away her concern.

I turned my head slightly to look at her and noticed how close her face was to mine. I leaned toward her and raised my eyebrows. She paused, her eyes searching mine briefly, and then she gave me a quick kiss.

"Feeling better?" Wendi asked.

I nodded and said, "I think a ride in the country would be good medicine, don't you agree, Dr. Carter?"

"Fine. Let's get your coat and hat and be on our way," she replied.

The ride was uneventful; other than a brief disagreement about who was going to drive, an argument I lost quickly. Either she drove, or she was taking me back up to my room. I kept my eyes closed much of the way, and somehow we arrived in almost no time, even though I knew it had to take almost an hour. The "going" with no sense of time or distance was happening more frequently.

I didn't say anything about it in the car to Wendi, but my trouble with time was really starting to bother me. If I thought about being somewhere, I soon found myself there, but without any memory of the "getting there." Was this what teleporting was like? Or was I dreaming? Maybe I hadn't even woken up. I could still be lying in my hospital bed with my head swathed in gauze. I could have dreamed everything that happened after Dr. Floyd unwrapped my head and gave me that hypodermic with the dull needle. This could all be a dream caused by whatever drug Dr. Feelgood had injected into me. *I could even be dreaming up Wendi!*

I pinched my leg through my pants. *Ouch!* No, that felt real enough. Unless… could I dream about causing myself simple pain? People in the movies always say, "Pinch me," to prove they're awake, but what if that was all part of the dream? What if it was a stupid line written by a $35-a-week writer in the 1930s or 40s with no research behind it? I decided pinching yourself only worked if you were already awake, which proved nothing.

Steffens suddenly rose up in front of us on the south edge of town. I saw the sign looming by the road before I saw the building. It said *Café* on the left side and had a pig in a chef's hat on the right. Underneath the pig, it declared simply, "STEFFENS." The sign hovered over a cluster of red gas pumps with white bubble-tops.

The restaurant building itself was set back from the gas pumps and sported a big yellow sign that stretched from one end of the restaurant to the other with two rows of text. On top in the middle, big bold letters announced redundantly,

STEFFENS. Right underneath in italics, it proclaimed *Air Conditioning*. The left side of the bottom tier of the sign advertised the Restaurant, while the right side extolled their Souvenirs. The building sported a red metal roof, or at least it *had* been red at some point. Some gray showed through where the red had come off. Some of the red could also have been rust, but I wasn't climbing up for a closer look. From the state of the roof, I got the feeling this wasn't a new building.

The parking lot was jammed with cars, which felt correct and normal to me. I don't know why it seemed normal since it was a new eatery, and I'd never been there before. It looked like a two-story building, but the second floor was windowless – at least, from the front – and I figured the top portion was only used for storage or maybe a small office. The first floor had plenty of windows: about eight across the brick front, and double doors right in the middle of the front—red doors to match the roof's color. For some reason, I hadn't been expecting a two-story building or gas pumps, but I wasn't quite sure what I was expecting.

Wendi parked the car, and we went inside. We decided not to wait for a booth or table and slid onto the first two side-by-side stools at the counter. Our coffee and water appeared quickly, and even as I perused the menu, I already knew what I wanted: Ms. Helen's biscuits and gravy. I must have seen them on the menu as I looked, and they stuck in my brain because they sounded good, but I felt as if I had ordered them before. *But that's impossible.*

Another couple sat down on the stools next to us. While they waited for their coffee, we introduced ourselves. They lived right on the Florida/Georgia line, right next to the St. Marys River. His name was Knud Olfort, and she was his wife, Nellie VanZant Olfort. They owned the Riverside Motel and St. Marys Liquors. Their motel and package store were located mere yards from the Blue Bridge on the Florida side. The liquor store got its name because it was on the banks of the St. Marys River, not from the town of St. Marys, located about ten miles northeast in Georgia. The liquor store was just barely on the Florida side, but it meant you didn't have to go all the way to Yulee to wet your whistle on a Sunday. Coming from the north, your car tires left Georgia as they climbed up onto the narrow Blue Bridge, and they deposited you in the Sunshine State on the south side of the river. The de facto border between the two Atlantic coast states, the St. Marys River and the bridge that spans it, are a quick five miles from Kingsland.

Camden County, Georgia, was a dry county before Prohibition and even after, until 1938. After liquor was deemed worthy of being sold again, Camden County was still under the jurisdiction of a Sunday Blue Law—no alcohol sales on the Lord's Day. That meant there was no place to buy a bottle of your favorite alcoholic flavor after church—but Florida was much more progressive. Hence the two establishments owned by the Olforts.

Knud and Nellie had seen the handwriting on the wall and figured correctly that people would be happy to take a little Sunday drive, cross the Blue Bridge, purchase a bottle, and drive back home to enjoy it. How ironic (or appropriate?) that both the law against Sunday liquor sales and the means around it were blue: a quick trip to the Blue Bridge to circumvent a Blue Law.

The waitress brought my biscuits and gravy, along with Wendi's eggs, bacon, and toast. As we chewed, we talked a little, but mostly we just enjoyed our food in silence. I was troubled by the names of the people sitting next to us, the Olforts. There was something about their names that was knocking on a door in the back of my head.

Something told me Nellie didn't belong there. I got an odd sense of doom from her, even though I don't generally believe in omens or portents and the like. There was some connection between her, the St. Marys River, and the Blue Bridge, but I just couldn't connect the dots. The more I tried, the worse my head felt.

Mrs. Olfort was friendly enough, but her husband, Knud, was pretty close-mouthed. She said, "Don't pay him no mind; he's a very private person." I thought it was ironic that a guy who owned a hotel and a liquor store and made his living from interacting with people would be so close-mouthed and withdrawn. He looked sad and angry at the same time: sangry.

We didn't linger long after we finished, mostly because there was a steady stream of people who wanted to get in and try the food. The place was run by the Steffens family, and the word was out that they were serving up good portions of good Southern comfort food. It was like having Sunday dinner at your grandma's house every day of the week.

Wendi and I wandered through the crammed parking lot, looking at all the cars sporting Georgia and Florida license plates, which was to be expected at a place so close to the state line. I also saw a couple of cars with plates identifying them as having strayed from North and South Carolina. I doubted they had come down just to try the food, but you never knew. Some people liked to get on US Highway 17 and just drive until the sun went down, find a motel, and then head back the next day.

Wendi had parked near the highway, and as I walked to the car, I looked to the north, toward downtown Kingsland. Staring off in that direction, I could see Elmo's Café about a block away, another place for good eats. Turning to face the south and the way we had come, all I saw were tall pines that were the perfect size and straightness for telephone poles and a two-lane ribbon of highway that stretched straight away, fading into the horizon. Even though the Blue Bridge wasn't visible from where I stood in front of Steffens, I knew it was out there.

I had an urge, like a tugging in my chest, saying, "Home is that way." I tried to rationalize the feeling, telling myself, *Of course, home is that way; my apartment is in Fernandina.* But something about the Blue Bridge said home, too. I saw a sudden image in my mind's eye of a dew-covered grassy yard as seen at dawn from a porch. I knew I was sitting on that porch, and Wendi was beside me. More than the image was the feeling that accompanied the image of the early-morning vista. Whenever and wherever that image had been formed, it carried good feelings, and I wanted to go back there.

In the image, a white sack out by the mailbox caught my attention, and I knew the white sack was bad. And then the image faded away.

"Well, you sure were quiet. You rode all the way back to Fernandina without saying a word. You just stared out the window. It's like you weren't even in the car with me," Wendi said.

I looked around and realized we were in downtown Fernandina, parked across from the Palace Saloon and my apartment. I had lost another chunk of time. Or had I just stepped from one dream into another?

"I need to go to the hospital for a while," Wendi said. "I should be back in time to have supper with you, though. Will that work for you, Jimmy?"

"Sure. I have some … work stuff to do," I lied. Or maybe I did. I couldn't be sure anymore. My grip on reality seemed to be getting more and more tenuous.

I stepped out of the car and looked up at the windows where my apartment was. When I turned around, Wendi and the car were gone. I couldn't remember her saying goodbye or driving off. Another gap.

I had told her I had work to do, but I started walking further up Centre Street, away from the waterfront and my apartment. I had just passed the Methodist Church with its massive white columns when a teenage girl stepped out from behind a tree and asked, "Are you Mr. Marlowe? The private Investigator?"

I figured she was about fifteen or sixteen, with light brownish hair and cute features—not what you'd call pretty – just cute. She still had time to grow into her beauty, though. She wore a plaid skirt and a white blouse and carried a leather bookbag. From the way the bag hung, I knew it had something heavy inside. *Probably school books.*

"Yeah, I'm Jimmy Marlowe." Inside me, a battle raged. When I told the girl my name, it felt more wrong in my mouth than it had since the day I woke up in the hospital. Marlowe isn't my last name, but I can't for the life of me remember my real one! *I want my name back!*

"What can I do for you, Miss …" and I waited for her to fill in her missing last name. She did not oblige me, revealing only her given name.

"My name is Darla. Do you know Muff Benjamin?"

"Muff? Sure. I know him. Why?"

"I'm trying to find him. How much would you charge me to help me find him?"

"Find Muff? I wouldn't charge you anything, darling. I know where he lives, and if he's not there, we can just come back down here to this area. He usually just hangs out here and waits for me to show up. What do you wanna find Muff for?"

"It's personal."

"Well, Darla, if you want my help in finding Muff, you'll need to tell me the nature of your search. That's the way it works with private investigators. We need our customers to be open and honest with us, and not hold back information. So, I'll ask you again: why do you need to find Muff?"

"He's my brother."

Whoa. Muff has a family? I mean, everybody has a mom and dad somewhere, but I never thought of Muff with brothers and sisters. Of course, I couldn't remember Muff any further back than twenty-four hours.

"Muff is your brother, Darla? He's obviously your older brother. How old are you?"

"I'm eighteen."

"Try again," I answered. "And this time, let's try being honest."

Darla wasn't wearing any makeup or carrying a purse. I felt like an eighteen-year-old would be trying out lipstick and rouge and starting to carry around the accouterments of a grown woman. She'd need a purse to cart them around, not a leather book valise.

"Fine. I'm nearly sixteen. Muff is the oldest in our family. There are twelve of us kids. I'm not even the youngest. I have two younger brothers."

"Okay. Now we're getting somewhere. Why didn't you tell me your real age to begin with?"

"I didn't want you to think I was just a dumb kid. It's just that … it's important I find Muff."

"Let's go down to Thompson's Luncheonette. Muff's been known to frequent that little gastronomic delight on occasion."

We went back down the street the short distance and went in. I looked around but didn't see Muff. We went back out and went back up the street in the general direction of the boarding house where I knew Muff lived. We checked in at a couple of other stores as we walked, but no one had seen Muff that day.

When we were about a half-block from the Strickland house where Muff rented a room, I saw him come out of the gate to the side yard and start down the walk toward us. I didn't say anything to Darla at first. I wanted to see how she reacted.

Nothing.

"There he is," I said as we got a little closer.

"Oh. Yes, it is," she replied.

"Hey, Muff!" I called out. "I've been looking for you."

"What's up, Jimmy? Have you got a case, or are you going to the junior high mixer on Friday night?" Muff answered with a laugh. He had almost reached the corner of Centre and Sixth Street, where Darla and I were waiting

"Whattaya talking about, Muff? Don't you recognize her? Your own sister?"

"Sister? I ain't got no sister, Jimmy. Just two older brothers."

Alarm bells began clanging in my head. I turned to Darla, who had reached into her leather book bag and pulled out an ugly, black .32 caliber handgun, letting the book valise fall to the ground by her feet. My brain shouted, *Gun!* long before my mouth could form the word.

Darla swung her arm around and fired the gun three times at Muff, who fell back in a heap. Just as quickly, the teenager turned on me. I expected the gun to start spitting bullets and began tensing up, but then the impossible happened. Darla flipped the gun around and handed it to me, butt first. I took it with trembling hands and held it, cradled in front of me. All I could do was stare at the instrument of death in my hands.

With a flat voice devoid of any shred of emotion, Darla said, "When the cops come, tell them I did it. I won't answer any questions, though. Just tell them I did it."

I woke up from my inactivity and shoved the gun in my coat pocket, trying not to rub it or put my fingerprints on it. I grabbed her arm, swung her around, and shoved her to the ground. She landed hard on her butt. I screamed in her face, "Sit there and don't move!"

Turning back to Muff, who I figured was dead already, I was shocked to see him sitting up and watching me.

"Muff! How bad are you hurt?" I shouted, my bloodstream flooded with adrenaline.

"She only hit me once, Jimmy. But … it's not good."

He opened up his jacket, and I could see his white shirt already soaked in blood. The bullet had hit him in the right side of his chest, and every time he breathed, bubbles and foam appeared from the hole. The bullet had hit his lung.

Someone had come out of a house, and another person from a store. Both were women. Luckily, they weren't screaming. I was doing enough for all of us.

"Call the police! And tell them we need an ambulance!" I shrieked at them. The woman from the house ran back inside. I hoped she did what I told her to do. I hollered at the woman who came out of the general store, "Do you have any chewing gum? Some Wrigley's Spearmint?" *I'll admit I sounded a bit hysterical.*

She looked at me like I was insane and started to back away. I realized I had to calm down if I was going to help Muff.

In as calm a voice as I could muster, I asked, "Do you have a stick of gum? I just need the wrapper."

She was wearing a green apron like shopkeepers wore. It had a pocket in the front, and her hand slid down into the pocket and came up with a pack of gum. She took one stick out and came closer, but not too close; not close enough that I might grab her. She tossed the stick of gum to me. More accurately, she tossed it *near* me. I bent down and picked it up from where it had landed on the sidewalk. I carefully peeled the foil away from the stick of gum, throwing the gum into the gutter.

"Hey!" Muff said. "I could have used that!"

I stared at him, incredulous. "Shut up, Muff!"

I took the gum wrapper and flattened it out; then I placed it against the bullet hole in Muff's chest. He yelped and winced at my touch; his eyes squeezed tightly together.

"Every minute or so, I need you to pull the corner of that wrapper up for about ten or fifteen seconds. You got it, Muff? You have what they call a sucking chest wound, and it's a very bad thing. That gum wrapper will prevent air from going out through the bullet hole. If the air goes out, you will get a collapsed lung, and that would be very bad. How's your breathing?"

"It's kinda hard to breathe, but I think I'm okay."

I looked at the little guy with the oversized schnoz. I picked up his pork pie hat and tugged it down on his head. We were just a few blocks from the police station, and I could hear the police sirens. I'd leave it up to them to decide whether to wait for an ambulance or haul Muff to the hospital in the squad car.

"I think you're okay, too. I think it's a good thing your so-called sister doesn't have a lot of experience with guns." I turned to where Darla was still sitting on the sidewalk and saw her sobbing.

My tone was harsh as I barked, "What are you crying for?"

"I forgot to give you the message," she wailed.

"What message?"

"He said to tell you, 'I'm tired of all the trouble you've been causing. I'm going to make you watch while I kill your friends one by one. This is just the first.'"

I was so stunned by her words that I couldn't move. I tried to clear my thoughts by shaking my head. *Ow!* Bad move. My head began throbbing, and a wave of nausea rolled over me. I did my best to ignore it. I had to talk to Darla before the cops got here and took over.

"Who gave you that message, Darla?"

She keened even louder now. The police sirens were close, and the combination of the sirens and her yowling made my headache even worse. *On top of it all, I had my friend, Muff, bleeding out in front of me!*

"You said you weren't going to answer any questions the cops asked you, Darla. Well, I'm not a cop!" I grabbed her arm hard, digging my fingers into her soft, "nearly-sixteen-year-old" flesh.

I shouted the question at her again, barking the words in her face. "Who! Gave you! The message!?"

"The Man!" she screamed at me before tearing her arm from my grasp and collapsing into a mass of tears and sobbing.

Chapter 22

THE MAN: DOYLE ABADDON. Except he wasn't called The Man. Not yet, anyway. I don't know how I knew that, but I did. He was just a good-looking, young guy of about twenty with a penchant for nice clothes and not-so-nice henchmen. He was someone who was going to 'make something of himself,' people said; somebody who was going places. With any luck, the place he'd be going would be a prison.

The cops arrived right after Darla – still no last name – told me who had given her the message to share with me once she had completed her assignment. Surprisingly, Officer Bill Crane wasn't one of the two cops on the scene. I guess that was a sign that Muff would be all right since Crane and I usually only bumped into each other when other people died.

"How did you know about the gum wrapper thing for a sucking chest wound?" the ambulance guy asked me.

"I saw it on an episode… I mean, in a … movie," I answered. My brain told me something that didn't make sense, so I kept it to myself. *What was M*A*S*H?*

"I thought you musta been on the front lines during the war," he said as they finished loading Muff into the converted cargo van. "That's the kinda thing people learned out of necessity when there was only one medic available for dozens and dozens of troops."

"I'm just glad it worked," I answered. "Take care of Muff. He's a good guy. And watch his head. He got a pretty hard knock on it last night."

The ambulance was a black 1942 Cadillac station wagon. I realized as it drove away that it was from the local funeral parlor. Hook a couple of lights on top when no funerals are scheduled, add a couple of sirens to the fenders, and boom! Instant ambulance. The drivers were usually just that: drivers. Most of them would have been hard-pressed to know how to check someone's pulse, let alone stop any bleeding. Their main skill was driving as fast as they could to get the patient to the hospital as quickly as possible.

I hadn't met the policeman in charge of Darla before. I found out his name was Canny Jackson. I went over and introduced myself, carefully gave him the .32 Darla had used, and gave him one of my business cards just because. Then I asked if I could come along when they took Darla to the station.

"She was talking to me before," I explained, "but when she shot Muff, she gave me the gun and said, 'When the cops come, tell them I did it. But I won't answer any questions.' I'd like to go along and see this through since Muff is a friend of mine. You know what I mean, officer? Since she said she wouldn't talk to any cops, but she was talking to me, maybe I could help. Okay?"

"Yes, sir. I understand," Officer Jackson replied. "I also know she hasn't said so much as boo to me since I got here. So, if I can't get her to talk, maybe you can. Hop in the cruiser, and we'll run the pair of you over to the station house." I had been there before, maybe more than once.

Two days ago, outside the police station, I saw my mom – my mother who had been dead for five years. *How do I know that?* But I did. After she and I talked briefly, I glanced away, and when I looked back, she was gone.

I suddenly realized Jackson was getting Darla out of the backseat. We were already at the police station. We had gotten there fast, but once again, I had no recollection of the trip. I had no time to sit and think about it, though. Jackson was taking Darla into the station, her hands behind her back, his shiny silver handcuffs reflecting the morning sun. I opened my door and hightailed it after Canny and Darla. I didn't want to get separated from them.

I nodded to the desk sergeant, but I doubt that was his rank. I've never been good at recognizing ranks. Some people said I wasn't very good at recognizing authority *of any type.* For all I knew, the desk sergeant was just a glorified secretary, answering the telephone and calling all cars on the radio when needed, and working on a crossword puzzle when he wasn't needed.

Canny, Darla, and I went down the hall and entered a small room. I looked for a big two-way mirror on one wall, but the walls were solid, with no mirrors. Each wall was painted a gross pea-green color. The room had a small table and two chairs. I guessed that I was the one expected to stand, despite being a guest.

"Do you need to leave the cuffs on, Officer Jackson?" I asked.

"I do," came his terse reply. I shrugged.

"Darla is a minor," I replied. "Don't we need to have an attorney or an advocate present for questioning?"

He looked at me like I had just sprouted antennas from my head. "No. We do not. She doesn't need any shyster's help. We'll get ahold of her parents if and when she tells us who they are. She just shot down a man in cold blood, Marlowe. We won't know for a while whether or not she was successful. Right now, she's only facing attempted murder, but that may soon change to first-degree murder if Muff doesn't make it."

I had been watching Darla to see if she might react to anything he said, such as the threat of a charge of first-degree murder, but she was as impassive as a rock. True to her word at the shooting scene, she hadn't said a word since the police arrived.

"I'm going to go and get Lt. Hargrave to question her. You stay here and keep an eye on her. I'll only be a minute or two," Jackson said. He turned around and left by the room's only door. Apparently, they didn't think a skinny teenage girl was a big enough threat to warrant locking the two of us in. Maybe they didn't have enough experience in this kind of crime to realize everyone brought in for questioning was a threat.

I sat down opposite Darla. "You doing okay?" I asked.

She lifted her head slightly, her eyes flicking across my face and pausing a fraction of a second to make the briefest eye contact before moving on. "Yeah," was all she said.

"Did you hear what Officer Jackson said about first-degree murder if Muff dies?" I asked.

She nodded.

"Do you know what that means?"

She shook her head slightly from side to side this time.

"That means they could execute you," I replied, keeping my eyes fixed on her face as she appeared to stare at the junction of the wall and floor. Her eyes flicked back my way, but she didn't turn her head.

"That means they could kill you, Darla."

"You mean, like, hang me?" she asked quietly.

"No. Florida uses the electric chair. And they call it Old Sparky. They keep it in a place not too far from here. It's down Highway 301 from Jacksonville, down in Starke."

Her eyes began to fill with tears, and her breathing increased until she was panting like a little dog that had been running.

"So far, though," I continued, "Florida hasn't actually executed any women yet. Both women who were on death row had their sentences commuted – that means changed from a death sentence to a prison sentence – and they were released in the mid-1930s."

Her breathing slowed to normal again, and she lifted her cuffed hands to try to wipe her eyes. I reached into my coat pocket and discovered a handkerchief, so I handed it to her. She wiped her eyes, and I made sure to retrieve the handkerchief.

"Now, tell me why you shot Muff. Remember, I'm not the cops. You told me someone wanted me to suffer. I get that. But what was in it for YOU?"

"I did it for Freddie," she said in a voice so low it was almost a whisper.

"Freddie? Who's Freddie? And what does he have to do with Muff?"

"Freddie Lee, my boyfriend. Or he was before I did this." She lifted her cuffed hands for a second. "I did it to save him."

"Save him? From what? From who? Muff couldn't do anything to him."

She nodded her head. "Uh-huh. Freddie was getting hooked on opium, on heroin. And that Abaddon guy said Muff was the one selling it around here. He said if I got rid of Muff, I'd cut off the head of the snake, whatever that means. And I'd save Freddie from becoming a dope fiend. Then Freddie would come back to me, and I'd be his girl, and we'd be together again."

Abaddon had played this young girl and used her as a weapon against me. He had played a tune with her heartstrings like they were a guitar, manipulating her emotions to hurt me. She would undoubtedly be better off without Freddie if he was getting into drugs, but her "nearly-sixteen-year-old" heart wanted what it wanted. An adolescent heart wasn't that different from a thirty, forty, or fifty-year-old heart. It was just the mind and experience that made the difference. That, and the memory of the pain from having your heart broken other times.

"What else did Abaddon say or do to help you save Freddie?"

"He told me you could help me find Muff. Then he gave me that gun, and he told me what to say to you when I did it. Except I forgot to say it." Her eyes welled up and overflowed again. I dug my kerchief back out and gave it to her.

"Listen, Darla. Abaddon lied to you. Muff helps me out, and I'm a private investigator. That means I help the cops, and so does Muff. He wouldn't be selling drugs to anybody. Abaddon told you that so you'd shoot Muff, thinking you were saving Freddie. But think about what he told you to tell me: 'I'm going to make you watch while I kill your friends. This is just the first.' Abaddon used you like you used the gun. He used you to hurt me. And he doesn't care that you're going to get hurt in the process, too, maybe killed. You're probably not going to see Freddie ever again except through the bars of a jail cell. I'm sorry to say this, but you might be the first woman Florida finally executes."

Darla's wailing ramped up when I said that. I held up a finger, and she reined in her crying after a second or two, reducing it to sniveling while I continued.

"Listen to me: I don't really think they'll execute you for being stupid and gullible. But they will surely throw you in jail for a very, *very* long time if you don't tell the Lieutenant everything you just told me. That's the only way you and Freddie have any chance for a future. Do you understand?"

She nodded, her nose still sniffling. I heard footsteps outside in the hall. I stood up and took back my kerchief, leaning my head down near hers as I did.

In a soft voice, I told her, "Tell the Lieutenant *everything* you told me and then ask for a lawyer. Tell him you'll only answer his questions with your lawyer present. I have to go check on some other people and then get up to the hospital and check on Muff."

The door opened, and Lt. Hargrave stepped into the room.

"Tell him," I said to Darla.

I said to Lt. Hargrave, "She's all warmed up for you," and I stepped out into the hallway, closing the door behind me.

As I walked down the front steps of the police station, I saw a police cruiser pull in and park right next to the building. Officer Crane got out of the driver's side and came slowly around the car. Someone was sitting in the backseat, but I couldn't see who it was.

"Don't go away just yet, Mr. Marlowe. We might have some questions for you," Officer Crane said as he reached for the handle of the cruiser's back door.

He opened it and then reached in to help whoever was sitting in the car climb out. The cop's body blocked my view momentarily, but as he turned around, I saw who he had in custody: Pepé! The young sailor!

Crane handed Pepé off to another uniformed policeman and sauntered over to where I was standing, my mouth hanging open in shock. The Fernandina cop stood in front of me, hands on his hips, and told me what had happened.

"We had to let Sean and Angelo go. They weren't involved in the shooting of the Sacketts, but your friend there, Mr. Perez, was, by his own admission. He shot Val Sackett, and he shot Angelo. He admitted to both shootings.

Sean said he didn't know who shot him, but he corroborated that Perez shot Sackett and Angelo. Mr. Abaddon is pressing charges on behalf of his employees, Angelo and Sean, and on behalf of Miss Dale Higgins, whose step-parents were killed right in front of her."

"What?" I shouted, incredulous. "You can't be serious, Bill. Pepé shot Sackett in self-defense, and he shot Angelo because Angelo had a gun to my head and was about to shoot me!"

"Well, that may all be true, and I'm not saying it ain't, but I gotta do what I gotta do when someone presses charges in a shooting."

I stepped closer and lowered my voice. "Like with the Brodys? Abaddon got his money from them and killed them so they couldn't point the finger of guilt back in his direction. You *know* that, Bill. He's the one behind all the killings and crime going on around here."

"Then prove it, *Marlowe*, or whatever your name is. I have to do what the city pays me to do, and right now, that means questioning your friend, Mr. Perez. We'll take good care of him, I promise. He'll have a bond hearing, and if he can pay, he'll be out soon enough. Now step back, sir, so I don't misunderstand your intentions toward me and arrest you for threatening a peace officer."

I stared into his eyes for a few long seconds, then did as Bill suggested and took a step backward, giving him some space.

"We've got things under control here, Marlowe. I suggest you go to the hospital to check on the condition of your friend, Mr. Benjamin." In a slightly softer voice, he added, "You have my word: I'll see to Mr. Perez personally."

With that, Crane left me standing outside the police station. I watched his back all the way until he reached the big glass doors. He didn't look backward at me once.

: : : :

THE ONE TIME I *wanted* to get someplace in a hurry, I was aware of every step of the journey. I walked down the sidewalk to Atlantic Boulevard and then turned up Atlantic and walked east, away from the downtown. No skipping on the details this time. I noticed every old, stately home along the street, the majestic live oak trees, and the towering longleaf pines that rose high in the sky above. The funeral home was situated in front of the hospital, so I saw it before I saw Nassau General Hospital. *It's kind of gruesome that you see the place of the dead before the place of healing and living.*

The same antiseptic smell I remembered from when I woke up in there *(Was it just days ago?)* filled my nostrils as soon as I passed through the hospital's front doors. I remembered the shiny tile floors, waxed and polished to within an inch of their life, the paste wax causing the nurses' soft-soled shoes to make little squeaky noises as they walked down the hall. And who could forget the nurses, angels in white, all adorned in crisp white uniforms with little hats pinned atop their heads?

What else would they wear? I thought. *Nurses wear white, right? They're angels of mercy.* So why did the uniforms seem out of place? Something was scratching at my brain like a dog at the backdoor trying to get inside during a thunderstorm. The word 'scrubs' surfaced in my mind momentarily, but that didn't make any sense, so I let it go. Besides, I saw Wendi coming down the hall toward me.

I walked toward her to meet her halfway, forcing myself to maintain my pace and not run. Once I was near enough to ask questions without shouting, I probed, "Any good news on Muff?"

She shook her head and replied, "No good news, but no bad news, either. Like they say, no news is good news. Sometimes. I heard *somebody* did a fancy little trick with a gum wrapper to prevent a pneumothorax. You wouldn't know anything about that, would you?"

I wanted to take her in my arms, but knew that wouldn't be appropriate here. I held out my hand, keeping it at waist height, and she reached over and gave it a quick squeeze.

"I'd seen it done before; it must have been in a war movie. That's not important, though. If Muff dies, a young girl's life is over for all intents and purposes. She'll be charged with first-degree murder, and that's not completely wrong. She went looking for Muff to kill him, but she went on that hunt because Abaddon lied and tricked her into killing or injuring one of my friends in front of me. She told me that he said he was tired of me causing him trouble, and – quote – 'I'm going to make you watch while I kill your friends. This is just the first.'"

"Jimmy, that's horrible. What are you going to do? Did you tell the police?"

"Abaddon has them in his back pocket, some of them at least, and my problem is that I don't know which ones. I need to arrange a meeting with him. Are Sean and Angelo still in here somewhere?"

"Sean is. Angelo was already released. His wound was smaller. Why?"

"I need to talk to Sean. I need to find out where I can find Abaddon."

"If you're going to see him, you better take Pepé along, Jimmy."

"I would if I could, but Abaddon beat me to it and took him off the board. He had the cops arrest Pepé for killing Val Sackett and shooting Angelo. I was at the police station when he was brought in. Abaddon's filing charges on behalf of his 'employees,' Sean and Angelo, and—get this—in the interest of Miss Dale Higgins. We know he thinks he can get at her money if he keeps her close until she turns twenty-one. I don't know exactly what he has up his sleeve, but he may be trying to ingratiate himself to her. They're about the same age. I've always heard good girls are attracted to bad boys. Is that true?"

Wendi and I had been walking as we talked, and we were near a lounge area with a large stone support column. Wendi steered me behind the column so we were out of sight and said softly to me, "Sometimes, good girls are attracted to good *men*." She draped her arms over my shoulders and drew us together, her mouth finding mine in a gentle kiss that lingered but not long enough.

She stepped back, and we both circled back to the public side of the column. I cleared my throat and asked loudly for anyone who might care, "So, how soon do you think you'll know anything about Mr. Benjamin, Nurse Carter?"

She smiled at me, and I wanted to go back behind the column with her for a day or three.

"Our doctors are doing their best, Mr. Marlowe," she answered in a similarly loud, public voice. She looked around, and no one was even near us or looking our way. She dropped back into her normal conversational voice. "I'll come find you as soon as I know anything. Where will you be?"

"That depends on what I get from Sean. I need to find Abaddon and have a sit down with him. What room is Sean in?"

She told me, and we walked in that direction.

:::::

"ROBERT? THIS OFFICER NEEDS to speak with you." Gwynn came into Jimmy's room and hurried over to where her husband sat next to their friend. Jimmy's sedative had been decreased, but it was going to be a day before they saw any signs of him waking up. Even so, he was still intubated and unable to speak if he did wake up.

Pepé stood and looked past his wife toward the door into Jimmy's ICU room. A Nassau County Sheriff's deputy stood in the doorway in his green uniform. Pepé kissed his wife and gave her a hug, then walked over to the peace officer, who held the door open. The two men stepped out of the room.

"What's this about, deputy? I thought I was already cleared of the shooting death of the man who put two of my friends in the hospital. It was a self-defense situation."

"Yes, sir. You were, but these are funny times. These days, when people disagree with the outcome of something, they find another way around it. If you are found innocent of criminal charges, they go after you with civil charges. Sometimes, the outcome of a civil trial is even worse than a criminal one. Do you know a Mr. Doyle Abaddon?"

"I know *of* him, deputy. To my knowledge, he was nowhere near the site of the shooting."

"That is correct, Mr. Perez. However, he claims to be the employer of the three men who confronted Mr. Favreaux and Mrs. Lyst outside her business. He claims you used unnecessary deadly force in that meeting, and he has filed a civil charge against you for the wrongful death of his employee, Damian Griffin. I'm going to need you to come out to the station with me for questioning and to file a statement."

The deputy reached behind his back, and Pepé tensed. He did not want to be perp-walked out of the hospital in cuffs. Every fiber of his being screamed at the injustice that would be. After all his years in law enforcement, protecting other peoples' lives, to find himself on the other side might be more than he could stand.

But instead of handcuffs, the deputy brought out an envelope he had in the back of his waistband. "Oh, and by the way, you've been served," he said, handing Pepé the envelope. Pepé relaxed marginally but realized this dance was far from over.

Wendi, Gwynn, and Hillary watched with mouths agape as Pepé got on the elevator with the deputy. As the elevator doors closed, Pepé gave a tiny finger wave and an even tinier smile.

Pepé and the Sheriff's deputy walked across the parking lot toward the county cruiser. "You want to sit up front?" the peace officer asked. "Professional courtesy."

"Sure," Pepé answered. "But when we get out on A1A, what's say you hit the lights and siren and show me what this machine can do? I've always liked to go fast." Pepé snugged his Vietnam Veteran cap a little tighter on his head as he waited for the deputy to unlock the vehicle's doors.

"No problem, sir. And thanks for your service, soldier, and welcome home."

Chapter 23

I WALKED INTO SEAN'S hospital room without knocking. The curly-haired thug was asleep, his red curls vibrant against the white pillowcase. Just like children who seemed like little monsters an hour ago look like little angels when they're sleeping, Sean didn't look like a guy who would shoot a woman in the head just because his boss told him to do it. I had no doubt he had done other despicable things to people who got behind in payments or simply backed the wrong "team," but lying asleep in his bed, he didn't look like a threat.

The hospital room Sean was sleeping in looked almost exactly like the one I had recently awakened in. These rooms did not hold fond memories for me, but to be truthful, they barely held any memories for me at all. Nassau General Hospital and an almost identical room was where my amnesia had begun.

Wendi agreed to wait outside in the hallway to warn me of anyone coming and to be close in case I needed anything. On our way to Sean's room, she grabbed a cart with various vials and pills splayed across the top. As she stood outside Sean's room, she sorted the various medicines aboard like they actually needed sorting. I figured she was just trying to give the impression she was supposed to be there, but I also hoped she was looking for something to keep Sean quiet if he got too loud and boisterous. *Something like the doc hit me with that first time!*

I sat down in the chair on the right side of Sean's bed to be close to the shoulder where Dale had shot him. I sat for a few minutes and watched him sleep, thinking about the thing I was about to do. I wondered if he was in the same drug-induced slumber I had been in not so many days before. Whatever drug Doctor Floyd had used on me when I started to get agitated had worked extremely fast. *That's the one I want on her cart!*

I picked up a glass from the table next to Sean's bed and filled it with water from a nearby pitcher. I considered pouring the glass of water over his head all at once but eventually chose something with a little more finesse. I dipped my fingers in the water, then dripped the water on his forehead, slowly, one drip at a time. He started to frown and look less relaxed. I stopped. He went back to looking calm and collected. I dripped a few more drops of water on his forehead. This time, he tried to bring his right hand up to wipe away the drops, but his right arm was in a sling.

A puzzled look crossed his face. The bottom half of his eyes opened, and he looked out at the sling lying atop the white sheets covering him. He slowly rotated his head to the left, opening his eyes a little more, and then back to the right, where he spotted me. His eyes shot wide open.

"Care for a drink, Sean?" I asked, holding out the glass.

"What are you doing here? For that matter, what am I doing here?"

Deciding Sean wasn't thirsty, I set the glass back on the bedside table.

"You are here because you and Angelo tried to act like pirates and take over the boat we were on, but the two of you didn't plan well enough. By the way, just in case the drugs they used when they brought you in have made you forget, you let a girl get the drop on you in the salon on Sackett's boat. And not just any girl; she's a nun with a gun."

"What are you talking about? Who's a nun?"

"Dale Higgins. Well, she's not a full-fledged nun yet, but she works at the nun's school, and I wouldn't be surprised if she becomes a nun after her twenty-first birthday. Anyway, you and Angelo are messing with supernatural powers beyond anything you're used to dealing with."

"Gimmee the water, Marlowe."

"Of course, Sean." I handed him the glass, then gave him the coup de grâce. "You know, nuns are *married* to Jesus. They even get wedding rings to show they're married to Him." I pointed up toward the ceiling as I said, "Him."

He choked on the water, spluttering as he tried to breathe.

"Listen, Marlowe. We had no idea. The boss said to go out to the boat and see what was going on. So, we did. Then we saw the two dead bodies – Val and his missus. We figured we should look around the boat and make sure there weren't any others. You know?"

"Oh, I know. Such civic-minded, good Samaritans. It's just that dead bodies seem to pop up wherever you and Angelo go. Once you pull a gun from its holster, you think you have to use it."

'Don't be a smart guy, Marlowe. I'm being straight with you."

I thought about it for a second, and I realized he probably *was* being straight with me. They had probably given him some derivative of sodium pentothal when they fixed his shoulder, and he was probably still feeling some residual effects. If sodium pentothal was really a truth serum, I needed to ask him where I could find Abaddon before it wore off. I could also ask Wendi if she had any on that cart of hers, but I'd save that for a last resort. I decided to try to get the information without giving Sean a booster shot.

"You know, I can tell that you *are* being straight with me, Sean. So, I'm going to be straight with you. I need to find your boss and have a sit-down conversation with him, just the two of us, man to man, you know? *Mano a mano?*"

"Oh, man, I don't think I can do that. The boss is kind of sensitive about that. And with Angelo and myself out of commission, he's probably going to be even more reclusive than usual, on account of he likes to have a little hired muscle around him to maintain the upper hand in case people come around. You understand, don'cha, Marlowe?"

I smiled before I answered. I've been told I have a nice smile. I decided to see what Sean thought of it.

"The thing is, Sean, I don't have time to wait for you and Angelo to heal up and be able to flex your muscles again. Abaddon has suddenly decided he doesn't like me, and he's trying to hurt me by knocking off all my friends. You can understand how that might make me feel a little edgy, right?" I stepped closer to his bed. I leaned my body a little closer to the bed and his recently wounded shoulder. He automatically leaned away.

I grabbed his upper right arm with my left hand to stop him. He winced, and a high-pitched keening sound began coming from his mouth. It made me think of a wolf or coyote crying in the wilderness.

Thinking someone might notice, I slapped my right hand over his mouth like I was slapping a gum wrapper on a chest wound. I let go of his arm, brought my left hand up in front of his face to make sure he could see it, and waggled a finger back and forth like I was chastising a toddler.

"Nah-ah-ah," I said in a singsong voice. "Be a good boy. No yelling or crying." I put my left hand back on his right arm just below the elbow. Lifting the bottom half of his arm made his shoulder move in the opposite direction, putting pressure on his recent gunshot wound. Beads of sweat immediately broke out on the curly redhead's forehead, and a look of panic filled his eyes. He groaned loudly, and I lowered his elbow. He quieted, but his eyes were still reflecting his inner panic.

"Where can I find Abaddon, Sean? I need to meet with him. Tell me what I want to know, and you can go back to resting peacefully."

"I can't, Marlo—"

"—but you can, Sean. It's very easy. You learned how to talk a long time ago when you were just a wee lad. All you have to do is tell me where I can find Abaddon. Even easier, just give me a telephone number, and I'll set it up myself." I paused to see if he would still be compelled by the sodium pentothal to tell me. He said nothing, so I reached out quickly and gave his shoulder a gentle squeeze before he could move away. Let me rephrase: it would have been a gentle squeeze any other time, but not this soon after doctors had been digging around for a bullet inside his shoulder muscle. My thumb wasn't even on his wound, but it was in the same township. His eyes flew wide open, his back arched, and he began to cry again. My hand went over his mouth for a second. I made a decision.

I stepped away from his bed. "Wendi," I said softly and evenly. "I need something that will help Sean remember where Mr. Abaddon is, and after he has, it should also help him sleep."

I didn't like what I was doing, but I needed to find Abaddon and weave a deal with him.

She picked up a hypodermic from her cart and stepped over near the bed. She wrapped up Sean's left arm tightly against her body like she had done it many times before and plunged the needle into his undamaged upper arm. I continued to hold down his right side, trying not to put my hand directly on his wound. Wendi set the hypo back on the cart. I stepped away from the bed for a moment to let the drug do its thing.

I recalled something my mother had told me once. When you get down in the dirt to play with someone, you both get dirty. Part of me felt dirty, but I needed to do this. I could find a therapist and deal with the dirt later.

It wasn't long before Sean was sleeping peacefully, thanks to Nurse Wendi's judicious use of the hypo, but not before he told me what I wanted to know. It would also keep him from contacting anyone who might give me trouble, namely Angelo and Abaddon.

While Sean slumbered, I gave Wendi the kind of kiss I had wanted to give her behind the column in the other part of the hospital.

I told her not to worry, and I hurried out, walking back downtown with a purpose.

: : : :

WHO WOULD HAVE GUESSED the guy I was looking for would hang out fifteen feet *beneath* my apartment in the Palace Saloon? It further explained why Daani, the barmaid, had warned me about him. She had apparently seen him on numerous occasions, and she recognized his true personality, the part of him not hidden behind the nice clothes, expensive haircut, shiny shoes, and winning smile.

I slid into the seat in the booth across from the man I had been seeking. "Hello, Mr. Abaddon."

"Mr. Marlowe?" There was a momentary look of surprise and even a touch of fear in his eyes, but he recovered quickly. "Did we have an appointment that I forgot about?"

"We didn't, but we should have one anyway."

We were interrupted by a visit from Daani. She set a glass of clear liquid in front of Abaddon and looked at me expectantly.

"What's he having?" I asked.

"Water," she answered with no inflection in her voice. "Plain old water."

"Then that's what I'm having."

"Great. The last of the big spenders. That'll be a nickel."

"You're charging for water now?"

"No, but if you're not going to drink anything from the bar, I'm going to charge you a butt charge for planting your butt in that seat where a paying customer could sit."

I glanced around the saloon. I didn't see anyone anxiously standing in line for my seat but decided against making a fuss over five cents. I dug around in my pocket and flipped a nickel to her through the air. As she pocketed the coin, I suggested, "You should call it a cover charge – a charge to cover the use of the seat."

I could tell she was thinking about my suggestion as she went to get my water.

Neither Abaddon nor I spoke as we waited for Daani to bring my glass of water. She was only gone a minute since there were no other customers to wait on, and all she had to do for my order was pour a glass of water from the pitcher sitting on the dark mahogany bar. Daani didn't bother with a tray; she just walked back to our table and set the glass in front of me rather brusquely before returning to the bar. She must have known our business did not involve her. I was sure she knew the water glasses on the table before us were a mere formality. She stood with her back to us, polishing drink glasses for customers who would arrive later.

"I know where you're from, Doyle."

He glanced at me with annoyance at my assumed familiarity, calling him by his first name. "It's not a big secret," he replied.

"No, but it can be a big deal. You're not from around here, Mr. Abaddon. You're not even from this country. You're from Canada, a Canuck."

"I'm a naturalized citizen of this country, Mr. Marlowe. I'm as much a U.S. citizen as you."

That statement stabbed at my brain, sending a zing down my spine. Something about what he said made me uncomfortable, but I chose to push it down and ignore it. I continued with my prepared remarks for our meeting.

"As a U.S. citizen, Mr. Abaddon, you're subject to a couple of little-known laws. The first involves being convicted of certain criminal acts, aggravated felonies primarily, and crimes that fall into the category of moral turpitude, such as contributing to the delinquency of a minor. Those crimes carry particularly harsh penalties for immigrants, including deportation. You might think the crimes under that heading aren't particularly heinous, but after you promised us you'd be a good American, we find them quite ..." I searched for the right word before continuing, "... helpful, advantageous, even. The law makes it easy for us to drag you into the police station, question you, and hold you while we check on your activities. The crimes and activities listed are such heinous acts as filing a false tax return and failing to appear in court. Have you been on the up-and-up with our local law enforcement for both of those?"

"This is ridiculous."

"Now, see what I mean? You're calling our laws ridiculous. That makes it sound like you're not happy living here, even after promising to abide by our laws and learn the National Anthem. You *have* learned the song, haven't you?"

"I'm not going to sit here—"

"Yes, you are. You see, I had a nice conversation with Sean up in the hospital. It turns out some of the painkillers and sedatives they use can make a patient much more compliant than they would ordinarily be. With surprisingly little prodding, a patient can become quite talkative. A little poke in the arm, and they can't help but tell the truth. It's like leading the proverbial horse to water. You can't *make* him drink, but if you make him thirsty, he'll drink on his own."

I took a drink of my water just for dramatic effect. He wasn't quite glaring at me, but his smile was nowhere in sight. I set my water back on the table and continued.

"Moral turpitude. Have you heard that phrase before, Mr. Abaddon? In addition to those so-called aggravated felonies I mentioned, there are *actual* crimes of moral turpitude, ones that typically involve deceit, fraud, or causing harm to others. Crimes along those lines carry additional penalties, including but not limited to the potential penalty of *deportation* for naturalized U.S. citizens. Now we're not talking about jaywalking and overdue library books. This is things like child molestation, drug dealing and smuggling, and – one I'm sure you'll appreciate – convincing minors to do your dirty work."

"That has nothing to do with me."

"Oh, but it does. Do you remember the young girl, Darla? The one who was so worried about her boyfriend Freddie Lee because she thought he was getting hooked on heroin? It turns out Darla Harris – that's her last name by the way – is only fifteen years old. Not only did you deceive her and convince her to cause harm to others, but she's also a minor. That sure sounds like it falls under the moral turpitude heading to me. And crimes of moral turpitude include what? Let's quickly review to make sure you were listening. What was that phrase I told you? '<u>The</u> <u>potential</u> <u>penalty</u> <u>of</u> <u>deportation</u> for naturalized U.S. citizens.' You already told me you were one of those – a naturalized U.S. citizen. Since you weren't born here, we can send you back if you do things we don't like. It's kind of like screwing up when you're on probation. We can and will arrest you and send you away."

Doyle Abaddon, the young man who was going places and going to make something of himself, stood up to leave. He had heard enough from me. He wasn't used to being denied or accustomed to being told "no" when he gave an order. As he pressed down on the table and rose to his feet, a big hand pushed him back down.

Abaddon swiveled his head to identify the source of the big hand. "Crane! What do you think you're doing? You know I'm one of the chief's 'special friends.' You can't touch me."

"On the contrary, Mr. Abaddon. Not only *can* I touch you, I am, as you can tell by my big, firm hand on your shoulder. By the way, I'd really love it if you resisted arrest, but you probably would find a way to use it to your advantage. So just hold your hands out where I can put these cuffs on you. Better yet, stand up and put your hands behind your back. We're going to take a little trip, you and I, over to the police station. And you probably haven't heard the news yet, but the police chief that you just mentioned? He just retired this past hour. That makes Lt. Hargrave the acting chief, and we both know he's clean as a whistle."

Officer Bill Crane of the Fernandina Beach Police grabbed Abaddon by the collar of his coat, hoisted him up, and cuffed his hands behind his back, making a click sound that I found particularly satisfying.

Crane marched Doyle Abaddon out the door of the Palace Saloon. I sat back in the booth and sipped my water. Daani came over and sat down in the empty seat across from me. She had been watching since Crane came in the back door. He had entered by way of the outside stairs and come down the inside staircase in the back of the room.

"What's going to happen to him?" she asked.

"If we're lucky, he'll go back to Canada. If we're unlucky, he'll get locked up here and get out in a year or so."

"He's going to be mad. He won't forget you, and Wendigos have long memories."

"Well, that's something he definitely has over on me. My memory is full of holes." I leaned across the table. "But I think I remember you, Daani. Don't I? We've met somewhere before. Or some other time?"

She smiled back at me – which was a rare sight to see in the short time I'd known her here at the Palace. She winked at me and stood up. "You don't know what you know, Jimmy. In fact, you don't know Jack!" And she broke into laughter, like it was an inside joke, and walked away, disappearing into a back room behind the bar. Uncle Charley remained, mutely polishing glasses.

I continued sitting in the booth after she left. It was quiet in the Palace Saloon, and there were no other customers around. I stared at my water glass, empty now, and as I did, the room dimmed, and the background faded around me. Another background moved into place like I was watching a play from backstage and privy to how they changed the scenery between acts.

I wasn't at the Palace Saloon anymore, even though I hadn't moved. The bench in the booth I had been occupying was now the stone bench located outside the police station, the one where I had seen my mom. I felt the presence of someone else sitting next to me, and their hand take mine. At first, I thought it was Wendi, but when I turned to look at her, I saw my mom, but not the image of her that slipped in and out of my Swiss cheese memory.

This was a younger version of her—somehow, inexplicably, even younger than me. This was the version of her that had greeted me each day when I came home from grade school. She was young, smiling, vibrant, and full of life.

"Marty! I'm so glad I got to see you again. It's been such a long time, hasn't it? I should go see if there's a cake in the icebox and something for you to drink."

She called me Marty. But my name is Jimmy. James … what? James … Martin … no, Martin James! I used to go by Martin, but then I switched to Jimmy. But Martin James … what? What's my last name? Not Marlowe. But it's two syllables… two parts feel right.

I squeezed her hand to hold her in place on the bench. "No, Mom. Just stay right there. I don't need anything else. Let's just talk. It's been so long since we did that." I didn't want to let her off the bench. I was afraid she'd disappear again like the last time I saw her.

"All right, Marty. Or I suppose you want to be called Jimmy. I could never understand why you switched your names around. It was such a silly thing with that Zamboni machine at the arena. Then the mayor and the council said it was best if you moved away because they were afraid you might sue them."

She added with a little sigh, "But you took their deal and moved away, and I hardly ever saw you after that."

"I know, Mom. I'm sorry about that." I looked away for just a second, feeling the guilt squeezing my heart. When I turned back, she was the older version of my mother, the one I had seen on this bench the other time, the version of her I saw during the last few years before I moved away. It was the image stored away in my wonky memory. It was the image of her I preferred, seeing her this way rather than how she really looked not long before she passed.

She patted my hand and said, "That's all right, Jimmy. Or Marty. We gave you both names, so whichever one you want to use is fine with me. It's fine with your father, too."

"Pop? Is Pop here, too?" I said, looking over her shoulders to see if I could spot my dad.

"Oh, no. The last I saw him, your father was busy clearing the last snowfall and laying up some more cordwood for the winter because it'll be here before you know it."

My dad was always busy taking care of his family; ironically, he sometimes did it to the exclusion of his family. He was so busy taking care of us that he didn't have any time to spend with us. Consequently, I didn't have bad feelings about him; I just had very few deep feelings about him, positive or negative. He was always so busy trying to take care of us when all we wanted from him was to simply *be* with us. I never truly got to know my dad, and suddenly, he was taken from us. I couldn't remember how, though. I tried to recall it, but it was a big blank. A man who was never there could just slip away without anyone noticing.

"Your father loved to go dancing."

Her comment came out of the blue. I looked at Mom, and she was young again, an even younger version than a few minutes ago when I first noticed her on the bench with me. I had never known her when she had just married and was in her early twenties. I had only seen pictures from that time.

Now she was as youthful and fresh as when she and Pop first married, more than ten years before I was born. By the time I came along, she was already thirty, still young but not youthful. I only got to know her for the last half of her life. She had lived another entire life before I ever realized I only knew about half of her life.

My scant memories and her appearance were linked; the earlier my memories of her, the younger she looked. But this woman—girl—sitting next to me wasn't the tired woman in her forties and fifties I had known when I grew up and moved into my adulthood. I was getting glimpses of her from outside my memories. *Are these her memories?* I wondered.

I couldn't picture the older Mom I knew dancing with my dad. For that matter, I couldn't imagine them on a date. I couldn't envision him courting her, doing silly things to try and impress her. By the time I hit my teen years, they were both exhausted from raising children and working to provide for us.

I think I would have liked to have known this young woman sitting next to me, holding my hand in hers. She seemed so full of life and potential, and that's how she talked about my dad, too.

"He had such dreams," she said, "so many things he wanted to do. But then our family came along, and with it came responsibility and duty. *We* – our family – needed him even more than I needed him, so he did what was needed."

I blinked and looked again, and she was older again, in her eighties, bent, faded, and shriveled. I saw the toll that cancer had taken on her. The young, carefree woman she had once been had been completely erased by this ancient woman who had lost the only man she ever loved, her children, and was now losing the fight to the sickness that would claim her. She seemed to be able to read my thoughts.

"I know you would have been there for me if I had asked you to be, Jimmy, but this isn't how I wanted you to remember me. I wanted you to remember me when we had fun, back when I could chase after you, climb trees, roll on the ground with you, and do almost everything you could.

No one wants to be remembered how they are when they're old and sick. We want to be twenty forever."

I blinked my eyes, and she was a newlywed again. But it was like fanning through a stack of photos, morphing from very young to very old, her features changing as the years flew by. Wrinkles appeared, and her hair turned gray, the lines around her nose, mouth, and eyes deepened.

No matter how her exterior changed, I noticed that despite the pain, exhaustion, frustration, and sorrow, her eyes always stayed the same. No matter her age or illness, there was always the spark of that twenty-year-old bride inside, shining in her eyes.

I blinked again, and suddenly it was Wendi's hand I was holding.

"W-wh—where did she go?" I asked her. "I wanted a little more time with her. I still had things I wanted to ask her. I just wanted a few more minutes …"

Wendi looked into my eyes, and, for a tiny second, I saw my mother reflected in hers. Then Wendi said, "It's time to wake up, Jimmy. We need you—I need you."

I remembered what my mom had said about my dad: *"We needed him more than I needed him."*

Was that my destiny, too? Would responsibility and other peoples' needs overshadow who I was, stripping away my desires and dreams to fulfill the needs of those around me? *The needs of those I love!* I realized I wasn't giving up anything; I was just going down a different path, one I could share with others. In that regard, it was a better path because I didn't walk it alone; I walked it with people I loved.

I heard my mom's voice again, but I didn't turn to look at her. I forced myself to see her the way I held her in my mind's eye, the way I wanted to remember her, neither old nor young. And though I didn't look, I listened as she spoke.

"Your father had dreams and aspirations, but his primary goal was to take care of his family. And he achieved that goal many times over. You have a family now, too, so don't be afraid to love them. If you take care of them, they'll take care of you. Always remember where you're from and who you are."

I looked down at the hand holding mine and saw my mother's care-worn hand for a moment, and then it became smooth and supple again. I knew it would be Wendi's face I would see when I looked back up.

"Jimmy." It was Wendi's voice.

I knew I would probably never see my mother again. But I was wrong.

At the sound of my name, I turned my head to look, and my mom met my eyes, a smile on her face. It was the younger version of my mother, laughing and smiling, not the vision of the old, sickly woman from the last time I saw her, shortly before she died. It was the picture of her from my childhood that I always kept of her. I realized there were two images of my mom in my heart: the adult mother I knew as an adult, the one I interacted with as a near-equal, and the young, vivacious mother who loved her family, her husband, and her life.

I felt a hand squeeze mine gently but firmly. Then I heard a voice.

"Jimmy. Jimmy Favreaux. It's time to wake up."

That's me, I thought. *I'm Jimmy Favreaux. That's who I am!*

Chapter 24

THE ROOM WAS DARK, the lights muted and dim. Jimmy flashed on a memory of another recent time in a dark hospital room, and the sounds and smells of the hospital were all his senses could decipher, his head swaddled in gauze, his unseeing eyes covered by layers of wrapping. Jimmy smelled the sterile, antiseptic air again and heard the hushed nearby sounds and voices. He was no longer sitting on the bench near the police department. Was it the same hospital where he woke up the last time? Was this like the movie *Groundhog Day?* Was he going to start over with his head wrapped in gauze like in the *Twilight Zone* episode and a doctor who looked and sounded like Floyd the barber?

"Jimmy. Are you awake?"

Unlike his previous awakening, there was no gauze swaddling his head, and the voice he heard was not Floyd's. Jimmy's eyes were like tiny slits, allowing only the most minute amount of light into his brain. Unlike the previous awakening, his throat felt like it was on fire this time.

"Water," he hoarsely whispered, holding out a hand.

Someone guided a straw to his lips and placed a glass in his outstretched hand. He sucked the cool, clear liquid into his mouth and tried to swallow. That hurt, too, like trying to swallow a golf ball covered in cactus spines. He let the mouthful of water slowly trickle down his throat, and slowly the pain lessened. The person near him took the glass away, and he heard the sound of ice being shaken in a Styrofoam cup.

A deep, earthy female voice said, "Stick to the ice chips for now."

A man's voice asked, "Can you open your eyes, Mr. Favreaux?"

Mr. Favreaux? Jimmy tilted his head slightly out of curiosity and opened one eye a quarter of an inch. He could see a man wearing a white coat sitting next to him, a stethoscope around his neck.

"Hello, Jimmy," the man said. "Welcome back. Do you have any idea where you are?"

Jimmy swiveled his head a little more and cracked open his other eye to match the first one, getting his first real look at the room he was in. It was a hospital bed; he was pretty sure. He reached up and found a remote control near his shoulder. *Modern technology!* The blinds were closed, the curtains drawn across the window, and the fluorescent lights overhead were off. The only light in the room was ambient light sneaking in around the blinds and curtains.

Jimmy cleared his throat, which still felt like he'd swallowed a flaming porcupine someone had tried to extinguish with gasoline. Reflexively, he put a hand to his throat.

"Yes, your throat is sore," the man in the white coat said. "You were intubated for a couple of days, and it will be sore for a day or so. Do you know where you are?"

"Hospital," Jimmy whispered.

"Good. Yes, you are in the Baptist Medical Center in Fernandina. Does that surprise you?"

Jimmy started to shake his head, but the doctor—Jimmy assumed that's who he was since he wore the white coat and had a stethoscope—put a few fingers of one hand on Jimmy's cheek and his other hand on Jimmy's hand. The hand on his hand got his attention, while the hand on his cheek stopped him from shaking his head.

"You might not want to be shaking or nodding your head quite yet. Do you know *why* you're in the hospital, Mr. Favreaux?"

It was so nice to hear someone use his real last name instead of Marlowe. *'I'm Jimmy Favreaux!'* he shouted internally, ecstatic to be able to connect the first part with the last. He knew who he was again!

"My head ..." he hissed in a whisper. "A ... concussion?"

"Yes, you received a nasty concussion a few days ago—"

'Only a few days?' Jimmy thought.

"—and a depressed skull fracture. You have assorted bruises, contusions, and welts – oh, my!" The doctor paused, but Jimmy didn't say anything.

The doctor continued fishing, "You know, like lions and tigers and bears, oh my? Hmmm. Sense of humor still in a coma. We put you in a medically induced coma for two days due to your TBI – that's a traumatic brain injury – to give your brain a chance to heal and to avoid swelling."

"Healed?" Jimmy rasped, lifting one hand and pointing in the general direction of his head.

"No, you're not completely healed yet, but the fact that we're having a mostly normal conversation is a good sign." The doctor got up and turned on the overhead lights before asking, "Do you know what year it is and who the President is?"

"2023 and Sleepy Joe," Jimmy replied hoarsely.

"Yes to the first one and close enough on the second part," the doctor answered with a smirk. "How about your name and address?"

"Jimmy Favreaux … and I live over by the Blue Bridge five miles south of Kingsland on Highway 17." His throat was getting a little better as he talked, and his voice was not quite as raspy.

"Kingsland … where?" the doctor repeated and then paused, waiting for Jimmy to fill in the blank.

"Kingsland, Georgia," Jimmy obliged, then added. "Go Dawgs," punctuating his statement with a weak fist pump.

"Hmm, yes. Georgia beat the Florida Gators 43 to 20 about a month ago in the Florida-Georgia game," the doctor said with a half-hearted, plastic smile that told Jimmy his doctor was a Gators fan.

"Do *you* have any questions, Mr. Favreaux?"

Jimmy took another sip of water before asking, "Do you need the curtains pulled over the window? I can hardly tell if it's day or night, and I'll tell you honestly that I am not sure what day it is."

The doctor stood and went to the window, pulling back the curtain panel on each side and then opening the blinds slightly to let a little more light into the room.

"Not too much. Your eyes have been closed for a couple of days, and you'll find, with the concussion and TBI, that your eyes are probably a bit light-sensitive, but that should go away in a week or less. Any other questions?"

"I feel like I just wasted a question," Jimmy said.

"On the contrary, Mr. Favreaux. If you have questions, you just need to ask me or one of the nurses. Questions mean your brain is functioning, and that's good. We can also tell how well it's functioning by the questions you ask. Not always, but sometimes." He moved toward the door.

"What day is it?" Jimmy asked again, afraid the doctor was going to leave before he finished asking questions.

"Day? It's Thursday, November twenty-third. It's Thanksgiving, Mr. Favreaux. And I think you have something to be thankful for. Welcome back to the land of the living, Jimmy."

"Where are my friends?" Jimmy croaked. He was supposed to celebrate Thanksgiving with Wendi and her former father-in-law, Hillary Lyst, and maybe Pepé and Gwynn, too. He scratched his chin – which was covered with beard stubble, he absently noticed – trying to remember something important, but the detail was hanging on the fuzzy fringe of recall.

"Is there a problem?" the doctor asked.

"Um, maybe. I was supposed to be spending Thanksgiving with my, ah, girlfriend and her father-in-law, and maybe some other friends, but I can't remember if it was just the three of us or the larger group."

The doctor smiled and put his hand on the big door opener button that looked more like a metal salad plate than a button. "Well, we expect you to have some gaps in your memory at first, but I wouldn't worry too much about them. I think you're going to do fine, Mr. Favreaux. We're going to keep you in here for another day or two, and we'll do some more assessments to make sure you're healing properly before we set you free. In the meantime – those friends you're asking about? Why don't you ask them?" He pushed the door opener, and the door began swinging open. Jimmy was greeted by the faces of his friends, standing right outside his door, crowding to get in.

Like a single entity, they swarmed into Jimmy's room. Wendi reached his side first, taking his hand in hers, putting her other arm around his neck, and pulling him close for a passionate kiss.

She suddenly broke off the embrace and leaned backward. "Oh, my! I forgot you haven't brushed your teeth or gargled or anything for a couple of days. That's some nasty morning breath, Jimmy! This is definitely *not* like in the movies!"

Everyone laughed, but Jimmy was mortified and, in his raspy voice, asked her, "Really? I'm so sorry…"

She moved back in and kissed him again. "Yes, but I can deal with it. It's worth it to have you talking to me again. You have no idea how awful it was to sit here with you unconscious for two-and-a-half days, not talking or even snoring. We all took turns sitting with you and talking to you so you knew we were here. That is, assuming our voices got through to wherever you were. Where were you, by the way? You did some weird things like smile and try to talk a few times, but with that tube down your throat, we couldn't catch anything."

She sat on the edge of Jimmy's bed. She looked marvelous. Jimmy looked up and saw the doctor wave as he left the room to Jimmy and his friends.

"I guess I was dreaming," Jimmy said. "It was really strange, like dreams usually are. But it was also very real. Wendi, Pepé, and Hillary were there. No offense, Gwynn, but I don't remember you being there."

"I don't think Pepé would appreciate knowing I was in your dreams, and I doubt Wendi would like it, either!" Gwynn said with a laugh.

"Where is he? Pepé, I mean," Jimmy asked. "He saved my life a couple of times in my dream."

Gwynn dropped her eyes from Jimmy's and looked down at the bed. Her hands were twisting his bedsheets, and she forced herself to stop. "He couldn't be here today, Jimmy. He… ah—" She looked around at Wendi and Hillary, and a tear began trickling down her cheek. She struck at the drop of moisture, batting it angrily away.

"The sheriff's department arrived and detained him yesterday," Hillary stepped in to answer. "It seems The Man – Doyle Abaddon – has filed a wrongful death suit against our friend for the shooting death of one of his henchmen, the big one they referred to by the comic book moniker, Kingpin."

"Pepé shot him?" Jimmy exclaimed, his eyes opening wide.

"He shot him to save you … and to save Wendi. Kingpin was about to shoot her at point-blank range."

The room had become decidedly quiet, and a somber mood settled over the gathering of friends.

"Wait. Do I remember Kingpin attacking us?" Jimmy wanted to know, trying to assemble the puzzle of time in his mind.

They nodded in unison.

"I vaguely remember him yelling something at me in that stupidly high voice that didn't fit his body shape and size. He was yelling at me to wake up because he was going to …" Jimmy paused and rubbed his temples briefly. "He said he was going to *kill Wendi*, and he wanted to make sure I saw it happen. But I couldn't get my eyes open, and I couldn't move or do anything to stop it. All I remember is everything going black, like a TV show fading out at the end, and then I heard a really loud … gunshot." Jimmy turned to Wendi and sat up higher in the bed. "Did he *shoot* you, Wendi?"

"No, he didn't, but he was going to. The worst thing is, I didn't know anything about it. Pepé and Hil told me what happened later. I was out cold on the sidewalk, just like you. I knew nothing of what happened after Kingpin body-slammed me to the concrete."

Jimmy looked at Hillary, who shrugged slightly.

"There was no way that Robert and I could get close enough to attempt to physically restrain him," Hillary said, describing the events from a few days before. "That giant was turned toward us, and we each fired our handguns, hitting him a total of four times. Amazingly, that gargantuan beast took four shots to center mass but didn't look like he even felt them. Whether due to distance or his immense size and bulk, our handguns were ineffective. It was like King Kong on the Empire State Building, swatting at planes. Kingpin was pointing his weapon at Wendi and screaming at you, telling you to wake up and watch. He turned and centered his aim on Wendi." Hillary closed his eyes and swallowed. It was not easy for him to share the scene that was replaying in his head.

"The big man was trying to get you to be a witness to what he planned to do to Wendi. That may have saved your and Wendi's lives. He was focused on completing his mission, so to speak, and would let nothing distract him, not even bullet wounds. It was evident by his stance that he was about to pull the trigger. I knew it, and so did Robert, who did the only thing he could under the circumstances, quickly sliding his rifle out of its case. Kingpin ignored us and only delayed to yell at you again so you could witness his triumph. From our position about twenty-five yards across the parking lot, Robert dropped to one knee and took careful aim, released his breath like he'd done many times before, and gently eased back on the trigger. It was a perfect shot, right behind Kingpin's ear. All bodily movement ceased, and he simply fell straight to the pavement, like a puppet whose strings are suddenly cut."

No one in the room said a word. Jimmy saw tears rolling down the faces of both Gwynn and Wendi. A distant voice in Jimmy's head recited, *"Any man's death diminishes me ..."*

"Robert hurried to your side, kicking Kingpin's gun out of reach in case he had somehow lived through it. After what we had seen, it wouldn't have surprised us a great deal if he had survived. But he didn't. While Robert saw to you, I quickly attended to Wendi, called 9-1-1, and told them to roll the ambulance. The local police and sheriff's deputies arrived just before the ambulance. As the EMTs worked on getting you and Wendi ready for transport, the police confiscated our weapons and took preliminary statements, as it should be. The sheriff's deputies threw a tarp over the body and called for the medical examiner, the M.E. As with many small towns, the examiner comes from the local funeral home. It didn't take our M.E. long to arrive. He checked for vitals, did a quick exam of the body and the wounds, particularly the last one, and declared the man dead. He had the deputies help him load the body into the hearse. I went with the police to make a formal statement, and Robert rode with you and Wendi in the ambulance."

"Okay, so that gets Wendi and me to the hospital. Then what happened?"

"Robert waited in the waiting room while the ER personnel took care of you and Wendi. A neurosurgeon was called in for you, and after they took you to the ICU, he checked on Wendi before catching up with you to oversee placing you in a coma. Wendi was held overnight for observation," Hillary continued.

He was trying to cover everything in as much detail as he felt necessary because he knew Jimmy was hearing it all for the first time, unlike the rest of their group who had lived through it once but who had relived it multiple times over the three days since the event occurred.

"When I finally arrived here at the ICU, I met Robert in the hallway," Hillary continued. "I explained to him that the police had cleared us in the shooting, but he would still need to go down to the station and give them his formal statement. A great deal of the police's decision to not immediately put Robert and me behind bars rests on their relationship with *you*, Jimmy." Hillary paused to let that statement sink in before continuing.

"Thanks to their relationship with you, Wendi, and me, along with the fact that Robert is a decorated Navy veteran and former police officer, the police gave a preliminary clearance to Robert and me in the shooting death of Damian Griffin."

"Damian, who?" Jimmy asked.

"That's our friend Kingpin. A rather apt name if you ask me. Damian means to tame or subdue in Greek, something Kingpin did quite a bit of, no doubt. And Griffin—"

"A mythological creature with the body of a lion and the head of an eagle," Jimmy interjected.

"Indeed," Hillary replied with a smile. "Another rendering of the name means 'a monstrous creature to be feared.' Quite apropos, wouldn't you say?"

Jimmy sat quietly for a moment, wondering to himself, *Maybe it's the goofy names all these guys have that draw them together. Doyle Abaddon and Damian Griffin—it's like they got saddled with names intended to attract bullies. Maybe it's not entirely their fault they turned out the way they did.*

Looking from face to face, Jimmy asked the question nagging him, "What's going to happen next to Pepé?" He turned and looked at Gwynn and waited.

"He was able to get ROR – Released on Own Recognizance. The judge told him to go home and stay there until he heard back from the clerk of court. I talked to a deputy in the hall here at the hospital, though, and he said not to worry. He said Kingpin – Griffin – and the other guys who work for Abaddon have been in and out of jail and the courts so many times there's no way anything's going to stick. The judge is going to toss the case, probably on Monday."

"Monday? Why are they making Pepé wait so long?"

"Today's Thanksgiving," Gwynn replied. "That means everybody takes a four-day weekend starting today. The judge won't be back in his chambers until Monday. It's a blessing that he let Robert out on ROR. That means we can have Thanksgiving at our house as soon as they cut you loose from this place. Did the doctor give any indication of when that might be?"

"He said another day or two. I don't know if that means today and tomorrow and out at the end of the day Friday or if they're going to hold me over until Saturday. I suppose it depends on how good a boy I am."

"Hmmm. I've seen how good you can be, Jimmy," Gwynn said. "It's probably best if we just plan on getting together *Sunday*. Then if you get out Friday or Saturday, you'll have at least a day to get back to normal, and maybe two."

"That sounds great," Jimmy answered. During the conversation, Wendi had shifted repeatedly until she was mostly nestled against Jimmy, her head resting on his chest. He still had an IV in his right arm, so he was careful to keep that away from where Wendi was lying on the left. His eyes sought Gwynn's, knowing Hillary would be oblivious, and she read the message he was sending.

Turning toward Hillary, Gwynn took his arm in hers and said, "Why don't we go out and leave these two young people alone for a bit? They haven't talked for a couple of days, and I'm sure they would like a few minutes to get caught up. Although I don't know why they can't just text each other like they normally do."

Hillary started to protest, but Gwynn clamped her arm even more tightly around his and directed him out the door.

: : : :

A NONDESCRIPT WHITE DELIVERY van pulled up across the end of the driveway of a house located on a short cul-de-sac. The driver got out and walked toward the house. He wore a grey jumpsuit and held a large envelope in one hand.

He paused just before he reached the front door, and looked over the front of the house, then turned around and looked around the cul-de-sac like he was making sure he was at the right house. He was checking the house number but also checking for security cameras and any incidental witnesses. He stepped up to the doorbell and rang it, then took a step back from the door.

A man answered the door, and the driver asked, "Mr. Perez?"

The man who answered the door nodded. As he did, the delivery driver pulled a wicked-looking knife from a pocket of his jumpsuit and plunged it into the chest of the man who dropped to the floor in the doorway. The driver let go of the envelope and hustled back to the van. He jumped inside, slammed the door, and, in a notable show of restraint, drove out of the short cul-de-sac at normal speed.

A few seconds after the van reached the corner and turned right to leave the subdivision, Pepé got out of the recliner in his living room and went to the door. The door was slightly open, and a nubby tweed cap lay on the floor. It wasn't his. He had never seen it before. He picked it up.

Before shutting the door, Pepé looked out the door a second time and saw something lying on the front step. A letter-sized envelope was just outside the door. Opening the outer door, he picked up the envelope and examined it, but it had no address label. He tore the flap open, removed a small piece of paper inside, and read the short, computer-printed message it contained.

"One down. More to come. See you at 7. The Man. PS— don't be late!"

'One down?' Pepé thought. Then his eyes opened wide.

Judge's orders or not, Pepé had to chance making the trip to see Jimmy in the hospital in Fernandina. After backing out of his garage and driveway, the former Charleston cop laid rubber as he tore off to make sure no one in their group was the "One down."

Chapter 25

AFTER HILLARY AND GWYNN left Jimmy's room, Wendi stayed exactly where she had been, snuggled next to him. The change wasn't visible, but Jimmy felt a noticeable relaxation in her body after a minute or so. He had his left arm around her, enjoying the smell of her hair just below his face.

After basking in her nearness for a long moment, Jimmy cleared his throat. He wished he could get a drink, but he didn't want to break the spell or have Wendi get up from where she was lying.

"First, there was a hurricane and then some severed hands, and now this – confined to a hospital bed!" Jimmy declared hoarsely. "Have you noticed that we keep ending up like this? On my couch, on your couch, on the front porch … Not that I'm protesting, you understand."

Wendi shrugged slightly. She spoke into his chest, "I know you're making light of things to try and make me feel better, but I was scared, Jimmy. I didn't know if the doctors were going to be able to wake you up or what you'd be like if or *when* you woke up. I didn't know if you'd have amnesia. What would I do if you couldn't remember me?" She held him a little tighter.

"If I had woken up with amnesia, I think we'd still have been okay," Jimmy answered. "I had a dream during my coma, and I had amnesia in my dream. I didn't know who I was, or you, or anybody, but when I was with you, everything felt right. And I assure you it didn't take long in my dream before I was kissing you."

She lifted her head and looked into his face, one finger gently tracing the colored outlines around his two black eyes. "Are you saying I was easy in your dream?"

He laughed, really wishing he could have a drink of water now to stall for time to answer. "On the contrary," he said. "You were playing hard to get. Sorta-kinda. You were married to a local guy who had gone off to war, but he died, so you were a widow again. But you were afraid people would judge you harshly because it wasn't long enough since he had died. He was a hometown hero, which made things worse."

"Gone to war? Which war? Afghanistan? The Gulf War?"

"Believe it or not, it was 1948, just a few years after World War Two ended."

"What?" She sat up, and Jimmy took advantage of her position change to grab his water glass and take a long drink before telling her more.

"I guess it must have something to do with all the old-time radio shows I've listened to and all the historical things I've read and studied. And it wasn't very long ago that I went on a tour of Fernandina's history. I went through the old jail, firehouse, and city hall. Some of those images and places are apparently stuck in my head. And you'll never guess where I lived in my dream."

"Where?"

"I was a private detective living in a two-room apartment above the Palace Saloon. You were a nurse at the old Nassau County General Hospital, the one that used to be behind the funeral home on Atlantic Boulevard, you know? Except you were also my secretary, but not very often. I woke up in Nassau General, and you were my nurse. I said, 'Hey, baby, I could sure use a sponge bath,' and you went and got the soap and water, a sponge, and a towel.

Jimmy turned red, embarrassed to reveal some of the secrets from his dream. He held her against his chest to keep her from seeing him blush and continued the details from his dream.

"There were some things left unfinished. I mean, some things were complete, but some things weren't finished when I woke up."

"Like what?" Wendi asked, sitting up and moving off the bed and onto the chair.

"Well, like a guy who got shot by a teenage girl. I saved his life long enough to get him to the hospital, but I don't know if he made it through the surgery. And there was a Pepé in my dream, too, but he was a little different. He was a young sailor who had enlisted just before Okinawa in the spring of 1945, so by the time he was done with basic training and everything, the war was over. His main job was working on the Victory Ships that brought our soldiers home from the Pacific Theater. It was a lucky thing for him if you ask me. Not having to be a part of the actual fighting, I mean. But this young dream-version of Pepé was helping me out, and he even saved my life a couple of times from a pair of thugs who worked for a young, local mobster named – get this – Doyle Abaddon. I apparently dragged him into my dream, too."

Wendi stared at Jimmy for a second before she spoke. "Jimmy, Abaddon actually lived in Fernandina back in 1948. He immigrated from Canada and was living down here as a naturalized citizen. Pepé dug around in the old police records until he found one that proved Abaddon was there. It was just a traffic offense, but it was him."

"That's too weird, Wendi. I wonder how much stuff my subconscious mind threw together to keep me entertained while I was in there."

There was a timid knock on the door to Jimmy's room in the ICU.

"Come in," Wendi and Jimmy said in unison. They looked at each other, grinned like teenagers, and said, "Jinx! You owe me a Coke!"

The door opened partway, and a head poked in. Jimmy and Wendi recognized an ICU nurse in her teal-colored scrubs. *No more white dress and cap,* Jimmy thought.

"Mr. Favreaux, there's an older gentleman asking if he could see you for just a minute. He said he saw Mrs. Lyst and heard her talking with some of your other friends, and he was hoping to see if you might be related to someone he used to know. Would it be all right?"

Jimmy and Wendi looked at each other, and Jimmy lifted his head slightly, settling a little higher onto his pillows. "Yes, that's fine," Wendi answered.

The nurse stepped out briefly and then came back in partway, holding the door open. She pushed the automatic door button and stepped out. The door danced briefly before deciding to remain open. The front part of a walker came into Jimmy's room, followed by a short, white-haired old man.

He came partway into the room and stopped. He was squinting at Jimmy, but Jimmy didn't need to squint to see him.

The elderly man was short and wiry. He wore nubby brown slacks, a white shirt with an unbuttoned tan vest over it, and a tan pork pie hat that was resting on the seat of his walker. A toothpick sprouted from his mouth, protruding from under a nose that was considerably out of proportion with the rest of his face. He was wearing glasses, which was unfamiliar to Jimmy, but everything else about the old gentleman screamed in his memory that he knew the man standing before him. Jimmy had saved his life *in a dream*, and somehow he was here seventy-five years later.

But that's impossible!

The old man parked the walker on the side of Jimmy's hospital bed and slowly maneuvered around it until he could sit down on the device's built-in seat. He faced Jimmy and Wendi, his arms resting on the tubular rails of his fire-engine red walker.

"Long time no see, Jimmy."

"Muff?" Jimmy said hesitantly.

"The one and only."

"Muff Benjamin? How is this possible?" Jimmy asked, wondering if he was actually awake or still in his dream world. "You must be ninety-five years old."

"Ninety-six, but who's counting?"

"Jimmy, who is this?" Wendi asked, her voice low.

"I'm truly hurt, Wendi," Muff replied. "You helped fix me up when that young girl shot me. What was her name again, Jimmy?"

"Darla?" Jimmy replied without thinking. In his mind, that incident was parked in his short-term memory, a short backward reach, unlike dredging up something from his long-term memory.

"That's the one," Muff answered. "Darla Harris. Shot me because Abaddon was trying to get back at *you* by killing off your friends."

"This can't be happening," Jimmy said, leaning back into his pillow. "I must still be in a coma."

Muff unbuttoned his shirt partway and pulled aside his undershirt to reveal a jagged scar on the right side of his chest. "It happened, boy-o. I can still see that girl's stone-cold face as she swung that gun around and fired at me. Three shots, but only one tagged me." He tapped the ancient, white scar with a bent, arthritic finger. "Right there. Jimmy, you put a Wrigley's Spearmint wrapper on it, and you, missy, you helped the doctor at Nassau General fix me up. But now I'm old, and you two aren't. I'd like to know why you haven't aged a day."

Silence hung in the room for a minute. There was no rational answer to explain how this meeting could possibly take place. Because a previous meeting had impossibly happened, one man survived, and the three were together again.

"There must be some mistake—" Wendi started.

"Wendi Carter," Muff said. "Right?"

"Well, yes, but …"

"And Jimmy Marlowe, private detective."

"Jimmy Favreaux."

"So, you got your memory back and remembered your real name. Good. You didn't need to piggyback on Philip Marlowe's fame anyway."

"But Muff, this can't be happening."

"I've seen a lot of weird things in my ninety-six years, Jimmy, things I can't figure out. Maybe you were where you had to be to save my life. Whatever stars had to align to create this dance between time and history, I'm glad it did. Me and Dale had nearly seventy years of marriage together because you saved my life."

"You and Dale …?"

"Who's Dale?" Wendi interrupted.

Jimmy knew, but looked back at Muff, who answered.

"Dale Higgins. She came to see me in the hospital, and we talked and got to know each other. She took care of my hospital bills. Told me she had more money than anyone should have. She had just turned twenty-one and inherited her father's entire estate, the one Val Sackett was after."

"Val Sackett. He's from my dream, too," Jimmy murmured to Wendi, but he knew she wouldn't get the connection.

"You say it was from your dream, Jimmy," the old man said, "but it was my life. Dale came up and sat and talked with me every day until I got out of that hospital, and then we just kept on sitting together and talking. After a little while, I asked her to marry me, not thinking for a second that she would. She was independently wealthy, but she said yes. We were married from 1949 until she passed in 2019, just short of our 70th anniversary. She made some very wise investments with her money, and since we never had any children, we spent our time helping children without parents."

"The nun's school and the orphanage down by Tampa …" Jimmy mumbled, remembering what Dale had told him in his dream.

"That one, yes, and others. After she died, I donated some money to the hospital here in Fernandina. That's how you got this fancy bedroom with all the bells and whistles for treating brain injuries. I never forgot how you said you got a concussion and lost your memory. Since you saved my life, I thought I'd help others in the same boat. Never figured I'd be helping you for real, though."

"Muff, this can't be real."

"Real or not, I'm here because of you, and in a way, you're here because of me. I just wish Dale was here to see you. She never got a bill from you, you know? And I never got the chance to properly thank you for saving my life."

"We can call it even," Jimmy said with a grin. "How does that work for you?"

Muff smiled; his eyes were nearly lost in the wrinkles that surrounded them. He sat quietly for a few seconds, then he got up and carefully moved around his walker. Cautiously stepping closer to the bed, Muff Benjamin held out a wrinkled hand. Jimmy took it in his, and they shook hands.

"Done," Muff said quietly. "Friends look out for friends. Always."

After releasing Jimmy's hand, Muff moved toward the door. He stopped in front of it and was going to press the automatic opener but then asked, "How did you end up in here, Jimmy?"

"I thought you knew. A big guy – a mountain of a guy – threw me into a wall and gave me a depressed skull fracture and a concussion. The guy's name was Kingpin, and he works – or *did* work – for Doyle Abaddon."

Muff stiffened and stood a little straighter. "Abaddon's still around? That's a shame. I know he got sent back to Canada at one point. I hoped he'd stayed there, but I guess he didn't."

Jimmy answered without thinking as memories connected and intersected in his mind. "I think he floated back and forth between here and Canada because he has or had at least two children – daughters, I think. Muff? Do you have more information?"

The old man turned around slowly and faced Jimmy and Wendi again. His eyes had a far-off look about them as he recalled memories from three-quarters of a century ago.

"Alice Mortel, the waitress at the luncheonette, married Doyle about 1964, which must be how he got back in the States – a marriage visa, you know? Alice had a daughter named Aurora back in 1947 – not Abaddon's. But Alice and Doyle had a girl – Casey or something like that. Casey

Abaddon. Alice's first daughter, Aurora, had a baby a year later in 1965, a girl named Sonja. Aurora never got married, so Sonja was a Mortel, too. Years later, Doyle took up with Alice's granddaughter, Sonja Mortel. He was 61 then, and Sonja was only 22. He and Sonja were no relation, so there was no blood connection. They never got married, but they had a daughter in the late 80s—"

"1987," Jimmy interrupted. "That girl's name is Aleesha. The daughter he had with Alice was born in late 1964 and named Kaycie, not Casey. Kaycie died in a plane crash in 1983."

Muff nodded and said, "The Man leaves heartache, chaos, and destruction wherever he goes. He needs to go."

"That's not all he leaves behind," Jimmy answered. "He leaves bodies behind, too."

"You don't have to tell me that, Jimmy. I was almost one of them—Dale, too. And from what I understand, you were nearly one, too, more than once from the sound of it."

Muff lifted his wrist and looked at the empty joint like he was checking a watch. "Well, it's time for me to go. You have no idea how good it's been to see you again, Jimmy. You, too, Wendi. Take care of him for me, ok?"

"I will, Muff. I promise," Wendi vowed.

Muff pushed the automatic door opener and waited briefly while the door slowly opened. When the door was fully open, he slowly guided his walker out. It began closing before he was completely through, but it closed smoothly and quietly right after he and his walker cleared it. It was as though he had done it many times before and had it all timed out perfectly—like a well-choreographed dance.

Chapter 26

WENDI WAS THE FIRST to speak after Muff left Jimmy's hospital room. The couple sat speechlessly after the old man's revelations during his visit, minimal though they were.

"I have to go get Hil and Gwynn," Wendi said.

"Yeah, good idea. I would, but I'm kind of tethered here," Jimmy replied, motioning toward the IV attached to his arm.

"I wonder if Muff's still out there," Wendi replied. "I'm sure Hil and Gwynn would love to meet him and ask him questions. As slow as he moves, he can't have gone very far; he probably hasn't made it to the elevators yet. I'll try and catch him."

"Okay," Jimmy said, frustrated at his helplessness.

He watched from his bed as Wendi walked out to the waiting area. The door stayed open after she left, the automatic opener holding it open for a set time. He could see Gwynn and Hillary through the door of his room, sitting in the waiting area, but he couldn't hear any conversation.

Wendi stood in front of Hillary and Gwynn, looking left and right. After a moment, she turned around and darted back into Jimmy's room.

"They said they didn't notice anyone coming out of your room, Jimmy; they were talking about Pepé's case. Gwynn said the door opened, but they weren't paying attention to who was going in or out."

Jimmy stared at her, his eyes bugging out and his breathing faster than normal. *He was here! I know it!*

A moment later, a nurse came quickly into the room. "Are you okay, Mr. Favreaux? Is everything all right?"

"Why?" Jimmy asked.

"Because your pulse just shot up, and your pressure spiked, too." The nurse went over and examined the electronic digital vital signs unit near the bed.

"Well, whatever it was, it seems to be settling back down now." She looked at Jimmy and Wendi, and a small smirk formed around her mouth. "Were the two of you … you know …?" She just left the question hanging in the air.

Wendi turned beet red and nearly shouted, "No! We weren't doing anything like that!"

The nurse held her hands up in a show of surrender. "I'm just saying, wait until he gets home! Give the doctor a chance to clear him and give you a list of dos and don'ts so we don't see you back in here anytime soon."

She took one more look at the vitals machine, gave it a little tap with the palm of her hand, and then turned and left, a knowing smile across her face. In her mind, she had already decided what had caused Jimmy's vitals to spike.

The door closed slowly and smoothly behind the nurse. Jimmy looked at Wendi, his eyebrows raised. "He was here, Wendi. We both saw him and spoke to him. I shook his hand. He answered questions. The nurse came in and asked if it was okay to have a visitor, for Pete's sake. I am not going crazy."

"No, you're not, Jimmy. And neither am I. But I don't have an explanation, either."

Wendi came back around the bed on Jimmy's left side, the side with no IV, and Jimmy scooted his hips to the right while she climbed up on the bed. She lay on top of the bedclothes next to him, curled into his side, his unencumbered left arm holding her tight.

After a few long moments, Jimmy said quietly, "The best thing is knowing that he made it."

"I'm more concerned that you made it," Wendi answered.

"Well, unless I start seeing *other* people from back then, I'm pretty sure I made it."

"What did you make, Jimmy?" Hillary asked as he strode into Jimmy's room, Gwynn trailing behind. And what was that business a few minutes ago with the door opening and closing?"

"You're sure you didn't see an old guy with a walker come into my room and then go back out after a few minutes?"

"We went out and sat in the lounge area. After a while, we heard your door open and shut – I can hear the motor when it runs. But we were talking, not counting how many times your door opened or who went in. At one point, I heard the door open and close twice in quick succession, but

I really didn't pay it much mind. Wendi came out and looked around before asking us if we saw an old man. I said no and decided we should come in and see what's going on."

"There was an old guy with a walker. He was wearing brown tweed, a white shirt, and he had a brown tweed pork pie hat," Jimmy said, his frustration rising.

"I'm sorry, Jimmy, but we didn't see him," Hillary said, and Gwynn agreed, nodding her head.

"But you saw him, didn't you, Wendi?" Jimmy said, his words more statement than a question.

Wendi looked at Jimmy for a long pause before answering as though she was carefully choosing her words. "Yes. I saw an old man with a walker come into your room, this room where we are right now. He talked to us. He wanted to know why we weren't old like him. And he talked about people I didn't know, but *you* seemed to know them, Jimmy."

"The people he was talking about were the people – at least some of them, anyway – from my dreams when I was in the induced coma. And he was one of the people there, too. I know I never saw him before I met him in my dream. I swear I've never seen him before in my regular life." Jimmy swept his arm around the room, and asked, "Is that what we're calling this? My regular life? Am I supposed to think a ghost came in here? Or that someone made a hologram of Muff to make me think I'm crazy?" His digital life signs monitor was beeping faster as he ranted.

"I don't know what or who it was, Jimmy," Hillary responded. "I know both you and Wendi saw it—or him— so he had to be real on some level."

"Jimmy, a Bible verse talks about unknowingly entertaining angels," Gwynn said quietly from across the room.

"Okay. I think I've heard of that," Jimmy replied. "So, are you saying Muff Benjamin is my guardian angel? Like Clarence in *It's a Wonderful Life?* He was just trying to earn his wings, and he needed to help me before he could get them?"

Gwynn looked down, her cheeks reddening. "No, that's not what I'm saying. I'm just saying there is a precedence for angels helping people and then disappearing when they've completed their mission. Things happen that have no rational, natural explanation. A person steps off a curb and feels someone pull them back up on the curb just before a truck speeds by, but there's no one there when they turn around. That kind of unexplainable thing."

Jimmy lay back against his pillow. He was struggling to understand that one. The last thing he wanted to do was hurt Gwynn's feelings or ridicule her faith. He'd never really considered it, so he didn't know where he stood on the idea of guardian angels.

Wendi gently caressed Jimmy's arm, trying to keep him calm. "Maybe he came to help you tie up some loose ends in your mind, Jimmy."

"But you saw him, too. You spoke with him. You can describe him to Hillary and Gwynn," Jimmy answered.

The door to Jimmy's room began its automatic opening sequence, and all eyes turned to look, half-expecting to see an old man in brown tweed again. Instead, the door was pushed open impatiently by an anxious, panting Pepé. Once in the room, he stopped and looked from face to face like he was counting heads.

"Robert, what are you doing here?" Gwynn asked. "You're supposed to be at home. Have you forgotten the terms of being released on your own recognizance?"

"I had to come; I had to make sure everyone was still okay. I had to see with my own eyes. Here! Look at this note!" Pepé thrust the message he had found in the envelope by his front door into Hillary's hands.

Hillary read it and frowned.

"Don't keep me in suspense, Hillary; read it to us," Jimmy instructed the older man.

"It's very short. It just says, *'One Down. More to come. See you at 7. The Man. PS—don't be late!'* That's all it says."

Pepé took his wife's hand in his and pulled her close to him before asking, "So, who's the 'One Down' they're talking about?"

"Back the truck up for just a second, Pepé," Wendi replied. "Where did you get this note?"

"It was outside my front door. I was napping, and I felt a breeze. I opened my eyes and found the front door open. I got up to check on it, and found a letter-sized envelope on the floor in the doorway with this note. And inside the door on the entryway floor, I found this ..." He held up the brown, nubby, tweed pork pie hat.

"That's Muff's hat!" Jimmy pronounced excitedly. "You found it on your front step?"

"*Inside* my house. The envelope was outside on the step, but the hat was inside on the floor."

No one said anything for a minute or two, and then Jimmy asked, "Did you look at the camera footage from the security cam we put in the birdhouse by your front door?"

Pepé shook his head. "I was in too much of a hurry to get here and make sure everyone was okay – especially Gwynn." He gave his wife a shoulder squeeze, and she smiled at him with mute, genuine thanks.

"Give me your cell phone, Pepé," Jimmy said, holding out his hand. He used his right hand without thinking, stretching the IV tubes in the back of his hand and giving him a pinch. The action made him wince, but he reached the phone. In just seconds, Jimmy brought up the stored security camera footage saved in the cloud. He laid the phone on top of the bedclothes so everyone could watch the replay.

Someone in a gray work jumpsuit walked up to Pepé and Gwynn's house, looked around, and rang the doorbell. The door opened almost immediately, but the person who opened the door was too indistinct to make out on the video, just a shadowy figure. The jumpsuit guy looked like he said or asked something and then pulled a knife out of his pocket and slashed at the empty air in front of him. He dropped the envelope, put the knife back in his pocket, and left. The door was still partly open. The security footage showed the driver running to his white van and driving away. A minute or so later, Pepé appeared on camera. He looked around, picked up the hat and the envelope, tore it open, and read the note. Then he went back into the house, shutting the door behind him. A few seconds later, the garage door rose, and Pepé's pickup backed out of the garage, and Pepé laid rubber in their cul-de-sac as he sped off. That's all there was.

"I don't know what to make of it," Jimmy said. Wendi nodded her head, and Hillary said, "I'm equally at a loss."

Pepé said, "But we're all okay. There is no One Down. That's what is most important."

"But I think someone was supposed to be removed," Gwynn said nervously, "and I think it was ... you, Robert," she finished, her voice a whisper.

They had all seen the camera footage. The delivery driver had deliberately gone to Pepé's house. But what—or who—had thwarted his orders? Why had he flailed about with the knife and then left?

"I think I was right before," Gwynn said. "I think there is a guardian angel, Jimmy, except he came to help *Robert*. And he came here *after* successfully protecting Robert. I think he made that delivery driver see what he wanted to see. The driver wanted to see Robert and stab him, so that's what the ... angel, for lack of a better term ... let him see."

"And Muff? And the hat?" Jimmy asked.

"Maybe that was what *you* needed to see," Gwynn replied.

"Perhaps unfinished business from your dreams, Jimmy." It was Hillary, adding his opinion. "Perhaps it is as Shakespeare said, 'There are more things in heaven and earth, Horatio, than are dreamt of in your philosophy.' Hamlet, Act One, Scene Five. We don't know or understand the line that delineates between the corporeal and the supernatural realms. The line separating the two is sometimes blurred. Other than that, I have no answer."

"I do," Wendi said quietly. Turning to address Jimmy, she said, "You saved his life, and he saved a life for you. You said you guys were even. Muff agreed. Maybe we should leave it at that." Wendi paused hesitantly for a second, then asked Jimmy, "Did you happen to notice the timestamp on Pepé's security camera video?"

"No, I didn't," he replied.

"It happened just *before* Muff came to your room. So, when you said you two were even, Muff agreed because he had just saved Pepé. Does that make sense?" Wendi asked.

"About as much as anything else," Jimmy replied. "One thing's for certain: our business with The Man is not over."

"Not now. And not by a longshot," Pepé agreed.

Epilogue

It was late Sunday afternoon before the hospital finally released Jimmy. He had to wait for the neurosurgeon to come in and give him one more examination before the doctor would sign off on his release.

"I could have just walked out," Jimmy teased. "You know, leave AMA – against medical advice,"

The doctor looked over his reading glasses hanging from his neck on a chain and said, "And if the Gators had been playing this afternoon, I might have let you."

Wendi was in the room with Jimmy and the doctor. "Be nice, you two. Jimmy and I are grateful for all you did for both of us, doctor."

"Glad I could be of service," the doctor replied. He finished signing some papers, then looked at both Jimmy and Wendi and said, "The two of you need to take care of your heads. I'm serious. Wendi, you've had a concussion now, too, and another head injury could be worse. They build up, getting worse and worse the more you have. And

Jimmy, your skull is far from healed. The older you get, the longer it takes our skulls to reknit the bones. I'm only letting you out because Wendi said she'd take care of you and make sure you keep your head out of harm's way."

"I know, I know," Jimmy responded. "My mom always said I had the hardest head of anyone she knew, but we never tested it against a brick wall when I was growing up."

The doctor wrote an unintelligible note on a prescription pad and gave it to Wendi. "Fill this at the pharmacy, just in case he still gets headaches. Don't forget to stop at the business desk, too. I'd like to get *paid* for coming in today."

The doctor shook hands with Jimmy and Wendi, and then he was gone. Wendi finished grabbing up the various articles of clothing and stuffing them in a duffle bag while Jimmy went through the overpriced toiletries the hospital had provided and decided which to take and which to drop in the trash can.

"Ready?" Wendi asked.

"As nice as they've been to me, if I never see the inside of this place again, it'll be too soon," Jimmy answered.

Hillary was waiting outside in the parking lot, sitting behind the wheel of Wendi's Audi A3.

"You're going to let him drive?" Jimmy asked Wendi.

"Pepé is still required to stay at home," Wendi answered as they dropped their bags in the trunk. "I think Hil makes a nice chauffeur, don't you? He's got the outfit. Or an undertaker. The outfit is the same."

"Have your fun, children. It is within my power to send you careening from side to side in the car and jostle your brains if you persist in your cheekiness," Hillary said from his perch in the driver's seat.

"We'll be good, Hil," Wendi laughed as they climbed in to the backseat.

"Yeah, we'll be good. You just keep your eyes on the road, and we'll take advantage of this backseat," Jimmy added, joining in the lighthearted repartee. "You know, I haven't been in the backseat with a girl in years, decades even!"

"And for this, I'm sure the girls are thankful," Hillary added as they pulled out of the parking space.

A couple of miles from Jimmy's house, Hillary took the on-ramp for I95 North. Jimmy announced, "I know I really messed up my head, but this is not the way to my house."

"We're not going to your house," Wendi replied. "We're going to Pepé and Gwynn's so you can finally have an American Thanksgiving. We decided an evening meal was just as good as any other time of day. Besides, we've been waiting for you to get out of the hospital, and we want to celebrate that, too."

The ride to Jimmy's partner's house was uneventful, and Hillary was actually an excellent chauffeur. Hillary had the radio tuned to an oldies station, and the old song about tan shoes with pink shoelaces came on. Jimmy had a vague memory of wearing that exact outfit at some point in his dream. He knew it was in his dream because Wendi would never let him go out in public dressed like that, especially wearing a big Panama hat with a purple hatband.

At Robert and Gwynn's house, the trio went in through the front door – the same one where one of The Man's henchmen thought he'd stabbed Pepé. That whole thing was still too impossible for Jimmy to come to grips with, so he was letting it simmer on a back burner in his mind. He knew he'd have to figure out the sudden improbable appearance of Muff Benjamin in his ICU room at some point, but for now, he was just thankful to be with his friends, all safe and sound.

Casa Perez smelled wonderful. The aroma of the roasting turkey filled the kitchen and living room, and Jimmy could see fresh dinner rolls, green bean casserole, mashed potatoes, cranberry sauce, and even a pair of pies at the end of the counter. When it was all ready, Pepé called everyone to find their seats around the dining room table. He took his wife's hand and asked that their guests do likewise, holding hands in a small circle as Pepé asked the blessing for the food.

"Our dear heavenly Father, we are so thankful to be here. We know it is only through your intervention that we are together today. We thank You for modern medicine and the ways You work through doctors to provide the healing we need. You are the Master Physician, and we are grateful for everyone who watched over Jimmy and Wendi during their stay in the hospital. Heavenly Father, we ask You to continue to protect us and keep us healthy. Be our guide and our Shepherd, walking with us through the valley of the shadow of death. Bless this food that we are about to share, and may our conversations be as sweet as the pies that Gwynn has for dessert. In Jesus's name, I pray. Amen."

Whether it was Muff or some other guardian angel's doing, their meal was undisturbed by anyone with evil intentions. For a few hours, they were just plain folks —

friends and family – enjoying each other's company and being thankful for the blessings they recounted as they ate.

When the clock over the fireplace chimed at seven o'clock, Jimmy was the only one who noticed. He remembered the note's admonition, "Don't be late."

"I won't be," he whispered to himself.

For right now, though, there was pumpkin pie with lots of whipped cream.

And somewhere in the back of his mind came a snatch of a table grace his mother used to say: "…and for this we are truly thankful."

Loose Threads

So MANY THINGS TO tidy up. But that's why I include this section: to explain some of those questions that are bothering you. *Did they...? Was it...? That really happened?* So, let's get to it.

Jimmy's treatment is consistent with treatment for a Traumatic Brain Injury (TBI). A nurse in nearby Jacksonville, Florida, told me a person in his condition would be in ICU, intubated, and on a ventilator. At a minimum, he would be assigned a Neurosurgeon for the neurological (brain) part and an Intensivist as his ICU doctor. The hospital has an Observation Unit whose specific job is to monitor everyone under observation.

The hospital where Jimmy thinks he has woken up is fictional but is loosely based on the old Nassau General Hospital, which was located behind the funeral home in Fernandina Beach, Florida. Nassau General is no longer there, but you can still tell where the buildings and parking lot were.

I thought getting Floyd from Mayberry to play the doctor might be fun. Actor Howard McNear was the voice of "Doc" Adams in the original radio version of Gunsmoke, years before playing Floyd the Barber in Mayberry. McNear was heard in many radio dramas in the 1940s and 50s with his instantly recognizable voice. He played drunks, bums, doctors, cops, hen-pecked husbands, thugs, drifters, and many other roles. Howard McNear passed away in Los Angeles in 1969 at age 63.

I have tried to stay true to as many of the late 1940s-era landmarks in downtown Fernandina Beach, Florida, as I could. You can find internet pictures of the 'old' downtown and see the cobblestone street where the trolley used to run, Thompson Sundries, the mural on the store's exterior wall advertising their Luncheonette, and the Western Union sign a few doors away. Seeing the Western Union sign gave me the idea for Jimmy sending a telegram to Wendi.

Web surfing uncovers pictures of the Palace Saloon on the main thoroughfare, located near the waterfront. Originally constructed as a haberdashery in 1878, Louis G. Hirth bought the Prescott building in 1903, replaced the shoes with booze, renamed it the Palace Saloon, and never looked back.

According to local lore, it was the last bar in Florida to close on the eve of Prohibition. A shrewd businessman, owner Louis G. Hirth stored up for one last hurrah, selling until midnight and grossing $60,000 in a single day. That's $60K in 1920 money.

Another first for the Palace: it was the first hard liquor bar to begin serving Coca-Cola around 1905 and allegedly the first to serve rum and Coke. The Palace survived Prohibition by selling Texaco gasoline, ice cream, special wines, 3 percent near beer, and cigars. The pirate out front of the Saloon is a popular spot for selfies and "Kodak moments" when visiting downtown.

Other locations in downtown Fernandina Beach are also accurate – or at least partially – such as Front and Centre streets crisscrossing by the waterfront and the locations of Thompson's Luncheonette, the Police Department, and the train depot, although the original train depot was across the street and about 200 feet down the block from its current location. There was passenger train service out of Fernandina, and the depot was located at the corner of Front and Centre, but there would have been no grassy lawn for Jimmy to "feed the ants on." And yes, David Yulee was instrumental in resurrecting rail travel after the Civil War (or the War of Northern Aggression, if you prefer).

The Ship's Galley bar, unfortunately, is pure fiction. It is fun, however, to go to the marina on the river in Fernandina and walk along the docks, looking at the many sizes and shapes of boats moored there.

Bonus points if you recognized the address Jimmy gave Dr. Floyd: 1313 Mockingbird Lane. That's where the Munsters lived.

I hope you enjoyed Alice's Restaurant; I mean, Thompson's Luncheonette. The Luncheonette was connected with Thompson's Sundries. I have no idea if an Alice was on staff or what they served, either. I would happily eat at Alice's. It's a blend of small diners and eateries I have enjoyed.

There was a Bill Crane on the Fernandina Beach Police Department, and he volunteered with the Fire Department, too, but I just borrowed the name. Everything else about him and all other law enforcement characters came wholly from my imagination.

The old radio shows of the 1930s, 40s, and 50s were rarely copyrighted. Radio shows created before January 1, 1978, are generally believed to be in the public domain due to the Copyright Act of 1909. There were many shows and not enough writers or actors, so plots and ideas were reused and recycled as needed. Sometimes, shows were re-broadcast with a completely different cast years after the original premiere, and other times, they just changed the title and the characters' names and called it good.

The main idea for the section of this book with Kendall and Catherine Brody is an amalgam of several radio episodes built on similar plots and titles like "Tree of Life" written by J. Douglas Ware and "Practically Foolproof," "Strangers on a Train, and "The Alibi." A more recent version of the plot is the 1987 Danny DeVito and Billy Crystal comedy movie, "Throw Momma from the Train." J. Douglas Ware's story aired on *Suspense* on January 2, 1947. The scriptwriter is announced on the broadcast as "J. Douglas Ware," but the author was actually his sister, Joan Ware, who worked at the CBS script department. Joan and her brother would talk about stories and their conversations would often result in some curious plotlines, like this one. Douglas was called to serve in the Pacific as a pilot, and was killed in action. She had the script attributed to him as a memorial. Only one recording of this episode has survived, freely available on

Youtube.com and from oldies radio apps. (https://tinyurl.com/2922h67n). In the radio show, the hitmen refer to the Jimmy character as Curly, rather than the other way around.

The Dale Higgins/Val Sackett portion of the book was inspired by an episode of The Adventures of Philip Marlowe called "A Seaside Sabbatical," which first aired on July 7, 1951. It starred Gerald Mohr as Raymond Chandler's famous detective. The original did not have Curly and Slick, nor did it end in a shootout on a yacht. The radio script for "A Seaside Sabbatical" was written by another woman writer: Kathleen Hite. In an interview in 2014, Kathleen explained, "CBS had a policy against hiring women writers, so I hired on as a secretary. I figured once I got inside the building I could destroy them from within. I badgered the head of the writing department until he gave me a chance to write." Hite's plan quickly succeeded, for within a year she became the first woman staff writer for CBS. She subsequently noted that World War II-related labor shortages also helped her to obtain that promotion, explaining that "a producer needed a radio scriptwriter— ANY radio scriptwriter. And there I was." She died in 1989 at age 71.

The idea of guardian angels goes back thousands of years. Whether we each have a guardian angel assigned to us – mine would have certainly earned his keep! – or whether the angels watch over us as a whole, I can't say for sure. I'm good either way. There are Scriptures used to support each side of the issue. That's where we'll leave that. For now.

Will we see Muff Benjamin in book #5? Beats me! I like him a lot, but he may have run his course. *(Unless ...)* I also liked Slick and Curly, but I haven't worked out how or, perhaps more importantly, *why* they should make a reappearance. They're from Jimmy's dreamscape, and besides, evil henchmen are a dime a dozen.

Something else I am kicking around in my head: a short story about Jimmy and Wendi on vacation in northern Minnesota, where Jimmy lived before moving to the borderland between Georgia and Florida where the Blue Bridge marks the boundary. In my head, Jimmy walks down to the dock outside the rented cabin where his parents stayed on their honeymoon and finds a floater in the lake – a dead body – under the dock. That's all I have on that for now.

Someone asked me if my books are about mysteries connected with the real Blue Bridge since at least one body was found in a car pulled from the river in that area in 1999. I introduced the very real characters, Knud Olfort and his third wife of record, Nellie VanZant Olfort, at the grand opening of the Steffens Restaurant (note the picture of the original Steffens in the Acknowledgements section in the front of the book). Perhaps I'll weave that story into another book in the future, or perhaps it'll be the basis for another Jimmy and Wendi short story.

Oh, yes. Someone asked if Doyle Abaddon would be back. What's Holmes without Professor Moriarty? Batman without the Joker? Superman without Lex Luthor? Jerry Seinfeld without Newman? Doyle needs to make at least one more appearance before relinquishing the evil nemesis role to someone else. I have ideas for him, but if you want to send me yours, hit the email below.

If you like this book, please leave a review at Amazon or Goodreads. If you read the earlier books and didn't leave a review, you can still go back to ~~fix your error~~ ~~make it up to me~~ leave one after the fact. It's never too late!

Need to contact me? Story ideas or questions? Send email to mkzpublishing@gmail.com

About the Author

Mike Zimmerli is an author, ghostwriter, and editor whose fingerprints can be found in dozens of books, some even intentionally. Although much of his previous work has been as an editor, he is now writing and publishing his own series, *The Blue Bridge Mysteries*, featuring Jimmy Favreaux. Mike continues to work as a freelance editor.

A Minnesota native, he lived in several places between the northern and southern borders of the Gopher State. In 2004, Mike and his beautiful bride, Mary, abandoned their empty nest, sold everything that wouldn't fit in their two cars, and moved to St. Marys, Georgia – as far south as you can go without stepping into Florida and as far east as you can go without getting your feet wet in the Atlantic Ocean. From 2004 through 2020, Mike was in church ministry, and from 2009 to 2020 at First Baptist Church of St. Marys, GA, serving as the director of music and senior adults.

After a lifetime of writing words for others – through radio, newspaper, blogs, and full-time ministry – Mike, partly prompted by the pandemic, became a freelance writer and editor in 2021. That year, he published his dad's memoirs, *One Soldier's Story* by Jacob Wesley Zimmerli, which recounts his experiences in the Pacific Theater of War in 1944-45. That same year, Mike started freelance editing full-time.

Since then, Mike has edited or ghostwritten dozens of books for other writers and now has his own series of clean, light mysteries – the Blue Bridge Mysteries, named for the famous blue bridge on Highway 17 that separates Georgia and Florida and spans the St. Marys River south of Kingsland, GA.

Zamboni Is Not A Pasta was the first installment in the series, followed by *Wanted: Dead or Alive (Again),* which continued where *Zamboni* left off. *To the Last Breath* – book number three in the series – chronologically picks up after book #2, and *Perchance 2 Dream* starts where #3 left off. The teaser ending from *To The Last Breath* is included at the beginning of this book to catch people up to speed who (*horrors!*) may not have read the first three books.

IN THE FALL OF 2024, Mike is publishing a special Christmas book. No, it's not about Jimmy and Wendi's first Christmas. It is a long-overdue Biblical Historical Fiction about the events leading up to and including the birth of Christ. Whereas the Bible gives us a skeleton view of the events, *The Annunciation* puts meat on those bones and brings back the sense of wonder that may have been stolen by the innumerable elves on shelves, Red Ryder BB guns, flying reindeer, and Christmas trains. *The Annunciation* fills in some of the blanks the biblical writers omitted, giving you conversations (albeit fictitious) that could easily have taken place. It looks at the angelic visitations to Zechariah – the elderly priest married to Mary's relative, Elizabeth, Jesus's mother, Mary, His earthly father, Joseph, and finally, the big reveal to the shepherds.

"THE HAIRS ON the back of Zechariah's neck stood up, a ringing began in his ears, and he almost needed to force himself to breathe. It was as though he was in the presence of something or someone with the power to erase his existence, but at the same time, he felt as insulated and comforted as when in his mother's arms as a small child.

Standing to the right side of the incense altar was a tall man dressed in robes so intensely white that they could have been woven from pure sunlight. There was something unusual about his countenance. Was he truly a man? If so, he was the first man Zechariah had ever met whose face shone like a mirror in the noon-day sun! Zechariah's head became light, and his aged knees felt as though they would give way. He quickly bowed before the shining apparition at the altar, then submitted to the feeling in his knees and stretched out with his face to the floor, completely prostrate.

"Do not be afraid, Zechariah. The LORD your God, Yahweh, is well pleased with you."

"AS THE SHEPHERDS walked through the streets of Bethlehem, they sang the words the angels had spoken to them, their words echoing between the houses: *"Glory to God in the highest, and on earth peace among men with whom He is pleased."*

Excerpts From
The Annunciation
Copyright © 2024 Michael K. Zimmerli